# Z2135

Z2134
Book 2

SEAN PLATT

DAVID W. WRIGHT

STERLING & STONE

*To YOU, the reader.*
*Thank you for your support.*
*Thank you for the wonderful emails.*
*Thank you for the thoughtful reviews.*
*Thank you for reading and loving our stories.*

# Foreword

## Z 2135

*It is the year 2135, after the zombie apocalypse. Society lives in six walled cities ruled over by the State and its ever-present City Watch officers. The Walls keep citizens safe from the zombies that wander the Barrens, but some would argue that the Walls are prisons, keeping people in blind servitude to a corrupt government. Hovering orbs patrol the cities, monitoring every movement.*

*And City Watch propaganda posters read:* Do you REALLY know your neighbor? Watch. Listen. Report.

Former City Watcher Jonah Lovecraft, a secret member of the rebel Underground, was framed for murdering his wife. While he didn't remember committing the crime, his 17-year-old daughter, Anastasia (Ana), witnessed the gruesome display in real time. Her testimony sealed his fate. Jonah was banished to the Darwin Games, the State's televised reality game show in which prisoners are pitted against one another and zombies. The prize: *freedom in the paradisiacal City 7.*

Jonah wins the Games against all odds and soon discovers that City 7 was all a lie. Instead of being delivered to a new life of freedom, he was dumped in a shack in the zombie-infested Barrens, the no-man's land outside the walled cities, and left to die.

Jonah was soon rescued, and imprisoned again, this time by a man named Egan, who held Jonah responsible for the loss of his family. Jonah managed to win his freedom from Egan, but was also told that the State had implanted chips in him years ago: an identity chip, which he knew about, and a mind-control chip, which he did not.

In the process of flushing out the chips, Jonah learned that he *had* murdered his wife.

Ana's younger brother, Adam, was now all alone in a State-run orphanage after his sister was placed in the Games. He found himself navigating friends and bullies with the help of his father's old boss, Chief Keller, who lost his son years earlier when an Underground rebel bombed a parade. Keller told Adam to fight back against the bullies, and gave him a weapon to ensure that he could. But after accidentally killing one of his tormentors, Adam was arrested and hauled out of the orphanage by City Watchers.

Ana, with the help of Liam Harrow, a troubled young man she'd grown up with who was also in the Underground, discovered that her father may have been set up by forces within City 6. After being found consorting with the Underground, Ana was thrown into the Games.

Liam wound up in the Games with her — after getting himself arrested intentionally to protect Ana.

Ana made her way through challenges and was forced to kill or be killed. During the Games, giddy announcer Kirk Kirkman informed Ana via a video that Liam had been a double agent, working for both City Watch *and* the Underground: *Liam was the one who had outed her father's involvement with the Underground.*

She and Liam were eventually saved by Duncan, her father's old friend and leader of the Underground, who helped them escape into underground tunnels beneath the Barrens.

Confronted, Liam admitted to betraying her father, but only to save his girlfriend, Chelle, who was living in a hidden village.

But they arrive at the village to find it in ashes, its citi-

# ONE

# Anastasia Lovecraft

*THE BARRENS*
*June 2135*

ANASTASIA LOVECRAFT CHEWED on her lip, anxious to get this over with.

Her knees were killing her. She had been crouched in the bushes too long, waiting off to the side at the south entrance to Narrow Pass Bridge.

She stared through the binoculars, Liam beside her. The just-wiped lenses showed a cracked and broken road, long since surrendered to vegetation. She felt the truck before she saw it — a barely-there tremor rising into a low rumble as the large armored vehicle rolled toward the bridge.

The truck was a quarter mile away. She looked over to Liam, wondering if he noticed the same thing: the truck was alone. Liam's eyes were covered by his own binoculars, and he was waiting with seemingly far more patience.

They watched as the truck rounded a torn section of road, navigating around something caused by what Ana had heard everyone in Paradise call the "April Cotter Incident," or "that thing at the bridge," though nobody had detailed the incident. It looked like some giant meteor had fallen from the sky and cratered the earth with a hole wide and deep enough to tickle the planet's core.

But she couldn't allow the mystery to distract her now. Paradise's leader, Oli, had finally allowed her to go on a raid, and she couldn't screw up. She had to prove herself capable, worthy of being on the twelve-person team.

Liam had briefed Ana on the drive over: three trucks, maybe five. "Nothing matters more than the unexpected. If it smells wrong, it probably is." Then he'd told her about a time back in March when they had waited too long after an orb appeared from nowhere. Liam had guessed it was *maybe* five seconds before it turned Tom Callow to foamy red oatmeal from the shoulders up.

Ana had seen some awful things since being "chosen" for the Darwin Games, but the thought still made her shudder. She shook her thoughts back to the present and looked at Liam. He wasn't happy, eyes off the road and scanning the opposite horizon — the other side of the bridge, where the rest of their team was positioned just out of sight. His binoculars peered into the trees and his jaw twitched. He lowered the lenses and looked at Ana, nodding.

They said it together: "Just one truck."

"How far behind do the others usually follow?" Ana asked.

"Close. There's no more coming."

"What about orbs?"

"None."

Ana wiped her brow, chewing her bottom lip. She looked from the road to Liam. "So what do we do?"

"Call it off. One truck's stupid."

"What? It's why we came out here. We can't go back empty-handed."

"No." Liam let go of the binoculars so they hung from his neck.

"We came out for a shot at a City Caravan. We're swapping camps in three weeks, and this vein is close to tapped. One truck isn't a caravan: fewer supplies, no vehicles, almost for sure no weapons."

"Maybe it's something small. Easy pickings?"

"No," Liam said, raising his comm, ready to call Daemon. "After what happened on the other side of Cactus, it looks like they were expecting it here. This is a trap." He half-smiled, like a pat on her head, then spoke into his comm. "We're done. One truck. It's yours any second. I suggest calling it off."

A crackle, then Daemon's voice, "Bullshit. The barb strip is down."

"Pull the barbs and let's get out of here," Liam pressed, though Daemon was the mission leader. "This isn't right, and you know it. There's one truck. When has there ever been *just one truck*?"

Nothing from Daemon.

"Look, I don't want to go back without a haul any more than you do. I *hate* it. But I want to live, and that means not chasing one truck into an obvious trap. Sometimes springing a trap's the only option; this time it isn't."

No crackle from the comm: Daemon still thinking.

Liam had raided many times since he and Ana found Paradise. She was new at this, but trusted him when he said they never sent fewer than three trucks into City 6.

This was *supposed* to be an easy raid, one of the final few before they swapped camps. Twelve people had left Paradise — an even match for a caravan, and overkill for a single truck. Low-hanging fruit, ripe for the fall ... if not for Liam's instinct.

Everyone — especially Daemon — knew Liam wasn't the sort to say the sky was falling unless it already was.

The comm snapped with static, then Daemon said, "We're hitting the truck."

Liam's fingers curled tight around the comm, and Ana worried he might crush the device. His nostrils flared. "You *know* that's a mistake."

"Not a mistake," Daemon said, the swagger back in his voice, probably to account for his earlier doubt. "This is too easy a target to ignore, Liam. We're *not* going back with nothing, *especially* with only one truck to take down."

"*No*," Liam insisted. "They wouldn't send one truck and you know it!"

Daemon got louder. "Everyone appreciates your contributions, City 6; you're a real asset to the team. But I've been packing with this camp since I couldn't shave and you'd barely left your daddy's sack. We're hitting the truck. That's an order, from *your superior*."

In seconds the truck would be tearing rubber to shreds on the barbs. But Ana could tell by Liam's slowly mounting snarl that he was edging eruption, and she knew it was wasted energy.

She grabbed him by the arm. "Don't," she begged, with eyes and words. "It's one truck, Liam. It probably *is* a trap, but we're prepared. There are twelve of us, and we have Shaw. He's like two people."

Liam didn't laugh. "We have no idea what could be waiting. This is dangerous. More importantly, bending to Daemon's ego is a fool thing to do."

"You're right." Ana let go of his arm. "But we're on thin ice. We don't want to piss off Oli's son, even if he is being an idiot."

Ana didn't want to remind Liam how he'd nearly gotten them kicked out of the camp in their first week because of his flaring temper, particularly now, when his caution was right. The last few months had taught her a subtle way to tap Liam's more thoughtful, analytical side, a layer beneath his anger.

"Sometimes, we have to play politics," she said. "Isn't that what *you* told me? We have to be nice and swallow the shit sandwich?"

"Well?" Daemon's impatience crackled through the com. "Are you ready to do this?"

"Fine," Liam said. "But if this goes wrong, it's all on you."

Daemon didn't reply.

The truck made its way around the crater, then tore by Liam and Ana, both still crouched low. The truck was going way too fast for a decrepit bridge over a deep ravine. If the 400-foot drop didn't kill the truck's occupants, the river's teeth — jagged rocks and alligators — would.

The truck was three-quarters of the way across the 700-foot bridge when its front two tires exploded. The truck screamed to a stop, the engine choking violently, stopping just short of the crumbling concrete guardrail — the only thing preventing the truck from losing complete control and plunging into the ravine.

Liam and Ana ran toward the vehicle's rear, keeping a good ten yards back, rifles out, as the rest of their raiding crew approached from the front. It was a cargo hauler with eighteen wheels, a large boxed back, and a retractable rolling door.

"Keep an eye on the rear door and watch out for crossfire," Liam said, even though they'd gone over the details dozens of times.

Daemon reached the driver's-side window with his grandfather's old lead shooter drawn. "Get out with your hands in the sky!"

The truck was surrounded.

The driver's door opened a crack, then swung wide.

"Out," Daemon ordered.

The driver hit the dusty asphalt, a young man in common clothes. A terrified rabbit in a human's body.

Daemon waved his gun at the truck. "What's in the back?"

Ana held her gun to the rear, both anticipating and dreading what would happen when the door rolled up. Her heart pounded hard in her chest, unable to shake the feeling that Liam was right and that they were stepping straight into a trap.

"Just supplies," the driver said. "I'm making a run to City 6."

"What kind of supplies?" Daemon peered toward the back, as if his squint could cut through metal.

"Flour, medicine, rations. No weapons."

"We'll see. Open it up." Daemon waved his gun from the driver's face to the truck in a universal gesture for *hurry up* before taking a step back.

Ana and Liam took a step forward, as did Manolo and Jor, who had circled from the front to stand beside them. The driver turned from Daemon, trembling slightly, and walked to the rear with measured steps.

With no hesitation, the driver swung the latch and yanked the door up by its weathered strap, then slipped his fingers under the metal bottom and shoved the paneled door high.

As the door started to open, Ana noticed that the

driver had something dark tucked away in his palm —
some sort of small device. And his eyes seemed wrong.
Afraid … but not of the men with their guns aimed
behind him.

*There's something else.*

Then the door rolled all the way open and hell spilled
from its gaping mouth.

Zombies exploded from the back, swallowing the driver
in a sea of limbs and gnashing mouths.

Ana fell back, staring in horror as they chewed
through the driver like ants devouring a speck of bread.
She thought of the thing in his hands, then noticed that
all the zombies wore black bands around their necks —
necklaces that must have kept them docile until the
driver pressed the button. He'd known what was coming.
Ana wondered how many rations and credits the State
had given the driver's family to make a suicide run like
this.

While the first group of zombies feasted on the driver,
the rest raced forward, searching for their own meals.

Liam pulled his trigger a beat before Ana, but both his
zombie and hers dropped at the same time with matching
head shots. They had been lucky, being farthest back of the
raiders, with time to draw a bead on the zombies. Manolo
and Jor were closer — overwhelmed before they had a
chance to aim.

They fell while emptying their guns in futility seconds
ahead of their shredding.

There were at least twenty zombies left, maybe more,
they were moving faster than any zombies Ana had ever
seen.

She pushed herself against Liam, feeling his side
against hers as they fired into the crowd, missing more
often than not, but still somehow keeping the horde away.

They could hear the other members of their party firing but were too busy to see how the fight was going.

"I'm out," Liam said, stripping a magazine from his rifle. Ana covered him, taking shots at a zombie racing toward them. She missed the first three times, the thing was moving so fast, but her fourth and fifth shots dropped the creature.

Liam swapped his ammo, then Ana did the same.

She was startled to see that the zombies were now ignoring them, instead chasing the remaining raiders in front of the truck.

"Come on," Liam said. "We'll hit 'em from behind and take out as many as we can."

They spotted Daemon climbing to the top of the truck for a better vantage. Zombies couldn't climb for shit, so it was a terrific position if they could make it up there too.

A zombie noticed Daemon before he reached the top, grabbed at his ankle, snarling as Daemon kicked at its face.

The zombie kept reaching, its teeth gnashing.

Daemon screamed, kicked again, and hauled himself to the roof before the zombie could sink its teeth into him. Atop the truck, he started nailing zombies one at a time, felling each with a head shot, including the three descending on Ana and Liam.

Zombies kept pouring out from the truck.

Ana couldn't imagine how tightly they must have been packed inside their rolling coffin. They were coming too fast; she couldn't reload quickly enough.

Neither could Liam. He fell back beside her until they were just far enough from the mass to get their bearings. Then — as they were taught and practiced each day — they spun their weapons, butt first in their fists, and rushed into the fray, swinging rifles like clubs at the zombies, aiming for heads when possible.

Ana and Liam dropped the zombies closest to them. With bodies sprawled across the ground, they held formation, waving their weapons, ready to either reload or keep swinging.

But it wasn't necessary. The truck was finally empty, and Daemon, with nothing to slow his reloading, was a metronome atop the truck until his shots finally fell silent and the bloody mist cleared to a metallic scent.

Their team had been cut to a third: just Ana, Liam, Daemon, and Shaw — the only one to survive the massacre in front of the truck.

Daemon reloaded one last time before climbing down, looking pained as he dropped to the asphalt, his right ankle fringed with bloody tassels of shredded denim.

"You were bit." Shaw pointed to his wounded ankle, stating the obvious.

Eyes were mostly on the ground — all four of them were thinking of Drey. Ana had only known Drey for a month, but she doubted she'd ever forget a day with the kind man. He was older than her father, but younger than Duncan, and knew how to turn every situation better by seeing it differently. If it was raining, Drey would say, "The world's getting washed so we don't have to scrub it!" If something was on fire, he'd say, "Sometimes a seed has to burn before it can sprout!" When he had been bitten on mission two months back, Drey said, "Everything will turn out, it always does!" proving he was unflinching in his optimism.

Too bad he wasn't always right.

Because things *didn't* work out for Drey.

Rules were rules, and after Drey got bit he was given a choice by Oli: head out to the Barrens and wait to become one of the undead or die while still clinging to his humanity.

Drey had fallen to his knees and told Oli to go ahead and end it. Oli did, putting a bullet between Drey's eyes without blinking.

Ana wondered if Oli would be as strict with the rules when it came to Daemon being bitten. Would he be given the same choice of banishment or execution? Or would the leader find some excuse to spare his son?

"Collect the weapons and any supplies we can salvage, and let's get back." Then Daemon emptied the magazine of his reloaded gun into a pile of unmoving bodies before climbing inside the truck and rifling through the cabin.

"What are we going to do?" Ana whispered to Shaw.

"About what?"

"You know what."

She looked at Shaw like he was stupid, both because of his question and because he was.

"Daemon's infected."

"You don't know that," Shaw said, as if their leader's ankle didn't look like raw hamburger. Shaw always followed Daemon like a puppy, was mostly indifferent to Ana, and slightly hostile to Liam. She got the feeling that he would always see them as outsiders, even if they went gray in Paradise. "The zombies were bloody. They could've got some of it on his leg."

"You know the sentence for infection," Ana said, ignoring his idiocy.

"Yeah, but that's decided by Oli. He won't kill his son." Though Ana had known Oli for only a few months, she was approximately a million times more perceptive than Shaw, who'd known him for at least a decade.

Liam was silent, too smart to argue with an oversized moron. Talking to Shaw was pointless.

Ana collected weapons from her fallen comrades, double checking as she went to make sure the downed stayed put, stabbing them through the head with her machete as she went.

Approaching Jor, one of the nicer among them, barely older than Ana, she had to turn away. As the sound of the blade squished through his face, she nearly lost her composure.

Liam was headed her way, a distraction from her grief. He pulled her aside. "Me and Shaw are gonna get the truck. You okay to stay here with him?"

"If he turns, I can take care of myself," she said.

Liam nodded, then left with Shaw to collect the truck they'd come in, parked just down the road and tucked away in the woods. But they wouldn't be filling their ride with supplies.

Daemon checked the truck's cabin for anything useful.

"Jack shit," he reported, eating a granola bar.

"Not gonna offer me half?"

He broke off a piece and offered it to her.

"No, thanks. You bit off of it."

"Suit yourself." He shoved it into his mouth, chewing with his mouth open.

They stood in awkward silence while waiting for Liam and Shaw. She tried not to notice his ankle. He made no attempts to hide it, as if daring her to look.

He should have listened to Liam. But there was no point in stating the obvious and rubbing salt in the wound that had already ruined him.

The truck was only a half mile away, and the boys returned in no time.

Shaw rode shotgun beside Daemon, while Ana and Liam rode in the back — an empty cargo box, which only made their losses seem more painful. Rather than delivering a truckload of supplies, they were going home with eight fewer campers and Oli's bitten son.

Their raid was a bust.

They had fallen into a trap.

*Liam was right.*

The back of the truck had a light, but neither Ana nor Liam wanted it on. The dark somehow seemed safer.

Ana whispered, "Do you think Oli will banish him?"

"We'll know soon enough."

TWO

# Jonah Lovecraft

*THE BARRENS*

JONAH STARED through the scope of his crossbow, hungry to pull the trigger, desperate to hit anything. Ever since seeing the faked footage of Ana's and Liam's deaths last winter, he'd wandered the Barrens alone in search of his daughter.

He was exhausted from the endless miles and near starvation he faced daily. The network had gone to great lengths to fake their deaths, which Jonah had seen on Egan's orb, showing direct network feeds of the Games, the footage that people back in the cities didn't see. The network was clearly attempting to hide the truth that Ana and Liam had managed the impossible by escaping the Darwin Games.

Jonah hadn't seen his reflection in anything beyond the muddy water for months, but his cheeks were hollow — thin skin caving in from both sides — so he assumed *gaunt* was an accurate description for both his physical and mental conditions. The winter had been too long and nearly had killed him too many times, yet it seemed like only yesterday when his life ended alongside Molly's. Only yesterday since everything he'd ever cared for was warped, ruined, or stolen away from him.

*No. I did it. I killed Molly. Even if Keller or someone somehow forced my hand, it was still me. I butchered her, in front of our daughter.*

Ana, if she were alive, probably hated him. Adam too. And Jonah deserved it for being a monster. He couldn't explain what happened, other than the State forcing him via the implanted chip that Father Truth removed. But Jonah could no longer lie to himself by calling it an artificial memory. His hands were still stained with the literal blood of his wife.

He should have been able to stop himself from doing it, his love for Molly overriding whatever programming the State had slipped into his brain.

He'd failed her, his family, and himself.

Keller had to be behind it, but Jonah needed to know why he'd put such a plot into motion. And needed revenge. But not before he found Ana — even if his daughter was still alive, she would no doubt be a different girl than the one he'd left last winter.

Jonah had done many awful things in the last few months, worse than the petty crimes for which he'd arrested citizens as a Watcher.

Two weeks back — he only knew the passing of time by tallying nicks on his machete's black handle; he wasn't sure of the actual day or date — Jonah stole food from a sleeping family.

There were more families scattered throughout the Barrens than he had ever imagined, at least in those areas clustered closest to City 6. Jonah wondered if populations thinned or thickened further in. Hard to know when his time was all spent wandering the same loops in search of Ana.

The State reported empty Barrens, except for the savages and scavengers. It was easier to control a populace too afraid to step outside their controlled environments and trade safety for a death sentence.

Jonah knew better. He had been helping the Underground move people to West Village. He'd found the camp in ashes, but still saw signs of life everywhere. Groups like Egan's were fairly common: clusters shoved into tiny pockets of the Barrens, too mistrusting of others to fall in with a larger family.

Small hordes of survivors (rebels, outsiders, aliens — Jonah didn't know what to call them) were common; seeing them starving, shaking, and near death only slightly less so.

Again he remembered his atrocity two weeks ago.

He had buried himself behind a thicket of trees, watching as the matriarch killed a deer. The father was weak, something wrong with his leg, and had stayed in camp with the two young girls and a toddler boy.

Mom dragged the deer to camp on a homemade wooden cart, which Jonah helped himself to as soon as they were all snoring. He crept up and stole what he could, silent and swift, excusing his thievery on grounds that the slumbering family wasn't also starving.

He was preserving his life to protect Ana's. Ensuring her safety was worth everything, including his soul. He had to know she was safe — or at least not dead — and make peace with the truth.

Every day he walked until he couldn't, then he set up camp in the safest place he could find or craft, swearing that he felt her in the wind. The instincts that had made him such a highly decorated major at such a young age —

and the best in City Watch according to Keller — told Jonah that Ana was somewhere here in the Barrens, alive and waiting to be found.

He had to stay strong, even if that meant living in shadows, stealing food, and contemplating murder.

The only person Jonah had seen that reminded him of Ana was a teenage girl, malnourished enough to resemble a zombie.

Somewhere behind her thin and haunted face quivered something still human, but nothing that looked like it would — or even could — smile again.

At spring's earliest notes, Jonah had come across a small village with the most people he had seen in one place outside the Walls. He'd found the place by accident after following a quad of travelers — one man, two teenage boys, and a woman who seemed late twenties —into a giant field of forsythia. The sea of bright-yellow bell-shaped blossoms had been a promise that warmer weather was finally on its way.

He had maneuvered around the village's perimeter, making sweeps for four full days, his eyes on the village, waiting for any sign of Ana. He had seen none, and his gut told him she wasn't there, especially after bearing witness to their handling of a stray visitor — a brusque response that escalated to the visitor's murder by the guards.

Jonah had thought it best not to introduce himself.

But the village had haunted him since. The largest gathering of people he'd seen looming farther behind him by the day. As his handle gathered tallies, he couldn't stop wondering if Ana were there *now*, just past the fields of forsythia, even if she wasn't before. Or maybe she *had* been in the village but left a day before he started watching and gone off in the other direction.

These thoughts — and many like them — plagued him

with indecision. He'd finally surrendered, figuring he'd return to City 6 to seek more information. It was dangerous, but Jonah knew enough people to help him stay hidden for a while — just long enough to get strong, lean on his contacts, and see if maybe word of Ana's whereabouts had reached back behind the Walls.

Resolved, he had trekked back to the outskirts City 6, only to find the place surrounded by an impossible number of orbs, swallowing the skyline outside City 6 and buzzing like bees through the hives of the hidden tunnels he knew. Something big was happening behind the Walls.

Having to turn away once there had been even harder than deciding to return in the first place — as hard as it was to leave that village beyond the forsythia. He had only seen The City on lockdown once, when a zombie had somehow been smuggled behind the Walls and threatened rampant infection.

He wondered if that's what was happening again.

He wondered about the other cities too, and whether they were also on lockdown. Even though Jonah had never thought of it before, he wondered if he could reach City 5 without dying.

It would be difficult to cross the Barrens, but if the other cities weren't on lockdown, then maybe he could sneak into City 5.

Jonah didn't have a network in 5 like he did in 6, but you only needed one connection to stay alive, and he had at least that in four of the cities. He had decided it was worth a shot, and it might have been the only option still open to him.

But he needed to round up supplies before he could make the trip. The provisions Egan had supplied him with were long ago depleted. The sphere he'd used to watch the network's direct feeds had died a month ago. He also needed basic survival gear, including first-aid supplies, material for fire, tape, and some rope.

More importantly, he had to find a gun and either some energy packs to go with the blaster or ammo if it turned out to be a lead shooter. Finally, he could use a new sack, as the one he'd been carrying on his back had torn through.

But in the two days since he'd decided on his journey to City 5 he had yet to find anything to eat, let alone additional supplies to reduce the danger of his trek.

Movement jolted him into the present. He finally sighted a deer. It was a far-off dot but definitely in range. He swung his crossbow toward it.

The deer looked up and over as Jonah pulled the trigger.

Something (hunger, fatigue, or mounting fear that his mind might soon leave him) tightened his reflexes. A slight movement, but enough to send the bolt flying too high over the deer's head, sailing between a matching set of trees before thunking into the thick trunk of a third.

The startled deer raced deeper into the woods.

Grumbling, Jonah lowered his crossbow, stood, then went to retrieve his bolt.

He couldn't go much longer without eating. Too weak to aim meant too weak to live, and surely too weak to fight if he crashed into zombies, bandits, or predator animals.

As his hand closed around the bolt and he jerked it from the trunk, Jonah heard death behind him. He turned to see a long gun, with an unfamiliar type of blaster, aimed by a woman on horseback.

He smiled, too tired to do anything else, then kneeled, set his crossbow on the ground, and stood with his hands in the air.

Horses weren't extinct, but were extremely rare. The

zombies had infected them, sometime after the Original Plague cleared most of humanity from the planet, and had altered the horses' ability to reproduce. Cities were too crowded for horses to be kept by commoners, though a few were raised behind the Walls, ridden by City Watch and select officials in parade lines like the trophies they were. In City 6, Keller's stallion was biggest.

In addition to riding a large City Watch-like horse, the woman wore City Watch-like body armor and leather. Yet, she clearly wasn't City Watch, so said everything from her careless posture to her wildfire eyes. Her hair was dark and cut short, a smart choice when it came to fighting.

She lowered her gun. "You're a hard man to find, Jonah Lovecraft."

He felt a burning in his gut, suddenly angry. The woman knew who he was, leaving him at a disadvantage.

He asked, "Who's looking?"

"Sutherland."

"Who the hell is Sutherland?"

"He's the Chief of Hydrangea."

"The Chief of Hydrangea? What are you talking about?"

"He's the Chief of Hydrangea," she repeated, hopping off of her horse as she eyed him up and down. "You're not going to do anything stupid if I give you back your weapon, are you?"

"If I wanted to hurt you, I would've already lodged my machete between your eyes."

She kneeled, retrieved his crossbow, looked it up and down, then handed it back to him. "As I'm sure you're aware, there's a network of camps scattered through the Barrens, filled with people who will one day bring down the Walls."

"Hydrangea? That doesn't exactly inspire fear."

"The camps are all named for flowers," she said, as if that were explanation enough.

"So what do you want with me?"

"*I* don't want anything." She started walking back toward her horse. "Sutherland asked me to find you."

"And what does *Chief Hydrangea* want with me?"

"That's between the two of you. But I will say that Sutherland might be your biggest fan."

Jonah tried to temper his growing hope, thinking it had already abandoned him, but it was hard in the face of good news from a stranger who wasn't eager to rob or murder him.

There were *camps*, plural. And they were part of a network. If Ana was in one, he might be close to finding her.

Jonah swallowed, waited a second for his breath and heart to both calm, then with his voice so ragged and cracked that it barely sounded like him he said, "Have you seen my daughter?"

"Of course." She smiled. "Ana is with us."

Jonah wanted to collapse in excitement and weep with the news, but he didn't dare allow himself to celebrate just yet. And it might be dangerous, revealing his desperation to this stranger.

She got on her horse, then patted its rump, waiting for Jonah.

He took her hand and climbed up behind her. They clomped off, his arms around her waist.

Jonah had felt dead ever since Father had shown him the truth of his crime.

Now, with the thought of seeing Ana again, the ghost of hope was alive.

THREE

# Liam Harrow

*The Barrens*

LIAM'S EYES WERE CLOSED, not that it made any difference in the truck's pitch-black hold.

For some reason, closed eyes usually made it easier to imagine the road back to Paradise. Judging by their time in the truck, number of occasions when they had slowed, and their approximate speed, he figured they were past the outskirts.

They had already driven through the area where Bird of Paradise flowers that gave the camp its name sprouted in patchy clusters, through the larger bushes and widest swath, then farther to where they surrendered to a small walled camp. One of the oldest and strongest in this section of the Barrens, it was filled with tiny homes and nearly a hundred campers — twice as many as Forsythia, the nearest camp, and nearly three times the number of Buckeye. Despite the camp's high walls and more permanent-seeming exterior, nothing in Paradise couldn't be torn down and loaded for flight in minutes.

As always, the truck idled outside the walls. Usually after a mission it would be driven to maintenance at the camp's rear, then emptied and scrubbed. But today the back rolled up and Shaw said nothing, just turned and walked toward the main gate after Daemon.

Avery waved at them from the top left tower, and Bobby from the right; then the doors to Paradise parted. Liam and Ana stepped through the gate, a beat behind Daemon and Shaw.

Oli looked pissed, and he didn't even know anything yet. "No trucks?"

"It was a trap, Father. There was only one truck, and it was filled with … *them*. Zombies." Daemon said the last word with a snarl.

"One truck?" Oli spat, then took a step closer to Daemon. "When did you know that, son? Before or after you laid the strip?"

"Before." Daemon held his stare. "One truck seemed easy pickings."

"Son, I know for a goddamned fact that you are *not* this stupid. So, ya wanna tell me what in the fuck possessed you to act like an idiot? Where the hell is everyone else?"

"We lost them, sir."

"Lost them? How many?"

"Eight."

Oli was boiling lava. Liam couldn't even guess what was next. The big boss always ripped into the guys, but it was *usually* good-natured, and funny. But there was nothing humorous about an angry Oli. Eight men was a big loss. Liam thought of all the old movies he'd seen in the Arcade, with men wearing faces like his: a cop waiting to inform a man that his wife has died in a car accident, a doctor informing a patient he's terminal, a uniformed man passing a picket fence so he can knock on the red door of a white house and tell a soldier's woman she'd gone from wife to widow.

Oli's anger simmered to a look of relief as he slapped a hand on his son's back. The strength of his voice could be counted on as much as anything in Paradise. Still it cracked. "You could've been bitten, son."

"He was," Shaw offered.

Oli's hand fell from Daemon's shoulder. He took a step back, searching his son's body with a long gaze — extra time at his neck, shoulders, and torso before scanning the rest of him — finally settling on the horror at his ankle.

Most of the camp was gathering toward the entrance, a physical wave of tension radiating from them as they took in Oli's demeanor.

Liam stared like everyone else. He could practically feel Avery and Bobby looking down from the watchtowers. Same with Lincoln and Maddie on the other side, probably peering through their binoculars. He could feel Ana's heart racing as she stood beside him, waiting for the horror sure to unfold no matter Oli's decision.

Everyone knew that the virus meant certain death for nearly all of those bitten, but it didn't work on a definitive timetable. Most often, the infection stayed dormant for days, even weeks.

Sometimes, infection took hold more quickly.

Because of the uncertainty, Oli wouldn't allow the infected anywhere near Paradise. The bitten or scratched were cast out immediately, or — if they preferred — given a mercy bullet in the forehead, since most people agreed that the slow fade to zombie was worse than death. Not everyone chose mercy, some preferring to haunt the Barrens, clinging to life no matter its form.

Oli's eyes were glassy and wet, but his gun was already pulled from his holster and greased in his palm. "Well, son, I'm sure you've had plenty of time to think on this during the ride over. You in or out?"

Liam had spent months thinking Daemon was a dick and wishing he would show some diffidence. Now, seeing Daemon's humility while facing his father, he wanted to break down and weep.

"You'll have to get a mark if you choose to be banished." Again Shaw offered what no one was asking for.

"I don't wanna turn." Daemon held his eyes straight and chin high.

"Well then." Oli nodded, losing his first tear, silent as it cut his cheek into two dry patches before splashing the dirt.

Daemon started to kneel.

"Not here," Oli said, pulling his son up by the collar and gently leading him toward the gate's entrance. He called for a blanket — like he always did for a mercy killing — then told his boy to kneel.

Liam was sure the boss would ask someone else to do it, especially once his hand started shaking like it might lose the gun, but Oli wasn't the sort to lose his composure or ask another man to finish his work.

"Sorry about this, son." He trembled once more, then filled Paradise with thunder.

Liam turned to Ana; she was crying as he grabbed her hand.

"Sorry," he said softly, squeezing.

She squeezed back, then whispered, "I can't believe how fast that all happened."

"Better fast than slow. No surprise that Daemon would rather die here."

Ana looked near catatonic.

"You okay?" He squeezed her hand harder.

"No." She released his hand with a sniff and turned, her eyes hard, like every time their conversation walked into an ugly yesterday: Chelle and him, her father, Adam, Charlotte, West Village.

Duncan approached the pair from behind, his abrupt voice like a salve. "Going to be a while before this one settles. We lost a lot today."

Liam turned to Duncan. "What do you think? What's Oli going to do?" Then, after barely a pause, "How bad is this going to get?"

"I don't know." Duncan shrugged. "He just lost his son, so it might send him into the depths of despair, in which case, he'll need me to guide him through it. Or, he might use this as a driver. He single-handedly went into City 5 and took down an entire City Watch squad after they nabbed Daemon, so anything's possible."

Liam nodded but wasn't so sure Oli would rebound so quickly this time. His face must have betrayed that thought.

"I'll talk to him and make sure everything's okay," Duncan promised.

Liam felt a little of his fear lift away.

Oli confided in few, but for some reason, he and Duncan had hit it off from the day they reached Paradise. The men might as well have been long-lost friends, or brothers. Duncan was one of those people you instantly trusted: the right blend of intelligence, compassion, and authority. As such, his words carried weight with the leader.

Oli was a man who needed an ear. Duncan was that and more. Oli had been corked for too long. Duncan showed him how to open the bottle, and trust was instant between them. Duncan never said what Oli confessed, and wouldn't, and that knowledge made Liam believe that the old man could make things okay.

Oli pointed his gun at the sky and swiveled his barrel — the usual sign for closing the gate. He walked by everyone, his jaw set. Some of the fear returned. Maybe Duncan was wrong about Oli this time — he looked like he wanted to hunt every zombie out there bare-handed.

"Think maybe you should talk to him now?"

"Not yet. Grief is like fear, Liam, it makes people act trapped. Oli needs time. Not a lot, but enough to keep him from lashing out."

"Hey, guys." Ana nodded toward the gate, which was slowly reopening. The camp was silent as a courier entered on horseback. "What do you think it is?"

"I don't know," Duncan said. Shaw approached the courier. Words were exchanged, then he followed Shaw's finger to the three of them. "But I think we're about to find out."

A courier wasn't looking to give them good news. Something was wrong.

He thought of Ana's brother, Adam, and hoped he was wrong.

The courier approached with a smile. "Anastasia Lovecraft?"

"Yes?" She looked as nervous as Liam felt.

"You have been summoned by Sutherland. He's waiting for you at Hydrangea."

Ana looked at Liam, uncertain.

"He's waiting with your father."

FOUR

# Jonah Lovecraft



*The Barrens*

KATRINA ONLY GAVE Jonah her name after her horse
had carried them at least ten miles toward Hydrangea,
where Sutherland, a man Jonah knew only by name, was
apparently waiting to speak with him. Considering that
they were offering to reunite him with his daughter, he
would have agreed to meet anyone.

Through those first ten miles — and every mile after
— Jonah was confused, mind swimming through fog as his
weakened arms barely clung to Katrina's waist. He was an
excellent tracker, probably as good as anyone born behind
the Walls, but between her meandering path and his too-
airy head, Jonah couldn't keep track of where they'd been.

He looked down at the canteen of water, provided by
Katrina. "You drugged me, didn't you?"

"Just a little something to make sure you don't
remember the way."

"You ask me to trust you enough to ride out to God

knows where, and *drug me*? How do you know I won't just stab you in the back right now?"

"Because you'll want the antidote."

"*Antidote?*" Jonah said, wanting to stab her.

"Yeah. Don't worry, we've plenty of time to reach camp. But … do anything stupid and you won't live to see your daughter."

"Do you handle your leader's entire social calendar?"

"Sutherland's not *my* leader. He's *the* leader."

"Not mine." Jonah leaned to her side and peered into the distance.

Were the trees on either side of the boulder the same as those that had been there the last three times they trotted by the zigzagging strip of river? Jonah would swear they were, except the bluffs rolling into meadow on the right seemed new.

"We'll see," Katrina said.

"What do you mean, *we'll see*?" She was pissing him off with her knowing way and infuriating quiet. She was more than a courier, but of what she refused to say. "I don't have a leader on either side of the Walls."

"Sutherland is the leader out here and the only one who can bring down the State. If you're not with the People's Party, that puts you with the State."

This sort of *us or them* sounded a lot like every other so-called movement and cult Jonah had ever known, that the State squashed for breakfast.

Jonah would have rattled off questions one at a time if he had the breath, or believed it wouldn't be wasted. More-over, he felt oddly obedient — probably from the poison — on the horse, behind a courier who wasn't a courier, on the way to maybe … *please, please, please be true* … see Anastasia.

Jonah looked up, for a minute having no idea who he was, or where he was going. His companion was a stranger.

He stared at the back of her head, trying to remember her name, only vaguely knowing the beast beneath his thighs was a horse.

Then he remembered *Katrina,* and trees cleared in the distance along with some of his thinking.

He had been drugged, just a bit, but enough to confuse him.

Minutes, trees, hours, wrong turns: all soup. Jonah wasn't surprised by the disorientation; its steady depth intrigued him. He didn't even mind feeling so oddly safe with Katrina.

They stopped in front of a bridge, blocked by a horde of zombies. He expected Katrina to kick the horse into running, maybe find a route around.

Instead she hopped off.

Jonah wanted to jump from the horse and help, but dizziness and fatigue had him nearing collapse. Plus, he wasn't exactly sure what she was doing.

Katrina screamed, drawing the zombies to her. Two bluish silver blades slid from under her cuffs. Then she charged: slicing, gutting, and tearing the undead to pieces in a crimson ballet.

He reached for his crossbow but couldn't find it.

Didn't matter. Jonah was going nowhere. He could barely focus, much less help. She didn't need it anyway.

Katrina finished off the zombies and returned to Jonah.

"Why didn't you go around them?" he asked as she rubbed her blades with a soft cloth. He imagined the blade humming as she rubbed it, unless that was real.

The blades retracted into her gauntlets. "If I leave 'em undead, I'm likely to think of them when I should be snoring. Hard enough to sleep as it is. Besides, there's no better exercise. Killing keeps you ready."

Sleep wasn't Jonah's problem. Even as she got back on the horse, he was already back to dipping in and out of the blur. This happened a few times until he finally surfaced, clearer than ever. The air smelled crisp, and he could feel every prickle. His skin was tighter, his core somehow fuller. Jonah smelled lilac, though that was impossible.

"Why do I feel better?" he asked.

"Because you're taken care of," she said, patting her saddlebag.

"You gave me the antidote?" He didn't remember drinking anything.

Katrina might be smiling. "About an hour ago. In between your naps."

She fell quiet, almost reverential, even after Jonah soiled her silence with more questions to ignore. Finally he fell quiet too. They rode like that for a while until they reached sweeping miles of breathtaking hydrangea.

They stopped among the deepest eggplants and auburns, crimson on blush, cream kissing lavender and green.

"Where's the village?" Jonah asked.

The ground answered with a mechanical grinding. He looked down — they were on a hidden platform covered in soil and grass.

The horse whinnied.

Katrina rubbed its neck and said, "It's okay, girl."

She turned to Jonah. "Welcome to Hydrangea."

JONAH WAITED in a room similar to where Egan had held him in the train station last winter. It was long and narrow, with several benches lined along one wall and a table running across the opposite one. Jonah imagined it used to be loaded with computers. But that time was gone and now there was nothing except for the stacks of books and folders full of papers.

Though he'd only seen a few tunnels on his way to the room, Jonah was sure they were in another abandoned train station.

This one was in much better condition. Well-lit and freshly painted, as if the upkeep was important. Jonah wondered what powered the lights.

After waiting awhile, the door opened and Katrina entered, with a dangerous-looking stranger just one step behind her. A 50-something-year-old with long red hair and a scruffy beard. Though Jonah had only seen him on the Reels, he would remember him anywhere.

A long time ago — Jonah was tempted to call it a lifetime ago — he remembered an uprising the State had brutally suppressed. Normally, such revolts fell into two categories: those led either by angry militants or by oddly charismatic cult-like leaders. Of the two, cultists were more dangerous because their followers were often fanatical, willing to kill and die for their leaders.

One of the State's primary directives — for obvious reasons — was the early extermination of emerging cults. All were considered a cancer to the general welfare. The same sort of cancer that started the Original Plague. City Watch always had spies or used the many surveillance options available to make sure seeds of dissent never sprouted too tall.

The worst cult Jonah had known about was the Children of the Last Light. They preached weird mystical pseudo-religious end-of-the-world nonsense.

The group had been created by a guy named Dennis Weaver, a cook in City 3. The man was unique-looking with his long red hair and beard. In addition to being a cook, he was a church pastor who had somehow spread his message via sects in each of the cities. Weaver was a minister's son, claiming ancestry to Jesus. He preached peace, according to reports, but then one of his parishioners squealed to a Watcher that Weaver was stashing weapons and planning a massive attack on City officials.

City Watch ordered the Reels to report Weaver as a lunatic, actively plotting an attack. A necessary lie to kill the cult before it could do any real damage. Anything to protect the State — the motto Jonah had lived by for so long.

They raided Weaver's compound beneath the bowels of City 3 and found an army's worth of guns. He had rations, vouchers for food, and supplies across all tiers. Plus links to agents who had infiltrated the government. It was the largest cult since the Plague, and it had grown up right under the observant all-seeing City Watch eye.

Weaver was executed in some of the most-watched Darwins ever. Everyone knew the round was probably rigged, but nobody cared. The State mandated harsher laws for public gatherings after the games, and required all City Watchers to take a new class called *Birth of a Cult*, which gave historical accounts of cult leaders going back before Charles Manson, though he was the first figure the curriculum spent any time on.

Now Weaver standing before him, was Weaver, the cult leader he saw die in the Games. "Hello, Mr. Lovecraft, I've been dying to meet you."

# FIVE

# Adam Lovecraft

*CITY 6*

ADAM LOVECRAFT SAT in the classroom with the other cadets, all of them watching a City Watch officer dispatching a horde of zombies on the wall screen.

The Watcher was caught outside the Walls, alone but not off guard, because he had been a good cadet and had learned smart ways to stay alive no matter the odds. That was the message Adam was supposed to get from the instructional, but he couldn't seem to keep his eyes on the screen or his mind on the topic.

He was lucky, considering all that had gone so horribly wrong. Adam's mom had been murdered by his father, who was now sitting comfortably in City 7 as winner of the Darwins. Then his sister was put into the Games for spying, and killed along with Liam, leaving Adam an orphan with no one to care for him. After that, he got kicked out of Chimney Rock and arrested for defending himself.

With so many things going against him, Adam should have been living in the Dark Quarter or dead — it still wasn't clear which would have been worse. A few months ago, Adam was sure he'd be the next Lovecraft exiled into the Games. Any of those would have been his fate if not for Chief Keller saving him.

The chief had said, "Lots of people have it tough, and I'll say you've got it tougher than many. But you know who else had it tough? Jack Geralt. He rose up from nothing to become a champion for the people. I see that same fire in you, Adam. A need to do what is right, no matter what."

Adam was surprised that anyone — outside of his family — saw anything in him. Most people thought he was dim because he was so quiet and expected little from him, if they thought of him at all.

But Keller wasn't like the others.

"You remind me a lot of your father, before his troubles," he'd continued. "And I'll vouch for you, if you promise to always live up to your potential and stop wallowing in personal miseries."

Adam accepted Keller's offer, because what else could he say.

In the months that followed, Keller taught Adam how to think positively and how to be an important citizen of City 6, putting the needs of his fellow man before himself. To Adam, the City Watch message wasn't merely words anymore but something truly important: *Love the State. Promote human dignity and the rights of all individuals by safeguarding the needs of the many.*

With that sentiment firmly ingrained in him, Adam joined the City Watch Junior Advancement Plan, a program set up for "special people who demonstrate an ability to put the needs of the State first and foremost."

Keller had compared it to being selected as a knight's

apprentice, a position of honor that Adam could grow into if he was truly worthy of the title.

He too could become City Watch, just like his father.

Adam was taken in and nurtured, steadily transforming into the best version of himself thanks to the program's constant encouragement. And since leaving Chimney Rock, he'd gone from a nobody to a valuable part of something important — something that mattered. For the first time in a long time, Adam belonged somewhere.

He derived satisfaction from daily challenges, having other Junior Citizens to share experiences with, and feeling good about *Adam* and what *he* could do for the City. Even talking to the other Junior Citizens helped him learn new things, especially about himself.

City Watch gave Adam ideals to strengthen his character like ten thousand pushups would strengthen his arms — Keller had said that. The City Watch Junior Citizen motto said the rest: *The City is Only as Strong as Its Weakest Citizen.*

Adam would never be a weak link again.

He usually had no problem staying upbeat and positive. But today was different.

Today he was thinking about Ana.

Tomorrow would have been her eighteenth birthday, and while he was usually good at being able to keep his sister out of his mind — today that was impossible.

He should be watching the screen, holding his eyes to the *Top 10 Ways to Take on a Horde if You Find Yourself Without a Weapon.* He liked the instructionals, but today's lesson made him think of how he would never see Ana again, and the horrible way that she'd died — overcome by zombies in the middle of the night after trying to escape the Games. The cameras missed filming the attack, but broadcast her grisly remains, torn to strips like boar food.

Adam turned from the onscreen cadet who was fighting rampaging zombies and thought back to Ana's thirteenth birthday. He'd been sad because Ana was getting all the attention. He was still little and used to getting most of it. He'd gone into a corner and pouted, not his proudest moment.

"I have an idea," Ana had said, coming over to her brother and pulling him into a hug. "Why don't we make it your *unbirthday*."

"What's that?" Adam had asked, trying not to cry.

She had laughed. "Any day except one's birthday. It's from *Alice in Wonderland*, I think."

"Unbirthdays don't sound very special."

"That's because no one takes the time to acknowledge them. We should acknowledge yours."

Adam had asked how they would do that. Ana said she would show him, then turned *her* birthday into one of his best days ever.

He looked back to the screen and felt bile in his mouth. He couldn't believe how much it was affecting him. Adam blinked, then turned, hoping Jason "Smoky" Bilson didn't notice him getting queasy.

The Top 10 instructionals had moved on to *Do Nots!*

A careless cadet was getting his face eaten in front by one zombie while a second chewed from the back. Four claws pawed at their meal. Like all instructionals, the footage was real, taken in training. But today's reminded Adam specifically of Liam's final footage, when the zombies were mangling his body and fighting over his head. Adam had watched in horror, both live and during the many repeated broadcasts. It took a while to identify the body, just like Ana's. He felt both better and worse once they finally did.

Better because at least he knew what had happened,

but worse because now they were both really dead. Adam hadn't known Liam all that well, but he was City 6, and you always mourned your own when they fell in the Games — unless the person in the Games had somehow wronged you or your family. Then you rooted against them as hard as you could.

Like with his dad.

As Adam started to wallow in self-pity, he remembered something else that Keller had said.

"Many people see the eye in the City Watch logo as a sign of oppression, that the government is always watching them. Often, those are the people with something to hide. Watchers see the eye as the beacon of hope it is, a sign that no matter how dark things get, our brothers on City Watch are always looking out for us. Things will be better when *we* make them better, Adam. Remember that."

Adam felt awful for Ana and Liam, but in his heart he knew that City Watch and Keller were right. Even in his childhood, City Watch had taken care of them. Daddy was proud to be a Watcher, before whatever happened.

Keller also said, "Family can be who you choose."

And now Keller was his family.

The *Do Nots!* finished and the screen went black.

Commander Nelson went to the front, faced away from the wall screen, and lectured on the virtues of victory and vigilance (the only *V*'s that matter!).

Class finally ended and Adam stood. He clicked his wristlet to ping his advisor; he was finished with Survival and on his way to Combat.

He left the room and heard "Adam" as he stepped into the wide wooden hallway. He turned around to Keller's smile.

"I missed you yesterday. Did everything turn out fine?"

Keller turned and started walking before he could

answer, expecting the boy to fall in step beside him. Adam did, like always.

"Yes," he said, four steps behind Keller, working his legs to make it three. "I hit Ruben in the throat. You were right, he defended low."

"Are you confident you could beat Ruben again?"

"Yes." Adam's pause was so slight, he barely felt it.

Keller heard it anyway. "Why aren't you sure?"

"Because he's the second biggest in class. When he hits, it really hurts."

"Of course it hurts. It will always hurt. You don't learn to make it not hurt, Adam. You learn to ignore it."

"Yes, sir."

"Your father was excellent at going against larger adversaries. Remember Bear? That man would have crushed anyone but your father. Maybe you will be that powerful someday." Keller turned without slowing. "You *are* him, you know."

Keller allowed Adam to catch and maintain his pace before speaking again. "Your father's actions were awful, Adam, and I understand why you might not be able to forgive him. I don't know if I could either, but Jonah Lovecraft wasn't all bad. Before the unthinkable, your father was the best. Never forget the part of him that City Watch was proud to claim. Banish the Jonah Lovecraft who murdered your mother in cold blood and ruined all hope for your sister. Wipe him from existence. Let's speak only of the Jonah I knew as a friend, and the father who loved you so."

Keller slowed his walking. "Don't let anyone get the best of you, Adam. Not ever again. Life tried that once. Don't give it another shot. If your opponent is slow to guard his throat, you be fast, no matter his size. Ready, *fire*, aim. Do you understand?"

"I understand."

Adam's friend Michael was the opposite. He would have told Adam to tire Ruben out, *if* he had to fight him. Michael stressed caution and taking the safe road. Adam preferred Keller's way: "Always do what no one's expecting. And strike when others are hedging."

They were almost to Combat — the part of their walk where Keller would say what he wanted if he'd been holding back. Every once in a while he didn't, and Keller would walk with him from Survival to Combat simply because he wanted to, simply to spend some time with Adam.

*"You don't have a father and I don't have a son. What kind of man would I be if I didn't try to make that hurt a little less between us?"*

Adam had been trying to work out exactly what that meant since Keller had said it, but he knew it felt good and that was enough.

"How would you like to go undercover?" Keller asked.

Adam had no idea what that meant. Real City Watchers went undercover all the time. But Adam didn't know they did that with the cadets and had no idea what sort of mission he might get if he agreed.

But he had also never been more excited by anything, ever. "I would love that!"

Keller smiled. "I'm trusting you to do this, and I will bring you on board, even though missions are never for cadets. I've not searched the archives and don't have access to other cities, but you might be the first to get one."

"Why me?"

"Because no one would suspect a cadet, especially you. And they already like you because they loved your father. You do understand this is serious?"

"Yes."

"There are traitors among us. We must excise the cancer. I can count on you, yes?"

"Yes."

"Excellent. Terrific to hear. This movement is insidious, having already claimed some of our best … it's awful. It's a weed. The only way to stop the problem from spreading is to yank it at the root. I had no idea how deeply the roots seeped into City Watch. Can you appreciate the danger we're in, Adam?"

"Yes."

"And it gets worse." Keller lowered his voice. "The only thing worse than a traitor is a nest of them. Can you imagine how terrible that would be, to have a nest of traitors in your family?"

"Yes," he nodded.

"I think we have a nest," Keller said, like a confession. "Will you help us squash it, Adam?"

"Of course." He was foolish for feeling sorry for himself just a few moments ago. Now he was on the verge of doing something big, something no other cadet had ever done.

He wondered if Ana — considered a traitor to the State — would be proud of him and what he was doing, or disappointed.

SIX

# Duncan Thomas



"HE'S PERFECTLY CALM," Duncan repeated.

But he could tell neither Ana nor Liam believed him. She looked confused; he seemed downright suspicious.

"So he's already over killing his son. Oli?" Liam said. "In two hours, without a rampage?"

"I'm not saying he's fine, or that he's not upset, or that the man isn't deeply grieving. But he just lost his son and eight others. And now you two are leaving. The man needs time to digest."

Ana, always quick, got there first. "Wait. What do you mean 'you two' — you're not coming with us?"

"No, I said I would stay here; it's best for everyone. If I leave now, Oli will fall apart. The camp will follow."

Liam looked suspicious but held his silence, knowing Duncan well enough to trust him, even if something smelled sour.

41

Duncan continued, "I know it sounds flimsy, but I promised Oli I'd stay and help get those three captured orbs up and running, programmable by his people. So far, I got one up and tweaked, so we're close. More importantly, though, I figure he also needs an ear … about Daemon."

"We're not leaving you," Liam said. "I don't trust these people."

"Nothing will happen to me," Duncan insisted. "I'm fine."

"You don't know that. Oli's flaky. And Shaw's downright psychotic. If you piss Oli off, Shaw will seize the chance to take you out. He's been eyeballin' us since our first day."

"Oli needs me, and Oli's still in charge. It wouldn't matter if Shaw and everyone else hated me, they all listen to Oli."

"Makes sense," Ana said, eager to cut the arguments short and find her father. "But when do we get to see you again?"

"I'm not sure." Duncan shrugged. "I imagine I'll either join you next time a courier comes through here. Or if you and Jonah return."

Duncan excused himself before they started digging deeper, especially Liam. Dinner was an hour away, once Shaw returned from the perimeter sweep he was told he didn't have to (then was asked not to) make.

It was absurd to say that Oli needed him that much, and even his fake admission of the cover story felt weak. Paradise had existed before Duncan's arrival and would continue to thrive in its way after he left. That was mostly because of Oli, one of the toughest men Duncan had ever known, well-seasoned by time with the Underground on both sides of the Walls. He also knew that even if Oli *did* fall apart, the village was well-organized enough to fall in step behind Oli's council, a set of three elders who served as the camp's skeleton government.

But Duncan couldn't tell Ana and Liam the truth, that he needed to make an immediate return to City 6 for medicine to keep his infection at bay.

It had been a month since Duncan had run dry of his supply. He never expected to be away from City 6 for so long, but even if he had never returned, West Village's doctor could have brewed a new batch of medicine from the formula Duncan had memorized.

Yet West Village was now in ashes, meaning City 6 was Duncan's only hope … and a place where he was a wanted man.

Duncan had been hiding his infection for two years. He was bitten by a zombie child he and his friend, Dr. Liza, had tried to rescue outside the Walls. The child, docile and in the early stages of infection, escalated immediately. It had nearly killed Duncan. It *would* have, if not for Dr. Liza's quick thinking and the shot she fired to kill the miniature monster.

Dr. Liza had brought him back to her hidden lab in City 6, and promised to keep his infection a secret, in exchange for his being a guinea pig. Duncan was the doctor's first human test subject in her campaign to cure the Plague.

The current serum wasn't a cure, but it was still humanity's present best hope. It worked by keeping the virus dormant in the bloodstream, but it required early administration to the infected, before the virus had a chance to do serious damage. The serum had tested successfully on lab primates. Duncan was the first evidence that the medicine also worked on humans, but Liza needed more subjects — not exactly something humans were standing in line for. And Dr. Liza could never tell the State about her work; they would want to turn prisons into labs.

She didn't want her research public until ahead of the actual cure. That meant waiting until she found subjects who had accidentally been infected, like Duncan.

The medicine worked in ninety percent of its subjects, but still only delayed the inevitable turning and required weekly injections, with five weeks being the longest any of the lab animals had gone without the medication before turning.

Duncan had run out exactly four weeks ago. He could feel himself changing, ever so slightly. Being around zombies, even though they were outside of the camp's walls, caused something to stir in his blood. He could almost feel their hunger and thoughts, like he was part of some sort of hive mind.

But their thoughts were never in words.

They were visual and emotional — fear, hunger, anger — flashes of emotion tainting his thoughts.

He could barely keep these feelings in check, and was cognizant enough to know it was only a matter of time before the collective thoughts would overpower him and trigger the change in his body.

Of course, he had no idea of *how* the change would happen, or how quickly he would turn.

Would his metamorphosis be instant, or a slow degradation? Duncan didn't want to find out, which was why he needed to return to City 6 immediately. Every minute spent in Paradise was another one in which he put his humanity and the entire camp at risk. Duncan had wanted to leave a few weeks back, but guilt kept him in Paradise, tending to Oli, Liam, and Ana.

As the weather grew hotter, zombie activity in the Barrens increased. The zombies seemed hungrier, more desperate to feast. As the undead wandered nearby, their thoughts increasingly seeped into his brain, threatening to trip whatever mechanism inside his cells caused the turn.

Duncan had thought about telling the others — specifically Ana, Liam, and Oli — that he was infected, so they'd let him leave and return to City 6. But if he told the others, he would be banished. If Oli wouldn't allow his son to stay, he'd never let Duncan return. Even worse, Oli would surely be angry that Duncan had withheld the truth of his infection. But he couldn't risk Dr. Liza's life by telling anyone, even if it might have saved Daemon's.

He strolled along the interior walls of Paradise as the sun dipped beyond the tree-lined horizon. It looked as if God had poured molten sun across the sky, casting the world in many shades of beautiful orange.

He felt a chill as he considered how few sunsets were left in his life without the medicine. Then as they often did, Duncan's thoughts shifted back to the well-being of others, Ana and Liam foremost among them. He wished he could escort the two on their trip. Not just to see Jonah again, but to ensure the kids made it there safely.

Duncan had spoken with Oli about sending a hunter orb on their trip. Since he couldn't afford any more men, Oli agreed to consider it, so long as Duncan stuck around to fix the other two orbs. He had agreed, adding that he'd finish training Balon on the schematics. But in truth, Balon had learned enough, which made Duncan feel less guilty about his plan to leave at his first opportunity, whether he was done programming the other orbs or not.

Duncan caught Oli's eyes on his final lap around the camp, looking down from the dining hall porch. He smiled as they exchanged an unspoken kinship from one warrior to another.

Oli rang the bell.

Then Duncan crossed the yard and strolled up the dining hall steps.

~

DUNCAN SAT beside Ana and Liam at a long wooden table, one of five in the dining hall that seated most of the fifty or so citizens left at the camp. Four girls, all from the Harrison clan, worked the kitchen and set the tables before joining Oli at his table for dinner along with the council.

The day's final meal was usually led with a prayer from Oli, but tonight he simply said, "Let's eat," as he sat at the end.

Meal times tended to be lively affairs, with conversation flowing as freely as the drink. Tonight, death was an elephant in the room. All had lost someone close to them, and people were clearly swallowing their feelings — anger, the frustration of a failed mission, and of course, sorrow — along with their food.

A pall of silence had settled over the hall, cut only by the sounds of the mourners poking forks into their meals. Three children who had lost their older brother stared at their plates with red eyes. Their mother, who'd lost her husband three months earlier, didn't even bother pleading with them to eat.

Just when Duncan began wondering if anybody would say anything, the dining hall doors burst open.

Shaw entered, Avery beside him, dragging a wheeled cage and a captured zombie. Everyone gasped, their collective gaze settling on the woman, her eyes wild as she thrashed in the cage, trying to break free or grab ahold of Avery.

Duncan felt her hunger in his brain, interfering with his thoughts. He clasped one hand tight in another, squeezing, trying not to shine any light on the struggle to keep his thoughts from tearing, ripping, feeding ...

Shaw stood as tall as the cage, his hulking frame casting the zombie in shadow. He looked at Oli but spoke to the room, "Anyone wanna have fun?"

He guffawed, dragging his club across the bars while the zombie snarled and gnashed behind them.

The zombie was too close. Her rage and hunger too loud in Duncan's mind, amplified by Shaw's taunting. He squeezed his eyes tight, trying to will the danger away.

But it wasn't working. The undead woman could smell his infection. He felt her staring. Something drew his attention: he wanted to get closer. Something in him wanted something in her.

That something made the caged zombie go crazier, growling like an animal, now on all fours behind the bars, as if preparing to leap, grabbing the metal and grunting at Duncan as if trying to broadcast intention.

"Look." Shaw laughed. "She likes Duncan!"

Oli looked from Shaw to the zombie to Duncan and back, then to each of them again. The zombie's nostrils flared, and there was a terrible scraping, almost a clawing, croak from her throat. Her spindly fingers opened and clenched, reaching out and stretching for Duncan.

Oli looked up from his dinner with tired eyes, turning from the cage to Shaw. "You know the rules," he said softly, then gestured toward the cage. "No infected behind the Walls. You need to get that thing out of here, now."

Shaw barked laughter. "Aw, come on, Oli. She's in a cage. She can't hurt anyone. C'mon. We all want to take out our frustration from today." He addressed the room. "Don't y'all wanna get even, just a little?"

Shaw was a pig, the one person in the village Duncan couldn't stand. Daemon had kept his oaf on a leash, but now Daemon was dead. It was only a matter of time before things bucked between Oli and Shaw and one of them ended up dead.

A few of the men raised their fists and grunted affirmation, but most of the others were too shocked or too scared to utter a word.

The children all cried.

Duncan looked at the courier, sitting three people down, and saw him simply looking at Shaw with no emotion either way. At least he wasn't laughing along.

"Come on, you pussies, you all get a free shot!" Shaw gripped his club tight and thrust the butt through the bars into the zombie's face.

The woman fell back, screaming.

Her pain shot exploded in his mind. Duncan yelped without meaning to, then noticed everyone looking at him. Especially Shaw.

Fortunately, as a preacher it wasn't odd for him to cry out against such an act of violence. "There's no need for that, Shaw. Not here. And especially not in front of these children. We've been through enough today. Nothing will bring back our loved ones."

Shaw's smile faltered, a flash of anger tearing through his eyes as if Duncan had insulted his standing and questioned his manhood. Silence yawned too long, and Duncan was certain something bad was about to happen.

Fortunately, Oli finally spoke. "Outside," he repeated, his voice so low and so barely-there that Duncan figured Shaw was just stupid enough to make the wrong move. The giant shifted on his feet, seeming seconds from protest.

Every eye was on Shaw, the cage, Oli, or some combination — everyone surely wondering what would happen next.

The zombie screamed, inhuman and screeching, boiling in Duncan's thickening blood. He was about to lose control, any second now, but the standoff between Oli and Shaw seemed even more explosive.

He tightened his muscles, trying to stay invisible, then looked to his left. Both Ana, sitting next to him, and Liam, on the other side of her, were looking at Duncan in concern. Both knew him well enough to understand that *something* was up, even if they weren't exactly sure what that might be.

"Fine," Shaw finally said, spinning the cage back around toward the door, to take it out the way he came. "I'll be outside the main gate if anyone wants to have a little fun. Bring your own weapons!"

Duncan stood, dropped his napkin on the table, then clutched a hand to his stomach. "I'm so sorry to leave, but I'm going to be sick."

Oli looked over and gave him a nod, then Ana and Liam both stood and followed Duncan to the door.

"Are you okay?" Liam asked.

Duncan passed Shaw and the zombie without looking back, eager to put distance between himself and the room. The zombie's barks were deafening, crashing like thunder into its thoughts.

He made it halfway to the door before remembering his companions and turning back to look at Ana and Liam. "The stress is eating me alive, staying while the two of you go."

The excuse felt brittle leaving his mouth. Neither could have possibly bought it, but Duncan barely cared as his mind mingled with the zombie's rage and confusion, hunger and fear.

"Be right back!" Duncan yelled as he raced toward the door, trying to make it outside before he lost the battle forever.

But Duncan didn't make it.

The infection took him instead.

# SEVEN

# Anastasia Lovecraft

*PARADISE*

ANA WASN'T sure what to watch, the zombie or Duncan. But something was definitely wrong with Duncan for sure. The preacher had seemed preoccupied ever since their return from the failed raid.

She figured he was upset about the loss of their people, or concerned that she and Liam had been summoned by Sutherland. But as they sat for dinner, he seemed more than preoccupied.

Something was wrong, and Ana wondered why he hadn't confided in them. She and Liam — and even Oli — went to Duncan with their problems, but who could the preacher turn to?

Had they overlooked something seriously wrong with their friend?

She looked over at Liam, who also seemed to note Duncan's odd behavior. And now here was Shaw, making it worse.

He had always been a troublemaker. Oli only tolerated Shaw because he was a hell of a fighter — maybe their best — and one of Daemon's best friends in a world where he would never have more than a few. Strong as an ox and exactly that smart. One of the only things that made him a solid addition to raiding parties was that Shaw and Daemon had complemented one another in the best possible ways. Daemon was a hothead, but he had some of his father's strategic intelligence, even if it had gone unused today. The two of them as a team had been one of the camp's best assets.

But with Daemon gone, there was no one to check his worst inclinations. Everyone — save for Oli, herself, Liam, and Duncan — was too scared of Shaw to ever speak up against him.

*What kind of an idiot brings a caged zombie to dinner when the entire camp is in mourning?*

Only Shaw.

Duncan was sweating. His eyes were big and bloodshot. Wet. His skin was ashen. Even his hair seemed in disarray. He mopped his brow many times each minute and kept stealing glances around the room, mostly from Shaw to Oli to the zombie, then all three again in that order, pausing only to eye her or Liam.

He was probably worried about having to stay while they went to meet Sutherland. Before dinner, Ana suggested to Liam that she try getting Oli's permission for Duncan to accompany them, but Liam said that if Oli wanted him to stay, then the preacher wouldn't be leaving.

Ana wasn't sure. Despite everyone tiptoeing around his mood, Ana saw Oli as perfectly reasonable. But her argument weakened if Duncan looked and acted sick or crazy.

"What's up with Duncan?" Liam leaned in and quietly wondered, before she could ask him the very same thing.

"I have no idea," she whispered back. "But it's *some-thing*. Any ideas?"

"You won't like the one I have." His eyes went from Duncan to Shaw's thrashing zombie.

A horrible truth surfaced in her mind as the zombie screamed in its cage. Duncan flinched, shrinking in his seat, then he was out of it and on his way to the door with Ana and Liam right behind him.

Then everything changed. Something terrible happened to Duncan's face, like blood vessels bursting beneath his skin, flushing his skin with a violet hue. His cheeks began to sag, as if someone had let out the air. Then he started to choke, until Ana realized he was actually growling.

"Duncan?" Ana was desperate for the preacher to be playing a trick.

But he looked back at her with empty eyes. Something was wrong, but she wasn't registering what it could be yet. Instead she stood frozen and staring.

"What the fuck?" Shaw said.

Oli was out of his seat, along with a few other members of Paradise.

Duncan leaped at Ana, his hands closing around her neck as she fell back.

The courier rushed forward, pulling Duncan from Ana.

Duncan spun around on the courier, fast as a lightning strike as he chomped down on his neck.

The courier screamed, falling to the floor clutching his wound.

Duncan turned back on Ana, intent to finish. Some-how, he'd become one of the zombies. She couldn't just shove him away, she had to kill one of her only friends in the world.

Instincts took over and sent her fist at his throat.

But he intercepted her hand as it came toward him … and bit into her wrist.

Ana screamed, brought her foot up and kicked him in the groin, then propelled herself back. Shaw, Liam, and Oli rushed Duncan as she scrambled backward, followed by nearly every man in the hall.

Ana stared in horror as they descended on Duncan and ripped him to pieces. Kicking, punching, and stabbing him with weapons en masse until his muffled death cries were replaced with the wet sound of flesh getting mangled and pounded.

"That's enough." Oli's voice was void of emotion as he set a tender hand to Shaw's shoulder.

There was no way to hide her wrist, as gushing blood painted the floor.

The room held its collective gaze upon her. She looked at Liam, helpless.

"So," Shaw pointed to her wound, "what the fuck are we gonna do about that?"

# EIGHT

# Liam Harrow

THERE WAS no point in hiding Ana's wrist, seeing as it was leaking like a ripped fuel line, blood all over her arm and in a pool on the floor.

Liam's heart was more rattle than drum, frozen in indecision — too many things going bad at once. He raced to Ana's side and grabbed her wrist to assess the damage.

It was bad, but he didn't think the wound alone would kill her. There was a lot of blood, but it wasn't spurting out enough to suggest a ripped artery. He tore the bottom of his shirt and pulled a long strip away. He met her terrified eyes and then looked back down at her wound.

"What are you doing?" Shaw yelled, pointing his gun at Liam.

"She's going to bleed out if I don't do something!" Liam shouted back as he began to wrap her arm.

"She's dead anyway! You wanna be a zombie too?"

Liam ignored Shaw while wrapping her wound. It wasn't like she could turn immediately.

Oli stepped toward them.

Liam didn't look over but could feel the boss on edge.

He'd lost nine of his people, including his son. And now his most trusted confidante — not to mention the camp's technical wizard — was lying in a pool of gore.

"What are we gonna do, Oli?" demanded Shaw.

Oli looked down, his face grave. His gun wasn't out, but those who came to dinner armed — about a third of the hall — had theirs drawn and aimed at Liam and Ana, every barrel awaiting Oli's word.

Avery's gun went from Liam to the courier, who was still twitching, snarling, and starting to turn on the floor. He walked over, and put three of Bruce Lindsey's home-made bullets into the courier's face.

The zombie woman screeched, rattling the bars in her cage. Avery finished her off too, glaring at Shaw as if to invite complaint. But the big man stood down to Liam's surprise.

"What the hell are we going to do about her?" Shaw asked Oli.

"I'll leave," Ana said. "Right now. I'm sorry for all of this."

Her words were heavy and blunt, as if they tore flesh on their way from her throat. The courier had turned fast, in less than five minutes. But he had been dead, or close to it. Ana was still in good shape, and might take longer to turn.

But did that mean five minutes? Five hours? Five days? He had seen too many varying responses to wager an accurate guess as to Ana's infection. He knew only that a bite or scratch was a death sentence in Paradise.

She would turn eventually, and there was nothing he could do.

Liam wished he had recognized the threat sooner, and thought to put a bullet in Duncan before he could bite her. It hurt him to think about how much the world had already taken from Ana. He wanted to help, to say *something*. Liam was often as skilled with words as he was with a weapon, but he had no idea what he could possibly say to improve this situation.

Oli's mood could be anywhere. He might order them from his sight — a best-case scenario that saw them leaving Paradise to find Jonah, assuming Ana didn't turn on the way.

But Oli could also add them to the mess in between Duncan and the courier. Shaw would have to heave the bodies out of the dining hall and burn them in a pile, and Hardwick would mop. But Shaw would be thrilled to double his load and be rid of them in style — with a blazing fire in the yard — and Hardwick wouldn't mind too much since the floor was already sticky.

"It's not that easy. This isn't just a bite, it's a violation." Oli sounded sad more than angry. He looked from Liam to Ana. "What did you two know about his infection?"

"Nothing," Liam answered. "I swear."

"I was asking Lovecraft," Oli growled.

"We didn't know, Oli," Ana replied, holding her bloodied, bandaged wrist. "We had no idea, either of us. Never saw him get bit or anything."

"I don't even know when he *could have* been bitten," Liam added. "He's only left camp while out on raids. But we were never attacked by zombies when he was with us."

"Exactly," Oli said. "If he's not been bitten since getting here, then he came in infected. Duncan knew the rules — you did too." He narrowed his eyes on Ana. "How long did you know?"

Liam opened his mouth.

"Shut it, Harrow. I asked Princess City Watch."

"I didn't know anything," Ana said. "*We* didn't know anything. I swear on my father in the Barrens, my brother at the Rock, and my mother in the dirt, Oli. We didn't know a thing, and we weren't keeping secrets. I accept banishment, and will go right now if you let me."

Ana bowed slightly, still holding Oli's eyes. Someone said, "Bullshit. They're lying. Kill 'em both."

The room rumbled with agreement.

Liam said, "She's telling the truth. You think we would've been sitting with Duncan if we knew he was infected? You think we wouldn't have been put a bullet in his head to protect Paradise? This happened to *all* of us."

Shaw stepped forward, waving his gun between them with the calculated carelessness that made it clear he didn't care who he shot first. "Don't matter whether they knew or not. She's bitten. We kill her now, before she turns."

"No!" Liam stepped in between Ana and Shaw.

He'd brought his weapon to dinner — didn't even go to the bathroom without it — but fought his every urge to draw. Another gun would only escalate this situation into a bloodbath. Bravery was easier when it was only him paying the price for a misstep.

"We're both leaving right now, so nobody here is at risk."

"No." Oli shook his head. "Like *I* said, it's not so simple. This is treason. The three of you came to Paradise together, with one of you infected." He looked at Liam. "How do I know *you're* not infected right now? Maybe this spreads in some other way, other than bites … maybe you've already infected us all."

A collective murmur rippled through the room.

Ana was chewing her lip, trying not to cry.

"Look," Liam said, perfectly calm and speaking only to Oli. "I can't claim to understand any of this, or how awful this day has been for you, but I watched as the worst thing that could have ever happened to you did, *after* losing eight of your people. Then having a friend turn during dinner, and one of your favorite among us bitten."

Everyone knew how much Oli thought of Ana, and while that affection wouldn't save her life, it might help Liam maneuver their way out of the room. "I'm sorry about all of that. I survived the Darwins, for a long month of horror before you found us, then plenty of hard times after that, especially the loss of friends and family — following a trap I warned us away from. We've all suffered horrors and been dealt the unthinkable."

The crowd grew restless. A few voices saw the sense and truth in his words — the ones who appreciated the sacrifices and hard work that he, Ana, and Duncan had all been putting in day after day — and probably appreciated the circumstances that had kept Duncan from revealing his infection to the camp. But such voices were whispers compared to those screaming for blood. Oli wouldn't be concerned about doing right so much as doing what was best for Paradise.

Liam had come with Duncan and Ana, so he was guilty by association. He looked around at the rising tide of bloodlust — any second now someone might pull a trigger. It was all he could do to keep his gun holstered.

Shaw shifted on his feet, hungry, eager to kill Ana and Liam, but still waiting on an *okay* from Oli.

Liam gave Oli a nod, followed by a necessary reminder. "Ana's been summoned to Hydrangea. And Sutherland wouldn't send a courier if he didn't want her. What will he say when she never shows? And worse, that the courier is dead? You really think that's going to go over well with Sutherland?"

"I'm sure he'll understand why we killed her," Shaw argued.

Liam wanted to maintain that it was against the Pact

between the camps to ignore a request by Sutherland, but in truth he didn't know enough about the governing rules to win the debate. Arguing politics might flare tempers further.

"She won't make it a few days with that bite, it's too deep," Bobby yelled. "No way she's making it long enough to get to Hydrangea."

Oli spun to face him. "Maybe not, but Harrow's right. It's not our call. Sutherland requested we send her, so we do. What happens after she leaves, that's not on us." He looked at Ana's arm, and then her with disgust.

"Hydrangea has doctors, right?" Liam asked. "If we can make it there, maybe they can treat her."

"There's no treatment for infection. But they are more tolerant at Hydrangea. They have doctors and the space to care for the afflicted without risking lives."

"You're not gonna actually let them go there, are you?" Shaw clearly couldn't believe his big ears.

"I'm the one who answers to Sutherland. I say she goes." Something flickered on Oli's face, and Liam knew what was coming. "Just know, I'll spare no escort. I wouldn't even allow you to leave, except I'm not sure you would last a week after what's happened here tonight."

"Fine," Liam said. At least they would leave Paradise alive.

"One other thing ..." Oli turned to the crowd and gestured for everyone to lower their weapons. The room reluctantly obeyed, lowering their guns and sheathing their swords. He turned back to Ana and Liam. "We need to mark her."

"No," Liam refused. Sweat was soaking his shirt, and he didn't dare turn to see how Ana was faring beside him. There was no way out, but still he couldn't bear to watch what was coming. "There's no way she'll heal by the time we get there. The bite will be obvious."

"It's nonnegotiable, Harrow. Bites are healed and hidden, as our friend Duncan proved. He's been living months, or longer, all the while hiding his infection. What if it takes a month to reach Hydrangea, or two?"

"*Please.*"

"Infected are branded upon banishment. You know this, Harrow. She can get it on her left arm instead of the right, seeing as the bite's done enough damage there already."

Ana was silent, her body braced, as ready as she could be for what was about to happen. Shaw reached out to grab her, but Oli swatted his hand.

"Does it look like she needs any grabbing?"

Those campers rooting for Ana's unharmed release left the dining hall and disappeared to their homes, the branding too awful to watch. But those with blood in their nostrils, desperate to see "justice," followed the procession outside.

Ana followed Oli, with Liam just behind. Shaw, Avery, and the other spectators walked behind them, hands on their weapons — just in case — as they made their way from the dining hall, through the yard, then over to the blacksmith's hut where Ana closed her eyes and kneeled.

Tears spilled from her closed eyes.

Liam stared, hoping for mercy that wouldn't be coming.

Unlike some of the crowd, the blacksmith had been kind to Ana since the afternoon of their arrival, offering his rations of wrinkled fruits, since he was indifferent and she loved them. Named Baker Gray, he now stoked the fire and readied the iron, until the backward $Z$ was glowing red. He looked at Ana — eyes welled with an apology she couldn't see — still on her knees and awaiting the brand, like a child at the doctor's trembling for their shot.

Baker pressed the molten $Z$ to Ana's flesh, and the silent room filled with a sickening sizzle. Liam wished he couldn't hear it, wished he couldn't smell the vile odor of burning flesh, and wished he couldn't feel the joy blooming from her misery. He wished he could do something to dull or numb her pain, or take it for himself.

But the hiss was nothing. What followed seconds later hollowed him out.

Ana's scream was the most brutal sound Liam had ever heard. He wanted to kill every fucker there who dared to find joy in her suffering. End them all before fleeing with Ana. But there wasn't a damned thing he could do beyond waiting for the nightmare to end. He scanned the crowd, taking in their bloodlust, quite certain that the monsters inside Paradise were worse than the ones shambling outside it.

Baker unwrapped the makeshift bandage of Liam's torn shirt, inspected the bite wound, then went to a long shelf on the wall where he retrieved a salve, smearing some onto his fingers and rubbing it on Ana's arm as she flinched.

"This will take some of the pain away," Baker said, wrapping her injury.

Despite the obvious fear in camp, the blacksmith showed no timidity about treating her wound, acting more like a concerned father extending mercy to the infected child. He wiped some salve onto the backward Z now permanently burned into her skin, then wrapped her left inner forearm.

Ana's eyes lit with gratitude at the blacksmith's concern.

Liam wanted to damn anyone who had turned their

backs on her. Oli was also looking out at the crowd. He caught Liam watching and turned his attention to Shaw and said something inaudible.

"Fifteen minutes, then get the fuck out. Johnson." Oli turned to a small woman who had spent a few minutes that morning flirting with Liam, but could now only look at him with fear and disgust.

"Yes?" she said.

"Tell Decker to get down here. They'll need a location for Hydrangea, but he can't draw them a map to take in case they run into bandits. Wait with him, then both of you make sure they don't leave with paper."

Johnson nodded, then Oli turned and left Liam and Ana to all the suspicious eyes, whispering mouths, and itchy hands wanting any excuse to shed more blood.

"It's going to be okay," Liam promised, hugging Ana close to his body, hoping that wasn't a lie.

# NINE

# Jonah Lovecraft

"I THOUGHT YOU WERE DEAD." Jonah stood but ignored Sutherland's offer to shake hands, staring at the man he'd seen die in the Games many years before.

Sutherland motioned for Jonah to sit back on the bench. His long red hair was pinned atop his head in a bun. A broad sword was sheathed on his back, with a pair of guns in bandolier holsters beneath each arm. His pale skin seemed enraged by the sun, pouting in splotches that smothered his red-pepper freckles. His visage reminded Jonah of a drawing he once saw of an Old Nation Wild West gunslinger.

He shook his head and kept staring, waiting for the man who summoned him to finally say something.

Sutherland finally spoke, his voice as dusty as Jonah had imagined. "You really believe everything you see on TV? I figured you knew better than to trust the State. I suppose you also believe all the lies they told about me being a terrorist and a cult leader?"

Jonah knew Sutherland as Weaver, and Weaver was a monster.

Though, so was Jonah to all who had watched him on the Games or his trial's Reels footage. But Weaver was supposedly responsible for some unconscionable behavior that was in no way befitting the Underground. There was a big difference between attacking the State and pursuing innocent civilians, as his cult did after his arrest but before they were flushed out by City Watch.

"So you're innocent? You didn't have plans to attack citizens? Your people weren't responsible for bombing the Arcade in City 3 after your arrest?"

"Of course not." Sutherland dug into his reddish scruff like he was lying, while holding Jonah's eyes like he wasn't. "I didn't kill a soul. I wanted to, yes, but never innocents. Only the corrupt government that has destroyed so many lives, trampling on our rights and eradicating every dissenting voice. We were a threat to the State, so they set us up and turned us into boogeymen. The government always destroys what it can't control. How about you, Jonah? Are *you* guilty of your supposed crimes?"

"I watched you die in the Games."

"All faked, same as your daughter's death."

"What do you mean?" Jonah tensed.

"You didn't see? The Games showed Anastasia and her *boyfriend* getting killed a month or so after escaping the Games. It's all a lie scripted for the sheep. I escaped, as did she. Same as you 'made it' to City 7. The people can never know when the State has been bested."

Jonah looked from Katrina to Sutherland. "Where is she? Where's Ana?"

"She was staying in another village, but is now on her way. I've sent for her. She should be here in around ten days."

"You fucking lied to me?" Jonah said to Katrina.

"Would you have come if she hadn't told you Ana was waiting?" Sutherland asked. "Would you have come if she used my old name rather than my new one? We say what we must to finish our jobs, something I've learned from our overlords."

Jonah didn't like being lied to, and sure as hell didn't trust these people. Unfortunately, there was no one else to believe in. He would have to play ball until Ana's arrival, assuming she was really on her way.

"Relax, Jonah. You and I are sharing a side, and both want the same thing."

"What's that?"

"To bring down the State."

Sutherland widened his eyes and set a hand on Jonah's shoulder, managing to look soft … and still like the most dangerous man he'd ever met. "You're safe, Jonah. I brought you here because though you might not yet know it, you are one of us."

Sutherland turned from Jonah and pointed to the bench behind him again.

Jonah finally sat.

Sutherland grabbed a chair from the long desk, dragged it over, and took a seat across from Jonah. "Do you know why the State thought I was so dangerous?"

"Because of your religious leanings? All that end-of-the-world shit?"

Sutherland laughed — an odd and unsettling laugh, a lunatic's chuckle. Jonah tried to reserve judgment, not hold the man to his State-created persona, but Sutherland wasn't helping his own cause.

"No, they don't give a shit about that. And yet, they went overboard, painting me as a deranged prophet. They needed me gone because I was *organized*." Sutherland tapped at his temple. "I've always had this ability to find things nobody else could, to see the patterns no one else saw. I spotted a weakness in the State and wished to exploit it, but first I needed men. The authorities were right: I *was* going to stage a coup. But they lied about the *hows* as much as the *whys*. I would never have permitted innocent bloodshed. I found a way to sever the hydra's head and replace it with a government by the people, for the people. Like the Old Nation."

"Why are you telling me all this? I can't do anything to change what happened to you. And besides, it seems like you've landed on your feet."

"I'm telling you because I'm closer than ever to reaching my goals. The State believed they were exiling me, but out here they have only empowered me further. I have found my people — thousands of like-minded men and women, willing to claim their destiny and fight for the liberation of our brothers and sisters trapped behind the Walls, victim to all their infinite lies. We're doing what the Underground started but could never finish. We have nine camps, and this base is as strong as anything the City has ever dreamed of creating."

"And you need me for what, exactly?"

"I need you to locate someone for me."

Jonah met the man's eyes. "Who?"

"A Dr. Liza Goelle. A scientist in City 6."

Jonah knew her. She'd been an Underground sympathizer, a friend of Duncan's ... and Jonah's one near indiscretion in his many years of marriage. "What is she to you?"

"Dr. Goelle is the missing piece of our master plan."

He could feel Katrina behind him, her curiosity subconsciously drawing her closer. Clearly she wanted to know about this plan too. "Missing piece of your plan? How so?"

"First, I need to know if you'll help."

"Why should I help without you telling me what the hell I'd be doing?"

"Sorry, Jonah, but I don't have that kind of faith in you. I need you to find Dr. Goelle and talk her into coming here to Hydrangea. That's all you need to know for now, all you *can* know. But no harm will come to her, you have my word."

"Then go find her yourself. You obviously have contacts inside City 6, people who are supportive of your cause. What makes you think I can retrieve her any better than the resources you already have?"

"Must I say it?" His eyes twinkled, flitting from Jonah to Katrina and back.

"Yeah," Jonah said, calling the possible bluff. "Say it."

"We are aware of your personal history with Dr. Goelle."

"You don't know anything," Jonah replied, his anger simmering, knowing he had to play nice until his reunion with Ana.

"You underestimate us," said Sutherland, seeming amused. "We've done our homework. We know everything about you, Jonah Lovecraft. *Everything.* That is why we have gone to such great lengths in getting you here."

"What do you mean?"

"Did you really think you won the Games alone?"

"You *helped* me?" Jonah stood, unable to hide his infuriation. He didn't remember anyone killing those zombies but *him*. Anyone fighting and escaping Bear but *him*. "How?"

"We did what we could. Eliminated some of your competitors, helped thin the zombie hordes, and interfered with orbs when we had to. It's difficult to pull off without being caught, but we managed. You had to defeat Bear, of course, and bravo on that. But we helped to even your odds where we could, as we always do after finding someone worthy of our cause."

Jonah stared at Sutherland, trying to digest his words. *Can it all be true?* "You have other winners here?"

"A few, though we lost some of the better contestants when we failed to intervene before they got killed off."

"Why didn't you get me before now? Why the hell did you let me get kidnapped by Egan?"

Sutherland looked over at Katrina, then back to Jonah. "She was *supposed* to pick you up from City 7, but unfortunately she got held up. You fell off our radar right after that."

"You must not have been looking hard. I've scoured the Barrens for six months. How could you miss me?"

Katrina said, "Maybe *you* weren't looking hard. *We* found Ana months ago."

Jonah glared at Katrina. "I want to see my daughter."

"As I said, Anastasia is on her way," Sutherland told him.

"I'm not waiting. Have your girl take me to her."

Sutherland said, "That's not possible. I've spent valuable time and resources getting you here. I won't hold you against your will, but I can't let you just walk out of here. No one leaves Hydrangea without an escort, and I don't have anyone to spare at the moment."

Sutherland reached behind his head and drew a long wooden pin from his topknot. A fountain of hair spilled red from head to waist.

"Patience, Jonah. Not long ago you had no hope of finding your daughter. Now, Anastasia's on her way. You are in a sanctuary where the food is good and the company warm." Sutherland smiled. "And Jonah, there are as many women looking for a warm man as the other way around — no reason you should be lonely tonight, or any to follow."

Sutherland stood, slapped Jonah on the shoulder, then led him from the room. "Anastasia will be here soon. We have much to discuss in the meantime."

# TEN

# Adam Lovecraft

ADAM DIDN'T KNOW if he was overexcited about meeting Michael at the Arcade, and that's why his stomach hurt so much, or if it was something else. Despite the acid, he grabbed some fried greens from the basket and shoved them in his mouth, listening to Michael while thinking about Keller and everything he'd said to recruit him as a spy.

The fried greens weren't good enough to justify the extra credits on Adam's ration card, but fortunately he wasn't paying. The breading was too hot and the greens were frozen beneath it, so a single bite both burned and frosted his tongue. Adam couldn't understand why Michael smiled while chewing — they were totally gross — and wondered if he would have noticed as much if he was still living at the Rock. Food at the City Watch Academy was much better than it had been at the orphanage. Nips was Michael's favorite place to eat in the Arcade because he liked the small baskets of fried foods. Adam used to think they tasted good, but like his time with Michael, Nips wasn't as good as he remembered.

Michael was rambling. "I have no idea who the other two guys were, but the one in the middle was *definitely* Predi Dawson. You think he knew?"

Adam had no idea, not if Predi Dawson knew, or even *what* he might have known. Adam drifted off, thinking about his walk to the Arcade, which he had spent wondering what he would say to Michael. He couldn't tell him, no matter how much he wanted to. Plus, the few times he'd brought up the Academy, Michael didn't seem interested. Adam was trying hard to think of anything they still had in common.

"Adam?" Michael said. Then, "Never mind." *Again.* Another few beats of silence followed by, "Did you do anything … you know, for her birthday?"

"Yes." Adam brightened. Keller had taken him to get ice cream. He said that ice cream couldn't make things better, or bring Ana back, just like it could never bring back his son. But that it was important to acknowledge things as they are and was unwise to ignore Ana's birthday. That was why he never ignored his son's. Sometimes you had to celebrate like your loved ones were there even when they couldn't be. "I had ice cream to celebrate the good times I had with Ana, when she was still alive and could be with me."

"Ice cream?" Michael raised his eyebrows. Ice cream was expensive.

"Yeah, Chief Keller took me. Ana liked to have ice cream on her birthday, though I usually asked for cake for mine."

Michael winced like he'd just tasted something bad. Maybe he finally realized how awful the food was. "Chief Keller? What did he want to know about Ana?"

"Nothing exactly. He just asked me to tell stories that I remembered, so I told him the one when she shaved her arms …" Adam laughed, then stopped to think. "Oh! And the one about the time when she climbed the tree in the Lookout Gardens and fell out, right into Dad's arms, but it was a perfect fall, like he had been waiting even though he wasn't. We joked that Dad was like Captain Republic." Adam laughed again.

Michael didn't. "Which is the 'shaving her arms' story?"

"Oh." Adam could feel his cheeks flush. "You didn't know that? My sister shaved her arms. She was really hairy. Like a dog."

Adam felt bad; Ana probably wouldn't want Michael to know that. He changed the subject. "So what's new?"

Thankfully, Michael just laughed and went along with the shift of topics. "Nothing, really. I still hate the shirt factory, but that'll change soon. I've saved enough credits for a new aptitude test. I'm taking it next month. Been studying a lot, and I'm sure I can score myself into something better. I hate it there," he added, like he didn't say it all the time.

"What do you *want* to do?" Adam asked.

Michael never talked about much of anything, other than Ana. Adam was pretty sure he had been in love with her but didn't dare ask. He didn't want to embarrass Michael or make him feel even worse that Ana was gone. He figured losing someone you were in love with was almost as bad as losing your sister. Even though he and Michael were on very different paths, they would always have Ana.

"That's easy." Michael smiled. "I want to go where I can fix stuff. One day I want to open a repair shop. It can be small, and I know I can save the credits. I'm good at mending what's broken, but I'll have to prove my worth with the State first. Putting in time at a shop now would be best, like saving for later. I can't work in that factory for the rest of my life, like my father."

Michael really could tinker. That's one of the reasons Adam's dad had always loved having him around.

He narrowed his eyebrows and looked closer at Adam. "You're following in your father's footsteps, aren't you? Was your dad a cadet in school, or did he only join City Watch after he graduated?"

"Yeah, Dad was a cadet," he said, reaching for some fried greens. "But not as young as me. Chief Keller says I'm one of the youngest ever, but after my background — good and bad — the State was willing to make exceptions."

"What made you want to join?" Michael asked.

"I joined to stay safe, and because Chief Keller saved me. I told you what happened with Morgan and Tommy and Daniel. If Chief Keller hadn't been there, I would have been sent to the Dark Quarter, or worse."

"Yeah, but didn't Keller give you the weapon? You never would've … well, you know."

"The weapon saved me. Keller saved me."

Michael's brow furrowed, then after a minute he said, "Why do they find *you* so interesting? I mean, you're fourteen. It seems a bit young."

"Because of my dad," Adam said, hurt and fighting to hide it.

"An exception from the State. You don't think that's a little weird?"

"No. I think it's nice."

Before Michael could explain why it wasn't, Adam told him more about City Watch and the work they did, both behind the Walls and on outreach missions into the Barrens. To make sure that his first point wasn't lost, Adam ended with, "And they're nice to me."

Michael looked so bothered that Adam finally had to ask: "What?"

"*What* what?"

"Why do you look annoyed that I'm talking about my job?"

"Doesn't City Watch make you mad? I mean, don't you care that they screwed your dad over?"

Adam felt his jaw set. "No, because he wasn't screwed over. Dad had to pay the consequences for his actions. What happened was *fair*." He took a second, regulated his breath — in and out just like they taught him. "Don't forget: he murdered my mom, Michael. I don't know what happened to Dad. He was good before that, but after, well, I can't blame City Watch. They were there for us when Dad was with them, and they were still there even when he wasn't."

"Seems to me that guys like your dad might be the real heroes, while a terrorist like Jack Geralt somehow rises to be the State's One True Leader."

Adam couldn't believe what Michael was saying, especially *out loud*. "Shhhh!" He slammed his lips with a finger while leaning forward. "Talk like that will get you picked up."

Michael laughed, softly at first, but then louder. "What are you going to do, Junior Citizen, arrest me?"

Michael had never spoken to him that way before, and Adam didn't like it.

He looked around, suddenly nervous. "You know I can't arrest you. But why would you say that, Michael? Why would you call ... *him* ... a terrorist?"

Michael laughed again, although this time instead of flying from his mouth untethered, it dripped like liquid from his lips. He shook his head, not wanting to meet Adam's eyes. When he did, someone Adam had never seen was sitting across the table from him. The Michael he knew was gone. Maybe dead.

"Sorry, kid, there's no other way to say it." He paused, and in that pause Adam wondered what Michael was about to let go. "You're not seeing the truth. I'm glad you're happy at City Watch bunking with the chief, except that I'm really not. They're feeding you with lies, man. And you don't see it. Geralt *was* a criminal. We're asked, I'd argue *required*, to hail a man who robbed, cheated, and murdered his way to a ruling seat, where he now sits in City 1 — high in a glass tower, airship, or ivory dome, depending on the rumor — living like a god on that lie, cracking down on people like your dad as history buries the truth."

Adam looked around again. "And where do I learn *the truth*, Michael? From you? Do you know all the secrets, all the stuff I never would've learned in Chimney Rock if I'd stayed, all the things they won't teach at City Watch? Do you know *the truth*, Michael? Tell me what *the truth* is in your world."

Adam was shocked that he had turned his back on the City. His stomach turned as he wondered if Michael was part of the Underground.

Maybe *he* was insidious; maybe he was part of the cancer; maybe Michael was going to get himself into big trouble because Keller was looking for people just like him, who were saying the exact same things that Michael was saying.

Adam didn't want anything bad to happen to him. Before the chief, Michael was all he had. But now Adam had City Watch. He had routine. He had Keller. And, in many ways, he had family again.

Michael stared at Adam for a truly terrible moment, like he knew he'd gone too far, said too much. His face burned, the muscles hungry to stretch. He finally tilted his mouth into something like a smile and made a sound that was almost like a laugh. "I'm just messing with you!"

Adam nodded, pretending to not be bothered.

But, of course, he was.

ELEVEN

# Anastasia Lovecraft

THE SKY WAS SLOWLY PULLING layers of charcoal onto its long sweep of blue. Under normal circumstances, Ana would stop to appreciate the beauty. But now she could only think about a similar darkness spreading through her body.

Her eyes watered and her head felt like it was about to explode. Pain singed her ears; they might even be bleeding. Angry prickles erupted from her cells, her body burning so hot that she might have been glowing. All of her bubbled — except for her throat, which felt clawed by something in her windpipe.

Ana didn't think she could go on much longer, but she was unwilling to stop a second before then. When she closed her eyes — which she could only do for seconds without Liam wanting to stop and make sure she was okay — Ana could feel where everything started: the wrist that promised her rotting end.

She kept her face from Liam as they stepped through a pack of decomposing bush dogs. There was nothing unusual, seeing fallen canines. Animals were usually faster than zombies, but the undead traveled in larger packs and were sometimes fast enough to surround packs of wild animals, close in on them, and feed. That was the oddity: there was flesh left to rot on the dogs — as if the zombies had scattered before they could finish.

Ana wanted to point this out, but she could barely keep her head straight through the pain.

"How are you doing?" Liam looked over, knowing the answer, but clearly unsure of what else he could say.

Ana was afraid she might cry if she opened her mouth. She tried not to wince, shaking her head and hoping Liam got it: *I'm fine as long as we keep moving.*

"Ana?"

*I'm dying.* "Yes?"

The single word, a syllable, seemed to take everything she had.

"Would you like to stop? We can stop."

"No." Ana shook her head and kept walking. They had to reach Hydrangea and her father. She bit her bottom lip. "I'm good for now. Let's walk until dark."

"Okay," Liam said, clearly hating the idea.

They trudged past the dead dogs. They were three or so miles outside of Paradise, following Decker's route, delivered in a hurry to get them the hell out of there.

Ana still wanted Liam to ask about the dogs. Wanted him to say something, to act like he used to. *Before.* But like everything else since leaving camp, the subject was a silence between them.

They needed to discuss what would happen if she turned before Hydrangea. There was slim hope waiting at the camp: maybe tolerance, temporary solace, or medicine in her best case scenario, but her cut was a ravine, deep enough to turn her blood itchy. Mostly Ana wondered how long she had — part of her thought the change could happen at any time, and there was nothing she could do to stop it. No matter how close she was to a reunion with her father.

"If we stop for the night, we'll go twice as fast in the morning."

"I'm okay, really." Ana measured her words to make sure each carried its usual rhythm. "I just need to keep my mind from the pain. Keep talking. Tell me a story."

Liam looked helpless, like he wanted to reach out and soothe her but couldn't, and didn't know what to say or do to make everything better. "What sort of story?"

"Anything." Her smile was barely a crack. "Just don't make me answer any questions."

Liam looked up at the sky, thinking. He opened his mouth, then closed it, as if undecided on what story to tell. Finally, he brightened as he turned to her. "Want to hear about the first time I had steak?"

Ana had eaten steak a few times, but only because her father was a City Watch major, and his rations covered red meat on most holidays, except for Fertility and a few of the other less celebrated days. She nodded.

"My Uncle Malcolm is a master griller. That's his job — he cooks for all the bankers at The Fidelity, except for when they loan him to Legal downstairs. His station wouldn't normally permit rations for steak, but I guess the State can only be so cruel, making a man cook every day of his life and never having any steak for himself. So four times a year, they grant him the pleasure. He gets enough to share, and Uncle M's a man who likes company. He's my dad's brother. The two of them were total opposites. Uncle M loved everyone, my dad hated them all — he was a miserable fuck a long time before he killed himself. Anyway, I think Uncle M always felt bad that the State wouldn't grant him guardianship over me and that I wound up at the Rock. So he started inviting me to some of his cookouts when I turned eleven. The piece was *this* big," Liam squeezed his fingers together so they were about the size of a pebble, "and I couldn't wait to see it on the grill."

Ana tried not to picture her searing wrist as pictures of cooking flesh entered her mind. She wondered how long into the story Liam would be before realizing he probably should have chosen an alternate tale.

"Uncle Malcolm says we're animals, and that all animals love to eat meat. But we're the *only* animal that knows how to cook our food, some better than others. He says grilling's an art. Starting with the right meat is everything. The bankers and Legal had fancy cuts — filets, ribeyes, and strips. Uncle M's rations never covered those cuts, so he cooked something called chuck. He said the cut didn't matter so much if you knew what to do with the meat."

Liam looked over again. Ana tried cracking her smile wider, not wanting him to know how much she hated his story.

"Once the meat was finished we'd pretend we were bankers, businessmen, or directors, living in the highest floors of the tallest apartments, eating the best meats from the fanciest cuts, sipping real wine from actual glasses, and feasting on the kinds of desserts we could only dream of." Liam looked at her, raised his eyebrows, and added, "That's where I first met Duncan, you know — at one of M's steak parties."

"Oh?" Stories about Duncan beat searing meat, even if they were more painful.

"He was a friend of my uncle. One rotation, M took the party to a few guys in the Underground. He invited me to the cookout, though I didn't know why at the time. M was like that after my dad was gone, there for me in ways I didn't expect or know I needed. I was twelve or thirteen then, so it was a couple of years before I knew more about the Underground."

Same characters, dramatic change of subject. "How long do you think Duncan was infected?"

"I don't know." Liam shrugged. "But I hate that he kept it from us. This didn't have to happen."

"Duncan was honest about everything — how could he lie about this?"

"You're honest, but you would've kept your infection a secret, too."

Ana considered the many secrets that Liam had kept from her, including his worst — the one where he ratted on her father to City Watch and got him sent to the Barrens, which led to her getting thrown to the wrong side of the Walls, and abandoning a brother who needed her back in City 6.

It had taken time to forgive him. Duncan had also been angry with Liam, but still he'd explained that Liam's seeming betrayal was his only real play at the time. Ana might have done the same to protect her family.

She wondered how Adam was doing, and how he might have fared out in the Barrens with them. The State made it sound like a sprawling wasteland. Even its name spoke of nothingness. But the Barrens teemed with life, with citizens thinly spread across the land.

Orbs broadcasting the Games were careful to show only contestants, zombies, and the occasional dangerous animal. Beauty beyond the Walls was never on display. There were never human survivors, much less thriving communities outside the Cities.

Ana could barely get her head around what was slowly

surfacing as an inarguable truth: *there might be more people outside the cities than in them.*

Ana wondered how she had willingly lived blind to the truth for her entire life so far. Sure, her family had been happy when her father worked City Watch. They didn't get to live in the high apartments or eat steak, but they had harbored no fear of the Dark Quarter, and celebrated every State holiday in style. Ana had friends, and a fair assignment even if she hated her job.

Now, everything was different, and it always would be.

Especially now that Ana was dying.

A searing pain shot up her arm to punctuate the thought, starting at her wrist, then screaming into her shoulder. She lost an involuntary yelp.

Liam stopped walking and turned to Ana. "We have to stop." He looked up at the sky for show. "It'll be dark in minutes. We need shelter, and you need rest."

"Okay," she agreed, too weak to do anything else.

He accepted her surrender with a smile, then softly grabbed Ana's left hand and gently pulled her behind him, headed toward a copse of trees she could barely make out in the distance, at the base of some hills.

"Tell me a story about Chelle," Ana said, curious, in need of distraction, and knowing that Liam would be more generous with his stories in light of her pain.

"Do you believe in love at first sight?" he finally asked, after a long and uncomfortable pause.

"No." Ana shook her head. "I don't think I do."

"It used to be the same for me ... I'm as far from a hopeless romantic as you can get. But with Chelle, it *was* love at first sight. This isn't retrospective pondering, and I'm not blurring love and lust. There was something special about Chelle and we didn't even have to talk before

I felt how much I wanted to know her. I'm a cynic, Ana, not an idiot. I know love when I see it."

She shouldn't have asked. Liam went on and on (and on) about Chelle after that. She tried not to feel hurt, especially seeing as she had been the one to ask, but Ana couldn't help but wonder how he felt about *her*. Over the past few months, she'd felt Liam's growing affection, but how much of that had been in her mind? Would Liam sacrifice everything for her like he had for Chelle?

But … hadn't he already? Liam had entered the Games to "make things right" and protect her as long as possible. But had that been out of obligation to her father, or because he felt something for her?

Not that it mattered. Her life was over now. It might happen in a few days, or even as she slept. Love was irrelevant.

They stopped under a large tree with drooping branches like tentacles, ten feet from a cave. Liam pointed to its open mouth and nodded at the tree. "Any preference between getting trapped in a cold, dark cave with only one exit, or up in those branches with nowhere to go if danger finds us below?"

A scant cackle left her lips like a whisper. "I guess the tree."

Liam smiled, climbed onto the first branch, then pulled Ana up gently beside him. Despite his intentions, her skin felt like it was ripping beneath the bandage.

She cried out as he reached down beneath her armpits and pulled her up the rest of the way. His hands brushed her breasts as she shifted onto the branch beside him, but neither of them acknowledged it.

After a few moments of uncomfortable silence, Ana finally found the words. "What happens if I—"

"Turn?"

"What if I try to kill you in the middle of the night?"

"You won't."

"Duncan turned, I could too. Please, Liam. Promise that you'll kill me if you see me turning ... before—"

"We're not discussing this," he said, turning away.

She grabbed his chin and forced him to meet her eyes. "*Please*. Don't let me become ..."

He hugged her tight, her tears flowing for Duncan and Adam, her mother and father, and, of course, her own looming death.

"*I promise*," he whispered.

# TWELVE

# Jonah Lovecraft

JONAH WAS SURPRISED to find himself intoxicated by the brunette to whom Sutherland had introduced him. He was exhausted and wanted to bathe, then sleep in a warm bed, more than he'd wanted sex.

But the brunette — whose name he had unfortunately forgotten the moment he heard it — led him to a shower for two, then to a dark room with a large bed. She fed him with food and words and warmth. It had been such a long time since he'd been with a woman, and the sex was over embarrassingly fast.

Afterward, when Jonah had expected solitude, the brunette asked if she could stay. She lay against his chest, seeming to enjoy the aftermath more than the event. Jonah too. Just to be with someone, after living alone for so long.

He heard a loud knock on his door while drifting off. *Of course.*

He extricated himself from the sleeping woman, padded quietly across the room, and opened the door to a tall boy with a shock of freckles neatly divided between his cheeks.

He stepped through the open door and announced that it was time to eat, even though the brunette had fed him well. Jonah told this to the freckled boy a few times, the last time the loudest, stirring the woman sprawled in his bed.

But the kid was insistent, so Jonah followed him out into the hall, then back to the dining hall for another large meal, this one entirely liquid — greens, sugars, proteins — and much better tasting than he expected.

After Jonah finished drinking his meal, he was again led to Sutherland. But Hydrangea's leader was taking forever to find his point.

"So what do you want with me?" Jonah finally interrupted.

Sutherland laughed. "I told you, Jonah. I need your help getting Dr. Goelle here to Hydrangea."

"Again, *why me?*"

"From what I hear, she's too afraid to leave the city. And we want her to come willingly. It's no use coercing her."

"Like you're doing to me?"

"Apples to oranges, Jonah. I'm only being honest with you, as I believe you're a man who respects forthrightness. We need Goelle's cooperation to seize control of City 1."

"And how will she help you with that?"

"I've told you enough to make up your mind, Jonah. Suffice it to say, we're going to war with the leaders of the State. With Geralt. The world's not what it once was, and not just because of the zombies. Power was once divided rather than broadcast from a single city, or one man's will. Our current government isn't for the people, it's *only* for those in power. We barely have a nation, Jonah, and what we do have was born behind locked doors and now lives in the shadows. But we can strike back. The people *can* reclaim what's been stolen."

Jonah was again reminded of a feeling he had upon first meeting Sutherland: This wasn't the Underground. This was something else.

The Underground focused on getting people out of City 6 and away from the lie. Talk of revolution was broad — something they'd eventually do — mostly because no one dared believe that the State could be defeated. Jonah squirmed, uncertain what was making him so uncomfortable. That these people might fail or that they might succeed at too high a price.

"That's a big fight," he finally said.

"The biggest," Sutherland agreed. "And absolutely worth fighting. In the Old Nation, back when they were still celebrating a new constitution, a revolutionary named Samuel Adams said, 'If ever a time should come, when vain and aspiring men shall possess the highest seats in government, our country will stand in need of its experienced patriots to prevent its ruin.' We must prevent its ruin, Jonah. Right now, we're the patriots, and we need your help to be part of something bigger than any of us."

Jonah didn't buy it, especially not any part that had him waltzing into City 6 and talking Liza into leaving with him, then somehow escaping undetected.

"I don't know what in the hell makes you think *I* can get behind the Walls — I tried, and there were more Watchers and orbs than I thought possible."

Jonah held up his hand, anticipating Sutherland's protest before he could even open his mouth. "But let's say I can get in. Let's also say I find Liza and talk her into joining me on some secret mission I can't even explain. How the hell do you think we'll get *out* of the City?"

"You worry too much, Jonah. You get Liza; I'll tend to the rest. This stage has been dressed for years."

Even if Jonah could buy it, he still didn't like anything

about this. "Why bat at the hornet's nest? The cities are networked and well-armed. We don't stand a chance. And if the State's provoked, it *will* retaliate. Right now, all these camps and villages are left relatively alone, but only because you're not proving yourselves worth stopping, despite the occasional attack or tampering with the Games. The moment you're a threat to the cities themselves, the State will slam its heel on the Barrens like a blanket crawling with ants."

Sutherland looked at Jonah as if he felt sorry for him, then clapped his large hands on his strong thighs. "You're right, and it doesn't matter at all."

His words were startling. Sutherland stared so intensely that it felt like the man's hot eyes were burning right through him. "Why do you wake up, Jonah?"

"What … what do you mean?"

"Each morning, you *decide* to rise. Why?"

"Because I want to live."

"That reason has no blood, Jonah. Why do you *rise*?"

*I don't know,* he thought, hating Sutherland for making him acknowledge the truth that he had only one thing to live for.

"I wake for Anastasia. To find her."

"You wake for Anastasia," Sutherland repeated, his expression thoughtful and kind, as if trying to understand. "A worthy reason. Before that, I imagine your purpose was your family? And duty?"

Jonah nodded, waiting for Sutherland's point, knowing it would sting.

"Those are all perfectly valid reasons to get up: family, duty, even love. But none of that matters to me. I rise for freedom, Jonah. Freedom is my Anastasia, my family, and my duty before that. I want to reclaim what has been pillaged from us. Too many live from first to final breath in surrender, or they trade freedom for safety and leave themselves worthy of neither. In this world, the most courageous thing people can do is think for themselves. Even braver are those that do it out loud. In this world, thought is crime. This isn't acceptable, Jonah, yet we live as if we've forgotten that inarguable truth. The world is asleep, but I am awake and wish to rouse as many sleeping souls as I can — to give everyone a reason *to rise.*"

Jonah could clearly see Sutherland's danger, for it was the same threat the State had seen in Weaver. He was a fanatic, and while the message sounded good, it sounded irrational as well. A dream in which Jonah could barely find a spark of reality.

He didn't want to get involved, *couldn't* get involved. Any battle destined to lose wasn't worth fighting. He'd seen it firsthand as a member of the Underground — they worked tirelessly getting people outside. A coordinated attack against City 1 seemed about as likely as Jonah curing the Plague.

Yet, he didn't *want* to refuse because, as crazy as it sounded, something inside him wanted to brush the hope he saw in Sutherland's goals. Jonah had been brought here, given food and clothing and companionship. Ana was on her way.

"You've given me much to think about," he finally said.

"Bullshit!" Sutherland thundered. "You're letting fear scream in your ear, Jonah. Ignore it, or better yet, lean in: expose your terrors, absorb them, strip their power until they're nothing. Then you will be free to do as you wish forever. Free to change the world."

"The world is too dead to change."

Sutherland spun on Jonah, as if his indifference had finally pushed him too far. Teeth gritted, eyes narrowed, and expression almost somber, he said, "We *can* change the world, Jonah. Even if we can't, we *can* change ourselves. *We* can be the free ones — birds through life's sky, serene above the atrocity. The secret, Jonah — and this is the treasure of thought that Jack Geralt and the State in their insidious natures dare to hide from its people above all else — is that freedom is contagious. When one brother feels that swell inside him, he cannot help but trumpet the truth to others. Freedom is an infection the State cannot inoculate, or afford to see spread. The State fears two diseases, and the Walls are as much to keep the zombies out as they are to keep the people *in*. You are our contagion. *You* must go behind the Walls and let freedom spread."

"But don't you understand? The State sees you as scavenging rats. You don't go after a few rats that aren't really causing any problems, especially when they're outside the house. Bring the fight to them and they'll crush you where you crawl, then they'll turn the Barrens to ash."

Again, Sutherland dismissed him with laughter. "If they could turn us to ash, Jonah, they already would have. They do what they can — last winter they destroyed West Village, the largest of the organized villages outside City 6. Tore open the gates and slaughtered every man, woman, and child unable to flee. They drenched the village in blood, burned corpses, and littered the gate with charred bodies and heads on pikes. Before leaving, they painted their filthy logo in blood on the gate. Is that the cities *leaving us alone*, Jonah? No, it wasn't. The State must pay for what it did to West Village if nothing else."

Hope churned violently inside Jonah. He *wanted* to say yes, and for a shocking second he realized that the part of him that had spent winter near starving was itching to fight.

But not before he was stronger. And not before he saw Ana.

Sutherland seemed to be reading his thoughts. "You have much to think on, Jonah." He smiled. "We've waited this long; fate now favors our patience. I'm not asking for a yes; I'm asking you to consider."

"Of course I'll think about it."

Sutherland nodded with yet another smile.

Jonah was closer than ever to seeing Ana. But what if she didn't want to see him? What if she still blamed him for Molly's murder, and being tossed into the Darwins?

How could Jonah expect her forgiveness when he still couldn't forgive himself?

# THIRTEEN

# Adam Lovecraft

ADAM HAD BEEN SITTING in Keller's office for nearly fifteen minutes, awaiting his arrival. He liked that the chief trusted him enough to leave him alone in his office and wondered if the same was true for anyone else. The office had to be highly secure. That sort of trust for someone his age — barely a cadet — was a higher privilege than Adam ever could have imagined being granted a few months earlier.

He looked at the sparse walls, papered with State accolades, photographs of Keller with officials, and a scattering of him with his son. The chief was an ugly man, with an almost beak-like nose, and a gaunt, long face, but in a way that wasn't scary — unless you were meeting him because you got in trouble. Adam thought Chief Keller's ugliness made him look extra strong.

The office door opened and Keller stepped inside, smiling. "Sorry to keep you waiting." He clapped Adam's shoulder on the way to his own chair. The chief sat on his side of the large desk, looking across at him.

Adam appreciated how Keller always apologized for

being late, or for inconveniencing him in any way. No one else seemed to care about his feelings, except maybe Michael, and probably not anymore.

"So, young Lovecraft, what can I do for you?"

Keller usually requested Adam's company. He would either show up as one class ended, then walk him to the next before it started, or send a memo requesting that Adam come to his office. This time, he used the com Keller had given him. He was eager to start his mission and thought that if he called Keller on the com, he might get taken more seriously.

"I'm ready to start spying."

Keller laughed. "I love what an eager young cadet you are, Adam." He leaned across the desk. "But would you believe me if I said you're already doing everything you're supposed to?"

Adam trusted the chief, but that didn't sound right.

"I haven't done anything yet, other than wait for instructions," Adam insisted. "That's why I wanted to see you. I was hoping you could give me something to do on my mission."

"But you're already doing it!" Keller cried out, as if so proud of Adam he couldn't hold his emotion. "And doing a tremendous job!"

"I am?"

"What do you think your mission is?"

"To help find the enemies among us?"

Keller smiled and slapped the desktop. "Exactly! To find the enemies among us. Now, Adam, do you think those enemies are wearing shirts with neat black lettering that says *Underground Scum!* across the front?"

Adam laughed. "No."

"Of course not! That means you have to listen. Your mission, Adam is to simply be yourself and keep your ears open. You never know what people might say around you, especially when they don't think you're really listening. Some people seem to almost *want* to confess. Allow them to confess."

It wasn't satisfying, but Adam understood. He didn't want the chief to think he wasn't grateful for the opportunity he'd been given as a cadet. He still felt he could be doing more, but if Keller said his work was valuable, then Adam believed him.

"I get it. And promise to do my best listening." He paused and added, "I promise to be my very best Adam!"

"Tremendous, son. Continue to stay invisible. You will be amazed at what you will learn when people are too dim to see you. Now, have I satisfied you, or is there something else I can help you with since you're already here?"

Adam wanted to ask about Jack Geralt — someone all the cities probably knew about, but Adam had felt especially curious about a few specific things after meeting Michael at Nips. Unfortunately, Adam didn't know how to raise the topic. He didn't want to open any doors that he wasn't supposed to, or get Michael in trouble.

"Say it!" Keller joked, trying to mine what Adam held behind his eyes.

"Do you know Jack Geralt?" Adam asked.

"You mean personally?"

"Yes." Adam nodded.

"Well, yes I do." Keller smiled with pride. "Would you like to meet him someday?"

Adam nodded, not expecting the question. "I would love to!"

"I'm sure we can make that happen ... someday. In fact, I wouldn't be at all surprised if *you* were chief of City 6 one day, sitting at this very desk. Then you could go to City 1 yourself."

Adam stared at Keller. He couldn't imagine going to City 1, by himself or with anyone else.

"I'm glad you're asking about Jack Geralt!" Keller turned the compliment faucet back on. "A boy like you could learn a lot from a man like that. No one's done more to change, or improve, our daily lives here in City 6, or any of the cities. Can you imagine what things would be like if we'd never had the Wallings?"

"No." Adam shook his head. "Is the story true? The one about Jack Geralt? How he single-handedly fought off a horde of zombies from City 1 and rode from city to city leading an army against them?"

"Well, yes, of course. At least mostly. The State makes things more exciting, takes out the dreary parts. He was with City Watch, just a young lieutenant, when the zombie uprising started for the second time. The Barrens once had villages and towns. They were allowed to live independently from the cities. But then the zombie Plague destroyed them all, and the dead rose and attacked the cities. It began near City 1, when our communications weren't quite what they are now. Geralt went from city to city, warning citizens of the threat. It took longer than the history lessons say, and we lost a lot of people, but we erected walls, and now everyone's safe, thanks to Jack Geralt."

"He must be so old," Adam said.

"Yes, he's nearly one hundred and forty, but he has our best science keeping him thriving. Believe it or not, the man doesn't look a day over fifty."

Adam swallowed, not knowing whether he wanted to say the next thing in his head or nothing else. Certain he would hate himself if he acted like a kid and didn't speak his mind. "I have a friend who said Geralt wasn't really a great guy."

"Oh?" Keller raised his eyebrows.

"Yes." Adam spoke faster, appreciating his quiet invitation. "He said Geralt was a crook, and that he did all sorts of bad stuff, but that history teachers buried it because the State made them. He said the official version isn't the true one and that the true one would make everyone think differently about the State."

Keller's face soured, then a second later he found a calm smile. "Since the beginning there have been those who have tried to soil Jack Geralt's good name — as is true with all of history's most significant men. Jack Geralt, like all great leaders, had the burden of doing what was necessary. Thomas Jefferson, one of the Old Nation founders, owned many slaves and regularly raped them — you do know what that means, yes, Adam?"

He nodded, hating both question and answer, trying not to shudder while accidentally thinking of the Games and rapes he'd seen on TV.

"Martin Luther King, Jr., practically a saint, was a serial womanizer. Yet, history rinses those men's misdeeds to highlight their more important accomplishments. I'm sure Jack Geralt stumbled occasionally on his way to changing the world, but who among us hasn't?"

Adam nodded.

The chief looked almost grateful. "I'm glad you ask questions, Adam. They are healthy — the more you understand the world, the easier it will be to find your place. His eyes bored into Adam's. "Now. Who said this about Jack Geralt?"

Adam felt icy, wishing he'd never said a thing about a friend. His guilty heart pounded, and he felt cut in two — half of him wanting to protect Michael, the other half (or maybe more) wanting to please Keller and show him what a great City Watch spy he had already become. It wasn't like Adam had a lot of friends, so Keller would know the guilty party without thinking too hard.

Still, Adam couldn't open his mouth. He stared across the desk at Keller, willing himself to speak.

"Who said it?" Keller repeated, his voice still like a song. "Who was sowing these seeds of doubt?"

Adam could feel his assessing eyes all over him. Though Adam felt bad doing what he was about to do, the part of him that was growing fastest — the part the State said had so much potential — wanted to do the *right* thing.

That wasn't protecting Michael. Even though he was a friend, he had also said bad stuff about Jack Geralt and probably thought similar things about the State, since he hadn't been at all happy for Adam when he found his home with City Watch.

He'd already decided to do the right thing when Keller nudged him.

"I promise I won't say anything or get this person into trouble. This is between you and me, Adam; whoever it is will never know you said a word."

"It was my friend Michael. He doesn't seem happy that I'm with City Watch, so whenever we get together — we have dinner at the Arcade a couple of times a month, usually at Nips — I always try telling him how well things are going for me, and that I'm happy, but he makes me feel a little bad for feeling good."

Adam was sure Keller would be angry. But he laughed loudly instead. Almost like a bark. He stood, still laughing, and pressed a button on his desk. The wood was replaced with a white computer screen and a blinking circle in its center, the kind Adam had seen but never used, at the Academy.

"You should be careful who you trust, Adam. There are snakes in every patch of grass and on both sides of the

Walls. This is exactly why Jack Geralt, the State, and the cities must remain vigilant. And this is why I was so right to trust you. You can see through the veneer these snakes hide behind."

"I'm not sure what you mean." Now Adam felt scared.

"I'll show you." Keller gestured over the screen. "Michael's confession."

A video started to play.

It was Michael, in Keller's office, speaking to someone off camera. "I want to report a spy. His name is Liam Harrow. I'm afraid he's getting my friend Ana in trouble."

# FOURTEEN

# Anastasia Lovecraft

ANA WOKE up slowly enough to believe herself turned. She had never been a zombie, but she wouldn't have been surprised to find that this was what it felt like inside their minds: soupy, no up or down or left or right. Ugly. Inner torment blossoming.

Searing pain reminded Ana of her arm, but she didn't want to open her eyes because that might make her burning lids hotter, and she didn't want to look at her arm because the results were easy to picture: black skin, cracked and blistered, festering as her body readied for its inevitable change.

Ana inhaled, trying to absorb her surroundings. She sensed Liam … and something else. Something below.

The realization shocked her fully awake.

She and Liam weren't alone, nor facing a single interloper. There were many of them, likely members of one of the Bands that swarmed the Barrens, robbing and raping and leaving their every encounter for dead. Bandits were no less lethal than zombies but were far smarter, organized, and harder to counter. There were at least a dozen in sight. Her cold shakes promised more.

She turned to Liam. His jaw was set, eyes were fixed on her, already awake and aware of the danger.

She wanted to ask him how long the bandits had been down there, if they had said anything, and what he thought they should do. But before she could utter a word, the closest bandit — a sunken-eyed man with a gleaming skull — stepped toward the tree and crossed giant arms across his chest, as if to prove he needed no weapon. He licked his lips like the monster she knew him to be and laughed.

"Well, well, lookey what we have here."

FIFTEEN

## Liam Harrow

LIAM LOOKED OVER AT ANA, helpless as the bandits circled the trunk below.

Surprise dilated her eyes as she blinked into the raw shock of an inescapable threat. He'd said nothing, not wanting to startle her awake. She would rise on her own, and he could see her calculating, her mind already dancing between the disaster below and the one on her wrist.

At the front of the pack, the leader — a large man with a monster's sneer — licked his lips and laughed. "Well, well, lookey what we have here."

Liam turned from Ana to the bandit, peering down over his branch and locking eyes with the man as he narrowed his squint.

"If you wanted us dead, we'd be dead already. So what do you want?"

The leader laughed at Liam, then turned to his men and encouraged their chorus. Guffaws and cackles quickly multiplied, rolling a shaking terror across an otherwise quiet dawn.

"Loaded my gun last night before closing my eyes,"

Liam promised. "That's fourteen shots, and I'm an ace every time."

The leader spoke, his voice a bag of rocks: "You'd be lucky to squeeze two before we blast you from the tree."

"I only need one." Liam winked at the leader, his gun drawn and aimed at the killer's head.

The leader smiled, looking satisfied, as if tearing the meat of fresh challenge from its skinny bone. He stepped toward the tree, smiling, baiting Liam.

And now Liam wasn't sure what to do. He was only good for whatever he had in his bag: weapons, supplies, and nothing more. He had a few of Duncan's homemade surprises, but the bandits couldn't possibly know their value or threat, or they would have already shot Liam from the tree. Besides, there was no way to use what was in the bag — if he so much as inched toward the zipper, one of the barrels aimed at his head would surely start spitting.

Unlike Liam, Ana was safe ... at least from death, and only for a while. But Liam had heard the stories of what bandits did to their captured women.

Once down from the tree, she likely would be taken prisoner as a slave until she was too used up, at which point they'd leave her for dead. Of course, she might not live that long.

The moment someone noticed her wrist or the Z — which they couldn't see from where they were standing below — they'd likely shoot her.

Liam *was* an ace shot, and as promised he had fourteen rounds in the gun handed down from his grandfather, and another fourteen in the gun in the back holster hidden beneath his black vest — enough to even the odds against any Band.

Any but this one.

This Band was the largest Liam had ever seen or even heard about. They usually traveled in smaller packs, but this one had plenty *in sight*. Not that it mattered — he hadn't moved his eyes from the leader long enough to count.

Judging from their grimy clothes, unkempt appearances, ugly expressions, and many weapons, this group was full of broken men looking only to inflict their pain on the world. He could kill a few of them, but that would only begin the nightmare for Ana.

There was only one thing left to do …

"She's hurt bad," Liam said, nodding toward Ana. "Real bad. Was bit by a zombie just yesterday. We were traveling with another group of eight, but we were exiled after April was bit. We can't go back. She's no use to you; neither am I. Let us be, and we'll go on our way. No trouble, sir."

The closest man, still looking up at Liam and smirking, said, "No one just 'goes on their way.'" After a pause, though, he added, "Where's she bit?"

"On her wrist, sir."

"How bad is it?"

"Like I said, it's bad. Real bad. I expect she'll probably turn by afternoon. She's my girl's kid sister, so I'd planned on staying with her until the end, then use one of my fourteen rounds — that's all the eight of 'em left us with. We lost my girl, Ashley, during the skirmish, after falling into a horde outside the Outback. Ashley's the one who bit April."

Liam nodded toward Ana again. "If we hadn't lost Ashley, she would've fought for us to stay, I'm sure, and they probably would've listened on account of the group's leader being Ashley's brother, but as soon as she turned — right after she bit April on the wrist — I had to shoot her in the head, because that's what I always promised Ashley I'd do."

"I didn't ask for your damned life story. I asked—"

"Sorry, sir, I just don't know how to stop talking once I start, especially when I'm nervous, and you've got to understand, we climbed up here last night to stay safe from the zombies. I sure didn't expect to wake up and see folks like you aiming guns! I get it, we all need to survive out here, and to stick with our own, you don't know us and you've got no reason …" He paused, then leaned even further over his branch and lowered his voice. "What I'm trying to say, sir, is that if you can see to letting me go, I'll make sure she doesn't give you any trouble."

The killer grunted. "No deal. You're as dead as she is."

"I'll give you my gun, my bag, and April. All I'm asking is that you take her instead of me and let me go on my way."

Ana, eyes wide, whispered, "*What the hell are you doing?*"

Liam winked, then reached over and grabbed his bag, resisting the urge to tear it open, shove his hand inside, and throw anything from a sonic nug to a zombie pineapple down at the Band — he'd been ignoring the nug in his back pocket, knowing he only had one shot.

He slung the pack over his shoulder, made a show of thrusting the gun into his waistband, then climbed down the tree with his back to who-knew-how-many guns before dropping to the dirt, not too far from the killer's feet.

Liam walked straight up to the leader.

"Please," Liam said, begging. "Just let me go. Like I said, I can help. Make sure *she* isn't a problem."

"And how are you going to do that?" the killer asked, interest — or maybe lurid curiosity — creeping onto his face.

"Same way I always do." Liam smiled, then turned to the tree and yelled, "April!" Nothing for a painful half minute, then Ana peered over her branch and stared down, bug-eyed.

"April, sweetie?"

Ana said, "Yes," but her *yes* sounded like old syrup, slow from the bottle.

Liam said to the leader, "She's slow. Makes for dull conversation, but she's great to have around. She'll do *anything*, and never tell no one. We did stuff all the time and April never said nothing to Ashley, not once for the two years we were doing it. Sometimes you've got to give her something extra, like some of your rations, but if you can find a pretty rock — there's plenty out in these parts — she'll take that. But it's not like you'll be needing to keep secrets from her sister, so you should be fine. Your real trouble will come if she gets spooked, and that happens easy. April's a party but not if she's scared. If she gets the terrors, well then, she bites and screams and scratches. She's all animal, and not in a good way. I'd tell you this anyway because I don't wanna die, but that don't make it not the truth: shoot me and you'll ruin her for good. But," Liam lowered his voice to a conspirator's volume and leaned toward the killer, "if I call her down and introduce you, I'm sure April will play nice. I think that's a fair trade, and you seem sharp enough to agree."

The bandit was looking at Liam, assessing. "Gimme the gun, and the bag," the bandit leader commanded.

Liam thought about resisting but didn't dare. Not yet. He retrieved the gun from the front of his waistband and handed it over, grip first, keeping his eyes on the man. He pulled the bag slowly from his shoulder and dropped it on the dirt.

The leader grabbed the bag and handed it, along with

Liam's gun, to one of his fellow bandits, who took them without rooting through the bag.

Liam kept talking: "Of course, she does have that shit on her wrist. I feel terrible telling you this, but just last night while I was trying to fall asleep I was thinking maybe I'd just cut it off come morning, seeing as how that would probably keep the infection away longer. I know it can't kill it, but I was only looking to buy time, not wanting to be alone any longer than necessary."

The killer opened his mouth, but before he could speak Liam turned to the tree. "April, sweetie. Get on down here. We have some new friends!"

Ana silently climbed down from the tree, slow and labored, nursing her wrist. Once her feet hit the grass, she turned from the tree and hobbled over to Liam. She stood by his side, slouched, looking up at the killer.

"He's a friend," Liam said, pointing to the killer who most certainly was not. "Good guy."

The killer looked baffled, as did every bandit Liam could catch from the corners of his eyes. He'd been surveying the situation ever since he came down from the tree, stealing glances past the bandits out to the tree line that he hoped might save his life. He wondered if he would be fast enough to execute the impossible. Failure meant death, but Liam had no other choice.

He stepped back from the killer as the disgusting man's eyes raked Ana's body, licking his lips, looking her over like she was meat on the grill.

"Ooh, could we have some fun with this one. You shy, girl?" He reached out and touched Ana's breasts through her shirt.

She flinched, and he laughed while withdrawing his hand.

"Ah, yes, she is." He turned to his men. "Y'all ready for a time?"

Liam wanted to cleave the fucker's head from his neck, but knew if he did, they'd both be dead.

The bandits were all staring at Ana and their leader, some of them already rubbing their cocks through their pants. Though Liam was disgusted, he was also grateful, as that meant less attention on him.

He slipped his hand to his back, hungry to reach for his second gun — also with fourteen rounds — but passed it in favor of the nug in his back pocket that *might* keep them living.

Liam drew the sonic nug from his back pocket with a silent *thank you* to Duncan for giving him two before the bridge mission, and to himself for thinking to keep one of the pair in his pocket just in case.

He flipped the nug's dial and hurled it into the sky.

Liam had his gun drawn before the nug screamed with a shrieking whistle that split the air. Liam was expecting the sound — Ana too, once she saw the nug go flying — but neither were protected, and the scream still hurt like the world had exploded inside of his head.

At least they had a chance to brace for it.

The bandits had no such warning and lost weapons as they clapped hands over their ears. The leader, with ears the size of melons, and probably canals to match, fell to his knees with a bellow.

Liam dove to the ground, landing on his back and aiming his gun at the killer. He squeezed out three shots, all to the face.

Duncan's sonic nugs made for a perfect distraction, especially since beyond the thunderclap it jammed every energy weapon in range. The nug's third and final benefit

— and curse, but one he was counting on now — was that it brought every zombie in earshot racing toward the fray.

Liam emptied his remaining eleven rounds into the closest bandits as the nug spun in the air, shrieking and dousing the area in rainbows of smoke.

He shoved the gun back into his waistband and looked over at his second gun and bag, both lying by the fallen leader. He longed for them both but Ana more. He reached out, grabbed her by the wrist, then ran away from the confusion and toward the forest.

Zombies spilled from the woods, first three, then what had to be thirty, all moving fast enough to blur.

Liam ran like an animal through an open cage door, dragging Ana, sprinting straight for the zombies as guns unjammed and shots erupted behind them.

He didn't dare turn around.

They tore into the forest, past zombies too busy racing toward the wailing's source, calling them to it like mother to child.

# SIXTEEN

# Adam Lovecraft

ADAM STARED AT THE SCREEN, watching as his friend Michael — *his sister's* friend — betrayed her. That was why she ended up dead in the Darwins.

He glared at the screen, unable to bury his anger.

"Remember that feeling, Adam. Know the truth: people in City 6 will betray you in a heartbeat, so long as it serves their purpose. You can count only on the brotherhood of City Watch and your fellow cadets."

"I can't believe he did that!"

"Would you not have turned your sister in, if you discovered she was Underground?" Keller said, his left eyebrow arched.

Adam realized he had shown too much anger. And in doing so had broadcast that he would likely lie for Ana. He wouldn't have reported her and had probably just proved himself unworthy of City Watch.

Adam looked at Keller, almost shameful. "I can't lie. I don't think I would have reported her. Ana's my sister. I would at least want to know what she was doing before deciding."

"Excellent," Keller said, folding his hands on his desk. "I wouldn't want a cadet who would turn on his family. Family is all we have, Adam. Remember that. You should *always* be able to count on family. I consider you part of our family at City Watch, Adam. That means you can always count on us. On *me*."

Adam smiled, relieved that he'd not ruined things by being honest.

"I wouldn't hold it against Michael too much. He didn't realize how deeply Anastasia was involved with the Underground. He believed he was helping her. *Try* not to hate him."

He nodded. That made sense. Still, Adam wasn't sure he could *forgive* Michael.

"Let's change the subject, shall we?" Keller swept his hand over the desk. "Do you know what a ride-along is?"

Adam could tell a ride-along was special by how Keller was asking. "No. But I'd love to find out!"

"A ride-along is when a cadet gets to spend a patrol shift with a Watcher. Ride-alongs give our cadets a good idea of what they can expect from their jobs. Like the instructionals, there's nothing held back. But unlike the instructionals, ride-alongs happen right in front of you and in real time, so they can be frightening for our younger or more sensitive cadets. We know you're quite mature for your age, but are you one of those sensitive cadets, Adam?"

Adam shook his head, even though Ana had always said that he was.

"Of course not. That's why *you* don't have to wait until your final year as a cadet to go on your first ride-along. You're going to get to go on your first one *tomorrow*."

"Tomorrow?"

"Absolutely. The State's already granted permission.

They are *very interested* in you, Adam. You've no idea how special that is, you making quite a name for yourself like you are. I've been reporting how well you are doing — with everything, really. I've told them about the strength of your intentions to City and State. They fully agree — your eligibility requirements are outstanding. So, Adam, how does it feel to have such accolades raining all the way from City 1?"

"Amazing," Adam admitted.

"Yes, amazing. Now, because we are smart City Watch officers, we know that we must always be vigilant, and that vigilance means managing more than one thing at once, yes?"

"Yes," Adam agreed.

"So this time we want you to have all the benefits of a City Watch ride-along, to see as a cadet what you will one day face as a Watcher. But I'd also like you to keep your eyes open for the other stuff we discussed — signs of cancer in the Watch. How does that sound, Adam?"

"That sounds great!" This got more exciting by the second. "What exactly am I looking for? Are the Watchers I'm with suspected traitors?"

"It's simple." Keller smiled. "I'd like you to keep your eyes open and stay on the lookout for anything odd. I don't think these particular Watchers are bad seeds. They might be, but there could be others. I just want you to tell me if you see anything strange or in any way out of the ordinary with either of the two Watchers from your ride-along, or with any of the people you meet on the streets. Does that sound simple enough?"

It did, but Adam was confused. "If these Watchers are bad, why would they do something wrong in front of *me*? I'm a cadet, and I could tell on them."

"Ah, young Lovecraft, you still have so much to learn

about people. Human behavior is rarely black and white, or people good or bad. Your father was an example of someone who snapped; the pressure was too much, and a good man did a horrible thing that no one saw coming. But your father is an extreme example. Most bad things that happen inside the Walls aren't the result of heinous acts, the sort of unthinkable things that often make the Reels. They come from small acts done by bad people who don't even realize they're bad." He leaned toward Adam and narrowed his eyes. "Once people justify something long enough, they can't see it as *wrong* or *bad*. If they're bad, they forget to hide it when their guards aren't up. Does that make sense, Adam?"

"Yes." Adam nodded, although he had questions. "What if nobody does anything on the ride-along, then what do I report? And if City Watch has orbs and cameras all over the City, wouldn't you catch stuff on them?"

"For all the good of the cameras and orbs, they don't match an individual's ability to see the little things." The chief seemed pleased by his questions. "As for not witnessing anything, we can consider that excellent news and mark our day as a success. I don't want you to find things that don't need to be found, I just want to make certain you're keeping your eyes open, so you can let me know if you see something you think I should know about. I trust your judgment and your integrity. I'll rotate you into the ride-alongs with a few of our older, already scheduled cadets, and different Watchers. With your high performance and youth, they will see you as a brother, rather than a threat."

Adam sat taller, feeling more confident.

"Besides, most of the Watchers know who you are because of your father. I imagine most will be loose around you."

Again, that made no sense to Adam. Why would anyone care about what happened to him when his dad was a bad guy who had done such a horrible thing? He looked up at Keller, hating the question and not wanting to hear the answer, yet knowing he needed to.

"But, don't they all hate my dad … you know, for doing what he did?"

"No, Adam." He shook his head, still looking proud. "As I said, City Watch is family. These men are brothers, through thick and thin, and now they're your family too. They were disappointed in your father's fall, but they still loved him. There wasn't one Watcher who was happy bringing your father in."

Adam sat on his side of the desk, hands in his lap, wondering what to say. Then Keller made it easy. "So, are we going for a ride-along?"

"Yes!" he shouted, his doubts dimmed by the excitement of seeing what potential wrongs might happen so he could report them to Keller and make the chief even prouder of Adam than he already was.

SEVENTEEN

# Jonah Lovecraft

JONAH WAS SITTING with Katrina in Hydrangea's small bar. It looked enough like the Saxon — a bar behind the Walls — that Jonah couldn't help but think of it every time he brought the glass to his lips.

The Saxon had been one of his favorite lazy hangouts, for those rare times when Jonah had been able to afford such a thing. The bar was meant for Watchers and regularly had special events like open mic and trivia nights. The shape of the bar and the color of the wood, as well as the warm light and lived-in walls covered with posters and framed photos from the refugees' former homes, all felt familiar to Jonah; but the Saxon was usually filled with people, while Hydrangea's bar had only him and Katrina.

Jonah had been sitting long enough to get drunk — his first time on the pleasant side of drink since Molly. He had a high tolerance, and it took a lot to feel the effects. He wasn't sure, but it seemed to him that Katrina had downed more than he had. Despite being two-thirds his size, she seemed far less soused.

"I didn't know that," Jonah said, laughing. They were

121

playing a game called *I Didn't Know That*, a game she made up to "see if new people at the camp were worth talking to." Judging by her smiles and laughter, which made Jonah picture birds pecking from their shells, he was apparently worth it so far. "Your turn."

Katrina took a long pull from her drink, swallowed, then gently set it on the table. "A long time ago when settlers first came to the Old Nation, there was a hurricane — a tornado that swept inland from the sea. The settlers were caught unprepared. Life was destroyed on the coast and in the interior villages nearby, wiping out the pioneers and natives living there. The hurricane was the Old Nation's first national disaster, from back in 1635."

"I didn't know that," Jonah said.

"Back then they didn't record things like they did later. And yet it's amazing that we know more about the distant past than our years since the Plague. I guess people were more interested in preserving the past back then. Now everything seems to be about shaping our future."

Jonah inhaled the silence before starting his story. "Ice cream was invented in the Old Nation in some place called Kentucky. A farmer took cow's cream and sugar, then flash froze it with liquid nitrogen, making those little balls like you buy in the Arcade. After the Wallings, the State wanted to bring some of the Old Nation amenities back, but the cities were still young and had limited resources, so they had to make the ice cream in a new way, by hand."

"I didn't know that."

For some reason, though, Katrina's expression had soured. "Come on," she said, "let's go for a walk."

She stood, packed their bottles into her bag, and strolled away from the table.

Jonah followed her out of the bar. They were through the doorway, just turning into a long and warmly lit hallway, when Katrina said, "So are you going to help us get the doctor, or have you buoyed our hopes for nothing?"

"Hey, I wasn't looking for you guys."

"True, but if you believe in fortune — and sometimes that's the easiest means of clinging to sanity — then you must believe that some things *are* destined. That there are pieces to move on a board. I *believe* fortune brought us together."

She sounded so earnest, Jonah didn't know what to think, or say. He *wanted* to say that fortune didn't bring them together, they came and found him. But that felt wrong. So he said nothing, listening as her voice softened into a honeyed tone left warm from the drink.

"Help us, Jonah," she persisted. "Anastasia won't be here for another nine days or so. That's plenty of time to reach City 6 and return. It's a two-day walk from Hydrangea."

"I said I would think on it, and I will. But I'm not leaving before Ana gets here. I can't risk anything happening before then."

"But Jonah, you could be *done* when she gets here. Won't it be a lot harder to leave the safety of Hydrangea *after* your reunion?"

He paused. Of course it would be. "Why are you so hot to help the fearless leader? What's in it for you? What's *your* Anastasia?"

Katrina's face flickered with something; Jonah thought she might want to hit him. Instead, she deflected right back. "I hear plenty of Anastasia — don't you ever think about Adam?"

She didn't hit him, but Jonah felt slapped anyway. "I think about Adam in between those seconds when I'm not thinking of Ana. Why?"

"That doesn't leave a lot of room for Jonah."

"No, it doesn't."

"Wouldn't you like to see where Adam is? Don't you wonder how he's doing? What if you could get *him* out of the City?"

Jonah could smell the bait like one of Molly's bribes in the oven. He would be tempted, but Katrina had already broken one promise when she said Ana was at Hydrangea.

"We could do that, you know. Get Adam out of the City," she said.

"Adam's better off without me. I can only make things worse than they already are. I'm a criminal."

"You don't believe that."

"Doesn't matter what I believe, it's what everyone behind the Walls will think the second they see me. Even if I wasn't an enemy of the State, I'm in no shape to be a father. Look at me, I'm starving. I can barely survive on my own. Ana's different, bigger, stronger, already out here. Adam's better where he is."

"But don't you want to know how he's doing? Wouldn't you like to at least *see* him? Check in with him from afar? You can help us, and we can help you. We'll be back for Anastasia before she gets here."

The drink was hitting her harder, words leaving her mouth in a light slur, almost a lilt. "This is right. You know it. Just say *yes*."

Of course Jonah wanted to see one of his children before the other, end his obligation to Sutherland, feel an inner solace he'd not known since before Molly's murder. But still he said nothing from the bar, all the way until they were nearly back at his door.

Katrina drew a keycard from her pocket and went to open it.

*Great, she has a key to my room.* "I have to know. What it is that makes you so loyal to Sutherland. I can't go if I don't feel safe. And right now I just don't trust you."

She opened the door, stepped inside, and turned to Jonah. Three steps through the doorway she removed her armor plates and set them on the floor, then doffed her long-sleeved top.

Katrina was attractive, but she didn't seem to have any interest in him, or in anything beyond the cause.

*Is she seducing me?*

Katrina peeled off the tight tank beneath her shirt and stood before Jonah, topless from the waist up. Her body was tight, and her breasts would have been attractive, if not so horribly scarred, lashes like tallies above, beneath, and around them. Her nipples looked many times burned.

Jonah stared, unable to swallow, barely able to think. "Who did that to you? Geralt?"

"Yes," Katrina said, pulling her tank back on. "For starters."

"Why?"

She pulled the long-sleeved shirt over her head. "Because I was a spy for the Underground, living in City 2, where Geralt gets most of his toys. He loves traitors most because, as he says, they make the best … *pets*."

Jonah felt a shiver through his entire frame, seeing too many atrocities at once, knowing she suffered them all.

Katrina recited her story with no shame: how she was caught red-handed and treated well, encouraged to turn informant. She wouldn't budge, so she was taken to City 1 and tossed into a giant room full of slaves owned by Geralt and offered with no limits to the Council Guard. Katrina was used by that lot for years. A girl could live well forever with Geralt, if so inclined. The more trouble they were before capture, the more he craved their compliance.

Katrina was trouble and then some, without a compliant cell in her body.

Geralt made an example of her, then left her for dead. She lived, and made it to the other side of City 1's Walls because a guard took pity and led her to the sewer instead of the incinerator as ordered.

She stared at Jonah. "Geralt must pay for his crimes. This will be done, no matter what. I'm going to City 6 regardless and will bring the doctor back. But I'd far prefer it if you talk her into coming willingly. I believe in you, Jonah, and hope you believe in *us* enough to do what you *know* is right. Trust *that*."

"I'll do it. But I want Sutherland to promise that Ana will be taken care of if we don't return."

"Of course." Katrina nodded. "Sutherland would settle for nothing less."

# EIGHTEEN

# Anastasia Lovecraft

THEY RAN through the woods without stopping.

Every time Ana thought she couldn't bear more, ill fortune surprised her.

Her arm was pocked with diseased, rotting flesh beneath the bandage, spreading out and up into her arm — yellow blisters itching, burning, eating her alive.

Liam blurred beside her. Running without ceasing, labored only by her pauses. He should run faster — staying with her was death.

*Are they following?*

She didn't know. What she thought was the rustle of pursuit might've been the forest mocking.

No, they were alone: her, him, and the burning inside her.

Liam tugged at her healthy wrist, pulling her harder. "We have to go faster."

They were headed for the Outback, an abandoned town bordered by eucalyptus shading the acres around it. They'd find the road leading to Hydrangea and her father on the other side.

They had learned about the real Outback at Chimney Rock — an endless desert in a place called Oz, from long ago. No one knew what the city was called before someone from the Barrens pounded a sign in the dirt where the eucalyptus thinned: *The Outback: Zombies Usually Flawking*.

Duncan had told them about the Outback two days before they'd found it, and five before Paradise had found them.

*I'm burning.*

Nothing good happened in the Outback. Most stories taking place in the Outback ended horribly, and Ana had no idea why anyone ever went there. She couldn't imagine how many uglier stories went untold.

They were lucky; their first time wasn't bad. They stumbled through, Duncan so hungry for contact after finding only danger after the burning of West Village. Camps and villages — even Bands, so Ana was told — all used the Outback as a training ground. There were always zombies near or around it, way more than usual and for no reason anyone could explain. Crowds seemed to self-spawn. Between zombies and training, the Outback was a churning nest of life and death.

*I am black inside.*

Pain surged like lightning through her body. She pushed herself to keep up, guilty because she was forcing Liam to drag a walking corpse behind him.

His voice rang out from somewhere in the blur. "Snap out of it!"

He stopped and spun her to face him.

She fought for his eyes. He put his hand to her cheek. "Ana, can you hear me?"

She looked at him, dazed, then nodded.

"Can you hear *them*?"

She listened. Far off — the crackle of leaves, the snapping of branches.

The scent of rage.

"Maybe." A stutter, then, "Yes, I think so."

*So.*

*Much.*

*Pain.*

"I know how much you're hurting, but we're almost there. A few minutes more, okay? We'll figure something out in the city. Just stay with me, another few minutes."

He didn't wait for an answer, trotting forward and tugging Ana by her unbitten wrist. They ran a few more minutes — three or thirty, it no longer mattered — then into a clearing before crossing it and racing through the mint-scented haze that surrounded the sprawling fields of eucalyptus.

They stopped at the sign where the woods surrendered to a once-thriving metropolis. The Outback was an iron reminder of what the world lost. Even if what they had heard whispered about Sutherland leading a revolution against the State was true and the impossible happened — that world could never return, warped past bent into broken.

Streets were crumbled or overgrown with vegetation. Ivy crawled up every structure. Buildings leaned at sharp angles as if stretching against nature. Ana pictured them eventually toppling, then shuddered with the sense of claustrophobia creeping in.

Mountains of concrete lay in broken piles that looked in some places to be randomly scattered and in others somehow neatly arranged. The Outback crawled with zombies, many on the streets and even more inside the buildings, sometimes drifting in front of windows like specters.

Despite that, the Outback was so big that it offered many places to hide for the careful. Liam hoped to lose the bandits behind them … without meeting more along the way.

He pulled her into an alley so they could catch their breath. "Everything will be fine. We'll stay alert and out of sight, get some rest, then leave when it's safe. Okay?"

Ana nodded. Then she looked at him for the first time since their flight. He looked so vulnerable, with one empty gun and the other gone missing. His bag of trinkets from Duncan — each one engineered to keep them alive — was gone. She hoped they'd find new weapons in the Outback, before something found them.

"In there." He pointed across the street to what looked like a hollowed-out liquor store.

They sprinted toward it.

Ana did her best to keep up as Liam held her hand, until he let go and ducked inside the old store. She followed, getting just inside the entrance before he said, "Stay here, I'll be right back."

He quickly and quietly plunged into the darkness of the empty store, soon returning with a brittle layer of calm.

She heard a commotion outside the store, not too far off. But before she could open her mouth, Liam caught her look and violently shook his head. He slapped one hand over her mouth, put a finger to his lips, and pulled her behind an empty, broken shelf, out of view.

The bandits were outside the shop, boots crunching on the caked debris. It was all over if they were caught, especially since Liam was empty.

Ana had no idea how many were left, but it sounded like a lot. They were loud, inviting zombies to join their hunt. She was crouched low, and Liam silently motioned for her to follow him. They made their way behind the counter in the store's rear, and when Liam looked back at her, she held his eyes, telling herself they weren't going to die, so he could see *that* instead of the truth.

Finally, the voices faded away and Liam peeked over the counter.

He descended with a nod: *all clear.*

They waited a few more minutes, then crept out of the store.

He went first. Ana followed closely enough that Liam was just the brush of a finger ahead. He paused in the doorway, looked left, right, and everywhere else with a glance. He turned back to Ana, nodded again, and stepped into the street.

They wove through the broken roads, navigating crumbled concrete, glass, chunks of rotted wood, and twisted metal. Tall buildings blocked the sun and made the Outback seem darker than the forest.

"Where do we go?" Ana asked quietly, able to speak now that her wrist pain had subsided to an ache less than murder.

"I don't know," Liam said, his voice just above a whisper as he crept toward the corner, ducking around a low-hanging sign. "Zombies could be hiding anywhere, in any building. We can take them out quietly if we have to, but killing leaves a path for the bandits. We've got to get through the city, and find the river to the west."

Liam made a sudden move to his right toward an ancient car, and Ana's heart leapt into her throat. But he reached in without hesitation and pulled a crowbar from the interior, the tool peppered in a thick layer of powder.

Just as quickly, Ana calmed down — they were armed now. Barely.

Ana pointed to a tall building two blocks ahead. At

least ten floors, plus a few after that. "Sorry, but I don't think I can go on much more. I need to rest."

His face said it all.

She felt like a hindrance and hated it. If Liam were on his own, he could probably navigate the Outback far easier. But her head was swimming, and she was short of breath. Fleeing the bandits had emptied her out. She needed to refuel.

"Sorry. I just need a little bit of time to rest."

He nodded. "Let's find somewhere to hide out."

She looked up at the tall building and pointed. "Didn't Duncan say that zombies usually avoid climbing stairs? Even if a few strays got ambitious, they wouldn't cluster. We could take them out one by one on our way to the top."

"That's a longer walk to the top than you realize. If the bandits happen inside, they'll find a trail of dead zombies to the top."

"That's assuming we're killing zombies in the lobby. If they don't see any evidence there, why go farther? At least not more than a couple of floors. We go as high as we can, avoiding, not killing, and that should throw them off. I can make it to the top, Liam." She straightened her shoulders. "Besides, if we go high, we can get a better view of the city and map a path out, right?"

Liam looked at her, thinking.

She added, "If they're coming up the stairs, we'll hear them. We'll know where they are, but they'll only be able to guess where we are. Eventually, they'll give up, right? Or get chased off by zombies or other bandits?"

Liam didn't exactly smile, but it was close, considering he was in the zombie-infested Outback. "Let's go."

They made their way to the building and ducked in through a warped metal door frame, long since missing its glass. They headed for the stairs, conveniently right in front of them.

The stairs rose from the lobby, narrowing into darkness. The lobby was wide, which made it hard at first to make out the zombies inside. Ana saw five. The zombies looked up, one at a time, each registering an undead version of surprise before ambling toward them. They were slow, the sort of zombie that only threatened en masse.

Liam and Ana easily ran through them — not bothering to fight, feeling they'd be safe once up the stairs. They saw two zombies — a man and a woman — one flight up.

So much for zombies not climbing stairs.

The woman was four steps up, blocking the stairs. Ana heard the shuffling zombies making their way after them as the bandits burst into the lobby below, one of them finishing a sentence: "—yeah, I'm sure."

Liam gently pushed Ana down two stairs, backed up beside her, then planted his foot one more step behind and drove his crowbar forward into the male zombie's face, killing it instantly. Then he pivoted toward the female zombie.

But Ana was running toward her.

She slammed her body against the wall.

The zombie gnashed and snarled as Ana ducked low and, she hoped, out of reach.

The zombie screamed, a siren to the bandits.

Liam leapt past Ana, crashing his crowbar into the zombie's face and dropping her to the stairs. Below them, in the broken doorway of the second floor, zombies shrieked.

"THEY'RE UP THERE!"

Liam grabbed Ana's hand, and they raced up the

stairs, making it one more flight before the bandits caught up with the zombies on the second-floor stairwell.

Screams, human and zombie; grisly gnashing; four energy blasts perfectly spaced; a wet slap; two thuds; a stumble and a curse; the scampering of feet.

Liam and Ana kept going. He screamed as they ran, drawing more zombies into the stairwell behind them.

They reached the rooftop doorway as more gunfire erupted several floors below. The bandits were too well armed to be delayed long enough for Ana and Liam to escape. They'd have to stand off against the bandits fourteen stories above the Outback with nowhere to go.

Ana was hoping the entire run up that they'd find an advantage on the roof. Somewhere to hide or something to shift their odds or change the game. As they raced from the doorway and toward what looked to be a large water tower, she asked, "How many bandits do you think there are?"

"Not many. Ten, maybe a few more."

"Think we can take them?"

"We'll do our damnedest."

They ducked behind the tower and looked around. The nearest building was at least four stories shorter. Even if they could survive the fall, the gap was too far to jump.

There were three other towers on the roof, along with several ten-by-ten wooden boxes. Ana had no clue what they were. But there were no other doors or places to run. "So this is it?"

Liam nodded, peeking past the tower — their only pathetic cover — ready to face whatever emerged. Ana knelt beside him, catching her breath.

The stairwell door exploded open.

His false confidence was gone, along with the color from his face.

# NINETEEN

# Adam Lovecraft

ADAM SAT in the City Watch van's passenger seat, noticing how different everything looked from a Watcher's side of the glass.

Keller didn't walk him down personally, saying it was better for Adam to serve as his eyes and ears without the overt connection in the other men's eyes. Adam had asked if other Watchers already knew that he went to the chief 's office all the time, and Keller said yes, but that everyone also knew he felt an obligation to look after Jonah's son. And it was well established that he couldn't stand to see young men lost to the Dark Quarter. Especially after what happened to his own child.

Keller had assured Adam that many of the men already considered him one of them. They'd loved his father like a brother, and by extension, they loved him. "You're already in the system. Simply give your name to Dispatch, and they'll send you out on the next call. This is a learning experience above all else, but you should also try to have fun."

So Adam had walked down to Dispatch alone, giving

his name to the man with the bulbous nose sitting at the front desk. "You're here for a ride-along, eh?" The man seemed friendly, despite his red face, which looked angry at a glance.

"Yes." Adam had nodded.

"Pretty young, huh?" His face broke into a genuine smile.

Adam nodded again.

"Good for you. Now, a ride-along is just what it sounds like: you're along for the ride to see what a Watcher goes through on a daily basis. You're allowed to ask questions, as many as you want. The Watchers will give you a good idea of what you can expect in a few years once you're out in the field." He looked at the screen, then turned back to Adam. "You have Fogerty and Carson, so you should have an okay time. Carson's a good kid; you'll like him. Fogerty's an old bastard like me — don't believe a word he says unless you plan on hating the world."

Adam had laughed and said, "Okay," then the man pressed a button on his desk and called for Fogerty and Carson. A few minutes later a good kid and an old bastard led Adam to their van.

Fogerty said he'd been on City Watch forever, and looked it. They were only gone from the station for a few minutes when Adam decided he didn't like the guy at all. Fogerty had a personality like Adam had expected Keller's to be. But while the chief was kind, Fogerty kept shaking his fist at the world.

Everyone they passed on the streets was suspect: a crook, dirtbag, or mouth-breather, whatever that was. Fogerty seemed like the sort of City Watcher Michael and others were right not to trust — an officer who probably caused more trouble than he prevented.

Carson was nice, and reminded Adam a little of

Michael. He was very tall and very skinny. He had a long neck and a soft voice. His eyes seemed too small for his face, and while he only spoke one word for every hundred of Fogerty's, Adam wanted to hear all of Carson's.

After they left Municipal they cut over to Commuters, across the Exurban, and through the manned checkpoint into the Dark Quarter — the scariest part of City 6, by far.

Since everything with his dad, Adam started having more varied nightmares. Before that, his bad dreams had *always* been about the Dark Quarter. Those had started after he saw them as a setting on some of his favorite shows.

While many parents and authority figures used the Dark Quarter as some sort of cautionary tale or to tell their own children how lucky they were in comparison, Adam's parents never did. He obsessed about the place anyway.

He remembered in school hearing about a kid born in the Quarter; he was so deformed that no one would claim him. Apparently the boy found people who would care for him a day or two at a time but no one to love him or take him in permanently. Worse, the State wouldn't allow him in the orphanages because of his deformities. The government didn't believe in helping weakness thrive. According to the One True Leader Jack Geralt, allowing nature to thin the herd of the sick and dying was always more merciful, especially to the whole. That was the only way to strengthen the State. And what was good for the State was good for all.

The deformed boy, over the years, grew bitter and angry. Eventually, he started killing people, and — for reasons nobody knew or understood — ate them.

He was known as the Dark Quarter Cannibal and became one of the most notorious Darwin Games contestants of all time. The moment Adam had heard the cannibal's story, he dreamed of getting lost in the Quarter, searching winding alleys for his parents. Adam would run through his dreams, every time winding up at the end of a dead-end alley. He'd hear the cannibal whistling, humming pleasant tunes as he cornered his victims.

He always managed to wake up just as the killer was raising a blade to stab him. The nightmares had plagued Adam for most of his life, until the ones about his father started late last year.

Now, to enter the very place that was the source for so many of his nightmares had him feeling both apprehensive and eager to put the childish fears behind him.

Adam remembered something Keller had said that made him wonder how a kind man like him could be so cold.

"There will always be a need for a place like the Dark Quarter, Adam. We could clear it tomorrow, and it would grow back in a month, slowly at first, until it was fat on its vice again. It *is* already what it needs to be. The City can't take care of everyone, not without hurting the many. Would you rather have a small family where you could feed everybody and keep them happy, or a large family with everyone starving?"

"A small family," Adam had said.

"Exactly. And that is why places like the Dark Quarter must exist, so the people who deserve happiness can find it."

Looking out the van windows, Adam started to understand. While City 6 was hardly a paradise, it was leaps and bounds above the rampant squalor in the Dark Quarter: tall, filthy buildings shoved so close together they seemed like an elaborate scheme to defy gravity; bags of trash like leaves on a tree; and people who looked so neglected, and haunted, Adam was sure they'd plague his sleep for years.

If Keller was right, and there were really only two choices — some people happy and well fed while others were cast to the Quarter, or everyone barely living — Adam supposed he was grateful for the better life. Still, as he looked around, he felt guilty that others suffered for his meager prosperity.

Carson pointed to a parking lot up the street, crammed with cars. A man with a large rifle stood guard. He wore some sort of uniform. Not City Watch, but still official. "We'll park there, then head out on foot. You ready?"

Adam nodded. He couldn't wait.

"Just stay with us and you'll be fine. We won't let anything happen to a Lovecraft." Carson winked.

They parked the van with Hech, the man with the rifle, who promised to keep a "real good eye" on it. The way they joked around with one another, Adam figured they'd been parking with Hech for a while.

For fifteen minutes they walked the Quarter.

Unlike his grousing in the van, Fogerty stayed mostly silent save for an odd grunt or to correct something Carson said — never the specificity of his words so much as *how* he said them — while showing the cadet "the City's seedy underbelly."

He told Adam that he would probably be doing most of his early Watcher's work in the Quarter and identified the crumbling tenements, decaying like the addicts inside them. He said they were getting through most days strung out on Crash, an illegal street drug that clung to the Quarter like paint to walls. It was cheap and kept users hazed for days, helping them forget the despair in their lives. The drug numbed them, pleasantly at first, then not so much, until it eventually fried their brains and left the users for City incinerators.

Adam was surprised by how many people he saw buying, selling, and taking the drug out in the open, just like he was surprised by half-naked women walking or hanging out windows of some of the rundown buildings. It seemed like everything was for sale in the Quarter, whether it was drugs, stuff (most stolen or refurbished trash, Fogerty told him) from homes turned into storefronts, or people themselves.

At the end of their walk, a tall man with skin stretched so tightly across his face it looked like paper, sold something from a crate called Beans — advertised in large block letters on a cardboard sign behind him.

"What are Beans?" Adam asked Carson.

"Nothing you want anything to do with."

Fogerty said, "They're dream pills. But you never know what you're gonna get. You could get a dream where you're surrounded by blondes and doing stuff in their mouths, or you could get one with zombies. You never know, kid. Beans are Russian roulette with your sleep."

Adam couldn't understand there being so much illegal activity, right in plain sight. They were Watchers. Even though Adam was only a cadet, it was *their* job to put an end to the bad stuff. But there was so much, and they were walking right by, watching rather than *Watching*.

"Why aren't we stopping them?" Adam kept his voice low. "And why aren't they afraid of us or hiding their bad stuff?"

"What, you gonna kill one roach so another hundred can skitter out from a rock?"

Carson looked over at Fogerty with a roll of his eyes and said, "Killing one in plain sight doesn't bring the others out from a rock, and even if it did, at least you got one." He turned to Adam and set a hand on his shoulder. "Great question, kid. I wondered the same thing. Why do *you* think it's the way it is?"

Adam looked from Fogerty to Carson. Fogerty had a point, about the roaches. "Because there's too many?"

"That's a part of it." Carson smiled. "See, there has always been crime, always will be. It's in people's nature. No matter what we do, or what sort of laws we pass — no matter how high we build our Walls or how hard we work to keep monsters outside — we'll always have some inside too. We can never stop all crime. That's impossible, and every society before ours has made the same mistake by thinking they *could* stop it. We can't do that, not ever."

He took a look around. Even just talking, Carson was every bit City Watch, and never seemed to let his guard down. Satisfied for the moment, he continued.

"But what Jack Geralt figured out that no one ever figured out before is that the best way to stop crime is to let it happen, but keep it in a part of the City where it won't affect the majority. The Quarter affects a relative few; they're all gated in like animals, and that's best for all of us. We patrol the Dark Quarter to make sure nothing too awful is brewing, but as long as people aren't killing one another or plotting against the State, City Watch leaves the drugging, gambling, and whoring mostly alone."

Adam heard Keller in his head: *No one ever finds themselves in the Dark Quarter entirely by accident.*

"Then why are *we* here? Why are there so many Watchers assigned to the Dark Quarter?"

From what Adam knew so far, patrols in the Quarter were mandatory for most new Watchers. Some (like Fogerty) never left. Special assignments were rare, though Keller promised that Adam was equally rare, and that he probably wouldn't have to spend much time there.

Carson was about to explain, but Fogerty cut him off.

"We're here because it teaches us to look criminals in their ugly fucking faces, and looking criminals in their ugly fucking faces teaches us to be ready and recognize our enemy better. More important, we can contain the threat before it spreads out to the places that matter." Fogerty jerked his thumb in no particular direction, indicating Municipal, Commuters, and all the rest of City 6.

They crossed the street, their van now out of sight. Adam was starting to feel claustrophobic, like the tall, dark buildings were closing in around him.

Fogerty stopped in front of a small market and looked at Adam. "We're going in here, so just keep your mouth shut unless spoken to, got it?"

"Got it," Adam said with a nervous gulp. He looked at the storefront, a shoddy-looking place with a boarded-up window and bars over the glass door.

They entered the shop and Adam looked around, trying to figure out why they were stopping here. Though old and poorly stocked, it seemed like a regular business, unlike the many crate shops lined up along the streets.

The shelves had barely anything on them, mostly food rations and small, seemingly random household items. The overhead lights were a low blue and hummed as they flickered. They passed a worn payment counter and went into a hallway that wanted to squeeze them like toothpaste.

Carson nodded at an ancient, dark-skinned man with a foot-long beard, sunken eyes, and hands shoved inside his long dark coat. He sat on a stool in front of an old wooden door with peeling purple paint. The door once said something in big black letters, but the letters had long ago faded, leaving Adam with no idea how they once read.

Fogerty stepped in front of Carson and rapped his

knuckles hard on the door in a pattern — once, twice, then once again.

The door opened following the final knock, and Adam found himself looking up into the yellowing eyes of a giant man with teeth that looked as big as playing cards and hands the size of melons. His hair shot out from his head like a helmet; he had more than anyone Adam had ever seen — thick and black, made from a million tiny curls. He was dressed in what looked like a giant sack — burlap stitched together — as if nothing else could possibly fit him. His pants were dark, with lots of pockets like the ones City Watch wore. His boots looked City Watch too. He looked from Carson to Fogerty, from Fogerty to Carson, and finally down at Adam with a laugh. Big and booming, the sound seemed to flicker the thin blue lights as it thundered the market.

"What do you have for us this week, Marquis?"

The giant ignored Fogerty, his eyes on Carson. "Who's the kid?" Without waiting for an answer he drove his jaundiced eyes into Adam's. "You wanna be City Watch?"

He bellowed more laughter, deeper than the first time. Adam had no idea if the man was usually so jovial, or if it was something specifically about Adam that he found amusing.

"If you've got smarts," the big man said, "which I can see in your eyes that you do, then you'll grow up to know two things: tinkle flower tastes good and you should eat it whenever you can — you do that and do it right, ladies are forgiving of most things — and life is *far* more lucrative on this side of the gates. Don't let either of these baton twirlers tell you otherwise."

Marquis finished with another laugh, then crossed his arms across his chest, as if waiting for one of the Watchers to challenge him. Adam wanted to ask what a tinkle flower was.

Fogerty said, "Yeah, but the kid's not a degenerate."

Marquis stood like a troll, seeming to stretch the entire width of the doorway. "See how they treat me? And after all the business I steer 'em?"

"What he means to say," Carson turned to Adam, "is that we have an understanding with Mr. Marquis. He gives us information about people we should maybe look at; we pretend he's another outstanding entrepreneur and not earning undocumented credits from humanity's misery." He turned back to Marquis. "So, what've ya got for us this week, Marquis?"

"Well, that depends on what you're looking for. There's plenty as usual, but like always, our time together is short. I suggest starting with specifics."

Adam was surprised to see a criminal talking to a Watcher like he wasn't afraid, almost like *he* was the one in charge.

Fogerty seemed tired, like he hated Marquis. Carson seemed to think he was funny and wore a half smile he'd not lost since the giant opened the door.

Fogerty sighed before finally saying, "We had a body on Third and Clover Wednesday. So far no one knows shit."

"Working girl? Redhead, no cyebrows?"

"Yeah," Fogerty said. "Exactly. Got anything?"

"Might wanna look at Little Mitch. He was bitching all over the Quarter about his little firestarter done fucking him for cash."

"Little Mitch — that a pimp or a john?" Carson asked.

"John?" Marquis barked. "Bitch has the wrong equipment to interest Little Mitch. He was her pimp."

Adam wasn't sure what a pimp or john was, and was even more confused by the "equipment" comment. He wanted to ask Carson but thought it best to keep his mouth shut and not embarrass himself. He was so excited to be here, among adults — City Watch *and* criminals — saying real things in real places, that he definitely didn't want to remind everyone he was still a naive kid.

"I've never heard of Little Mitch," Fogerty said. "Where can we find him?"

"You won't have to look hard. Little *bitch* is always lying about at the Orient. Good luck catching him not all fucked on Crash. You'll be lucky to get a sentence."

"Anything else?" Carson huffed. "Underground?"

"No, ain't heard dick since you all busted last month's party. It's mum in the Quarter. Give 'em time. They'll start back. Always do."

"True that," Carson agreed. "They always do."

Now it was Fogerty who rolled his eyes at Carson.

"It was a pleasure doing business with you, sirs," Marquis said, still smiling. "And hey, kid, you ever need a gig better than the loserfest you'll get thrown as a Watcher, come back and see old Marquis. I'll hook you up. Innocent face like yours, that's a lot of credits in not a lot of time."

Marquis winked.

Carson stepped in front of Adam. "He ain't interested."

Adam wasn't sure if he was being complimented, joked with, or threatened, so he laughed nervously, feeling dumb.

Marquis closed the door without another word. The Watchers turned — Fogerty in front — then left the market and walked back down the block to their van.

Adam paused while climbing inside, turning to Carson. "What did he mean about my innocent face making lots of credits?"

It took too long for Carson to find the right words. He

stuttered twice, then Fogerty cut him off. "He meant men would pay to fuck you in the ass."

"What the hell is wrong with you?" Carson looked at Fogerty, angry.

"What? The kid wants to be a Watcher, he can't be naive and stupid forever. Right, kid?"

Adam nodded. Fogerty was right, though Adam didn't like being called stupid.

Fogerty started the van, nodded to the man with the rifle, and pulled into the street. Adam decided to ask what a pimp was.

Fogerty laughed. "You're about to see for yourself."

The van fell silent. A few minutes later they were pulling beneath an overhang in front of another dilapidated building. The overhang had lit-up lettering that read Orient Hotel, every letter burnt out except the *i* and the *e* in Orient, and the *t* in Hotel.

As they got out of the van, Adam thought about asking them what a tinkle flower was but figured he'd been the butt of enough jokes already.

## TWENTY

# Jonah Lovecraft

"Sutherland will be pleased," Katrina said, turning back toward Jonah's door and leaving his room. She walked down the hall, Jonah a tentative step behind her, already wondering if he had made a mistake by agreeing to infiltrate City 6 to rescue Liza, even if it also meant a chance to check in on his son.

"Thrilled I can please him." Jonah was bothered by Katrina's affection toward Sutherland and not quite sure why. He drained the edge from his voice and added, "I'm glad we're doing this. It feels right, I think."

Katrina led Jonah to Sutherland's chambers. He looked up as they stepped through the doorway. He seemed neatened, refreshed. Almost rosy, from drink or exercise, or perhaps a bath. He didn't look surprised to see them, smiling at Jonah as he welcomed them into his company and nodding at Katrina as she slipped out, closing the door behind her.

"Jonah, have you come to compliment the drink or the company? The bed? Surely I'm not so fortunate that you're already visiting with excellent news?"

Sutherland was a magnet like few men. When he smiled, Jonah wanted to smile; when he laughed, Jonah wanted to laugh; when he asked for excellent news, Jonah wanted to declare nothing but the best. He could see why the man had risen to power not once but twice in his life.

"All of it. But the part you actually care about: yes, I'll do what I can to reach Dr. Goelle." Jonah could see Sutherland wanted to say something in approval, so he quickly raised a hand. "But I want to see my son once in the City, I want to know how he's doing. And …" Jonah paused, trying to figure the best way to say what he meant, and understand it himself. "I know something could happen to me while I'm back there. I want to make sure Ana's taken care of if it does, and that she no longer has to fight."

"I understand. You want your daughter to have a normal life, without all the suffering."

"Yes."

"Truthfully, Jonah, you know as well as I do — that's not possible. There is no *normal*. Everyone must fight. Even the poor sheep behind the Walls are fighting; they're simply in the dark about the battles and stakes. *This* is what we're trying to change, and what we *will* change, slowly at first, then like a cracked dam burst onto arid land. We will attack Geralt and alter the current. Do you see why you're so important to us all?"

Sutherland didn't wait for an answer, shaking his head instead. "No, I cannot promise you a normal life for Ana, nor can I promise that she'll never have to fight. Hydrangea is the safest place in the Barrens, but still, the State could attack us tomorrow. Surely Anastasia would fight then. I can promise a comfortable place as long as she's with us. How does that sound, Jonah?"

"Makes sense." He nodded.

"Excellent!" Sutherland beamed on his way to a short counter lined with mostly tall bottles, picked one up — short and squat — then poured amber liquid into a glass and handed it to Jonah.

He thanked him and swallowed it off before Sutherland could propose a toast, then set the glass on the counter. "What next?"

A deep and hearty laugh, then Sutherland promised to show Jonah Ana's quarters and amaze him after that. He led Jonah back into the corridor.

The layout of Hydrangea was confusing. He couldn't still the frames in his mind enough to decode the picture. One underground hallway followed another, some cold and made of steel, tinted blue, others ancient and wooden. Most looked like the tunnels where Jonah spent days tied to a chair after his capture by Egan. They wandered through several twisting corridors — Jonah was positive they were going deeper, though they had yet to descend a stair — until they reached a small cluster of three rooms at the end of a warm hallway with impossibly plush carpet. There was a door to Jonah's right, another to his left, and a third directly in front. They were marked A, B, and C. Sutherland pointed to Jonah's left.

He said, "I thought A, for Anastasia," then opened the door.

Jonah gasped. The room was small but cozy, about the size of her old room in the City. The magic wasn't in the room's size or its furnishings — a dainty bed, a dresser, a mirror, and, most surprising to Jonah, a small pink-and-white area rug, embroidered with hydrangeas. It was a shock that such a room could still exist in this world, offering his daughter something he thought impossible: a spot to forget the Barrens.

He turned to Sutherland, overwhelmed, imagining the

look on his baby girl's face when introduced to her own little slice of heaven. Sutherland clapped him on the back. "Glad you like it, friend. Now, let me show you something you'll *really* love."

His mirth made Jonah curious; the man was clearly pleased with whatever he was about to show next. Sutherland walked one step ahead, long strides down the hallway, going faster than during their relative stroll to Ana's apartment.

He turned back to speak with Jonah as they walked. "Of course I watched all of your Games. Remarkable how much they stacked against you, and how well you managed the odds regardless, pulling them toward you, even when we couldn't help."

"I was well trained," Jonah said, the words sour on his tongue.

"As was I. Now we both must use our training to reclaim what was so unceremoniously stolen from our world. Are you ready to do that, Jonah?"

He was surprised to feel a strong *yes* bubbling inside him, but there it was, fire rekindled where it had been cold and dark for so long. He kept it inside, but Sutherland could clearly see it in his eyes.

"I was most impressed with your use of the machete. How you held it like a whip and swung it like a conductor's baton. When those three zombies had you surrounded, backed in that corner over by the Bone Pit, all of them gnashing and snarling, closing in, leaving you nowhere to go … instead of shrinking, you roared, then proceeded to kill them all. It was beautiful, Jonah. I cheered for days. Everyone thought I was crazier than they already do."

Jonah didn't comment on that last part. "I've been trained in many weapons, but the Darwins were the first time I'd ever held a machete. I didn't want to carry anything after that. Tool *and* weapon, it kept me alive when I had to hack through brush; the chopping power of a hatchet, but the finesse of a knife."

"It *is* a tool. Did you know Nepalese warriors were once farmers? They took their tools into battle when provoked, and the machete was born."

"I don't even know what Nepalese are."

Sutherland laughed and fell into silence, until they reached a metal door. He laughed again, then opened it with a smile and nodded for Jonah to enter.

A sparse room, filled with long metal tables, no benches or chairs. There were what looked like refrigerators and tall cabinets lining every wall, screens filling the spaces where there was room. It was all black. The room felt cool, at least ten degrees cooler than the hallway.

"This is our lab." Sutherland waved his arms around the room. "We're just traditional enough to take Sundays off, so today we have the lab to ourselves. Perfectly convenient, you'll have the chance to admire it in private."

Sutherland crossed the room to one of the tall metal cabinets, punched something on the door's keypad, waited a second for a hiss to indicate the latch had unlocked, then opened the door and reached inside and withdrew a black sheath with a familiar shape.

He handed the leather-clad machete to Jonah.

"I had this made for you, wanted it done for when you got here. Herb, our resident doctor and weapons specialist, finished it a few weeks ago, though I had no idea when I'd find you." Then, with a wink: "Never doubted I would."

Jonah drew the machete from its sheath, admiring the blade as Sutherland spoke.

"We're plenty armed here, and there are tons of machetes, but none are quite like this. I wanted you to have the best. I had one like that." He nodded toward Jonah's new weapon. "It's beautiful, yes?"

He looked up at Sutherland and smiled. It sure as hell was. The blade was all black, its weight perfect in his hand, slightly smaller than what he'd had in the Games, about fourteen inches from tip to the hilt's interior edge.

He swung the blade and it whistled through the air. Then he anchored his weight and pulled back from a second swing, wrist and elbow singing in key. "Amazing blade."

"It is." Sutherland was still beaming, as if he'd forged it himself. "May I?"

He extended his out and Jonah set the machete inside it. "There are a few additional features I had Herb add to your tool; I think you'll appreciate them. This sheath is important." Sutherland patted the leather as he slipped the blade back inside it. "It keeps your machete charged."

"Charged?"

Sutherland was practically glowing. "Yes, charged. I wouldn't send you back out into the Barrens with anything less than the best, Jonah. This," he patted the sheath again, "is the best that I can do."

Sutherland handed him the sheath. Jonah drew the blade and studied it with newly interested eyes.

"Your blade is a perfectly weighted weapon, tailored to you from the data we could gather watching the Games. Even better, as you already said, it's also a tool. Your machete has a jamming signal that will disable any orbs within range, charged by solar cells in the blade and sheath. It can burn hot enough to start fire, and if you press this button at the bottom and hold it for three seconds before throwing it, your machete will serve as a high-powered explosive and detonate on impact."

Jonah didn't know what to say.

Sutherland made it easy. "I'm glad you like it!"

"It's perfect." And it was. Jonah could have stood there holding the weapon forever, but instead he simply thanked Sutherland and said he wanted a good night's sleep — alone, he added, to which Sutherland grinned. He also said that he'd be ready to leave first thing in the morning. They reached the door when Jonah paused, turned to Sutherland, and asked if the lab had any sort of recording device he could borrow. He wanted to make a video for Ana, in case something happened on his way to or from City 6. Sutherland said of course, then went to a cabinet three feet away, opened it, and handed Jonah a vox.

Minutes later Jonah was in his quarters, recording what he knew could be his farewell to Ana.

"Anastasia." Jonah stared into the green light, trying not to lose it. "I'm so sorry for everything that's happened. It isn't fair and you don't deserve it. I can't explain what happened with Mom, but you must know that I loved her, just as I love you and Adam. I would never do anything to harm either of you and would give anything to spare you from the horrors rained unjustly on you. You are my first-born, Anastasia, and have made my life better for every day I could share it with you. I may never know what happened, but you must know I've never stopped loving you or your brother and …"

But there was nothing more to say.

Jonah ended the recording, brittle, not wanting to cry through his goodbye.

He set the vox on the floor beside his bed and fell asleep hoping Ana would never see this video.

# TWENTY-ONE

# Adam Lovecraft

ADAM SAT in the corner of a filthy apartment on the Orient Hotel's third floor, watching Carson and Fogerty interrogate the pimp.

The apartment Adam once lived in with his family was small. Basic. Slightly larger but no fancier than those of most of Adam's friends. He had one friend, Arnold Denny, whose father was a lawyer. They lived in the high apartments. Adam had seen his place three times; it was big, and the ceilings were tall. The paint at his place seemed extra clean. Standing in Arnold's apartment, Adam had felt somehow taller and stronger, like he could do anything he wanted, and that feeling had made him want to do more.

But this place made him feel smaller, less significant, and almost like he wanted to die. The Orient Hotel was filthy from floor to ceiling — wall to wall the most disgusting place Adam had ever been in. There were rats and roaches, along with things he'd never seen and hoped to forget. The place was brown and smelled like its color, reeking of piss and shit. Paint peeled where the walls weren't caved in or broken. The building weighed on Adam like a wet blanket, and while he'd only seen one apartment in the Orient, Little Mitch's *had* to be the worst.

"So where were you, Mitch? This is a simple question, and I'm not sure you're seeing how patient I'm already being. My partner Carson's a nice enough guy, but I'm starting to lose it. Word at the station is that I'm a total cock, and I'm at my worst since my old lady hasn't wanted to fuck me for a week. You're either gonna spill or not, and if you're not, we're gonna do some stuff that will spread through the Quarter fast enough to get us a month full of *Yes, sirs!*"

It went on like that for a while. A lot about the Quarter had surprised him, but nothing more than the way people were willing to argue with Watchers. These were bad guys doing terrible things, yet they were acting like the Watchers had no power.

Little Mitch laughed, as he had been doing since they stormed his apartment and Fogerty ordered Adam into the corner. "I ain't saying shit and don't have to. You don't scare me. You got questions, you can ask my brother. He'll tell you everything you wanna know."

"And who's your brother?" Fogerty smacked Little Mitch hard on the back of his head.

"Mac Callum," Little Mitch said, then leaned back in his chair, smiled, and watched the Watchers trade a glance. "Yeah, that's right. Mac Callum. So don't fuck with me."

Carson's face changed. He walked up to Little Mitch and punched his face.

"We don't give a shit who your brother is," Fogerty yelled from behind him, then stood back as Carson shocked Adam by beating the crap from their suspect.

Beating the man had to be wrong, but Adam knew rules were different in the Quarter, and that maybe Carson was doing what was necessary to keep Little Mitch from hurting innocent people. Adam would have expected Fogerty to do the beating; he was gruff and mean and it seemed in character. But Carson was kicking the shit out of the suspect without hesitation.

Little Mitch whimpered. Blood rained from a face that was starting to look like an open wound. Finally, he started talking. Adam was bothered by the beating, maybe even scared, but he finally confessed to killing the woman.

"That bitch owed me," he whined, as if it were a decent defense for murder.

Fogerty wrapped a bloody Little Mitch in cuffs and dragged him downstairs, through the filthy Orient, and into the back of the van. He got in and turned back to Adam. "Look, kid. We don't like to get physical, but sometimes us Watchers don't get a choice, especially here in the Quarter. It's our job to show the criminals who's boss, and sometimes what we did up there," he glanced toward the burned-out letters in the sign, "well, that's the only way we get people to listen."

Adam nodded, wishing he were anywhere but in a City Watch van, sharing space with a pimp and a pair of thugs. He thought the ride-along would be exciting, or maybe scary in a good way. But right now he felt sick, and desperately wanted to go back home to the Academy where he could climb into bed.

Fifteen minutes later, they were hauling Little Mitch into the station. Fogerty agreed to book him so Carson could take Adam to the dining hall before the end of their shift.

The station didn't use ration cards, so Adam ordered what he wanted — a protein sandwich, macaroni salad, and an apple — then sat beside Carson.

"Listen, kid," Carson said as soon as Adam sat, like

he'd been waiting to say it. "Fogerty wasn't bullshitting you in the van. What you saw, we don't do that all the time, but today it had to be done. I know we set a bad example, and I'm sorry about that. I don't want to tarnish your image of City Watch because we lost control with an asshole who wouldn't fess to murder. That's not who we are *outside* the Quarter; that's important to understand. You'll be in the driver's seat someday. You have to be able to disconnect yourself from what's required from this job. I've got a lot of respect for you, Adam; I was good friends with your father. For what it's worth, I don't think he was guilty." He smiled. "But that's between you and me, K?"

Adam nodded, swallowing uncomfortably, then smiling back at Carson and eating his food. He didn't want anything to stay just between the two of them, at least not if Keller asked.

# TWENTY-TWO

# Anastasia Lovecraft

IF LIAM HAD AMMO LEFT, this would've been easy — or at least easier. Six bandits total: poor odds, sure, but they would've had a better chance.

"We know you're there. Come out now with your hands up!" yelled one of the bandits as he approached.

"Come on." Liam shoved the crowbar into a tool loop on his belt, held his hands in the air, nodded a *trust me* to Ana, and slowly stepped out from behind the tower to face the six men.

Ana walked with hands in the air behind him. Five of the six bandits fell back, all holding their weapons on Liam. One had the old gun that had belonged to Liam's grandfather. The man in front, a thick man with a pure-black goatee, stepped forward and punched him hard in the gut.

He cried out, clutching his stomach as he worked to regain his balance. He wobbled and swayed, then stood straight, looking at the man, defiant, eyes searching the roof for solutions, unwilling to surrender to what he couldn't see. That was Liam — taking punishment to buy them time.

Liam wasn't standing straight long before the bandit hit him a second time, this time with a fist to his jaw. He cried out, louder and with a warble, clapping hand to jaw as he staggered back, again at war with his footing.

Liam surprised the bandit — though not Ana — by regaining his balance much faster than he had let on and charging straight for him, lunging toward his gut and sending them both to the rooftop.

Neither of them could know if the bandits behind the goateed man would start blasting. And Ana wasn't about to find out. She put one foot behind the other and started slowly backing away from the melee.

Goatee had untangled himself from Liam and was now standing up. He waved his hand and his men fell back, holding their barrels on Liam as the leader punched him enough in the jaw to prove that the first two were tickles.

Liam, who was also back on his feet, fell back, landing on his ass. He wheezed and looked like he might vomit as the bandit rushed him and slammed a boot on his chest.

Ana, now backed up to the roof's edge, called out, "Stop! Don't hurt him. I'll do whatever you want — just leave him alone."

"You'll do whatever we want anyway," one of the men said, stepping toward Liam so he was standing beside the goateed man, aiming an energy rifle at Liam's head.

Ana looked down from the rooftop, fourteen stories to the street below. No way she'd survive. She remembered how the bandits were leering at her earlier, with such ugly looks in their eyes, touching themselves. She'd never been with a man, but she knew that sex short-circuited a man's thinking. She hoped that the men were more interested in having their way with her than exacting revenge on Liam.

"If you hurt him, I'll jump. Let him go, or else!"

"You ain't gonna jump," said one of the bandits from behind an uncomfortable-sounding laugh.

She stepped onto the ledge, nearly losing her balance as a gust of wind whipped at her, somehow managing not to fall as she looked back at the bandits. "I'll fucking do it! Let him go!"

The bandits looked at Ana, hesitating, as if assessing her willingness to follow through.

But if they really hurt him, there was zero doubt about what she would do.

# TWENTY-THREE

# Liam Harrow

"IF YOU HURT HIM, I'll jump! Let him go, or else!"

Ana teetered at the roof's edge, insanity rimming both of her eyes. If he half-believed that she'd do it, the bandits must have no doubt. She was trying to buy him time to reach safety. Liam knew she wanted him to run.

But he stayed put, rooted as bandits looked from him to Ana, then back, clearly wondering what might happen next — and if Liam might be foolish enough to make a move with his silly little crowbar.

He might get out alive if he ran now. And if he were able to escape, he could maybe find a better weapon, then return with a fighting chance and save them both.

But he looked around at the half-dozen bandits with their bloodlust and rape eyes and felt hopeless. Even if he got away, it would take too long to find a weapon and get back. He didn't dare leave Ana alone that long. Not with these men.

Liam had thought all was lost seconds after waking up. But even with only a quarter of the attackers they had faced at the tree's base, Liam figured their odds were better earlier in the day. The bandits were primed for attack, not seeing Liam or Ana as much of a threat. The remainder were angry. They had been outsmarted by their victims and dragged into a pursuit through the forest, then the Outback, and up fourteen flights of stairs through a zombie-infested building, losing at least four more men along the way.

These bandits were out for blood … and more.

The world froze around him as he sized up the situation.

Of the six, three held guns. The one in front — the goateed giant — had picked up the wooden club he dropped when struggling with Liam. Nails pounded through it glinted in the sun. Another held a spear. The third bandit without a gun, standing off to the side of the group, swung several feet of heavy chain, links whistling with a mild scream as he swung it in wide circles against the wind. Liam had a crowbar, two fists, and the willingness to die if it meant protecting Ana, still teetering at the roof's edge.

Ana stared into his eyes, urging him to go. To flee. To leave her be.

But he couldn't, even with murder approaching from every angle. It was better to die himself than see it happen to her … or live with the knowledge of what they'd do to Ana if they caught her.

If she failed to jump, or they somehow stopped her, they'd take her as a toy, using her fast, brutalizing her body on behalf of their fallen brothers and their own sordid lusts. Liam had seen the atrocities leveled on women forced into the Games all too many times on TV.

*This* wasn't televised. God only knew how much worse they would treat Ana if given the chance.

He couldn't let that happen.

Liam charged past Goatee and toward the bandit behind him — the one holding the spear — and tackled him hard with what little energy he still had. The move took the man by surprise, and Liam dropped him hard to the rooftop before he had a chance to raise his spear. The bandit scrambled for his weapon, crawling on his stomach, his fingers touching the shaft ...

Liam slammed the crowbar into the back of the bandit's skull.

He wanted to go back for seconds, across the man's face to make sure he didn't rise as a zombie, but he heard footsteps approaching and the sound of metal swinging. He glanced up just in time to see Chain Man charging him.

He managed to roll out of the way as the chain whistled and slapped the roof beside him, then sprang back up and swung the crowbar, taking aim at Chain Man's kneecap.

The solid steel hit with a bone-shattering crunch. The bandit's leg folded the wrong way, collapsing him to the roof in a scream.

He bent over, clutching his bloody knee, dropping the chain out of reach.

Liam swung the crowbar into the top of his skull, twice, ending his screams.

Liam had been expecting gunfire to erupt, but a shot had yet to be fired. He leapt to his feet — *two down* — then looked over at Goatee and saw why he wasn't yet riddled with bullets: Goatee was waving his brothers back. His eyes were as red as they were yellow, hungry for Liam's blood.

Goatee took a step toward him, but Liam held his space, crowbar poised in front of him, ready to swat or swing or parry. Eager to kill. Goatee grunted and swung his club from what might as well have been a rooftop away.

Liam laughed, trying to get under his skin, rattle him.

Goatee swung his club again, this time coming closer to Liam, but not enough for him to launch a counterattack. He darted out of the way.

Goatee was strong and big but lumbering. If his club struck Liam, it would probably mean instant death. But even exhausted, Liam was faster and lighter. If he could hang in long enough to get behind the man, or even just near enough to strike, he could take the giant down.

Liam didn't dare move his focus off the big man. He could only hope no one else was taking aim. Hoped no one was moving closer to Ana. Hoped Ana was still on the ledge and hadn't already jumped.

Goatee took two steps toward Liam, pushing him farther from both Ana and the other bandits.

Liam stepped back, holding the crowbar tight, watching the giant's arm muscles to try and predict when he might swing.

He was too close, but Liam didn't dare step back too fast or too blindly, lest he trip over the decades of debris that littered the roof.

Goatee snarled and jerked his head toward Ana. "After I kick your body over the side, we're gonna hold her down while the others take turns fucking her, one from each side." He smiled, a gruesome sight. "I called pussy on the way over."

Liam said nothing. He just kept watching Goatee's arms and feet and moving out of the way in response. His enemy was growing more out of breath as he continued to swing the club.

But Goatee wasn't tired of tugging on Liam's nerves. "When we're finished, we'll take her back to camp and let everyone have a go. She'll be begging us to kill her. But we won't. We'll use her up until she's wide as a valley. Then we'll flip her, maybe cut some new holes."

Goatee expected Liam to charge.

But Liam wasn't biting. Instead, he picked up his pace, moving faster even though he was stepping back blindly. Maybe he could tire the giant, then make his move.

Goatee grunted as he took another swing.

This time, Liam dashed to his right as the club went left. Liam raised the crowbar, hitting Goatee in the elbow with a satisfying *crunch*.

Goatee's grip didn't weaken on the club even as he screamed out in pain. His eyes met Liam's, and Liam felt as if he'd spit on an angry bull.

The bull charged, faster than Liam expected.

Goatee was feigning fatigue. The club flew at Liam's face.

Liam's foot slipped on something and fell back, smacking the rooftop hard and sending the breath from his lungs.

Goatee was quick to recover. He lifted the club overhead, ready to deliver the death blow.

Adrenaline coursed through Liam's body. Before his brain found a defense, his foot responded, thrusting straight into the Goatee's knee.

His leg collapsed, just like Chain Man's, twisting the club's arc and causing it to plummet hard, inches to Liam's right.

The giant toppled, and Liam raised his crowbar, thrusting the sharp end into his gut. Goatee fell forward on top of him, driving the metal deeper into his own stomach even as he pinned Liam down.

The bandit screamed as his hot blood spilled onto Liam. It bubbled from the man's mouth, and his eyes rolled back, wide, scared, and angry. As his blood frothed onto

Liam's face, Liam twisted his head away, closing his lips tight against the taste of warm copper.

"You fucker," the man managed, bringing his hands to find Liam's neck.

Trapped, his arms pinned beneath the massive weight, Liam felt the fear tighten its hold on him, just as the man squeezed his neck.

Liam wrestled with the crowbar, twisting and turning it to damage the internal organs, ensuring that he bled out before Liam could be strangled.

But Goatee's hands didn't slacken.

Liam kept struggling with the crowbar, twisting and turning it, feeling even more of the man's blood gurgling out. And yet his grip somehow tightened.

Liam felt himself weakening, struggling for breath as the man continued to choke him. He struggled to keep his chin down hard on the giant's hands, lest they close around his windpipe and collapse it immediately.

Panic enflamed his face as a lightheadedness began to take over.

*Can't. Pass. Out!*

He managed one last surge of strength, turning the crowbar up severely. Then an awful crunching as his enemy's eyes comically widened.

Goatee went entirely limp.

Liam wanted to collapse as air filled his lungs again, but then he heard the guns. Pieces of the roof flew up in chunks as the bandits opened fire.

Liam twisted the corpse to put it between him and the bandits as a shield. It shook and jolted as bullets and energy blasts beat into it.

He glanced up at Ana, still teetering at the edge, watching and waiting, see-through pale, exposed but reasonably safe until Liam was dead.

He wished she'd run while the bandits' attention was on him. But she might have had no clear escape, or was too weak to risk running. She had to keep suicide as an option.

Liam tried yanking the crowbar from the giant, but it was slippery and stuck.

The bandits moved closer, firing.

Most were shit shots, otherwise Liam would be dead. He might as well have been, with nowhere to run. He had only a fucking crowbar, which he couldn't even pull from the giant's corpse.

Amazingly the gunfire stopped as one of the men said, "Surrender now, and we'll let you live."

Liam didn't believe a word, or dare peek over the corpse. But he couldn't help but wonder why they'd stopped firing. They easily could have finished him off, firing until they finally broke through his shield.

Instead, they were advancing.

There were three men left. The odds had shifted significantly, giving Liam a glimmer of hope that he might survive, despite their guns.

The wind picked up, making it impossible to hear their footsteps. But he could feel them coming.

Liam continued to wrestle with the crowbar, finally pulling it from the giant's body. It was coated in a thick stickiness. He had no time for disgust. No time for anything but to—

He heard footsteps running toward him. Too late. Hands pulled his hair and yanked him from his hiding spot. A hard fist slammed in his back.

Liam dropped the crowbar, helpless, struggling to turn and fight off the bandit, but the gun was already pressed against his head.

He froze, watching as the two others approached,

barely able to bury their rotten-toothed smiles behind their smacking lips.

"Well, well, well," said a tattooed man with long, dirty curly dark hair. "Whatcha gonna do now?"

Liam looked past them to Ana, still on the ledge, crying as she stared.

The man with the tattoos turned back to her. "Don't jump, honey. We'll let lover boy live, just step away from the ledge."

Liam finally understood: he was their pawn to talk her down. After all they'd been through, to wade through the zombies without any prize must have been crushing. Leaving without Ana was just not an option.

"Don't trust them!" Liam couldn't tell her to jump, but he needed her near the ledge. Jumping was her final card — she *couldn't* just hand it over.

"They're going to kill me anyway!"

"Shut up!" Another of the bandits — a skinny rat of a man — grabbed the fallen Chain Man's weapon. He slinked toward Liam, rat grin intent and teasing.

He gripped the chain and said to Ana, "Get your little ass over here right now, or we start whipping your boy."

"Stay there!" Liam shouted.

"Shut up." Rat Man swung.

The chain hit Liam in the back of his calves and dropped him back to the rooftop. Pain shot through both knees.

"Get over here, NOW!" Rat Man commanded, laughing as he walked behind Liam.

Liam flinched, balled his fists, ready to fight back, but then the bandit with the gun reminded him to sit still by shoving the energy blaster against his head.

"I'm gonna count to three!" Rat Man said. "One ..."

Ana cried out, starting to step away from the ledge.

"Stay!" Liam said.

"Two!" Rat Man said.

Ana was frozen, shaking her head, her distress breaking Liam's heart.

"Three!" Rat Man swung again, this time hitting Liam across his back.

He screamed and fell forward, hunched over in pain.

"I'm gonna give you one more chance, bitch! One!"

"Stop! I'll come!" Ana started to step away from the ledge.

But Liam just couldn't allow it. He'd either take them down, or die trying.

"Two …"

Liam stood, pain like lightning through his joints.

"Get back down," said the gunman to his left, pushing the weapon harder against Liam's head.

"No." This was it. Two more bodies lost to the Outback.

"Three!" Rat man swung again.

Liam braced for impact. The chain was a split second from his chest when a bright blue light vaporized the chain into black ashes in a scream of crackling sparks, along with Rat Man's body.

Liam fell to the ground, instinct taking over, as the remaining bandits aimed their weapons around in search of the enemy.

A hunter orb screamed through the air, stopping on a dime ahead, then whirling around in an urgent circle, facing the bandits, its digital eye fixed on them.

The bandits fired their blasters.

The orb dipped and stopped as the burst of energy went over its body. One shot hit the orb without felling it, knocking it only momentarily askew.

The orb calibrated, corrected its position, then fired

another bright blue blast, white heat following, turning the second bandit into molecules and memories.

The last bandit fired several shots in desperation. Taking advantage, Liam stood and limped, as quickly as he could, toward Ana still at the edge.

She met him halfway. He grabbed her hand, but she resisted, her feet stuck to the rooftop as she stared at the fallen bandits in shock. They were all gone.

Only the orb was left, hovering and turning toward them.

Hunter orbs were non-thinking machines. They couldn't be outsmarted or reasoned with. Six bandits were bad.

One hunter orb was worse.

It whirred toward them, slowly, as if assessing. Liam wondered which city had sent it. He'd witnessed orbs hunting people almost indiscriminately in the Barrens on two occasions. He didn't know why they had targeted people outside the cities, if the orbs were specifically hunting enemies or just brushing up on target practice in a place where nobody would notice. He imagined someone on the other end of the transmission, seeing both Liam and Ana in its sights.

If the City, or the network, had been looking for them ever since they escaped the Games, the fugitives had finally been found.

Liam looked at the door to the stairwell — too far to reach. No way they could make it before being vaporized.

The best he could do was distract the orb and tell Ana to run. But hunter orbs were too fast. Their only hope was to find something to bring it down.

They'd just pulled off the miraculous by surviving the bandits not once, but twice. He wasn't about to lay down for the State.

A spark of hope as he spotted a blaster on the ground, ten feet away.

He might be able to bring it down with a clean shot, or at least disable it long enough to escape.

He stepped in front of Ana, his heart still racing and body still broken, and inched toward the gun. If the hunter orb — or the person watching its feed — recognized what Liam was doing, it would vaporize him before he reached the blaster.

He kept stepping forward, eyes locked on the hovering orb, silently watching him. He braced for the energy blast as he inched closer.

The gun was four feet away.

If he dived and rolled he *might* be able to get off a shot, maybe two. His heart pounded so hard he could feel it in his throat.

*Three feet. Two.*

The orb zipped toward him.

He dropped to the ground, reached for the gun, raised it, sighted the orb, and pulled the trigger.

But the blaster was empty.

The orb raced toward him, stopping just inches from his face.

"I'm here to help." The orb's screen lit with a familiar face on the other side of the transmission: Balon, Duncan's apprentice. "You two okay? Looks like I found you just in time!"

Ana steadied her breath, rubbing her arm above the wrist. She looked like she wanted to ask Balon why or how and in some way understand the impossible, but her mouth wasn't working.

"How did you find us? And why? Does Oli know you're helping?" Before Balon could answer, Liam added, "And thanks. You saved our lives. There's no way either of us would've left this roof alive without you."

"You're a lucky man, Harrow, but yes, even you might not have seen your way out of that one."

"How did you find us?" Liam asked again.

"Duncan asked Oli to send an orb with you, when the courier arrived. Oli agreed, but then everything happened, and well, I never finished prepping the orb. Then you guys were gone, and I wasn't about to ask Oli if I could send the orb with you since he was pissed in ten colors. But then this morning, I thought I should send it off. Your trail was easy to follow: I found the skirmish about twenty minutes ago, then sent the orb into the Outback. Just followed the gunfire from there."

"Thanks," Ana managed through her tears. "Thanks for caring, and the risk. I know it's not easy to keep stuff from Oli."

Balon's smile filled the small screen. "You can *thank* Oli. He gave me permission, actually ordered me not to do anything including eat, sleep, piss, or shit until I found you. That was this morning, before tea."

Ana was still teary, probably finding it hard to believe that even after everything, Oli wanted to help them, wanted to help her.

Liam was about to ask Balon how many of the bandits were left, if any others had followed their sorry asses into the Outback. He wanted to ask if Duncan's bag of tricks was still at the tree, and if so, if it was worth returning for. But before he said a word, the orb started to sputter and tilted a bit off kilter.

"What's happening?" Ana stepped back from the orb.

Balon's voice warbled through static as it spun and sparked and whirred. It sputtered again, lost another two feet from its hover, then said, "Looks like we took too much damage. I'll have to bring her home."

"Will you be back?" Liam asked.

"Let's hope so." The sound went dead along with the picture.

The orb glided jerkily over the rooftop, descended fourteen stories to the wrecked streets of the Outback, then flew away and out of sight.

Liam hoped it wasn't the last they'd seen of Balon.

# TWENTY-FOUR

# Jonah Lovecraft

*CITY 6*

GETTING into City 6 was easier than Jonah could have possibly dreamed. They were met in the sewers by a man named Anthony Walsh, whom Jonah had known before losing Molly, though not as a member of the Underground. Everything about Anthony was square: head, jaw, and shoulders. As he and Katrina clapped one another on the back and traded familiars, Jonah realized that although he'd seen himself as an important — or perhaps even essential — member of the Underground, the truth was clear that he was but a small cog in the machine.

They were deep in the City's bowels, the same tunnels Jonah had once used to coordinate evacuations. The musty corridors were monitored by sensors and orbs, but the Underground knew the location of every sensor, and wore bracelets that intercepted orb frequencies and alerted refugees to their presence.

The State wasn't stupid; it knew the sewers weren't

secure, but solutions were never permanent since manning the sub areas was expensive, and the maintenance even worse. Cities tended to lose orbs in the sewers, thanks to the resistance regularly rigging traps and disabling the flying machines.

After about forty minutes of walking through winding tunnels, Anthony veered to the right and stepped into their trek's final leg.

The new tunnel led them gradually higher as promised until it crashed into a false wall. Anthony slid that wall aside and revealed a passageway into the basement of a shop belonging to one of Jonah's old associates. The word *friend* nearly fit, and would have if Jonah allowed it.

Marquis hefted Anthony from the tunnel first, followed by Katrina, then Jonah.

At Sutherland's suggestion, Jonah had shaved his head, save for the sides. They colored what was left of his hair gray and trimmed his beard to a small mustache. The disguise was rounded out by Sebastian, a man at Hydrangea with the odd title of *Accessories* who was responsible for the prosthetic nose that changed the shape of his face, and the injections of whatever he'd used to round Jonah's cheeks.

Jonah looked different, but not enough to fool anyone who knew him well. Katrina had introduced him to Anthony, so Marquis was the first true test of his disguise.

"So what can I do for you three jolly members of the Underground?" Marquis looked at Anthony, giving Jonah no sign of recognition.

But Katrina led the conversation. "We need temp IDs, a skin tab to get through the Quarter's gates—"

"Ha!" Marquis barked laughter, cutting her off. "You're gonna need more than a skin tab and some lame disguise to hide Lovecraft." He gestured at Jonah and slapped a giant hand on his shoulder.

Jonah stared in surprise, then shook his hand. "You recognized me!"

"Of course I recognized you. Only place you ever need look is in a man's eyes. Everything else is window dressing." He slapped Jonah on the shoulder again, harder than before. "Good to see you, man."

"So you think I'll get spotted?"

Marquis shrugged. "Normally I'd say you'd be fine. Watchers see what they're expecting to see, and getting in and out of the Quarter is easy enough when they're looking for nothing in particular. But you're a fallen Watcher. You've been in the Games. Your daughter followed behind you. I don't expect you can bury that history behind a fake nose or an ugly comb-over." He smiled and added, "I've got a doctor's uniform you can wear. People tend to recognize uniforms rather than faces, so that should help."

City doctors wore all white suits for the men and long dresses for women, with small black crosses where the collar closed. It reminded Jonah a bit of the priest collars from the Old Nation.

"You sure I should look like a doctor? There aren't that many. Seeing a new one might raise some hackles."

"More have entered the workforce in the last year or so, especially with all the sickness spreading through the Quarter."

"Rats?" Jonah asked.

"Venereal. The State tends to take notice when men from the decent parts of the City start getting the sickness. They sent in doctors to treat the whores — and even some of the men — on the hush-hush."

"So I'm a dick doctor?"

"Well, dick and ass." Marquis laughed. "Don't forget the ass, man."

Katrina rolled her eyes as Jonah laughed. Given the Watchers' gallows humor, it explained why so much of the force tended to get along with Marquis while they cracked down on other, lesser criminals.

"Your lady friend will have to wait here, though, since I don't have a female uniform," Marquis said. "That okay?"

"I guess," Jonah said.

"I was askin' her." He grinned at Katrina. It was rumored that Marquis had slept with north of one thousand women, and Jonah had no problem believing it.

"I have some people to look in on, anyway." Katrina nodded. "Is Jericho Joe still down on Baker Street?"

"Yes, ma'am. You need an escort? These streets are rough to strangers."

"I'm a big girl." She ran a hand along her bladed gauntlet.

Marquis turned back to Jonah. "You should be able to walk right through if you take the south gates — Del Toro's working them. Tell him the Gentleman said 'no cover charge,' and he won't look too close. But first I need to give you one of these."

He led them from the basement and into the shop's "stockroom" in back. There, at a table full of various body mod tools, sat a shifty-eyed bald man with tattoos covering every inch of visible skin. He smiled with a mouth full of metal teeth, a common thing to see from people who'd smoked too much Black Mist.

"Set my man here up with this ID tab." Marquis reached into his pocket and pulled out a small carbon envelope.

"Sure thing," said Tattoo as Jonah sat.

"Your name is now Dr. William Baker," Marquis

informed him. "You work at several clinics, including Clinics 17, 14, 12, and 9. That means your ID allows you to be in any area of City 6. Can you remember that?"

"Dr. William Baker. I work at Clinics 17, 14, 12, and 9."

"Glad to see the months in the Barrens haven't robbed your blue-ribbon recall."

"Sometimes it's a curse," Jonah said.

Tattoo took his right arm, wiped off a spot on his inner wrist with a swab of alcohol, then dried the spot and grabbed a small pair of tweezers. Reaching into the carbon envelope, he retrieved a small silver-colored disc about a half-inch in circumference. He peeled the backing, then pressed it onto Jonah's skin.

Jonah had seen plenty of bad fake ID discs in his day, most of them awful and able to fool practically no one. But Marquis wouldn't go through all this trouble just to give him a bad ID disc.

Tattoo grabbed a metal tool that looked like a cross between a pen and a screwdriver and held it over Jonah's arm above the disc.

"What's that do?" Jonah asked.

"Gets your skin color." The instrument beeped, then Tattoo pressed the metal tip to the disc.

Jonah watched as it changed color to match his skin. Then felt a warmth as it melted into his flesh.

"Wow," Jonah said, barely able to tell where his skin ended and the disc began. "How long is this good for?"

"A few weeks," Marquis replied. "Just don't fuck with it, or pour anything other than soap or water on it. And it'll dissolve if you try and take it off, so don't."

Jonah nodded, impressed with the level of tech Marquis had at his disposal. He was friend to more illegal activities than Jonah could imagine, but also friend to

Jonah, and the Underground. Duncan and Marquis had probably saved close to the same number of lives, even though one was a preacher and the other something close to the opposite. Temp IDs were expensive, and the risk for Marquis immeasurable, and yet he never asked for a single thing in return.

Jonah was ready to enter the Quarter, but Marquis stopped him with a gentle hand to his shoulder, looking like he wanted to talk.

"I saw your boy in here, just the other day."

"Adam?"

"He was in here with two other Watchers on a ride-along. Word is he's cozy with Keller."

"Why's he with Keller?" Jonah felt the anger on his face. "Isn't he at Chimney Rock?"

"I looked into that. Right after I saw him. Turns out Adam got into some trouble, right after Anastasia was tossed — sorry about that, by the way."

Jonah waved the apology away, and Marquis continued.

"Guess some kids were bullying your boy; he went all Captain Republic on their ass, and one of 'em ended up dead. Keller stepped in, pulled some strings, and now he's a cadet."

Jonah kept his rage from showing. Marquis wished him well, then handed him keys to a mobile waiting outside. They were smaller and slower than cars and only fit two people, one in front of the other, like an enclosed motorcycle, but they were better at navigating the pedestrian-filled streets.

"Don't do anything stupid," Katrina warned him as they parted. "With Adam, I mean."

Jonah ignored her and went to his mobile.

He approached the South Bridge gates. The Dark

Quarter was walled off with only four points of entry and egress. Normally, they'd take the sewers and tunnels in and out of the area, but according to Marquis, someone at City Watch had recently placed thick bars on all of the choke points. There was a small City Watch substation at each gated area, with at least a half-dozen Watchers on duty. Each gate also had a battery of weapons and hunter orbs, making it nearly impossible to breach the walls without help.

Jonah approached the gates and saw two armed Watchers, one manning the pedestrian exit with its long line of people, and the other manning the lane of cars — three waiting to go through.

Jonah hoped Del Toro was working his lane.

As the metal spikes retreated to allow access to the car ahead of Jonah, he got a look at the Watcher. He wasn't sure if it was Del Toro, but the man — not wearing a full-face helmet like many of the Watchers — eyed Jonah's vehicle with recognition.

He pulled up, his heart racing. The mission was finished if he got busted here. He'd never see either of his children again.

The Watcher approached, looked Jonah in the eye, then nodded. The name on the uniform read *Del Toro*.

Del Toro pressed a button on the device in his hand, then a green light on the wall between the lanes indicated that it was now safe to pass.

Jonah drove through the gate, crossed the bridge over the Big River, and saw the warm skyline of the lonely City he'd spent a lifetime serving. Countless orbs dotted the horizon, hovering, scanning, and observing every movement below.

## TWENTY-FIVE

# Adam Lovecraft

ADAM WAS HANGING out with Jeremy Hatch at the arcade.

Hatch was two years older than Adam but never made him feel like he was a stupid kid, maybe because he was also new to the cadets. He talked to Adam more than most of the other cadets — and definitely more than any of the Watchers — so when Hatch asked if he wanted to hit the Arcade, Adam jumped at the chance.

They had been there for more than an hour already. Hatch was having a blast. Adam felt scattered and wasn't having fun. He blamed Michael, not Hatch. Though Adam had worked through Michael's betrayal — of course he would never knowingly put Ana in harm's way — Adam still couldn't *forget.*

"Your turn." Hatch stepped out of the game box and gestured for Adam to enter.

He wasn't in the mood but didn't want to disappoint Hatch or have him think he was a stupid 14-year-old cadet, so Adam smiled, then stepped inside the box and closed the door behind him.

Suddenly, he was no longer a cadet in City 6: Adam

was Captain Republic, taking down virtual bad guys two at a time with a single squeeze of the plastic trigger. He'd already made it past the hydrofoil (his favorite part) and was now blasting through the bank, quickly finding himself surrounded by robbers.

He gripped his gun, sighting one smuggler at a time, then squeezed the trigger and sent each of them down to the marble floor. Gunfire exploded behind him — a smuggler had tagged Adam (Captain Republic) in the shoulder. His helmet sent a jolt of electricity — not much, but enough to nab his attention.

The game was one of Adam's favorites, but even Captain Republic couldn't wipe away the thought of how stupid Michael had finked on Ana.

He was angry, not just at Michael, but also at his own inability to confront him. Saying anything meant telling Michael that Keller had showed him the video. But the chief told him not to let anyone know he was wise to Michael's betrayal.

Easier said than done. He pulled the trigger three times and brought down an approaching trio of robbers with matching head shots. He spun around, looking for more, but everything behind him was dead.

Just like Ana. Adam couldn't help but blame Michael, now that he had someone to blame. He moved into another room and immediately pulled the trigger twice more, ignoring a sharp whistle of pain as another bullet tore into his back. One more hit like that and the game box would be ready for Hatch.

Adam didn't care. He remembered Michael had asked him if he wanted to meet at Nips, but he was afraid to see Michael because once Adam started screaming at him he'd never be able to stop.

A small part of Adam would be happy to see Michael

dead. Like Keller said, an eye for an eye was best sometimes.

He ducked, swiped his thumb on the gun's butt to roll Captain Republic across the sand, then emptied his firearm into the remaining smugglers. The level shifted after a short cutscene that put Captain Republic on train tracks.

Adam opened the box's door. "Your turn."

"You died already?"

"I just don't want to play anymore."

Hatch raised his eyebrows but stepped past Adam into the box and closed the door behind him without a word. When he emerged a few minutes later, Adam said he was done. Hatch offered to play a new game from the beginning, his treat, but Adam still couldn't get in the mood to play, or fake it.

"It's cool," said Hatch with a shrug. "I told Lorena I'd be over soon, anyway. Her parents are both gone from the apartment after six, so I don't have *that* much longer to kill anyway. See you tomorrow?"

"Definitely." Adam appreciated that Hatch wasn't making him feel bad about not wanting to play. "Have fun with Lorena!"

Enthusiasm came easier outside the arcade.

Hatch grinned, looked like he was about to say something to Adam — probably about Lorena — then swallowed whatever it was and said goodbye.

Hatch hung a left at the end of the block, toward Commuters and Lorena's. Adam kept walking straight toward the Academy and his dorm.

Within a half block, his thoughts returned to Michael, enough to make him oblivious to the guy racing behind him until it was too late.

The mystery man slammed into Adam and sent him sailing to the asphalt.

He fell hard and stayed there for many seconds, staring after the running man — a skinny guy with scraggly brown hair, dark-blue pants, and a matching jacket.

His heart pounded as he stood, looking back to see if there was someone in pursuit. Nobody. *Yet.*

Then he looked ahead again, eyes following the fleeing man through the mostly empty street. The man paused at the corner, glancing between a busy marketplace and what appeared to be an abandoned storefront before darting over to the abandoned shop and ripping some boards off the front of a covered door without hesitation — as if he'd done this many times before — then slipped inside.

Adam stared in disbelief, wondering who the man had been fleeing, and what he might have done, when he heard a familiar whirring behind him.

He turned as a hunter orb whizzed overhead, then zipped into the market, followed by another two. Adam watched, open-mouthed, as two City Watch cruisers and one van pulled up to the market and six Watchers ran inside.

The lights inside went black.

Shots were fired, followed by screaming, then more shots.

*What's happening? Are there bad guys in the store too?*

*Who are they shooting?*

He choked on his fear, frozen in place. Until his training kicked in. Then Adam did what he had to without even needing to think.

He raced across the street, passing the Watchers' vehicles on his way to the marketplace. His adrenaline surged as he entered the market and saw dozens of people huddled on the ground — men, women, children — many crying, some soaked in blood. A few of them dead.

A helmeted Watcher approached Adam, black glass mask hiding his face, stick poised to strike him.

"Stop right there!" he said through the helmet's speakers.

Adam raised his hands, shaking his head, desperate not to be seen as one of the bad guys. He didn't want to be stunned, or worse, embarrassed.

"I'm Adam Lovecraft. I'm a cadet: ID number 51166. I think the man you're looking for is there, across the street."

Adam turned and pointed toward the other store, the one that looked abandoned. The Watcher studied him, his helmet likely reading Adam's body for signs of lying. He hoped his fear wouldn't cast him as a perjurer.

"Thanks, kid." The Watcher turned and barked at his team.

Three orbs flew from the market.

Four Watchers followed across the street and into the abandoned shop.

After a few minutes of waiting and listening for signs that they'd caught up with the guy, Adam crossed the street, curious despite his terror.

It seemed like forever before a Watcher finally emerged from the empty store, followed by another Watcher, both empty-handed. The third and fourth Watchers came out next, dragging the man — bruised and bloodied and bound by an electronic leash around his neck.

Adam felt proud enough to wish the Watchers weren't wearing masks, just so he could see their admiring eyes. He had taken care of Tommy and Morgan and Daniel like the chief told him to, and had done a few other things for Keller — like going on the ride-along with Fogerty and

Carson, while constantly keeping his eyes and ears peeled for insidiousness — but this was the first thing that Adam had ever done that *actually* made any difference.

Something *he did* helped City Watch catch a bad guy.

Adam kept staring as the Watchers led the apprehended man to the van, then opened the door and threw him inside. He glared at Adam, eyes full of hate, foaming at the mouth as his new electronic leash sent sparks into his brain.

For a moment, Adam felt terrible. Until he reminded himself:

*It's his fault. He shouldn't have broken the law.*

The closest Watcher slammed the van door. "Aren't you Lovecraft's kid?"

"Yes." Adam nodded, not knowing if being Lovecraft's kid was a good or a bad thing with these guys. He heard Keller in his head telling him that City Watch was a brotherhood, and that his father would always be loved by his brothers, despite his heinous crime.

But that was hard for Adam to believe.

"Great job, kid! Way to keep your eyes open! You'll be a helluva Watcher someday."

"Thanks." Adam smiled, wanting to stretch the conversation and maybe impress the Watcher further. But his work was waiting, so he nodded at Adam and climbed back into his cruiser, face still buried behind his visor.

More Watchers showed up and entered the busy marketplace. Eventually, one of them came out and told Adam to get lost.

He walked back to the Academy full of pride, more excited than ever to be an important part of City Watch.

# TWENTY-SIX

# Jonah Lovecraft

JONAH DIDN'T HAVE to look hard for Dr. Liza's office, though it did require a painful detour through his past to remember the way. He had loved Molly, even through their most tumultuous time — two years after Adam was born, when every exchange led to a new argument. She was his best friend, but still, after many years with City Watch, Jonah eventually found himself playing the *What If?* game like so many of his colleagues.

It was regular for Watchers to cheat on their spouses, and most of them thought nothing of it. Something about the uniforms seemed to drive men and women behind the Walls totally wild. And there was something about the job that pushed Watchers (especially men) into risky behavior — from gambling to drugs to illicit sex. The bosses were fine looking elsewhere, so long as their Watchers didn't get caught.

Jonah wasn't like the other men, or at least hadn't thought so. And yet, he heard enough to know, and to recognize, the symptoms as they started happening to him.

Liza had been a consultant for the Watchers, serving as

one of their medics for a few years before eventually switching her allegiance to the Underground. She and Jonah got along great. She had laughed at the jokes that Molly always seemed too tired to smile at, and was the kind of woman who understood the stresses of Jonah's job in a way his wife couldn't seem to at the time.

She started coming on to him. Not overtly, but enough for Jonah to clearly see her interest. She was beautiful, with long strawberry-blonde hair, a scatter of freckles across the bridge of her nose, and small blue eyes that made up for their size with their deep intoxication.

Jonah had been flattered and excited — until he finally felt the danger to his marriage. He never had acted on a single impulse — and never had planned to — so he figured it was best to keep his mouth shut and deny her flirtations. He had made sure to put distance between them and found excuses to speak with her less, until eventually he never saw Liza around his part of the station.

What Molly hadn't known couldn't hurt her; and Jonah had seen no reason to mention his momentary thoughts of another woman. It might have alleviated his guilt to come clean but would have done nothing for Molly, instead adding a toxin to their love that would have forever cast doubt on his feelings for her.

Now Molly was dead, and Jonah wondered how leaden the guilt might feel at his shoulders. But at least he'd never taken things all the way.

He entered her office in Clinic 17, and found himself in a crowded reception room. The receptionist's name was Charlie, an attractive blonde with bright blue eyes and a smile perfectly suited to warming the ill and miserable.

She saw his uniform, and looked puzzled.

Jonah had always liked Charlie, but she looked at him without recognition. He hoped the code word Liza had always used when helping the Underground was still in use — or at least made sense.

"Yes, may I help you?" Charlie had a clipboard in hand, stacked with forms for Jonah to fill out.

"Yes." He leaned in and disguised his voice. "I'm here to see Dr. Liza about my measles."

She yanked the clipboard back through the window. "What did you say?"

He repeated the phrase, softer rather than louder. "I'm here to see Dr. Liza about my measles."

"Absolutely." Not yes, but *absolutely*. "Please wait a moment."

A half-minute later a nurse opened the door to his right. "Sir?"

Unlike the receptionist, Jonah didn't recognize the nurse, a stout older woman who reminded him of a teacher he'd had as a child. He smiled, stood, and followed the nurse through the door.

Liza entered about five minutes later, trying to seem casual as she studied him, looking even more beautiful than he remembered.

She seemed to know something was off but wasn't sure what. She was probably afraid that he was a City Watch spy trying to bust her with an Underground code word. She held her eyes to her clipboard, trying to mask her nerves.

For some reason — his own nerves, fear, embarrassment, a quiver of arousal — Jonah wanted to laugh. It swelled inside him, then exploded from his mouth.

"Do I know you?" Liza had an edge to her voice when she finally looked up, seeming uncertain, ready to flee or perhaps fight this laughing stranger in her office, using code words he shouldn't be using.

But maybe she would see the truth in his eyes. So Jonah stepped closer and held her stare.

"Oh my God," she gasped, crashing into Jonah's parted arms, hard and unguarded. He pulled her tightly to his body as she whispered, "I'm so happy to see you, but are you crazy, Jonah? *What are you doing here?*"

"I need your help."

"Underground?"

Jonah shook his head. "Something more, Liza. It's big — the Barrens. I've been out there, and you can't believe how many people there are. And some of them are organized." He drew a breath to punctuate what was coming. "They want to hit City 1."

"Oh my …" Liza covered her mouth. "What can I do? What do they need? Medicine? Stims? And why aren't you in City 7?"

"There is no City 7. Never was."

Liza gasped again, louder.

"It's worse than you think. There's so much to tell you. The world is … different."

"Do you *live* in the Barrens?"

"Like I said, there are a lot of people, small pockets spread out well beyond West Village. And there are tons of wanderers. Lots of Bands — thieves, murderers, and rapists stalking together, taking what they can." Jonah needed a moment. "The State burned West Village to the ground … I don't think there were any survivors."

"That's where Duncan was headed the last I saw him. Now I'm worried. He left the City to find Liam and Ana and take them to West Village. He never returned, and a month later I got word it was torched. Have you seen him?"

"No, but supposedly I'll be seeing Ana soon. No word on Liam. Maybe they're together, or at least maybe she'll know where Duncan is. You can ask her yourself — she's riding with an escort to the same place I need you to go."

"Need *me* to go?" Liza paled, her bright eyes now dull and mouth drooping open. "This is bad … There's something you don't know about Duncan."

"What don't I know?" Hairs prickled his neck. Shoulder blades tensed. Every muscle was suddenly twitching.

"Duncan is infected."

"*Infected*? You mean he's a zombie?"

"He's not fully turned like the others out there, but yes, he carries the virus. I found something that keeps the virus from running rampant in his cells. It's not yet a cure, but it keeps him from turning. He needs a weekly dose, and I'm guessing he must've run out by now, even if he were cutting his dosage in half, or even in quarters. I gave him an ingredients list and directions to replicate the serum, assuming he could find another trustworthy doctor. I'm hoping that's what happened."

"Why the hell didn't anyone tell me?"

"I couldn't. Duncan didn't want anyone to know that he was infected. He said it would've changed everything, impeded his ability to effectively manage his role in the Underground, or even his congregation. Besides, I'm a doctor, not a scientist. This sort of work is illegal. The State wouldn't just put a stop to my research and experiments if they knew what I was doing, they'd probably put me in the Games."

"You'd think the State would be happy that someone was making progress."

She snorted. "I used to think that when I started. But from all I've seen, and heard from others, it's almost as if they *don't want* a cure."

Jonah couldn't be sure, but what she said — after all

he'd witnessed in the last year — *felt* right. A scary thought, but so was his next one.

"So you think Duncan's a zombie?"

"If he hasn't found help, then yes. His is the first case I've seen, living a full, productive life with the virus inside him, but if he's been out of the serum for a while, and hasn't found someone to make it, the odds of him still being the Duncan we know are slim."

Jonah held her gently at the wrist. "I know I can't make you come. But I need you to come with me to the Barrens. I'll take you someplace safe where you can finish your work, a place where they actually *want to* find a cure. Consider the possibilities of not having to look over your shoulder while working in your lab."

"*That* sounds great. But what expertise could I possibly have in taking down a city?"

"I'm guessing they know something about your experiments."

"Nobody knows about my experiments."

"Maybe not the State, but I'm sure there are others who have helped you, others you trust. Like Duncan."

"That circle is *small*."

"Sutherland has people in the Underground. He's the closest thing to a leader outside the Walls."

Jonah considered telling her that he was in fact Weaver, the cult leader whose name she would recognize. But there would be time enough to explain after they left City 6 without confusing the issue now.

"I'm looking for a *cure*, not something to use against City 1."

"Maybe he thinks you know something that can help him and give his people an advantage."

"How am I supposed to just pack up and go if I don't know what I'm agreeing to? If I leave now, there's no way I can come back. You want me to follow you, and *you* don't even know specifics? You're asking me to risk everything. That doesn't sound like you, Jonah."

"You're right. I wish I had more to tell you. But I understand why Sutherland might not want to overly inform someone heading behind enemy lines. I could have been captured or tortured or drugged."

He shook his head and continued. "If this is too much to ask of you, I get it. And I'm sorry. But I'm hoping you'll come with me to at least see what they want."

She met his eyes, considering the impossible but still needing a push. "There's no one to help these people here if I leave."

"They'll assign another doctor."

"In a month, maybe. The other clinics won't take transfers. People could die, Jonah."

"People could die if you stay. I know that's harsh, but aren't some things worth the risk? How risky was it for me to enter the City? I'm dead if I get spotted, but I came here instead of doing nothing while waiting for Ana. I returned for two reasons: Sutherland, and *you*."

Something in her eyes relaxed. She got harder and softer at once, straightening her posture as her voice suddenly warmed. "I need the rest of the day to close shop, and I'll have to ask someone to take care of the lab animals. How long do you think we'll be gone, assuming I can get back into the City without being missed?"

"I don't know, but be prepared to never return. Do you have family or anyone you'd be hurting if you leave without notice?"

She shook her head.

"How long do you need?" he asked.

"Meet me here tonight, after the clinic shifts to Dr. Berkley's care. I'm not here tomorrow anyway, so that will give us a day and a half before anyone starts asking questions."

Jonah smiled and threw his arms around Liza. "I'm happy."

Liza smiled back. "Stay invisible, Jonah. I can't take losing you again."

He looked down, unable to meet her eyes as he wondered how she could feel so strongly about him after what he'd been accused of doing to his wife.

He finally looked back up to see not only compassion in her eyes, but also understanding. Some part of him wanted to confess everything, get everything out in the open. He really did the things she couldn't believe that he had done, it really was his own bloody hands and not mind control at all.

But there wasn't time for that now. So instead he said, "See you tonight."

Then he left Liza's office and went to find Adam.

# TWENTY-SEVEN

# Adam Lovecraft

ADAM HAD NEVER BEEN to Keller's apartment before. Even though they had been spending time together — the chief had spent hours walking him to and from class, speaking to him on his personal com, and sending mail for Adam to check in with him once finished with his Academy day — he was still surprised to see the dinner invitation.

Work was work, but home was home.

Keller lived in the high apartments, and his place was even bigger than Arnold Denny's. The ceilings were high, the walls wide and white, sparse but for a few pictures of his son. His wife, Jacqueline, barely said a word, though she did smile a lot and made Adam feel like she was happy that they were sharing a meal.

Before coming over, the chief had asked Adam what he wanted for dinner and said that he could pick anything — rations didn't matter. Adam told him that he had once tried something called lasagna, and he thought it was the best thing he'd ever eaten. Adam asked if he could have that and Keller said, "Of course."

The scent was the first thing to hit Adam's nostrils

when Ms. Jacqueline opened the door. Adam had already finished thirds — Keller must not have been kidding, rations really didn't matter in the high apartments — and Ms. Jacqueline had already left the table when Adam finally gathered the courage to ask about his unexpected invitation.

"Why did I invite you to my place?" Keller repeated his query. "Because *you deserve it*, son!"

"Why?" Adam asked, insistent as he thought of the many things he'd started but not yet finished. He still didn't know how to best help Keller after his ride-along, and the chief had changed the subject every time Adam raised it.

Keller laughed. "You are so modest … and yet, it isn't even modesty. That's just *one* of the things that makes you so special, Adam. You are well beyond your peers in every way that matters. You might not score the highest on aptitude or be the fastest on field, but you are always strong where it matters most. Living your life with honor and dignity, clinging to a better future despite the odds, and knowing that it's always best to be alone if the choice is inferior company. *You* are a remarkable cadet, Adam, and even if I'd not been hearing stories about you since before you could walk, I'd still be impressed with the cadet you are and the Watcher you'll most certainly be."

Keller always talked about things in general terms, instead of saying exactly what he meant. Adam wanted to know what he was doing right and what he was doing wrong, because only then could he really do better.

"I can see you're looking for something more." Keller smiled, reading Adam's mind as usual. "Why don't we start with yesterday: your walk home from the Arcade, where you helped *six* on-duty officers apprehend a terrorist. Six officers and three hovers. Nine assets on the street and not one of them was able to locate the perp. But *you* did, Adam. Excellent job."

"But I didn't *do* anything. The man ran by me, then I saw the Watchers searching in the wrong place, so I just told them where to look. He was right across the street."

Keller slapped his hand on the table with another laugh. "Most cadets act like they know everything, but it's your quiet confidence and humility that makes you ideal Watcher material."

A shiver of pride fluttered down his spine and filled him with confidence for his follow-up question. "Who was he ... the terrorist, I mean?"

"Underground scum," Keller spat, like spoiled milk from his mouth. "The one you helped find had somehow managed to escape custody. He must have had inside help. And *that's* the cancer I'm talking about. Grabbing this man was a big victory for City Watch, Adam. And we have *you* to thank for it."

"What did he do?"

"It's not what he did; it's what he *could have* done, and what he was surely planning. An Underground killer's ill intent could be focused on anything: destroying City infrastructure, murdering random citizens to stir unrest inside the Walls, blowing up a school filled with innocent children. The Underground is infested with weeds strangling all the good we're doing here. But thanks to you, we've yanked another weed by the root. If all goes well, this man will lead us to other rotten spots in our garden. But once found, we will crush their resistance and keep our City safe. One down and many protected. So when I say *thank you* on behalf of City Watch and the State, shed your humility long enough to take your bow."

"You're welcome." Adam wanted to ask if the dead

people in the store were terrorists too, but Keller changed the subject.

"Tell me about your ride-along."

Adam had been waiting for him to ask, but now sitting across from Keller in his apartment, Adam was having a hard time deciding which words to use.

Telling Keller what happened wasn't quite right. He could see where Fogerty and Carson were coming from. They seemed like good Watchers, trying to do their jobs. He didn't want to get them in trouble.

"Just tell me what's on your mind," Keller prompted him.

"Everything was fine at first," Adam started, nervously scratching his left palm. "We went into the Dark Quarter, which was scary like I always imagined, but even dirtier. There were a lot of people doing bad things in the streets like everyone always says, mostly selling stuff, including women."

He turned away from Keller, embarrassed. "We parked and walked for a block, then went into this market where Fogerty and Carson met this guy who looked like a giant. The guy gave Carson and Fogerty a tip about someone named Little Mitch and told them about a dead woman, then we went to this place called the Orient Hotel to question Little Mitch. We were in there for a while, and I had to sit in the corner while they questioned him, but Little Mitch didn't want to talk … and he wouldn't, no matter what."

Adam stopped for a second, considering his words, still not wanting to get either Watcher in trouble. But Adam also didn't want to disappoint the chief, who was looking to him for the best possible information, counting on Adam to see what he couldn't — things people did when the boss wasn't looking.

Keller sat across from Adam, patiently smiling like always. Adam drew a breath. "They finally got Little Mitch to talk … but only after they started hitting him."

"Which Watcher did the striking, Adam? Was it Carson or Fogerty?"

"Carson."

"Very well." Keller smiled. "Is that it?"

Adam nodded. "Was that bad? Did the Watchers do the wrong thing?"

"What do you think?" Keller leaned back in his chair.

"I don't know." Adam shrugged. "I guess it's good if they got what they needed to stop other bad stuff from happening. And that the man who killed the woman got justice." He thought for a second, less certain over his next words, but thinking they seemed like something the chief would want to hear. "It probably matters less in the Quarter, doing that to someone there, I mean, than it would out here, right?"

"Yes." Keller nodded. "That is correct. But it isn't just about the Dark Quarter, Adam. It's about safety for us all. Realize: most things aren't black and white, especially now, when our survival depends on us thriving here behind the Walls. I'm going to tell you something, and I want you to listen carefully, Adam: *Violence is sometimes justified*. Take the Underground scum you helped to apprehend. Do you think we should leave that man to rot in his cell, or question him to learn what he knows and who he's working with, digging deep to prevent the atrocities that he and his cohorts have planned?"

"We should prevent the atrocities," Adam said.

"We stop the monsters by finding their den and burning the nest. If we don't protect our citizens, then nobody will. You will face this sort of situation constantly as a Watcher. Say you know a man who regularly beats his wife is about to go too far. He's spiraling out of control and is eventually going to kill her. If we wait for him to commit the crime, we're too late and the poor woman is dead. Isn't it the right thing to prevent that murder ahead of time?"

*Of course it is.* Adam nodded.

"What if there were a simple sign to follow? Would you stop something awful before it happened, or would you wait until it was too late?"

Adam felt guilty, suddenly sick as he stitched two and two together, realizing he was at least partly responsible for what had happened to his mother. He should've seen the signs that his father would kill her.

He tried not to cry. "I would have done something, but I didn't know! I *couldn't* have known. I wasn't a cadet — I didn't know how to see the signs yet!"

Keller leaned forward, his face relaxed and friendly as he set his hand atop Adam's. "Don't feel bad, son, or blame yourself. Your father's signs weren't obvious. None of us saw them, not even me. You can't blame yourself or feel guilty. But now that you *are* able to see it, don't you think that you *ought* to do something?"

"Yes." Adam nodded.

"So, don't you think that Carson and Fogerty were doing what they were *supposed* to be doing? What was best for the City?"

It did seem that way ... but Adam didn't like all the gray that changed so many things between right and wrong. Like when Keller told him to stick up for himself with Tommy and Morgan and Daniel, then gave him a weapon to teach them a lesson.

"How do I know when doing bad things is right?"

"That's one of the things that's great about you, Adam. The fact that you would even ask. I can't pretend that City Watch is pure — we have our share of thugs who should probably be in the Games. But that's *not* what we stand for. The fact that you're asking all the right questions further proves that I've been right about you all along. You have a strong moral core and believe in the greater good, even if it means you must sometimes soil your fingertips to execute an unfortunate but necessary decision."

His voice fell to a whisper. "Sometimes being good requires you to be around bad people. And maybe even be a little bad yourself sometimes. Wouldn't you agree?"

Adam nodded.

"Good." Keller leaned back in his chair. "Because I'd like to discuss your friend, Michael."

# TWENTY-EIGHT

# Anastasia Lovecraft

Ana's pain had mostly subsided, but it was still a dull and throbbing echo. She wondered if that was a good sign, that maybe the infection had seeped into her body enough to become a part of it, rather than a disruption. That meant she was hours from turning, or her body was finally fighting the virus.

Ana didn't want to turn but loathed the thought of losing control and becoming a liability. She mostly feared turning in her sleep and endangering Liam. She wanted to beg him to kill her but knew he would endlessly argue with her.

Even with the pain mostly faded, her thoughts were still muddy. Nothing made sense like it should. Good thoughts clashed with bad, and she had trouble stringing one event into the next. They left Paradise, found camp — the flight from Paradise to the tree was a blur — and woke in the morning to a Band below them. Liam towed her to the Outback and kept them alive long enough for Balon to send a miracle, but her memories were wavy and barely seemed real. Some of them might even be a dream.

She couldn't stop thinking about Adam, or worrying about what might be happening to him at Chimney Rock. It was hard for her brother to connect with people. Kids like him didn't belong in a place like the Rock. Without her protection, he must be at the mercy of miserable bullies wanting to ease their own pain by smearing some of it onto others.

She fought her tears so Liam wouldn't ask what was wrong. Her few mentions of Adam so far had ripped her apart. So she kept moving forward, trying to sort out the past.

Her life had irrevocably changed in a year. She missed her parents and brother, but more than anything, she missed the life they shared. She missed her friends and Michael, she missed her father's stories and Adam's compassion, she missed the miracles her mother made with their rations.

Finally, after hours of walking mostly in silence, Ana said out loud what she'd been thinking since the Outback. "I think you should kill me tonight."

Liam laughed. "Maybe someday, sweetheart. When you're foaming at the mouth and chomping for my face. Right now I like you better breathing."

"I'm serious, Liam." Ana couldn't stop thinking about Duncan turning, so sudden and unexpected. Duncan had loved her like a daughter in their short time together. If he didn't hesitate when biting her, that meant she probably wouldn't be able to stop herself from biting Liam.

"I'm not discussing this, Ana."

"Making it to Hydrangea would be easier without me. Once there, you can tell my dad everything. I'm sure you can help Sutherland with whatever he wants. Probably better than I can."

"No, Ana. The infection might subside if you're resting

somewhere. Duncan must've been infected for a while. You don't know how long you have, and we don't need to do anything rash before we know what will happen. You're fine right now, and I'll keep my eyes out. That has to be enough."

"Okay," she said, not particularly *wanting* to die, grateful for Liam giving her reason to believe she shouldn't … for a little longer, anyway. Maybe there really was a glimmer of hope. "I just need you to keep talking. Otherwise my mind circles the worst."

"Sorry. I thought you wanted to be alone with your thoughts."

"Alone with my thoughts is the *last* place I want to be. It's torture; I'm feeling too much in all the wrong ways — my insides and outsides aren't matching. Does that make sense?"

"No, not at all, but it doesn't need to. You've been bitten, you're sick. You were almost raped or killed. You want something to move your mind away from the pain. That's what I'm here for." His face brightened with an idea. "Let's play *I Wish.*"

"What's *I Wish?*" Ana asked.

"You've never played *I Wish?*"

"Nope." She shook her head. "Not even once. What is it?"

"A game we used to play at Chimney Rock."

"Who's *we?*"

"Everyone. You're the first person, maybe in history, to ever ask what it is." Liam laughed at her like he always did when she felt clueless.

Ana punched him in the arm, softly, like she did when feeling exposed by his laughter. "Well, sorry for having an okay life before all the murder and the Darwins."

He laughed. "All you do is make a wish: if you could

change one thing, what would that one thing be? Then you think about that wish for the rest of the day, pretending it was true."

"That sounds great, Liam. I would very much like to engage in some wishing this fine afternoon." Ana spoke like she was fancy, living in the high apartments.

"What's your wish? It can be for whatever you want."

"Oh, *I* don't want to go first," Ana said. "Let's start with your wish."

"Ladies first."

"Nope." She shook her head. "I'm the one who was bitten by our friend the zombie preacher; that means I decide. Okay, done. You're going first."

Liam laughed louder. "Okay, fair ... let me think." Then after a moment, he said, "I wish that West Village hadn't been burned."

"You're not going to wish that your father didn't kill himself, or that you got to live with your Uncle M after your father died, or that you'd never been thrown into the Games?"

"Sure. I wish all that stuff. But when you play *I Wish* you have to pick one wish and focus on only that wish. All the smaller ones revolve around it. There's no limit to how many times you can play *I Wish*, or what you can wish when playing. The point is to pick a spot in time, then think how your world would change on the back of that wish."

"So how would things have changed if West Village was never burned?"

"Well, we still would have had the Games, but they brought us closer, which I'm happy about. And the Games led you and Duncan to the truth about me, which I would've been too scared to ever admit on my own. Once you were safe, the only other thing I wanted was to stay outside the Walls. Maybe Chelle and I could've been happy in West Village. Maybe your dad would have found us. Maybe Duncan wouldn't have turned. Maybe we could have all had our own little *Happily Ever Afters*."

"I wish I'd given my dad the benefit of the doubt ... that I'd had it inside me to believe him."

"That's not your fault, Ana." He stopped walking, turning to look at her. "You witnessed something awful, and your mind had no other way to process what you saw. That has nothing to do with the relationship you have with your father — wrong, right, or indifferent. You can't beat yourself up about it."

"I'm not beating myself up, Liam. I'm making a wish, like you told me to. You never said there were *rules*. You said I could wish whatever I wanted."

"You can. I'm sorry. I'm not trying to tell you what to wish; I just don't want you to flog yourself any more than you already—"

"Fine. I wish for a cure."

He sighed. "That's a good wish."

"Do you think there will ever be one? A cure? It's too late for me, I mean in the world. Do you think scientists are still working on it?"

"I think they'll always be working on a cure, but I don't know enough about science or medicine to guess that we'll ever get one. Every so-called breakthrough so far has led to nothing. The Reels report each one like it's *the one*, but it never is. Still, a cure must be possible since some people aren't even infected."

"What do you mean?"

"Infection isn't guaranteed." Liam looked at Ana, apparently surprised by her ignorance. "Did you hear about the research assistant who killed himself around five years ago?"

Ana shook her head. "No."

"He was part of a State team researching a cure. The labs have the highest levels of security because they have to make sure the virus never leaves. But the research assistant was suicidal and wanted to put it in his body. He tried, but the virus didn't take. The State discovered what he had done and wanted to run experiments, see what was different about his blood or DNA from everyone else. But he outsmarted the State and killed himself while they waited."

"Do you think Duncan might have been temporarily cured? I can't imagine how else he stayed alive for so long. Unless maybe there are different strains like you said, and some of those strains take longer."

"Anything's possible, I guess." Liam stopped. "You sure you're not hungry?" It was his fifth time asking in the past two hours or so.

"I'm fine, I promise. Can we please keep going?"

Liam agreed like he had four times before, even though Ana could tell he didn't want to. They walked through another hour of *I Wish*, then a few other similar games, and finally made camp just inside a cave that seemed reasonably isolated from any passing bandits or zombies.

Ana was exhausted and couldn't have walked another foot, even if she'd wanted to. Liam made her comfortable, gathered wood for a fire, secured the area, and then went out to catch, skin, and cook a hare.

After dinner, Ana lay on her side and asked Liam to tell her a story. "Just, please, no more stories about Uncle M and his steaks."

Liam laughed, and she liked the music. As he started talking about the first time he realized how beautiful the Barrens actually were — after getting over their danger — Ana began to drift, trying not to think about how she might not wake up as a human, working to convince herself that she'd live long enough to see her father.

Ana must have fallen asleep. She could feel Liam lying beside her when she woke, but his story was over. Only the crackling fire interrupted the silence as the warmth of its flames licked her skin.

Despite everything, in that moment she felt safe and cozy.

And even warmer when Liam's lips brushed her cheek.

"Goodnight, Ana," he said.

# TWENTY-NINE

# Adam Lovecraft

ADAM WAS BACK with Michael at Nips.

The fried greens were still disgusting, and Adam was still angry with his "friend." But he'd promised Keller to meet with him so he could see if there was "something worth seeing."

But it was hard to pretend. Hard to keep Michael's betrayal a secret. Especially since he acted like he hadn't been the one to destroy what little life Adam had left after his mom died and his dad was sent to the Games.

"You should've seen it," Michael said. "It was *exactly* what I'm talking about, the sort of stuff that worries me. Amos is a good guy and wasn't doing anything wrong. The Watchers nabbed him anyway. Who knows where he is, or how long it will be until he's thrown into the Darwins."

"They had to have *some* reason, right?"

"No, Adam. That's what I'm saying, that's what's wrong. It's a book club; it meets every other week. City Watch says the meetings are congregations even though they're not, the number's small and they're not public —

like dinner with friends. But that still didn't stop City Watch."

"So what happened?"

"They were outside the book club, calling for Amos to come out, announcing to the floor that everything was fine, everyone was safe, telling them all to stay aware, know their neighbors, report what they see. Then they went in and turned the place inside out, but Amos wasn't there because he'd already bolted."

Adam got a sudden horrible and uneasy feeling. Could Amos be the guy he saw running? Then ratted out? "Why did he run if he didn't do anything wrong?"

"You'd learn to run too, if you were always being questioned by Watchers instead of eating with them."

*Ignoring questions meant there was something to hide.* Adam's classes had taught him that. He ignored Michael's insult. "How did he know the Watchers were coming?"

"He didn't. Amos was going to meet our friend Omar at the Arcade when he spotted a Watcher following him. He didn't want to be seen with Omar, on the chance that Omar had gotten into trouble like he was prone to doing, so Amos bolted. That's last anyone knows. I saw on the Reels that an unnamed suspect was apprehended after running inside an abandoned storefront. That happened a block from the Arcade, right around when Omar said Amos took off running."

Adam wanted to puke but shoved more of the crappy fried greens into his mouth instead. He couldn't tell Michael he had seen Amos running from City Watch, that he led the arresting Watchers to his hiding spot, or that it had felt amazing in the moment.

As guilt swelled inside him, Adam reminded himself that Michael was a liar, and he couldn't allow those lies to undermine his job as a cadet.

Michael kept talking, but now Adam watched his eyes, trying to see if he could sift fact from fiction as the words flowed from his mouth. He tried to consider both the Michael he knew — the one who was his friend, and had nursed a crush on Ana forever — with the secret Michael he barely knew.

He finished chewing and looked up at Adam. "Sorry. I know I shouldn't be going on about all of this, and I know City Watch is a sore subject between us. I'm sorry about that, really. I'm not sure what to do, other than to keep talking until we get more comfortable with one another. This is hard, what we're doing, keeping on because of a memory." Then Michael said something Adam couldn't believe. "Loyalty is important."

He wanted to climb across the table and punch Michael in the face. Adam pictured himself doing to Michael what Carson had done to the pimp.

"I'm sorry for offending you the other day," Michael was saying. "I know I did, and that wasn't right. I'm proud of you, Adam. For everything you've done since losing your family. It's not easy, but you've kept your head above water and stayed out of trouble. More than that, you've actually grown into quite the young man. Like you've said over and over, you could have ended up in the Dark Quarter and didn't. I'm proud of you, and Ana would've been too."

When Keller praised him, it was all he could ever want. But with Michael saying similar things, Adam only felt madder and madder. He didn't have any right to talk about her, or talk *for* her after what he had done. Michael couldn't say that Ana would've been proud of Adam, because Michael was the one responsible for making sure she could never be proud of anything, ever again.

Adam remembered what Keller had said, about how

sometimes you had to be around bad people if you wanted to do something good. The key wasn't to be bad, he told Adam, because bad people never saw themselves as bad — at least not the kind of bad City Watch was most concerned with catching. The key was to be the version of good (warped as it was) that the bad guys saw in themselves.

"It's okay," Adam lied. "I didn't understand at first, but now I do. A lot of what you're saying about City Watch and the State makes sense. I've even started to wonder about some of the things you told me about Jack Geralt."

"Really?" Michael raised his eyebrows. A smile teased his mouth.

"Yeah." Adam nodded. "Things have been weird lately. It's hard to look at City Watch the same way."

Adam fell silent, a tactic he'd learned in the Academy as a way to get guilty people to talk with confidence.

*Shame doesn't like silence.*

Michael spoke. "It's okay if you don't want to tell me, but I'd love to hear. Maybe there's a way I can help, even if that only means listening."

"I went on a ride-along with two Watchers—"

"A ride-along? What's that?"

"It's when you go on a Watcher shift, in their car. You don't get to *do* anything, you're still a cadet, but you see everything. I rode in their van when we went to the Dark Quarter."

"The Dark Quarter?" Michael seemed both bothered and surprised. "That doesn't seem like a smart place to take a boy."

*What happened to 'quite the young man'?*

"I'm a *cadet,* Michael. And almost fifteen. I won't be a *boy* forever. If I'm City Watch, I'll probably be in the Quarter all the time. At first, anyway."

"*If* you're City Watch?" Michael repeated.

Adam said *if* on purpose and was happy Michael had noticed.

He shrugged. "Yes, *if.* I'm not sure if I want to be a Watcher after what I saw in the Quarter."

"And what was that?" Michael seemed more interested in what Adam was about to say than in anything to come from his mouth since he once told Michael, *I think my sister likes you.*

"We went into the Quarter, which is just as scary as it's always been in my dreams. It's really dark, even in the daytime. There are bad people doing illegal stuff everywhere. We met this guy who gave the two Watchers I was with — an old guy who is really mean and a young guy who is nice, even though he has a temper — a tip about another bad guy, then we went to go meet that bad guy and, well," Adam swallowed, "when that guy wouldn't confess to what the Watchers knew he'd done, they beat him. And kept on beating him. It was awful, Michael. They pounded and pounded until the bad guy — he was a pimp — was bleeding and crying and willing to say whatever the Watchers wanted."

Adam was surprised that he felt so genuinely upset. More so than when he'd watched it happen. It was different telling Michael the story than it had been saying the same things to Keller. The stuff that irked Adam about the story bothered him more with Michael; the things that had made it seem *acceptable* were somehow less so at Nips.

"You can't tell anyone, Michael, okay? Do you promise?"

Adam wanted Michael to keep his secret and make a promise that he would — partly out of fear that Michael might actually say something to someone that could get Fogerty or Carson in trouble, or even worse, him. The last thing Adam wanted was for Keller to be upset with him or think *he* was an insidious cancer. And Adam had another reason for wanting Michael to stay quiet. He wanted it to seem like he was betraying the Watchers, or at least that he was willing to do so.

"So, how did that make you feel?" Michael asked, exactly like Adam expected.

"Awful, and it made me wonder about a lot of stuff."

"What do you mean?"

"I just mean that things seem different; I don't really know what to think about City Watch. Stuff I saw in the Quarter … it's the opposite of what I always thought about Watchers. They were scary, like actual bad guys. My dad was always like a hero. His job as a Watcher, that was the kind of thing you idolize. But now … I don't know. To see another side of it all—"

"So what does that mean? Are you having second thoughts about cadets? About being a Watcher?"

"I'm not sure." Adam shrugged. "But I'm starting to wonder if I made a mistake in joining. I know it's better than Chimney Rock, and whatever god-awful job I'd get after my aptitude tests, so maybe that makes it the best place, for now at least. But I'm not sure it's the best after I'm a grownup, you know?"

Michael nodded. *Of course he did.*

"I just wanted somewhere to belong," Adam continued, warming to the subject. "I figured I'd follow in Dad's footsteps. But the more I think about it, the more I wonder *why* I would want to. He murdered my mom and broke up our family. *He's* the one who got Ana killed." He shook his head. "I just don't know." Adam started to cry, surprising himself with genuine tears.

"Do you *really* think your dad killed your mom?"

"Yeah." Adam nodded, surprised that Michael would

ask something so stupid. "That's what I keep coming back to: if you have to do bad stuff as part of your job, and you have to do those things over and over, maybe it changes you after a while. Makes you crazy murderer bad."

"That's what I used to think ..." Michael's voice had softened; his compassion seemed real. Something in his whisper seemed to Adam less like him hating City Watch and more like he wanted to help Adam feel better. He leaned forward and lowered his voice so much that Adam strained to hear him. "Now I'm not so sure ... maybe he was set up, just like your sister."

That made Adam so angry that he balled both fists beneath the table. *Not yet.* "Why do you think my father is innocent?"

Michael glanced around every corner of Nips, swept fried greens from the table's center and hissed, "Can you keep a secret?"

"Of course." He leaned forward, his heart pounding, certain that his old friend was now just seconds from confirming Adam's growing suspicion that he was part of the Underground.

# THIRTY

# Jonah Lovecraft

JONAH LEFT CLINIC 17 FEELING … uncertain.

Liza was amazing, and seeing her was electric. It was barely physical, but still, looking into her eyes gave Jonah part of his soul back. Sutherland had filled him with an odd sort of hope, but Liza reminded him of who he was, back when Jonah was willing to stare into his hunger.

He had no idea how he would engage Adam, or if he would even be able to find him, but he had hours until Liza was free, and figured he would know the right plan when he found it. Jonah was about to head off on foot instead of his mobile, which might stand out more near the Academy, when he spotted Ballard — or Balrog as Watchers preferred to call him — on foot patrol.

Like everyone, Jonah hated Balrog because he was a miserable pile of shit, not to mention a marginal Watcher. A run-in with Balrog was certain to end poorly, so Jonah kept walking straight instead of turning, figuring he'd keep going for a mile, then double back and grab the mobile after all.

Despite his anxiety, Jonah smiled while passing a

fortune-teller working the street, amused as always that people were willing to surrender valuable credits so a woman in rags could tell them obvious nothings. No fortune-teller could have ever predicted the things that had happened to Jonah.

Another two blocks and he heard the whirring behind him. He couldn't afford to freeze; the orb would know because they were programmed for such behavior. If his gait made a hiccup, he would be scanned. The only thing that had kept it from happening so far was his intimate understanding of what data orbs gathered before alerting the nearest Watcher.

But he must have had a twitch in his movement, something that held the orb at his back for a full block before it hovered in a wide circle around him.

"Citizen, please extend your wrist."

Jonah held his wrist up like he wasn't terrified.

The orb scanned the skin, then turned silent. After four painful seconds it said, "Thank you," then drifted away.

Jonah kept walking. He wanted to hurry but was forced into strolling. He had no idea where the orb was. It could be behind him, high up in a place he couldn't see without looking. And even the slightest glance would surely broadcast his guilt.

He couldn't be sure, but Jonah would bet his disguise that Balrog had kept walking when he did and was now a block behind him. Jonah saw the man cut across the street and enter Bakery 4 from the corner of his eye.

Jonah waited in line for five minutes, subtracted two credits from his wrist for a baguette (Marquis had loaded it with a hundred), and stepped back into the street.

Sure enough, he saw Balrog one block up, but the big man's eyes weren't on the bakery, or anywhere near Jonah.

He looked both ways and crossed. Balrog's face was still turned away from him, and Jonah no longer felt the orb.

He set the baguette on the ground, then ran toward the alley and ducked into the dark. And there, Jonah felt the Watcher behind him.

"Don't move. Hands on your head."

# THIRTY-ONE

# Adam Lovecraft

THE ARCADE'S NOISES — people laughing, yelling, and talking, all crashing against the bleeps and bloops from music, games, and aimless entertainment braying in the background — waged war with Adam's attention as he hung on Michael's every word.

Adam said that he could keep a secret and now was leaning across the table — heart pounding — dying to know what Michael was about to say, already picturing himself back in Keller's office, ready to report whatever this was.

His lips parted, but then Michael closed his mouth and leaned back against the table instead. "I think we should go somewhere private first."

"Where?" Adam looked around Nips. Everyone appeared to be talking or playing. It seemed safer to talk among the crowd, where no one was paying attention, than out in the open where an orb could sneak up above them at any time. As Adam learned in the Academy, orbs didn't even need to be that close to see, hear, and record you.

"Anywhere but the arcade. Come on, let's go."

They left Nips. Outside, Michael walked the main boulevard, avoiding wall screens broadcasting the latest Games — Brian Handler was the momentary favorite for City 6, arrested for beating a man to death after he accosted his wife. Brian was in the game's final stretch, on his way to the Mesa for a toe-to-toe with a City 4 serial killer, Bridgette Phillips — the "Black Widow," they called her — from their own version of the Dark Quarter.

Adam followed, scouting the sky for orbs but not yet seeing any. After about a block, Michael started talking. "I used to be just like you. Did you know that?"

No, he didn't — and wasn't sure what Michael meant. Grownups had been saying they were once "just like him" forever — it was a way of getting him to lower his guard and trust them. Adam understood this, always had, but didn't like it when people said things that weren't true just to make him think better of them. He didn't mind when Chief Keller said he was a little like Adam, because Adam could see that. Plus, he really just meant that maybe Adam was a little like his son, who Keller would never ever see again, so even if it wasn't true, at least it was easy to understand. And that made it okay.

But Michael hated the State, so Adam didn't think they were similar at all.

"How do you mean?" Adam asked as they turned off the boulevard into a back alley snaking between the back of two rows of ten-story apartments. Adam was thankful that the backs of the buildings were all brick without any windows through which people might spy on them.

"I used to be faithful to the State and believed in City Watch. I was loyal to the system, like you. I believed in it, Adam. Then something happened ... and everything changed."

*You mean sending my sister to the Games?* "What changed it?"

Despite the fact that they had left the Arcade because Michael had something to say, he now seemed like he was still trying to decide whether he was going to. He wore the same look Adam imagined on himself just before getting into trouble, when he had to tell the truth about something wrong or embarrassing. He was showing some of the same signs City Watch had been teaching Adam to look for: the back and sides of his neck were blushed like his ears, his breath accelerated, hairs rose along the length of his arms as he glanced nervously around him.

"What is it, Michael?"

Michael stopped walking, then blurted, "It was me — I'm the one who told City Watch about Ana and Liam. I got them in trouble. I'm the reason your sister was sent to the Games."

Adam wanted to punch Michael, then kill him, then beat on his dead body. But at least he wasn't lying — at least Michael had finally told him the truth.

So Adam said nothing, waiting for his former friend to fill in the blanks.

Michael spoke fast, as if hurrying to expel his remaining confessions. "I'm so sorry, Adam. I was never trying to do anything bad. I wanted to do the right thing; I wanted to help Ana, not hurt her. I went to Keller and told him what I knew but never expected that would get her into trouble," his voice cracked, "at least not like it did."

"How could you do that?" Adam's rage was a controlled boil. He wondered what he would be feeling if Michael's confession wasn't old news.

"I wasn't trying to do anything other than be a good friend. I wanted to *protect* her. Liam was bad news and I didn't want her falling in with his group. But I had no idea that she'd get in so much trouble. The State started lying about her, saying she was up to things I knew she wasn't. Trusting Keller was the biggest mistake of my life. I wanted to fix things but didn't know what to do. So I started asking around, then met a group of guys who knew Liam. We all got to trusting one another after not too long, and this time the trust wasn't misplaced. Eventually, they asked me to join them."

Keller was right about Michael, like the chief had been right about everything else. Adam hadn't wanted to think his sister could be part of the Underground, but Keller explained how she had been tricked by Liam. *Used*, he said. And while her heart surely held no malice, she had to be held accountable. That Michael didn't see this made anything he said about Keller, City Watch, or the State, ignorant at best.

"Are you in the Underground now?" Adam wasn't shocked by the information itself. After all, Keller told him what to expect — that was why he agreed to meet Michael at Nips in the first place. But he was surprised at the speed in which he had discovered the truth, just three blocks from the Arcade.

"Yes," Michael said, meeting his eyes.

Adam had thought that he wanted Michael's confession. But now the reality of the situation was sinking in. Now he was obligated to tell Keller. As much as Adam hated Michael for what he'd done, a small part of him still didn't want to see his friend rounded up and thrown in jail, or probably the Games.

"Why would you tell me that? You know I'm a cadet, Michael! You can't expect me to keep your secret!"

"I believe you'll keep my secret because you promised that you would a few minutes ago. And I believe that even though you work for City Watch, you still have principles.

You're not a cadet because you want to exercise power or hurt people, or because you believe in the State's evil cause. You're in the Academy because you're a good kid who doesn't know better."

Adam was about to argue, but his attention was captured by the soft whirring of an orb floating by overhead. It stopped and hovered, looking at them — probably recording them together to show back at City Watch.

The towering buildings on either side of them were closing in. Adam wondered if a group of Watchers would suddenly rush at them, grab Michael, and throw him in a van.

He shook his head violently back and forth, upset, wishing that Michael had never told him anything. "I don't want to know that, Michael! I don't want to keep that kind of secret." Adam punched him on the arm and yelled, "I'm a cadet!"

"I know. And I know it was a risk, but I had to tell you. I'll take my consequences, including you being angry with me for getting Ana into trouble, and for getting her killed. But I had to tell you the truth, Adam. You're my friend. You're practically family to me. You deserved to know."

He was seconds from crying. Michael was like a brother. And since Adam would never see his father again, and his sister and mother were dead, Michael was the only person in his life who'd been there for him since the beginning.

"You have to know what you're getting into," Michael continued. "The State, City Watch, Watchers, Keller — none of it's what you think. And the Underground is nothing like the terrorist group described by the State. The Underground is considered an enemy of the State because the State stands for tyranny and the Underground fights for people like you, working to get the oppressed out of the City, beyond the Walls to where we can live truly free."

"But the Underground kills innocents! I've seen the Reels, Michael. Shootings, bombings, all sorts of stuff the Underground's been responsible for. How does that make you the good guys?"

"Because those are all lies, Adam. The Underground doesn't do any of those things. And it never has. It's made up of people like me and … your father."

"Dad wasn't in the Underground! Nobody ever even accused him of that."

"He was," Michael said, his voice soft. "The State didn't accuse him because it didn't want to admit that one of its top Watchers had turned. So the State set him up for your mother's murder instead. But he didn't kill her, Adam."

Adam surprised himself by taking a swing at Michael.

Caught off guard, he took Adam's blow hard to the jaw.

Michael reeled back, nearly losing his feet before regaining his balance. He looked like he was about to clock Adam back but stopped short, wobbled, then met Adam's eyes. "I'm sorry. But it's true. Your precious City Watch has lied to you from the start."

Adam shook his head, refusing to believe and not wanting to hear, knowing Michael had to be the one telling lies.

"The State set up your dad and your sister."

"Why would it do that? Ana *saw him* kill Mom!"

"I'm not sure how, but the State rigged it, tricked your sister into thinking she saw something she didn't. Once silenced, they threw your father into the Games, then did the same to Ana."

"Because of you!"

"Yes. And I told you that, knowing how much it could hurt you — hurt *us* — because I want you to trust me. I need you to know that I'm telling the truth."

"If my dad didn't kill my mom, then who did?" Adam hated himself for not knowing what to believe.

"I don't know." Michael shook his head. "We're still trying to find out. I know you hate me right now, but you don't have to take my word for it. Let me introduce you to some people who can answer your questions better than I can."

"What do you mean *some people*?"

"I want you to meet some of the Underground."

Adam was shocked how far he was getting without even trying. Chief Keller would be proud … if Adam could still bring himself to betray an old friend, like that old friend had betrayed him.

# THIRTY-TWO

# Anastasia Lovecraft

ANA'S SKIN was on fire, her body one big ball of flame.

The world had dug a deep hole in the hottest desert, then planted her inside, buried her to her neck, leaving her to an angry sun with no sense of humor.

Earlier in the day, she'd seen that the blisters and peeling had spread past her bitten wrist and up to her elbow. Now, though it was the middle of the night and too dark to see herself, it seemed to be spreading onto her shoulders and chest.

She'd seen this happen on the Games many times, the infection working its way from one limb and then through the body, starting slow, a hand bite that moved to the wrist, then to the arm, and eventually to the entire body, sometimes in as little as an hour.

Ana was living on borrowed time.

Viewers loved it when someone got bitten in the beginning and tried to outrun the turning. But even if the infected player won, there was no way he or she could ever be allowed into City 7 — not that there was one.

But Ana didn't want to outrun it. She wanted to close

her eyes forever, even if that meant never seeing her father or knowing how Adam was doing. Before her bite, her future was open. She could picture living out her days in the Barrens with Liam. In the past few months, she had come to like him a lot more than she would have ever thought possible. He was kind to her, funny, and even sweet on occasion. Beneath his gruff exterior, Liam was a good man. Yes, he had betrayed her father, but so had she. If things had been different, perhaps they could have fallen in love — not that Ana had ever been prone to such frivolous thoughts.

But everything was different now. Life as she knew it, and life as she might have dreamed it, was over. Better to go out now. At least she wouldn't be a dead woman walking, or a constant danger to Liam.

Her eyes snapped open.

Ana's body was itching because she was changing. The something she couldn't quite explain was under her scalp, deep in her armpits, between her legs, and all over her arms. She felt an army of ants, but bigger, with claws that burrowed deeper and deeper under her skin. She wanted to scratch and scratch and keep on scratching until her skin was in ribbons, but she wouldn't stop if she started, then that would be the end of her.

She would be a zombie by the end of the night, in minutes if not hours.

*It's happening.*

Ana looked over at a deeply sleeping Liam. It shouldn't have been possible to feel safe. For some reason Ana still couldn't figure, Liam wasn't afraid of her. He was snoring, somehow able to ignore the monsters in the forest and the one waiting to be born beside him.

Ana slowly stood, her head swimming, wanting to retch so badly that to avoid doing so, she took a full minute to go from flat on the floor to kneeling, then twice that to standing. Once vertical, she wandered to the edge of their impromptu camp and stared out of the cave and into the pitch-black forest. The pain made her desperate to scream, just to let some of it out. But her volume would attract the countless monsters in the night and endanger Liam.

The woods were silent, but Ana didn't trust them. Too often she'd been a fool to believe they were empty, when really the forest was waiting, preparing to spit its undead at her. The forest would start writhing soon. The zombies could smell Liam and her.

*My sisters and brothers.*

Ana had to leave. She couldn't trust that she'd be able to later. She was almost too woozy for intelligent decisions. Her head swam as acid sloshed in her stomach and the itching grew worse. She wanted to rake her skin with anything sharp.

*Broken glass would be nice.*

She pulled at her shirt to see that while the infection hadn't spread to her shoulders as she'd thought while lying down, it was getting closer.

*It won't be long now.*

Liam snored loudly. Ana crept closer to his body, inching toward the bag of supplies and weapons they'd retrieved from the bandits. She needed only one pull of the trigger — Liam's lead spitter or one of the clumsy energy guns they looted from the bandits — to fry her face and brains.

She unzipped the bag, slipped her hand inside, and slowly fished, timing her movements with Liam's loud snores. He held all the weapons — they both thought it best considering her condition, so she didn't want him seeing her with her hand in the bag. He'd immediately know what she was up to. Her fingers found the polished wood handle and drew it from the bag. She tightened her grip and stood, then crept away from Liam and back to her spot.

Ana opened her mouth and shoved the barrel inside, eager to end it, hungry to quit the itching and silence the change she couldn't stop from coming otherwise. The cold metal tasted clean in her mouth — a cool punishment for being stupid enough to get bitten. She should've seen it coming. Life in the Barrens was "Be Ready or Be Dead." She had failed, so death found her.

*Pull the trigger; then it's done.*

Ana closed her eyes to make things easier, but that didn't work. She kept her finger tense over the trigger.

She looked over at Liam, suddenly imagining the life they might have shared. But hope was the enemy of bold decisions. She couldn't go down that road. She had to act. Now.

Her heart pounded, slamming hard and begging for her death.

*I can't leave him to thunder and blood.*

Ana thought of her friend Stacy, who had found her brother hanging dead in his bedroom. She had knocked on his door for ten minutes before finally stepping inside to find the lights off and her brother dangling so low that she couldn't believe she'd missed his feet. A sheet was coiled tight around his neck, and small blotches of reddish-purple depressions and lesions pocked his skin. His eyes were frozen in a death stare. Stacy told Ana she screamed for minutes.

Ana couldn't do to Liam what Stacy's brother had done to her. She still had to end it, but not within earshot. Ana didn't want Liam to wake to the song of her murdering herself.

She stood, shaky, then moved the gun to her left hand

while creeping through camp past Liam and away from their shared ground.

She entered the forest, wondering how far she should go. Ana wasn't sure how loud the gun would be or how far the sound would carry, and didn't know how deeply Liam was sleeping or how much distance it would take to muffle the noise enough that he'd snore through the gunshot.

*Crap.*

It wasn't enough to get out of earshot. Once she was dead, the zombies would come. They would feast on her, and Liam if he was nearby. She might turn and make her way back to camp.

So Ana trudged deeper into the darkness — if she wandered far enough, Liam might stay safe even after she turned.

Every step better prepared her to die. She was no longer scared. She knew her life was over from the moment Duncan's teeth had ripped into her wrist. She saw it in Oli's eyes, just like she later saw it in Liam's. Every minute since then had been prolonging the inevitable.

Now finally moving away from camp, Ana felt better, calmer, more capable of a hard pull of the trigger.

She saw a clearing ahead and walked faster. Now only a minute away from ending it all, the pain had faded to barely an ache. But the reprieve was temporary, she was sure, subsiding only so the undead could slip comfortably into her cells, changing her into the wandering terror that haunted the Barrens and frightened the citizens living blindly inside the Walls.

Ana stopped short, realizing that she should have found a way to leave a message for Liam — a way to let him know what she was doing so he wouldn't waste any time looking for her. She thought of him desperately searching, never knowing what happened. It was even crueler than killing herself in front of him.

*You're just stalling. Do it now.*

She made it to the clearing, put the gun in her mouth again, and heard Liam calling out for her.

But he couldn't find her now, not when she was so close to ending everything, so close to sparing him from the pain of seeing her turn.

She took the gun from her mouth and ran into the woods on the other side of the clearing, farther from Liam, thankful the throbbing had dimmed.

Branches snapped in her wake. She ran faster. Liam screamed louder.

"Ana, please! Stop! You don't have to do this."

He must've seen the open bag and missing gun. He thought he could stop her, which meant she had to be strong, do what was necessary.

"Ana, *please*! We can get help at Hydrangea. I won't want to keep going without you. Please stop, you have to trust me. You're *supposed* to live, *supposed* to make it to Hydrangea, *supposed* to see your father, and *supposed* to stay with me. You can't leave me alone, Ana — I need you!"

She felt the same way, but it was almost too much. She wanted to turn back and run into his arms.

But that would be for her, not him. To Liam she was a danger.

She fought the urge to run to him, murdered the desire to lose herself in his eyes. She closed them instead, drew a deep breath, rooted her heel in the dirt, then opened them back up as she launched herself forward and tore deeper into the forest.

Ana had to be strong enough to do the hard thing and leave Liam behind forever.

# THIRTY-THREE

# Jonah Lovecraft

JONAH TRIED to keep his knee from bouncing as he sat in the small, windowless, gray-walled cell.

Nerves were the last thing he wanted them to see on him, knowing his every movement was captured by the tiny eye in the corner. He didn't know why they made the cameras so small — it wasn't as if they were actually hidden or like every person who had ever come into the checkpoint Detainment rooms didn't know they were being recorded. The State seemed to believe that by shrinking intrusions, or making them less conspicuous, people wouldn't mind as much.

The orbs had picked up on Jonah's odd pattern of walking and sent a rookie Watcher to bring him in for questioning. The first round went nowhere. His ID checked out for now, and they had nothing on him beyond a peculiar gait. They'd send a career Watcher in next to see what he could draw to the surface.

Jonah was agitated, not that he had been caught, but his being sloppy and getting nabbed might prevent him from seeing Adam, or getting back to Ana. They were all that mattered, the only reason he had gone to Hydrangea — then back inside the Walls — in the first place.

The only reason he hadn't already found a high place from which to jump.

Jonah wondered which Watcher would come into the room for further questioning, and hoped it would be someone he was friendly with from back before his world went to hell, ideally one of his old men. Sure, there was a higher chance of them seeing through his disguise, but he also felt that loyalty, even among Watchers, had to count for something, and there were a few who would still help him. *Maybe.*

He got a chill thinking of Keller, imagining the chief entering the holding cell with his serpent's smile, sauntering over and sitting across from Jonah — too close, the way he liked to get, his face bloated from gloating. Jonah had already been thrown to the Games as an example. The State couldn't admit there was no City 7, so Jonah could imagine what sort of torture and torment he'd suffer if discovered.

But Keller wouldn't be coming. If the chief knew Jonah was in The City — if the guard had seen through his disguise — then he wouldn't be alone in Detainment, sitting in one of the small cells just miles from the Precinct. He would be surrounded by half the City's orbs and then locked in the tower prisons.

The holding cell opened, and sure enough (because sometimes the world was still good) one of his old men stepped through the door. Sam Fogerty, a good guy and old-school Watcher. Jonah once thought the man saw the world through too harsh a lens; now he wondered how Fogerty might see things after knowing the truth.

He didn't even glance at Jonah when entering. He felt sweat on his forehead, wondering if his disguise was too thin to cover him. Fogerty finally looked up at Jonah, then *into* him, recognition barely perceptible but there.

For the first time since being led to the holding cell, Jonah felt an honest ray of hope. There was a chance he'd be leaving the cell soon, finding his way to Adam, Katrina, then Ana. In the last six months, he had been wrong more than right, but Jonah felt certain that Fogerty wouldn't throw him to the wolves.

He rolled his eyes up and to the right, indicating the camera. "ID."

Jonah raised his wrist and Fogerty scanned it. "State your business in Municipal."

"I'm a doctor. I was checking in with Clinic 14 because one of the physicians, Dr. Blair, was ill. When I got there she was fine, so they sent me home."

Fogerty's face was stern, his eyes smiling. "You were a ways from Clinic 14 when you were picked up. Why?"

"Just wanted to walk. I live in the mids and don't get down to the street much. I'm on sub call, so if no one's sick, I'm home all day. I was happy getting out of the apartment, so once I got sent home it was the last place I wanted to go. Figured I'd walk around for a while instead."

Jonah spoke in a tired rasp, worthy of a man who felt crushed by his day-to-day.

"Hey, I remember you!" Fogerty turned his body so he was half-facing the camera. "Were you the doctor called in on sub for Clinic 11 back in March, when that toddler took a nasty spill at Grassland?"

"That was me." Jonah nodded, cocking his head and feigning embarrassment.

"Got it, right. Sorry we pulled you in; plenty of heat on the streets right now. It's time for vigilance. Know your neighbor and all that."

Fogerty tapped the wall pad for less than a minute,

scribbled a few lines on his clipboard, hung it on the wall, unlocked Jonah's cuffs, then opened the holding-cell door and waited for him to step through. Then he led Jonah outside the room, down a short hallway, and out to the front desk.

"You're free to go." He turned and walked off without ceremony, turning back after six steps. "Do you have a way to get home?"

Jonah shrugged. "No, but I can walk."

"Jensen, the good doctor here was detained by mistake. Do we have anyone who can escort him home?" Fogerty asked, but then he glanced at the clock and turned to Jonah before Jensen could answer. "Never mind. I'm done here. Give me five and I'll take you. Not far, right?"

"Right," Jonah agreed. "Long walk, short drive."

Jonah waited an excruciating ten minutes, then Fogerty returned to the lobby seeming agitated — his usual look, though this time it felt like a show.

"Follow me," Fogerty said loudly, then muttered to Jonah as he passed. "Good to see you." They walked for another half-minute with his back turned to Jonah, then Fogerty pointed to an older cruiser. "We're in that one. Camera inside's been broken for three weeks."

Fogerty opened the driver's side door. Jonah climbed into the passenger's side and closed the door behind him.

"So, where are we headed?" Fogerty asked.

"You're smiling?"

He laughed. "I've never seen a ghost. Feels damn good to know they exist."

"It feels good to be a ghost." Jonah laughed with him. "Can you take me to the Quarter?"

"Sure thing." Fogerty sparked the engine and pulled out of the lot. City 6 had no better hiding spot than the Dark Quarter, since far fewer of the expensive-to-maintain orbs were assigned to the area. "Where we going in the Quarter?"

"To Marquis Odenkirk."

"No shit." Fogerty slapped the steering wheel. "*Just* saw Marquis, and, no shit, you're not gonna believe who I was with. It's what I've been dying to tell ya. You're never gonna guess."

"I have no idea." Jonah had never seen Fogerty so giddy. He went ahead and guessed. "Captain Republic."

"Would you believe me if I said little Adam Lovecraft?"

"No shit," Jonah growled. "That was you? Marquis told me he saw him on a ride-along. Didn't know it was you. Never thought to ask who the Watchers were, I was so pissed that Adam was getting cozy with Keller."

"Whoa, relax, Jonah. It's a good thing."

"Convince me."

"We were going into the Quarter to look in on a murder during Adam's ride-along. Pimp named Little Mitch cut a whore up. It was connected to Beans, so worth the meddling. Your kid was a star, Jonah; you would've been proud. He's growing up nice. Keller's taking him on like his own, which is why he got a ride-along after only just starting Cadets."

Jonah cut in, furious, wanting to punch the window. "Adam's *not* Keller's kid, though. He's *mine*."

"Look, Jonah, I get it. Keller's a throbbing cock of unholy proportions, and I'm sure he fucked you good. I've known you since you were a cadet, and I know you didn't do nothin' to Molly. I imagine you want to kill Keller twice, and I get that. So would I. Especially if he was stepping in for my kid when I couldn't. But I'd hope to have a friend like me — someone with the balls to say what's what. And you know *what's what*, Jonah?"

"What, Fogerty?" Jonah said through gritted teeth.

"Your boy is fine with Keller. Better than he was, or would be, at Chimney Rock. Better than he ever could be. He's learning smarts and discipline, and by all accounts is happier than any kid in his position would have any right to be. You can't give him any of that and you know it. You wanna do what's best for Adam, then you've got to let this go."

Jonah was silent.

"Cadets made you who you are. You're only alive right now because of the skills you've learned over a lifetime. Be a man, Jonah: *want* the same for your boy."

There was nothing to say. Fogerty was right. So they rode the remainder of the way in silence. Once they arrived, Jonah got out of the cruiser with gratitude, told the old Watcher that he couldn't thank him enough, then looked up at the darkening sky.

"What time you got?" Jonah asked.

"Six-forty."

"Shit. I forgot something. Could I ask you for one more favor?"

"What's that?"

"I was supposed to meet Dr. Liza Goelle at seven. Could you bring her back to Marquis's shop without anyone connecting you to her?"

"No problem. See ya soon." Fogerty left him with a two-finger salute through the window before flipping the cruiser around and driving out of the Quarter.

Jonah walked three miles to Marquis's market. It was late and the streets were busy. Everything seemed darker: sky, buildings, and people.

He went to the market's rear and into a room where Katrina and Marquis were playing cards.

Katrina looked up as he entered. "This asshole is a cheater. Why are you friends with him?"

"It ain't never cheating if you don't get caught," said Marquis with a smirk.

Katrina dropped her cards on the table and looked up at Jonah. "Did you see Adam?"

"No, and I don't want to talk about it. Let's just get the hell out of here."

Marquis managed to eat only high-apartment rations, despite a life confined to the Quarter. He made sure Jonah left with a pack full of meals he'd remember for a while, then gave Katrina the same. He winked, saying he hoped it made up for his cheating, and that they could play again next time.

Dr. Liza showed up at 7:10 p.m., seeming apprehensive.

"You ready to do this?" Jonah asked.

"I'd be lying if I said yes. But … yeah."

They thanked Marquis before heading into the secret tunnel under the market and then through the bowels beneath City 6.

Jonah couldn't help thinking about his conversation with Fogerty. He *was* glad that Adam was thriving. Fogerty was right about at least some of what he'd said. Still, Jonah looked forward to the day when he could return to City 6 and usher his son to the other side of the Wall.

But first, he had to make sure that his daughter was safe.

# THIRTY-FOUR

# Liam Harrow

LIAM PLODDED through darkness in search of Ana. The forest kept yelling in whispers, but every minute or so he chanced the flood of zombies anyway, drawing a gust into his lungs, then unleashing his trumpeted cry.

"Ana!" Another few steps. "Ana!"

A rustle ahead grabbed his attention. Liam was certain he saw her in the distance, so he moved fast to reach her and risked another call.

"Ana!" He walked faster, pursuing movement. Whoever was ahead — it had to be her — rushed away when he called. "Ana! You don't have to do this!"

He grabbed a blaster once he saw she was gone, threw the pack over his shoulder, then raced through the forest. It was too dark to follow a trail, so he chased instinct, running behind a ghosted scent of Ana that he kept telling himself had to be real. Because if it wasn't, then Liam had nothing.

He kept moving, grateful he'd yet to hear the thunder of a gunshot, knowing that Ana was still with him and waiting to be found until he did.

Again, to hell with the zombies. "Don't do this, Ana! We can find another way out of this together!"

He was too loud. Surely, the zombies had to be coming. Their hunger was worse at night, but he had to believe that between his eyes and his brain, being human gave him an advantage in the dark.

No room to think otherwise. He was the only one who could stop Ana from her intentions. After everything that had happened, Liam could never go to Hydrangea without her, let alone look Jonah in his eyes and admit that he'd failed to protect his daughter. He would be nothing as a man. Not to Chelle, or their baby aborted by the State, or the Underground he betrayed.

The rustling ahead seemed louder. He had to be catching up with her, and yet after another minute of running — and seeing regular movement ahead, the crashing through shrubs as she kept rushing forward and ignoring his calls — Liam also heard new sounds rolling in from both sides, around and behind him.

He tightened his grip on the gun as noise grew louder ahead, more insistent as Liam neared. He saw the sway of a low branch and smiled — he was seconds from Ana. If that was her.

He hurled his body the last few steps. "Ana! Please let me help you!"

She turned around and he nearly crashed into her.

But while regaining his balance Liam saw that it was a zombie, not Ana. A young woman wearing light-colored clothing, tattered and blood-stained, turning around and stepping into a sliver of moonlight that seeped through a split in the canopy of trees above.

She growled and snarled, lashing at Liam.

He stumbled backward, managed an about-face, then took off running in the other direction, wondering how long he had been chasing the zombie rather than Ana, and if he had ever really been pursuing her at all.

Liam ran without any real direction, suddenly scrambling, unsure of where to go. He was angry that he'd followed the zombie for so long. He had to find Ana, but he couldn't effectively search when running. He felt an overwhelming urge to go back and kill the zombie just to clear his head.

Swallowing fear and nursing his courage, Liam spun around and roared toward the zombie. He didn't slow when he reached her, grabbing her by the hair, pulling her down to the ground, and slamming her face-first into the forest floor. He got up and started kicking the back of her skull, once, twice, then repeatedly, even though its brain had ruined to bloody bits of mush like gum on his boot.

He stood above the zombie, slowly catching his breath, perking his ears for Ana but hearing nothing. He listened harder, then rushed toward the wood's only sound. A minute later he nearly ran into a pack.

The group was small, about four strong, but the moon had dipped back behind the clouds, and Liam could barely see. The trees were too thick to allow for much light. Mostly he could see the thin blur that his eyes had already adjusted to. One miscalculation — thinking there were four when there might be five, focusing on the zombies in front of him and not staying aware of what might be at his sides, engaging in a spot where it was too dark to win — and Liam would surely end up dead.

He wanted to take out this pack, but his odds were poor.

He slowly backed away instead, unsure of whether he'd been spotted. Liam stepped back and onto a branch — it might as well have been a tree crashing to the forest floor.

Liam couldn't be sure, but it seemed like all four

zombies turned at once. He ran as more zombies crashed through the woods behind him, calling out to their brothers in hungry pursuit.

Sounds were everywhere, but none coming from Ana. He had to get clear of the danger and find her. He could turn and shoot, empty his gun and maybe clear the threat from behind him, but then he'd be running without ammo, and with even less direction than he already had.

If he ran too far in the dark, he'd get turned around, unable to find Ana and powerless to help her.

The forest got louder as more zombies spilled into hazy shapes in the dark, circling, narrowing his choices and chances to nothing. He screamed in desperation, hoping to scare the shapes away, and that Ana might hear him if her part of the woods was anywhere near his.

The zombies were on him. If he didn't turn and shoot, he'd never get the chance. They would be on him, and then he'd be dead.

Liam spun, sighted, and squeezed the trigger.

Despite the overwhelming darkness, his first blast slammed into the nearest zombie's forehead and sent it flying to the ground. He pulled the trigger four more times and dropped a pair from the pack.

But it wasn't enough. There were more, countless more, approaching, shadows within shadows.

Liam fired blindly into the pack. He had six shots left in the energy clip. He had replacements in the bag, but no way of reaching them and reloading his blaster before getting torn to shreds.

He raced blindly into the dark. Made it about nine feet before he felt the first hand, lunging from the shadows, brushing him on the shoulders as he passed.

He cried out but kept running, the world a chaos of darkness and limbs — trees and zombies — kicking and punching and snarling. Gnashing teeth. The stench of rot all around him.

If Liam were capable of surrender, he would have already relaxed and let the inevitable wash through his body. But he hadn't admitted defeat in Chimney Rock, or when he was told by the State that he couldn't have a child with Chelle, not even after getting thrown to the Games, or when he and Ana found themselves surrounded by the largest group of bandits he'd ever seen.

Defeat had no chance now.

Liam would fight until—

He was thrown hard to the ground. Undead bodies piled on top of him, clawing and gnarling. He kicked, screaming, desperate to break free.

But there were too many, the sudden weight holding him down.

He reached up with his blaster, tried to squeeze, but it was yanked from his hand with a savage swing. This was the end.

A shrill scream ripped through the forest, loud even over the mass of snarling bodies atop him. Movement paused as if lured by the sound.

He couldn't understand why they would care about far-off prey when they had meat on the grill already, but he wiggled breathlessly out of the pile, barely making it to his feet as a dream come true approached.

Ana had been the one to scream like a banshee, and now the zombies were rushing toward her.

Liam grabbed his blaster and pulled the trigger three times, taking out the two zombies closest to Ana. He ran behind the others, to their right, and screamed, "Run! Over here, Ana! Run to me!"

She was moving too slow and the zombies too fast.

They were everywhere, surrounding her in an instant, and there was nothing Liam could do.

He dropped his bag and was about to grab more ammo, but then he realized that the zombies weren't attacking her.

They were clustering around, same as they had done with him a moment before. But they weren't trying to kill her. Their heads were turned, regarding her, as a lion might examine a new feline entering the pride.

Ana moved toward him, walking a straight line, slow and steady, pushing through the growing horde that was still spilling out from the forest — as if she didn't care if they killed her.

She was usually fearless, but this was suicidal. Given that she had probably run off to kill herself, that wasn't too surprising. But still, it was one thing to blow your brains out, another to greet a horde of zombies without flinching.

Ana's bite seemed to make her immune to their threat.

Liam stared, astonished as he approached her. She parted her arms as their distance narrowed, palms up and facing him. She handed the gun to him. Her eyes were wide, brimming with tears. Her lips quivered.

He took the shooter, then her hands, and pulled her body against him. Zombies made noises around them, but none growled or gnashed like before.

Liam felt certain one of the growing horde would swipe at him, her, or both of them, but they seemed unwilling, staring as if awed or confused. It was impossible to see intent through their vacant stares.

He ignored the largest zombie growling at him as they moved through the crowd. They kept moving away from the horde, neither speaking as Liam tried to remember the way back to camp, and tried not to notice Ana's scorching hand burning his.

# THIRTY-FIVE

# Adam Lovecraft

THE UNDERGROUND MEETING was in a dingy dung heap of a forgotten apartment in the Edge, a sector of Commuters that had "moved on." Apartments in the area were from during the Wallings, fashioned by budget contractors as the City was first being built. The dwellings were made from the cheapest drywall and stucco, never intended to last, and — as the rest of the City was built — the oldest apartments fell into disrepair, then, eventually, abandonment.

Adam's dad had said the Edge was a final resting stop before people surrendered to the full despair of the Quarter. Not everyone stopped at the Edge before falling all the way, but even for those who did, their stay was temporary.

The meeting was held in the cement basement of an interior building, scheduled on a day when there would be no sweeps (unless the Underground's information was wrong or the informant turned unreliable). No one in the basement lived in the Edge — according to Michael, the Underground was made up of people in every type of apartment, even the high-rises, though Adam found that part hard to believe.

There were people of all different shapes and sizes, but everyone other than Adam, Michael, a fat man named Belly, and a rail-thin woman named Erin — slimmer than his mom but about the same age that she would be — were wearing colorful balaclavas to hide their faces. Adam could only see their eyes and mouths. There were men, women, and even a little girl, maybe as young as ten.

They looked almost like superheroes, except they wore normal clothes.

*Like superheroes off duty.*

The notion made him laugh, but then Adam felt bad for laughing. These people weren't heroes. They were, save for maybe the little girl and Michael, monsters.

Michael told Adam to listen. And that if he did, he would see the Underground for what it was: important people doing important things that truly made a difference to people living behind The Walls. He said that Adam knew enough about one side of the world, but that it was time to flip it upside down and see what leaked.

The meeting began with a brief recounting of some of the horrors people had experienced during the week, most of it mistreatment from City Watchers. The pronouncements were shocking, but much of what he heard sounded like exaggerations of things that had happened earlier, and after a while all the stories sounded the same, almost competitive, with each person trying to top the one that came before.

Adam soon understood why Erin didn't want a mask. The dark-haired woman had no fear of being recognized, seeming ready to brawl at the slightest provocation.

As she paced the basement, arguing truth with a fist in the air, he could see every twitch of her nostrils. Her face screamed through quiet delivery. "We are all that stands between the government and the people! Without us, this City is lost."

A man — tall, with wide shoulders and a deep but kind voice — said, "We stand for people's rights, and we help them when needed. Enemies of the State are our friends. We help the oppressed get out of the City."

The entire evening had been filled with so much of the same that Adam wondered if perhaps they were purposely not talking about more important things because they were in the presence of a Watcher cadet.

He suddenly got a chill, like something was wrong.

Adam looked around at all the people in masks, trying to figure out the source of his discomfort.

He had a horrible thought: it would be just like Keller to initiate an unscheduled sweep of the Edge to ferret out insidious, cancerous cells and destroy them.

"We shouldn't be here," Adam whispered to Michael.

"We'll be fine. Don't worry, just listen."

But Adam had been listening for a while, and no one was really saying anything new. They were exchanging large ideas, not actual plans. If Keller asked what he'd heard, Adam wouldn't have been able to tell Keller anything that didn't sound like a generic quote from a random Reel on any given day. If Adam had to be in an Underground meeting, he wanted to leave with *something*.

"Why do you fight?" Adam asked, leaning forward in his chair. "There's no way that anyone can ever win against the State. Aren't you wasting your life by trying?"

A loud man sitting at the farthest part of the basement's circle shouted, "You waste your life by giving up!"

"Why is being good giving up?" Adam looked around; almost everyone sitting in the circle looked back at him from behind their anonymous masks. "What makes it so bad in the City? Don't you have everything you need?"

"We have exactly enough to keep us sucking the tit," said a soft-spoken man near the center. "And never a drop more than that."

A young woman laughed coldly from a few masks beside Adam. "Have you ever been to the Dark Quarter?"

"I went there last week with City Watch. It was on a ride-along — that meant I was with two Watchers. I saw lots of stuff."

"And what did you think?" Erin asked.

"It was awful, of course, but maybe you're seeing things the wrong way. Think about the whole City, not just the Quarter. We all have to stay safe inside the Walls, right? People having the hardest time are usually the most violent. The Quarter keeps those people together in one place so everyone else can stay safe. Doesn't that make sense? Most people don't find themselves there by accident — what if places like that are necessary to keep everyone safe? Would you rather have a small family where everyone was fed, or a large one where everyone starved?"

Groaning and laugher rippled through the circle.

A man yelled, "Why'd you bring the junior White-washer, Michael? What were you thinking?"

A woman agreed. "Get the Whitewasher out of here and don't bring him back. Our meetings are for people who know how to open their eyes!"

Belly cleared his throat. "Let the kid speak. There was a time when everyone in this room was living in the dark. Lovecraft's had some hard months. Cut the boy a little slack — he deserves it by association, and every one of you knows it. Not his fault he's living with Watchers. You'd do the same for a meal in his shoes, once your belly got to rumbling." He laughed, patted his own large stomach, then looked at Adam. "The floor's yours, kid. Don't waste it."

"I'm not a Whitewasher," Adam said, feeling defensive.

"I'm just like you all. I've lost a lot, maybe as much as anyone here. My dad was exiled, and so was my sister. I always want to do the right thing. I came here today because Michael asked me to. He said I'd see the truth if I came here tonight, but I haven't heard anything except 'the Underground is good and the State is bad.' Sad stuff, yes. But I'm not hearing anything that convinces me that the State is some sort of evil overlord controlling our lives."

"It is evil," said a woman from behind her mask.

"And how do you know that?" Adam asked.

"We just do," echoed someone else.

Words exploded from Adam's mouth. "But *how*? Tell me something that can't be called the wrong place at the wrong time or a streak of bad luck. City Watch isn't evil. I've spent enough time with the Watchers to know that they're trying to protect you all. Trying to keep you safe."

"Not evil?" said a smaller voice directly across from Adam. The girl stood and pulled off her pink-and-purple mask. But she was maybe eight or nine, not ten, and her eyes were a new kind of sad for Adam.

"My dad wasn't even in the Underground, but he was nice and cared about everyone, so he gave some of his food rations to someone in the Underground who needed them. City Watch came and snatched him away. He's been gone for a month now, and we haven't heard a thing. He'll probably be in the next Games, or the ones after that. But we know we'll probably never see him again, unless he's running from zombies. My family is barely surviving. Because Dad was an 'enemy of the State,' we're not even entitled to death rations. Chimney Rock has offered to take me and my brother and sister, but only because they want the three per diems. Mom doesn't know if she can fight the order since we were barely making it with Dad bringing home what he did."

"Is that the fucking government looking out for us, Whitewasher?" asked a man in black.

Adam felt awful for so many reasons and wanted to leave. He stood, nodded to the room so they could see his manners, then turned from the circle and went to the door.

"He better not rat us out!" someone yelled from behind as he opened it.

The door slammed, then swung back open and Michael came out a step behind Adam. "You're not gonna rat us out, are you?"

He looked at Michael, insulted. "No, I'm not. But thanks for *trusting* me."

Michael stared back at Adam in silent apology.

Adam turned and left Michael standing.

"Wait, I'll get you a ride," offered Michael.

"I'd rather walk." He needed time to think, away from these people.

Time to decide what he could possibly say to Keller.

# THIRTY-SIX

# Jonah Lovecraft

THEY REACHED HYDRANGEA, and Katrina brought them to meet Sutherland in the same room where the leader and Jonah had first met. He barked laughter on sight, elated to see them.

"Welcome. It's so good to see you. Dr. Liza Goelle." Sutherland bounded to her side. "I'm honored you came. I've heard so much about you, and couldn't be happier that you're here."

"I wasn't aware that my work was being followed." Liza took a step back.

"Relax." Sutherland soothed her with a smile. "Your discomfort is natural, but I'm no Peeping Tom. I search high and low for those who can change the world, and … those who can keep it from changing."

Liza seemed equally curious and uncomfortable. She shifted on her feet, holding his stare, as if turning away meant losing power she couldn't surrender.

"Is it true?" Sutherland asked. "That you are close to developing a cure?"

Jonah could hear Liza in his head, demanding to know

how someone in the Barrens had intimate details about work she'd kept buried. "Yes," she replied, still holding his stare.

Sutherland scratched his chin scruff and narrowed his eyes. "How close?"

"I've no idea, really. Just guesses. We've had some success in stalling the virus, and have even partially reversed its damage in a few animal subjects. But cure? I can't say. The virus has mutated so much from the original that destroyed our people."

"So what's stopping the cure?"

Sutherland asked Liza as if curing the virus was like pouring milk into cereal.

"A lack of subjects, funding, staff — there's no shortage of issues. The biggest being that all of my research has to be done in secrecy, which, if you knew about it, I guess wasn't so secret after all. Getting freshly infected subjects sometimes feels impossible."

She paused, looked at Jonah, then continued. "I had one human patient. He was infected but managed to keep from turning for two years. Unfortunately, I've not heard from him in a while."

She glanced over at Jonah again. He felt grateful for her eyes, and apologized with his.

"That's quite unfortunate." He looked disappointed. "What is fortunate, though, is that I think you'll find that what you've lost by leaving City 6 will be more than made up for here. You can continue your research in our lab, which is state of the art and, I'm sure, better than anything you have access to at Clinic 17." Sutherland smiled. "Hydrangea scientists are here to help you and are fully at your disposal. Our Dr. Oswald is eager to meet you. Here, your research isn't a secret; it's a godsend. Experiment in the open; loudly celebrate your victories."

Liza looked almost happy, but Jonah could see she wasn't letting her guard down yet.

Sutherland laughed again, clapping his large hands. "Yes, Dr. Goelle, this is meant to be. Someone like you belongs *here*, with people like us. You'll have patients to work with, infected who are desperate for your help. We find a lot of freshly bitten in the Barrens, and they aren't exactly picky."

Liza stuttered through a few seconds, seemingly unsure of what to say. Finally she cleared her throat. "I'll need some supplies, some of which might be hard to get, especially out here. Shall I make a list? Who should I give it to?"

Even uncertain, Liza seemed ready for whatever it was she'd be doing.

"Not to worry about any of that." Sutherland pawed the air. "As I said, our lab's state of the art. I'm sure we have everything you need already. If not," he grinned, "I think you'll find that supplies are often *easier* to get out here in the Barrens than inside your Walls."

"The Walls aren't mine," Liza said tartly. "When can I see the lab?"

Even with only the side of her face visible, Jonah could see that something about her had changed. Liza was a passionate woman, full of ideas and an always-whirring brain. But Jonah didn't understand science well enough to participate in her world, so her work was always something she did, rather than something they shared. Still, he could see the thrill of promised experimentation coloring her cheeks and brightening her eyes.

"Well, there's no reason not to take you there now." Sutherland went to the door and stepped from the room, expecting them to follow.

A few minutes and four corridors later, they stood outside a wide metal door.

Sutherland turned toward them, winked at Jonah and then smiled at Liza. "I expect that Oswald's inside. I should probably warn you, our lead scientist is a bit … odd."

Before Liza could ask what he meant, Sutherland's fingers were dancing on the wall's black keypad. The metal door hissed open and he entered the lab. She followed, then Jonah.

The man who had to be Oswald looked up as they stepped inside. He had been hunched over, examining something on his exposed torso. He turned and looked at them, putting down a small screwdriver.

Liza, like Jonah, seemed to be swallowing her gasp. The scientist's bare chest seemed neatly divided into three parts: human, zombie, and metal. She stared in awe, then ran up to Oswald and started running her hands all over his body, mostly on the metal, as if the man were a display.

"Was this to cut infection?" Liza asked with her hand on his metal shoulder.

The corners of his mouth were heavily damaged and cracked, and they wrinkled like a zombie when he smiled. "Yes, the infection spread fast, but it's now equalized. Any damaged body parts that could be replaced were swapped with bionics."

Still brushing her fingers against Oswald's shoulders, she whispered, "I've never seen anything like it."

"That's because there isn't anything like it," Sutherland said, circling the lab with his hands spread in the air. "Welcome to Hydrangea!"

He stepped behind Oswald and clapped the scientist on his fleshy back. "Oswald will give you a tour of the lab, answer any questions you have, then show you to your room. It's over there."

Sutherland pointed to the far wall, made of glass. Jonah assumed there were dorms behind it. "In the meantime, if you don't mind, I'd like to borrow Jonah for a moment."

Liza offered Jonah the most beautiful smile he'd seen in half a year.

"Are you good?" he asked.

"Yes, Jonah. Thanks. I'll be great."

Sutherland took that as his cue and led Jonah from the lab. "It looks like we still have another four days until Anastasia's arrival. There's one more thing we need you to do before she gets here."

Jonah's heart started racing. He didn't care for the unexpected — the only thing Sutherland seemed to traffic in. Whatever Hydrangea's leader was about to say, Jonah had the feeling that he wouldn't like it.

"I need you to go to City 1 and deliver a package."

"No." His refusal was simple and fell right from his mouth.

Sutherland was quiet as they walked, but his silence was heavy and had Jonah squirming beneath it. He and Ana were only days from their reunion; he wasn't risking his life — after he already had — to do anything more before he saw her. Jonah didn't owe Sutherland, Katrina, or Hydrangea anything else. He'd already gone beyond the call of duty.

"I have to wait for Ana. I can't go to City 1, or anywhere else. Not for anything, at least not until I see her."

"You're the only one who can do this, which means that you must. Not to be overly dramatic, Jonah, but the future of our world depends on it."

*Asshole.* Jonah hated feeling obligated and loathed Sutherland's manipulations.

"It's simple. And really, there's no danger to speak of. We could send anyone, and would, if the mission wasn't coded to you."

"What do you mean?" Jonah cursed himself for the question, hated how smoothly he was falling into Sutherland's familiar line of bullshit.

"You're the last person to get a fake ID chip." He pointed to Jonah's wrist. "Unfortunately, we can't get another because I just got word that Marquis has gone into hiding. It doesn't happen often, but when that man dips low he means it. He'll be down for a while."

"But what's so goddamn important that it has to be delivered *now*?"

Sutherland stopped to look directly at Jonah. "The package is a poison. A special delivery for Jack Geralt."

"And you think I'm going to walk into City 1 and hand Jack Fucking Geralt some poison?" Jonah was almost shouting. "What then? Pour it into a decanter and serve it with fucking cheese and crackers?"

"No," Sutherland replied, his voice still perfectly calm. "You won't need to. Get it to our courier, and *she* will do the rest. This is easy, Jonah. There's no reason to say no."

"And what happens if I refuse?"

"You can retire to your quarters. Eat well, drink well, sleep well. Enjoy the company of a woman or two — I don't care what you're doing if not your duty. But Hydrangea will buzz with news of what you didn't do when you could have. I'm not sure you'll want your daughter to arrive with that sort of chatter burning in the background — at least not in light of such a glowing alternative."

"I never cared much for what others thought of me."

"I know. And I admire that about you, I truly do. But I also know you care about your daughter. And you care about Katrina, right? She went and found you, made it possible for you to see Ana again. Don't you want to help take revenge against the monster that hurt her?"

Jonah didn't reply. And because the carrot had yet to move him, Sutherland showed him the stick.

"We've spent a lot of time and effort creating a safe haven here and in our other villages. A place where people like Ana can live in relative safety from the horrors of the Barrens. Don't you want that for your child? A place where she can live without worrying about zombies or bandits? A home where she won't have to ever find food or a doctor? But as a veteran Watcher, you realize that safety has a cost, and someone must pay for it. We all do our part here. Today, I am asking you to do yours. You're free to refuse, but there's no way I can allow you and your family to stay if you won't help us preserve what we've built. My leadership would be questioned, and chaos would erupt among the citizens. I don't want to say 'do this or else,' but you've given me no choice."

"Let's not fool ourselves here. This isn't a onetime request. There will always be one more thing you need me to do."

Sutherland smiled. "You're too smart a man to know I won't make other requests, Jonah. We're in a war, and until we bring Geralt and his corrupt system down, some of us will have to make more sacrifices than others. But what father wouldn't sacrifice everything for the safety of his children?"

"How long will it take to get there?" Jonah asked, swallowing the bitter taste of Sutherland's manipulations. "City 1 is at least a week away, right?"

"We have alternative transportation, provided you're not afraid of heights."

"Fine," Jonah said. "I'll do it. But I want to go now."

# THIRTY-SEVEN

# Adam Lovecraft

IT HAD BEEN two days since the Underground meeting, and Adam had yet to see or hear from Keller. Just when he was starting to wonder if he'd done something to disappoint him, Adam was summoned to dinner.

"There's nothing like a meal between friends."

Their best conversations usually happened when eating. Keller said that breaking bread loosened tongues. Tonight, Adam could pick any place that he wanted. He chose Bastion because he liked that they had plenty of screens, and that none of them broadcasted the Games.

Bastion played old movies and comedies, mostly from before the Plague. One of the movies was called *The Fifth Element*. Bastion was the only place Adam had ever seen it. Mom and Dad had taken him when he was three, because Ana loved the movie. That was the first time Adam had ever seen a piece of *The Fifth Element*, and he'd anticipated every piece since. He was pretty sure he'd seen most of it over the course of several years.

Adam stared at the closest screen: Cornelius was instructing David to prepare the temple before sneaking aboard the passenger ship. He had a hard time paying attention to the scene thanks to constant thoughts about Michael and the Underground, about Keller wanting to know all about them both, and how they went together.

Keller read his mind and filled him with chills. "So, your friend Michael — does he strike you as a problem for the State?"

Adam looked him in the eyes. "Michael isn't in the Underground, Chief Keller, and I don't think the City has anything to worry about." He paused, then started swinging his feet under the chair. "Still, I don't think I want to hang out with him anymore, and not just because we only go to Nips and never do anything fun. Michael is boring and never has anything to say. He's not really happy for me, but that doesn't make him one of the bad guys. And besides, he's too weak for the Underground."

He couldn't stop his leg from bouncing. Keller hooked his eyes into Adam's and clawed. He couldn't flinch without looking like a liar.

The chief knew, and Adam could see it in his icy stare. Everything harsh about the man seemed twice so beneath the weight of his gaze. Until he finally granted mercy by looking away, Adam would be stuck in his panic, leg bouncing, sweat beading, heart rate irregular, desperate to alter his story. Terrified.

Keller was waiting for Adam to crack. Everything would change when he did. It wasn't too late. The chief would understand if he admitted—

"Well then. That's a relief. Michael's Underground involvement *would* leave you in an awful spot. On one hand you'd feel an obligation to protect your friend — this is righteous and in your proven nature. On the other hand, you do have an obligation to your State, City, and role as a Watcher cadet."

The chief leaned across the table and set his eyes to Adam's bouncing knee, pleasant as always. "Do you need to use the restroom, son?"

Adam stopped his knee. "Yes, I have to go bad."

He laughed. "Well, why didn't you say something? A real man knows not to hold it. Go!" Keller swatted a hand toward the restrooms.

Adam half-smiled, then stood and went to the bathroom on the other side of the Bastion with a pounding heart. The only reason his knee wasn't rattling like a Barrens snake was because he was finally walking somewhere.

He entered the bathroom, closed the door behind him, and started to freak.

He waited about the length of time he thought it would take to pee, then turned on the faucet and splashed his face, telling himself over and over not to be stupid.

*You have to tell him. The chief knows Michael's in the Underground, and he probably knows that you know. You'll be in SO much trouble if you keep it a secret. Tell him about the meeting. Just get it over with. You have to. You don't have a choice. It's Michael's fault for trusting you. You're a cadet. A Junior Watcher. A Whitewasher. You wore your uniform to the Edge!*

Adam dried his face well, trying to pat as much of his hair into place as he could. He didn't want it to look like he'd been doing what he had, even though Keller would know anyway. The chief always knew about everything, which was why it was stupid not to tell the truth about Michael.

He took a final look in the mirror, then stood tall like a man and turned toward the door. He left the bathroom prepared to tell Keller the truth, but he was talking on his comm when Adam returned to his chair.

Adam sat as the chief finished his call.

"I have to go." Keller looked across the table at Adam, no longer smiling. "Yes," he added to whoever was on the other line.

The call went dead and he looked at Adam, his face different than usual. Harsher than before, as if brimming with anger.

"I'm afraid our time is up for today. There is a situation near Barnes Square that requires my immediate attention."

He waited for Adam to respond. Or blink. He stood, pulled his uniform jacket from the back of his chair, put it on, and started buttoning it up as he walked toward the exit, seeming to expect Adam to follow.

"Is there anything I can do to help?"

Keller turned to Adam in the doorway. "Absolutely. The best way you can help me, and yourself — as well as the City and the State that support you — is to know your neighbors and report what you see."

He smiled like he meant it, then turned and left. Adam was out of the restaurant two steps behind him, but Keller was already far off in the parking lot. Adam wondered why he was being so cold. Treating him just like anyone else. Was he that distracted by the situation in Barnes? Or was he disgusted by Adam's deception?

He left the restaurant with slumped shoulders, his head down, lost in thought as he started the two-block walk back to the Academy and his dorm.

He heard footsteps quickly approaching from behind.

The dark sent a chill up his spine as he turned to see Michael running up beside him.

"So," Michael said as he came to a stop. "Did you rat us out?"

# THIRTY-EIGHT

# Liam Harrow

LIAM AND ANA traveled in silence.

They were wide awake and too scared for sleep, so they kept going, aware but exhausted, moving forward like machines.

Or zombies.

Liam would've been happy to talk, but she clearly didn't want to.

She seemed angry rather than grateful that he had rushed through the forest to save her. She seemed upset that he'd interrupted her from the important work of ending her life. He longed to hear Ana say something, wanted her to see that she didn't have to die, and that he would do anything in the world to protect her until the last second.

She finally spoke. "You should have let me die."

"You shouldn't be an idiot." He cursed himself for already ruining what had taken so long to start. He figured it would be a while before she spoke again.

He was wrong. "We all have a right to decide exactly how long we want to live, Liam. And I'm done here. Why can't you be okay with that? Why can't you let me die in peace? I'm a danger to you, and I'll be a danger to Hydrangea if we get there."

"*When* we get there. And that's bullshit. You're just feeling sorry for yourself. I'm not going to assist your suicide. That doesn't make sense."

"I'm half zombie already. You saw how those damned things acted around me! It's only a matter of time before I'm one of them all the way."

"You should already be dead, but you're not. I would be for sure if it wasn't for you. I had one at my neck before you came through the forest. I was nearly bitten. But you came in and saved me! Don't you realize what that means?"

"It means I saved your life, so you should let me do whatever the hell I want with mine."

"It means you're like a half-zombie superhero. Like *Captain Republic: UNDEAD!*"

"Shut up," she said, but Ana managed to laugh, her first in a while.

"Seriously, though, how did you know you wouldn't be hurt?"

Ana said nothing.

"Oh ... you didn't *care*."

"By gun or zombies."

"Ana ..."

She slowly turned and met his eyes. Everything about her seemed faded, mostly gone. What little was left seemed sad without end.

The moon was full, casting Ana in a white light that belied her dying. Despite hollow eyes and obvious sorrow, she somehow looked as beautiful to Liam as she ever had. Not just sad, but sweet. There was something inside her — always had been — that was willing to believe in the impossible and preserve what was right. That was the quality in Ana that Liam wanted to take care of most, the thing he felt so driven to protect.

But that quality was dying.

"Yes?" Eyebrows raised.

Her face flickered as if in memory. Her expression wrinkled, starting at her brow. She cried out with no warning, losing barely a whimper as she fell to the ground with her eyes closed.

Liam dropped to her side, frantic and searching for her pulse. She was alive, but he wasn't sure what sort of alive that might mean.

"Ana?" He shook her but got no response. She was unconscious. Maybe turning for good.

He slipped his arms under her body, then stood, hefting Ana into his cradle, hoping to find somewhere to lay her down before she grew too heavy.

After twenty minutes of trudging along with Ana in his arms, Liam found shelter: a small, fenced-in house, fashioned from wood and various materials from old cars, planes, and other detritus from the Barrens — the sort of house he had seen plenty during his time in the wastelands, built by people living lives, zombies be damned. Liam never would have seen the house if it wasn't in a clearing by the water, easy to find under the full moon and no trees to hide it. Unlike many of the shelters they had stayed in during their time in the Barrens, this house looked lived-in, nestled beside a river with a pair of small canoes tied to the wooden dock in front.

Liam called out to see if anyone was home. Nobody answered. He would have to get closer; maybe someone was home, unable to hear him.

He laid Ana on the ground and started working on the fence. It wasn't difficult — the enclosure was built to stop zombies, not humans. He swung the gate wide, then returned to the other side, scooped Ana back into his arms, and carried her to the front of the house, where he again called out to see if someone was home.

The windows were boarded shut, but there were plenty of holes, and he could see no light source inside the home. "Hello! Is anyone here? We're friends in need. My companion is unconscious. We're no trouble, just need to rest."

After a long silence, he tried again. "Hello?"

With Ana in his arms, he couldn't knock, so he kicked instead, surprised — and relieved — when the door opened.

Liam was wrong; the house was abandoned. Everything wore a thin skin of dust. The furniture was well preserved, but it had clearly been a while since the space was home to anyone. A carcass of something sat on a plate on the kitchen table, so old and dried that even flies were uninterested.

He closed the door with his foot and crossed the small house to the corner, where a bed with a thin mattress stood, covered by a barely-there pillow and threadbare blanket. He kneeled, laying Ana on the bed, then pulled the blanket from beneath her and tossed it on the floor.

She was burning up; it wouldn't be good to cover her.

He swept the hair from her face, then stood, not knowing what else to do other than check out the house.

He locked the door, set his bag down, and retrieved both his blaster and lead shooter, then loaded them with ammo in case someone else stumbled upon their shelter. He looked through cabinets, searching for supplies, figuring no one would be missing anything.

The Barren's unspoken rules said that a house found with no one in it, where no one had been for a while, belonged (however temporarily) to those who found it — locked or otherwise. His search was brief and turned up little, but it was still enough to improve their morning. Liam found seven empty cabinets, but one that was filled with four boxes of supplies, each tin in the box stamped with the City 6 logo, and an entire shelf filled with water canisters.

Liam emptied the cabinet and set everything by the door, mostly so he had something to do, then dragged the kitchen table in front and found a small lantern with some fuel. He lit it and illuminated the cabin with the warmth of an orange glow. He hoped it wouldn't be bright from the holes in the boarded-up windows, but he didn't want to sleep in the dark again — not tonight.

He went to Ana's bed, sprawled on the floor beside it, grabbed her hand (much cooler than it had been), and let himself fall asleep.

LIAM WOKE IN THE DARKNESS — the lantern's wick had either gone dry or the fuel had burned out — to Ana growling beside him: the sound he'd been dreading since leaving Paradise.

It didn't come from her mouth; that's just where it left. The growl sounded like it was made of rocks and bones banging against one another on the bottom of a metal cage, starting in the pit of her gut, then clawing its way to the top of her throat before belching in fury.

Liam had heard the sound in person too many times since losing his veil of safety behind the Walls, and had heard it countless times before that, starting when he could first decode the savagery of the Games during broadcasts and recaps. The sound of turning sometimes crept, more often erupted, and always meant the death of a soul and the start of a living corpse's torment, clinging to fibers of being, so thin and barely there they were like a tornado's vapor.

Liam lay still, his body knotted and tense as Ana's growling grew louder and harsher, less of a rattling hacking and more of a throaty bark. He didn't want to get up, or look.

But he had to. Liam stood, then looked down on Ana's face, glad it was shrouded by darkness, knowing he had to see the infection's brutality no matter how much it hurt.

Liam grabbed his flashlight from the bag and shined it on Ana. She was waxen and still, growls leaving her mouth but somehow escaping her frozen body without a tremble. Her face wasn't yet warped like Liam expected, but she seemed somehow worse for it, icy and white.

Like a corpse.

He shifted on his feet, thinking. Liam loathed the thought of what he had to do. He kneeled to his spot and picked up his gun, rubbing his thumb on the butt while wishing for miracles.

He felt a shuddering bubble in his depths, rising inside him, shaking his body and making him want to weep. He stifled it because he couldn't afford to be frail. Liam owed it to Ana — he had to stay strong enough for them both, enough to do the unthinkable.

She was already dead; now they were stretching agony like a rubber band.

She'd begged him to kill her, but he wouldn't listen. She tried doing it herself and he stopped her. She pleaded for death, and he had selfishly kept it from her.

She wanted to die. Liam wouldn't allow it.

He put the gun to her head, his finger tensed on the trigger.

*Do it now. Before she wakes and turns all the way.*

*Just. Fucking. Do. It.*

His fingers curled around the trigger's metal. He started to squeeze with the slightest of pressure, trying to force himself into action.

He looked at her, tears streaking his cheeks, and whispered, *"I'm so sorry."*

He put the gun closer to her, and then — he dropped the gun on the bed.

He fell to his knees, sobbing.

Ana stopped growling.

For a long moment, Liam watched, waiting for something to happen. He wondered if that was it and she was about to wake as a zombie. If so, could he pull the trigger then?

She started to snore.

Liam, foolish as he knew he was being, took it as a sign that her soul wasn't yet lost to the monster inside. As long as that was true, he couldn't lose hope.

And so he fell asleep.

WHEN HE WOKE, everything was different.

Rays of dusty sunlight spilled into the house through the holes in the boarded windows. The light grazed his cheeks, warming him awake.

He opened his eyes and slowly sat up. He looked over at Ana, heart beating fast, certain she'd be dead or turned.

His body tensed, prepared to roll from harm's way. Ana turned toward him, as if sensing his presence, then slowly blinked her bright eyes — awake, alert, and appearing … happy.

Her cheeks had color and she seemed strong. Her hair

no longer looked dull, but instead almost as if she'd recently washed it.

Even her cheeks, which had looked hollow the night before, appeared fuller.

"Ana?" Liam couldn't believe his eyes.

Impossibly, she laughed. "I feel amazing."

# THIRTY-NINE

# Jonah Lovecraft

JONAH DIDN'T WANT to open his eyes. He just wanted to be back on the ground. This … flying … didn't feel natural.

He had never flown before. Planes were rare. There were only a few known Barrens Flyers, pilots who made their living renting out courier services to the State. Their planes weren't state of the art like those flown near the end of the Old Nation's reign. They looked more antiquated, like those from the early days of flight — rickety machines that had no business in the air.

But Captain Pete assured him, "Twenty-five years and I ain't crashed yet."

Still, sitting in an open cockpit surrounded by clouds, with the wind about to rip off his helmet and goggles, Jonah felt anything but safe.

"Yer gonna miss it if you don't look," Captain Pete shouted over the loud, sputtering engine of the glider plane.

"I don't wanna look! Just land the glider!" Jonah shouted over the loud wind.

"Only chance you'll ever have to see City 1 in all its

glory," Captain Pete yelled back from the pilot's seat as they drew nearer to their destination.

Jonah braced himself, grabbed his seat tight — even though he was belted in and probably couldn't fall out of the glider — and looked down.

Details of City 1 weren't reported on so much as whispered about. No two descriptions ever sounded the same, probably because so few people — people Jonah had met, anyway — had ever actually been to City 1. So far as Jonah knew, most people thought City 1 was just like the other cities, filled with common, working-class people crammed into apartments. While some citizens spoke of large castles or dark spires stretching into the sky, few people outside of City 1 truly knew what it looked like. Sometimes, Geralt appeared on City broadcasts, but such transmissions were always filmed from inside the State's High Tower, so the City itself wasn't visible.

In City 6, transports were all handled through a single depot, and the drivers had even higher clearance than Jonah at City Watch — all personally chosen by Keller.

Due to the nature of urban legends, everyone claimed to know someone — or know someone who knew someone — who had once seen City 1, but Jonah knew for a fact that he did know someone who had seen City 1: Chief Keller, who routinely traveled there for high-level State meetings.

But Keller had only spoken of the City in generalities, and had described it as anything remotely close to the grand spectacle Jonah was looking on now.

Staring down at the City, Jonah realized with a sickening certainty that he'd been wrong. The paradisiacal City 7 promised to winners of the Darwin Games and shown on the broadcasts *wasn't* a lie. It was City 1.

He doubted any winners of the Games actually made

it to City 1 — he knew *he* hadn't been brought there — but the place shown on the broadcasts was real.

Jonah looked on in open-mouthed wonder, staring down onto the sprawling locale he'd seen advertised as City 7 so many times on the Games. The same low and almost decorative Walls along the borders, the same ribbon of luxury with large sparkling pools, sprawling out-of-doors restaurants (rather than the Arcade's cramped food court), wide walkways, and row upon row of spacious living quarters spread over plenty of space. The most shocking thing to Jonah was the sheer amount of green, so rich and in such vast quantities, it looked bright even from the sky.

West of the homes, green grass, and rolling pastures was a long stretch of stunning white beach. A bright blue sea churned on the other side and stretched to the horizon. He had only seen the ocean in movies, and could never have imagined how infinite it seemed in person, or how small he felt in comparison.

After many miles, the homes and green grass areas he recognized from City 7 disappeared. Rolling knolls crashed into large white brick Walls. Behind them, everything was different.

High, gleaming glass towers rose into the sky, unlike anything Jonah had ever seen in real life — though they did look a lot like city skyscrapers he'd seen in movies from the Old Nation. These buildings were shinier, cleaner, and gleaming with everything City 6 was not.

He couldn't imagine the manpower or resources needed to create, let alone maintain, such things. Nor could he fathom what he would see inside the City.

"A thing of beauty, eh?"

"I don't know what to think." Captain Pete turned and winked at Jonah as he turned the glider. "Here's the bumpy part." The tiny engine sputtered as he used a combination of brakes and the rudder to guide the craft toward a long runway stationed just outside the City's northern Walls.

Jonah braced as the glider descended toward the road. The front wheel hit as Captain Pete applied the brakes. Jonah's knuckles were white on either side of the seat. The glider bumped, shook, and rocked as it slowed to a gentle roll before turning into an open hangar marked Hangar 14.

Only after the glider stopped did Jonah finally exhale.

Captain Pete arched over and unbuckled Jonah. The captain clambered out and then helped Jonah from the glider before going to grab his medical bag, which the captain had stored in a compartment in the glider's rear.

Jonah took the bag, wondering if the captain had any idea what was inside it. But no time to dwell as they were met by a young man in a tan jumpsuit. On his chest was a blue tag that read: *City 1* and beneath that, *Danny*.

"Hey, Pete," Danny said.

"Hey, Danny." He handed Danny paperwork that ostensibly detailed Jonah's identity and purpose in the City.

Danny gave the papers a cursory look and shoved them in his pocket. "So, how was the flight?"

"Good. No storms this time."

"Great to hear." Danny smiled ear to ear. "Thought you'd want to know — I asked Joyce to marry me last week. And she said yes."

"Great!" Pete slapped him on the back. "Glad it all worked out."

"Thanks again for the advice." Danny kept grinning.

Jonah felt uncomfortable being part of such a private conversation, and relieved by the soft security. If this were City 6 — not that City 6 had air hangars, all their couriers were trucks — City Watchers would have been all over both pilot and passenger, screening them carefully.

Here they had a guy named Danny, who seemed more interested in chatting than checking Jonah's papers.

Jonah almost had to laugh. But just as they were leaving the hangar, Danny called out to them. "Oh yeah, I need to check your ID!"

Jonah turned, keeping his face friendly and hiding his nerves. He'd been wondering since he left whether the ID would still work. Maybe Marquis had been caught by City Watch and Jonah's ID was no longer a suitable disguise. City Watch might even be looking for him.

Danny grabbed the portable reader from his belt and lifted it to Jonah's wrist.

Danny didn't appear armed, and there were no orbs or people beyond the hangar. If shit went south, he'd have to kill Danny before the guy could sound an alarm. Captain Pete was safe. He knew Jonah wasn't who he said already, and that Sutherland had paid Jonah's fare into the City.

"Okay, sir, you're cleared."

"Thank you." Jonah nodded and smiled in relief.

But it was temporary and artificial seeing as Danny would be dead soon enough, after the infection spread through City 1.

Captain Pete said, "I'm going to walk the doctor out, then I'll come back and tell you a story that'll have you pissing yourself."

They left the hangar and walked back onto the runway. Jonah glanced back to make sure Danny wasn't following them, then said, "Wow. *This* is security in City 1? Anyone can just fly in? And they have *one guy* checking ID?"

"They get a lot of couriers, and many citizens have their own gliders and take them out on safaris. City 1 keeps things low-key for its residents."

Jonah couldn't believe it. "You can't get within a mile

of City 6 without going underground unless you don't mind a City Watch escort."

"City 1 has a large military presence outside and along the eastern Walls, which you didn't see because your eyes were probably closed. They keep all the trouble out so their own people don't have to live in fear."

Jonah laughed. Most citizens inside the Walls in other cities lived under constant terror of both City Watch and its ubiquitous orbs. Here the wealthy must truly live free, without a care in the world.

"You've gotta remember, folks here are the best of the best. They're the State leaders, the brightest scientists, farming and industry leaders, many descendants of Old Nation power. If I were you, I'd try not to think too much about these people and what they have, or it'll depress the hell out of you. Trust me, I've been coming here for years, but I'm a City 4 man, through and through. We don't have anything like this back home."

Jonah shook his head.

Captain Pete led him toward the edge of the runway, reached into his pocket, and pulled out a comm. He tapped out a code, then waited. Finally, he spoke into the device: "Yes, we're here ... okay"

He handed it to Jonah. "The boss wants to talk. You can keep it."

The captain turned and headed back to the hangar without another word. Jonah looked at the com, then brought it to his ear. "Yes?"

"Good, you made it," Sutherland said. "Are you still at the hangars?"

"Yes."

"And you've bid farewell to Captain Pete?"

"Yes."

"Perfect. Now, look around you. Do you see the Pegasus?"

"The what?" The word seemed familiar, but Jonah didn't know where he had heard it, or what it might be.

Sutherland repeated, then clarified: "A Pegasus — a horse with wings."

Jonah looked around and at first saw nothing, then squinted at a sign past the hangars, far on the other side. A blue square with a white circle. In its center, a red horse with wings.

"Yes. I see the Pegasus."

"Great! That's a glider fueling station. City 1 gives its citizens free fuel, and the Pegasus is their sign. Your contact will meet you at the station. You'll know her as soon as you see her, and she'll definitely know you. Good luck."

"Wait! When do I call you next?"

"At the right time." And then Sutherland was gone.

Jonah passed the hangars, then approached the flying red horse — the Pegasus — and the place where his contact supposedly was waiting for him.

He saw four people at the station: a couple, a man filling his glider tank, and a woman at the farthest pump, washing her glider down with a wet rag.

The man who was alone wasn't dressed all that differently from Jonah, who wore casual gray pants and a blue shirt, though the other man's attire seemed like a much higher quality, with creases sharp enough to cut all the meat he was surely so lucky to have. The man from the couple wore clothes that reminded Jonah of suits and ties from the Old Nation, but the fabric seemed thinner and lighter and brighter, a screaming blue for his jacket and two slightly different shades of unnatural yellow for his patterned necktie. The woman on his arm was bedecked in many strips of multicolored fabric that wrapped her body in fuzzy crisscrossing layers. Her hair was bright blonde, and her skin flawless. She was probably the most beautiful woman Jonah had ever seen in real life.

The woman who had been washing her glider looked up at Jonah as he approached. She wore khaki pants and a white button-down shirt. She looked crisp, gorgeous even, with tight chestnut curls sweeping her shoulders just under the blades, but she wasn't a jaw-dropper like the other woman.

She looked up at Jonah and smiled. "You're the flower man, right?"

"Pardon me?"

The woman kept on as if Jonah hadn't pardoned himself. "Sorry I had to cancel yesterday. I thought today would be better because we were both out here and you could tell me all about the treasures you found. Come on, let's walk."

The woman waved her hand in no particular direction, then started walking away from the Pegasus station. After a few steps she pulled something from her pocket and pointed it back at the glider. It chirped as she turned, then started slowly rolling behind her. As they continued walking, Jonah turned to see the glider rounding itself into the hangars and parking in an empty space.

"That's my regular spot," the woman explained.

They walked for another few minutes, past the hangars, to another long building with many doors, each about twenty feet apart. The woman took the same small black box from her pocket and pointed it at the wall between two of the doors. She pressed a button and the wall split at a seam. A door appeared and rolled up from the floor. A sudden bright light illuminated the interior of what appeared to be a small garage with a smaller version of the supply trucks that made runs between cities. It was old and dusty from what looked like a million miles of use.

The woman entered the garage, and Jonah followed her. The door closed automatically behind them. "My name's Maya. And you're Jonah Lovecraft."

"Yes."

"If you get caught, Jonah Lovecraft, I suggest you find a way to kill yourself. They'll torture you until you wish you had."

"You live here, in City 1?"

"I do." Maya nodded.

"What's it like?"

"Better than you think."

"Paradise?"

"Nicer."

"So why are you helping?"

"Maybe one day the world will get to a place in which I'll want to hear reasons for things you do, and I'll have the time to tell you mine. For now, we need to get you into the City proper."

"I'm ready," Jonah replied, trying not to be insulted. "Sutherland said you had a secret way to get inside."

Maya laughed. "He said I had a secret way, did he?"

Jonah thought. "Well, no, I guess he didn't. I guess he said you had *a way.*"

"That sounds more like it."

Without another word, Maya turned from Jonah, went to the truck's cabin, then opened the door and pulled out a change of clothes from the driver's seat. With no regard to Jonah, she started undressing, removing her white shirt and khakis and replacing them with an all-brown jumpsuit with a City courier insignia on the left breast.

She finished dressing, reached inside the truck, then tossed Jonah a matching uniform and spoke as he dressed.

"We need to go through two gated checkpoints, but it shouldn't be hard with our credentials. City Watch here isn't on high alert, so you should be good once we're past the gates."

"What about orbs and such?"

"We don't have many orbs here. A few for emergencies, but for the most part, the City Watch blends in more than it lords over. Most of the citizens here live with blinders on, thinking nobody would ever wish them harm. They can only get hurt when people like me are willing to help." She met his eyes and smiled. "And people like me don't exist. Now get in."

Jonah went to the passenger side and got in. Maya got into the driver's seat, backed out, and the garage door closed behind them. A minute later they were driving on a concrete road, heading for the front gates.

"If they're suspicious of you at all, it will be now, when we're trying to pass through the main gates."

"Great," Jonah said, trying to bury his nerves.

# FORTY

# Adam Lovecraft

ADAM STARED AT MICHAEL, too shocked to stutter.

Michael asked, "So, did you rat on us to your buddy, Keller?"

Adam wished cadets were allowed to carry shock sticks in the street so he could belt Michael on the head. "No! Why would you think that?"

"Are you kidding?" Michael peered down at Adam. "You left in a huff, angry and yelling. Like *we* were the bad guys."

"But you *are* the bad guys!"

Michael wasn't getting it. Most of City Watch's tasks revolved around monitoring, anticipating, and ending Underground activity. Maybe there would be more chances to fix things in the Dark Quarter if there weren't so much time wasted stopping people in the City's way.

Michael shook his head at Adam, practically wagging his finger. "No, *you* still don't get it. They've blinded you."

Keller had already told him to anticipate this, to be wary of Michael's tactics, warned him that his old friend would use all the words he was using right now. It was the way of the serpent, confusing you until you were acting on its behalf.

Adam wished he *had* ratted Michael out when given the chance. But he had chosen friendship over allegiance to the State. Friendship with a terrorist.

"Whatever." Adam turned from Michael and started walking away, not wanting to fight.

"You know I'm right," Michael called out from behind him.

Adam spun back around. "No, I *don't* know you're right, Michael. All I know is that *you* don't get it. From ratting on my sister to hanging out with the Underground, you're obviously the one who's confused, *not me*. I know up from down and right from wrong. I know Municipal from the Edge."

Michael looked back at Adam in surprise. His body swayed back as if Adam's words hung with weight on his body.

"I can't even pretend to get why you think the City's persecuting you, but I don't think you and I will ever see things the same. I don't want to get you into trouble, so … so I don't think we can be friends anymore."

"I can change your mind."

"How?" Adam asked.

"I need you to come with me."

Adam didn't like that. He had just told Michael that they couldn't be friends, and now Michael wanted him to go somewhere, away from the street? If the Underground was willing to kill kids — which they were known to do — and of course they were willing to murder Watchers, maybe they would be willing to off a cadet like Adam who knew at least a few of their faces.

He had endangered himself by going to the first meeting. No way he was willing to go again. Even if Michael wouldn't try to hurt him, he had zero doubt that others in the Underground would love to punish a Whitewasher. "I won't go to a meeting. I can't. I don't want to be around you people anymore. And I won't lie to my superiors. It's best if you and I just stop talking right now."

"Come back to my apartment, Adam. Not for long. I just want to show you something. You'll thank me. I promise."

Adam didn't trust Michael, but he shouldn't say no. If Michael *was* a bad guy, he could stay aware like he was taught in Survival and defend himself. Watchers sometimes had to put themselves in danger. That was the job, and the task that Keller had assigned him.

Sometimes you had to be around bad people to do the right thing.

Maybe he could find out more about what was happening, then report it to Keller and make up for everything he failed to say earlier. If Michael wasn't a bad guy and really *did* have something important to show Adam, then he could be open-minded enough to listen to his friend.

"Okay. But if anything bad happens, we can't be friends anymore."

They started on the few miles or so to Michael's one-bedroom in the Back. Clustered apartments weren't as old as those at the Edge, or as rundown, but they were already on their way to forgotten, two-thirds occupied as the State neatened its ratios and built out better parts of the City. Even with its reduced population, apartments in the Back were small and crammed together.

They passed under an arch that opened into a courtyard behind the fourteen-story building where Michael lived as an orb floated by. Adam made sure to look and make eye contact. If someone was watching, and things went bad, then they could come and save him.

They walked through the rear entrance, climbed seven floors, and stopped just outside of Michael's apartment in the dimly lit hallway. He put a hand on Adam's chest and whispered, "I'll go to the bathroom first. Soon as I come out, you go in after me. Turn on the pad inside — I'll leave it on the sink. Whatever you do, *do not* talk about what you see when you get back in the living room. TVs have eyes, and I mean it. *They watch us.*"

Adam's heart was racing. Something in Michael's tone said he was telling the truth. Or at least he believed he was.

"Who watches us?" Adam asked.

"How can you not know that, Adam? You're *inside*. Don't they tell you the extent of their surveillance? How can you be a part of the system and not even know what they're doing? Don't you see how much worse that makes it?"

Adam whispered back, "What do you think they're doing?"

"There are rooms under the City, large ones, filled with people, all of them staring at feeds. Their only job — all day long — is to keep on watching us."

"How would you even know if that was true?"

"I just know," Michael said.

That was a terrible answer. And Adam would know if something like that was actually happening. Rooms like that would need lots of people. Where were all those people? They sure weren't sharing the dining hall with him and the other cadets. Michael might be right about some things, even a lot of things, but when he was wrong and refused to admit he might be — like right now — he sounded crazy, and that made it hard to believe him about anything.

"Fine," Adam said, not wanting to argue. He had to get inside Michael's apartment, because that was the only way he could get back out on the street, then to the Academy, where he could finally put the night behind him.

Inside, Michael went straight to the kitchen sink, leaving Adam to close the front door. He poured two cups of water and filled them with ice from the fridge. He handed one to Adam, drank from the other until it was empty, then excused himself to the bathroom.

"Be right back," he said.

Adam nodded, sipping from his glass as he looked around Michael's apartment — tiny, but neat. He had been here a few times, and always thought the place seemed sad. Not just because Michael lived in a nearly empty building in the partly abandoned Back, or because it was only one room, a tiny bathroom, a couch, a kitchen table, and a long mat on the floor for a bed, with a trunk at its foot. There were no books, games, plants, or anything to prove that someone lived there.

Michael *did* have a Boxie, and the Boxie made Adam gasp. They weren't technically illegal, but officially, Boxies didn't exist. He'd heard of them plenty. Everyone had. They were small black boxes, preloaded with hundreds and sometimes thousands of movies. You never knew how many movies your Boxie would come with, or what kind they would be. Adam didn't know anyone who actually had a Boxie, but he had known lots of people, even at Chimney Rock, who knew someone who knew someone who did.

Adam wondered why Michael's house seemed so spare. The trunk at the foot of his bed might have some of his stuff, but even that couldn't hold much. Maybe he had his stuff hidden somewhere because he was afraid someone might break into his place and steal his things. Or maybe he was a sad person who found his only joy in the Arcade and hanging with the Underground.

Adam set his glass on the counter and plopped down on the couch. The TV came on, as most TVs were programmed to do when they detected someone.

The TV was recessed into the wall, the same kind that came with every City apartment, exactly the same as the one in Adam's apartment growing up. Even the recesses in the Edge houses were the same size. They only looked different in the high apartments. The Reels were broadcasting weather. Adam wondered if Michael had that set as his favorite channel. He was boring enough.

Adam looked up at the screen, squinting as he wondered again where the camera was. The weather report spilled into the day's Darwin report, perking his interest. Adam hadn't been paying attention to the most recent round at all, at least not live. Of course he couldn't help but hear the latest news among the cadets. It was all some of them wanted to talk about. Adam probably would have watched more if he wasn't spending so much time with Keller.

He supposed he would have to make time for the Games, just to keep up and be able to discuss it with others, but the magic was gone, and Adam suspected it would be forever. Ever since Ana was thrown inside, and killed, the Games made him sick. He was good at pretending they didn't, but they always did. But he held his eyes to the TV now, seeing if this time might be any different.

The video showed an old man — at least sixty — running from three zombies, trying to reach a ladder leading to one of the platforms spread throughout the

Barrens. He somehow managed to reach the ladder and climb to the top. He was about to raise himself to the platform when a fat man with bright red hair sat up on the platform, suddenly revealing himself. He stabbed the old man in his skull, then pushed him down to the zombies below.

The cameras cut to a studio-audience reaction. People were laughing at an old helpless man as he was eaten by zombies as Kirk Kirkman's voice piped over the replay: "Whoops, looks like another player down thanks to sneaky Fat Matt who has somehow made the Final Four! Anyone who bet large on Fat Matt is raking in the winnings. Could he go all the way? Stay tuned, citizens!"

Adam stared at the screen in disgust.

Michael came out of the bathroom, then went to the couch and sat beside Adam, his eyes on the TV. "Did I miss anything?" he asked as if he cared.

"Yeah, it's going to rain tomorrow." Adam stood. "I have to go to the bathroom."

Michael nodded, acting absorbed in the recap. "Thanks for sharing."

Adam stepped into the bathroom and closed the door. He immediately saw the black tablet sitting on the sink. He recognized the kind — a Nova, same kind the cadets from the high apartments usually had. They cost more than twice what the Omegas did, the kind Adam was issued. He wondered where Michael got enough credits for a Nova. The device was worth as much as everything else in his apartment added together … and multiplied twice.

Maybe that's why Michael didn't have anything else in his place? Maybe he used all his credits to buy the best device for all of his entertainment. Maybe he synced it with his Boxie and could see all those movies wherever he went. Maybe Michael wasn't as boring or sad as Adam thought.

Holding the Nova made him nervous. He stared at the screen for a half second, then pressed a sideways triangle with the word *Play*.

The screen flickered with footage recorded by an orb floating over the roof of a tall building where a bunch of scary-looking men were surrounding a guy, and beating the tar out of him with a chain.

It had to be something from the Games, but the setting didn't look like the Barrens, or anywhere in or near City 6, not even the Dark Quarter. The skyline was crammed with buildings, but they were in horrible shape, the worst Adam had ever seen — crumbling and tilting like something from one of the Arcade box games.

The men were launching fists and feet into the fallen man, knocking his body hard enough to make it blur and lurch. Adam couldn't see who the person was or why Michael had insisted that he watch this video. The footage was too grainy and blurry, until the orb dipped lower and the camera became clearer.

The victim came into focus. Adam gasped, nearly dropping the Nova.

Then he stared, without any idea what he was seeing, his heart pounding for a man who couldn't be in danger ... because he was already dead.

Then Adam saw Ana, standing on the edge of the building like she was going to jump.

*When did this happen? Why didn't they show it on the Games?*

Then the orb attacked the men, blasting them into nothingness before hovering down to the rooftop. The footage ended abruptly and a man's voice filled the bathroom.

"This is Mr. X from the Underground, broadcasting

raw footage captured last night: proof that Ana Lovecraft and Liam Harrow are not dead. The City has lied to you yet again. Can't say we're surprised, though."

The video ended, and the play circle popped back up.

Adam swallowed and pressed the triangle to watch the impossible again.

# FORTY-ONE

# Jonah Lovecraft

As THEY APPROACHED the first checkpoint, a booth with a gate and two City Watchers checking vehicles, Jonah's heart started to pound.

Maya looked at him with arched eyebrows, and Jonah realized he was telegraphing his fear.

"Relax. No one inside worries about much of anything. You look like that and we're dead. I'm willing to help, but I don't want to die, so you need to get control of yourself. Think happy thoughts, count backward from one hundred, or do whatever will make you calmer before we hit the checkpoint."

Jonah looked up at the three vehicles ahead of them, dampening his panic as the first one was waved through.

"It's simple," Maya reassured him. "We'll pass through two gates before we're inside. The first checkpoint's purpose is to draw your blood. Just a prick to make sure you're not infected. This takes less than a minute, and you have nothing to worry about. Sutherland isn't stupid, so that means you're clean. The next gate is an X-ray and questions — they just want to make sure there aren't any extra bodies or weapons stashed inside the vehicle. Again, we're good. I'm sure you weren't stupid enough to bring a weapon. If you did, now's the time to tell me. The Watcher at the second gate will ask some questions, specifically about your business in City 1. He may or may not scan your ID chip, depending on his mood. Say nothing unless directly spoken to. You'll have to hand him the medical bag and hope to God that whoever secured it did his job and it passes. The second checkpoint is the only one to worry about, but it will mean death for me and worse for you if we're caught."

The first checkpoint was just as she promised. Jonah lowered his window, felt a tiny prick; then less than a minute later a white light in front of them turned green and the truck was moved forward on the belt toward the next gate, about a dozen truck lengths in front of them.

Jonah saw a trio of trucks leaving the City on the other side, all in a row, one behind the other. He wondered if they had dropped supplies and were returning to their cities empty or if City 1 was sending something out — surely their only export was misery.

"It's showtime. Don't say anything stupid." She sparked the truck and went forward a bit, now that it was off the conveyor and slowly rolling toward the second gate. She lowered her window, laughing like Jonah had just delivered an award-winning punchline.

The Watcher wore a loose-fitting, white-collared shirt, perfectly tailored pants, and a warm smile. The only indication that he was City Watch was the belt with the shock stick hanging loosely from his left hip.

"Hey there, Amy."

"Heya, Percy," Maya said. "I'm so glad to finally get off the road. Can't wait to get a nap. Feel like I'll sleep nine days when I do."

"It's good to see you again. You're the brightest spot of my week so far." The guard smiled, then glanced toward the rear. "What are you bringing this week?"

"Only the latest linens and garments from City 6."

Percy smiled and gestured toward Jonah. "What about him?"

"In addition to him making it hard to drive all the way here from City 6 without peeing on my leg on account of him always cutting up like Dr. Chuckles, Dr. William Baker here is delivering medicine and test samples to Dr. Hollier. His truck died en route from City 6, so I was asked to bring him along. They really ought to spring for some better trucks for the other cities."

Percy nodded. "It's not like they don't have the money."

"Exactly," Maya said with a flirty little wink.

"Is he staying long-term?"

She shook her head. "He'll be leaving with me when I head out, and I'll drop him back in City 6."

"And what are you delivering, sir?" Percy asked Jonah.

"Just some medicine," Maya answered for him. "You'll probably need to see it, right?"

"Yes, please."

"Hey, doc." She nodded at Jonah. "Can you hand that case to Percy?"

His heart pounded as he reached between his legs to grab the bag, then handed it over to the guard. Percy smiled as he pulled it through the window, tipping his head on his way to the small machine just off to the side. He set Jonah's bag onto a belt, which fed it into a machine.

He was carrying poison, but he had no idea what kind or how it acted. The vials looked like medicine to the untrained eye. Unless Percy had some sort of chemical scanner or something to detect poison, Jonah should be okay.

But his heart refused to stop pounding as cold sweat slicked his head.

Percy squinted at the screen, smiled, then pulled bag from scanner, returned to the truck, and handed it back to Maya through the open window.

He nodded at Jonah as she set the bag on the floor between his legs. "Now, I just need to scan you, Dr. Baker."

"Sure thing," Jonah said.

"Can you step out of the truck?"

"Of course." Jonah stepped out as the Watcher came to him and placed the ID scanner over his wrist. The screen showed his credentials, then something flashed.

"Checked at Hangar 014 fifty-nine minutes ago." Percy looked up at Jonah.

"Something wrong?" Jonah said, playing dumb, trying not to look at the other Watcher standing at the gate looking out at the cars behind them, even as he surveyed the situation to plot his escape.

Percy looked at Maya. "Says here he checked into Hangar 14 an hour ago."

She laughed. "Sounds like a glitch."

He glanced down at the screen, then back up at Maya. "I should call over to the hangars."

Jonah glanced at the other Watcher, preparing himself.

He could probably grab Percy's shock stick and use it to stun him, then kill the second Watcher.

Maya looked at Percy with a mischievous smile. "How's your friend, Jocine?"

"I'm sorry?" Percy said, his eyes suddenly wide.

"I asked how Jocine was." Still smiling, her eyes locked onto his.

The other Watcher strolled over, a beefy guy with his hand loose on the shock stick. "Everything okay here?"

Percy looked at Maya nervously, then at the scanner, then to Jonah, and then to his fellow Watcher. He swallowed.

"Yeah, yeah, everything's good. Just catching up with Amy here."

"Speed it up — we've got a line to get through."

Percy met Maya's eyes, and then Jonah's, not disguising his anger. "Y'all have a good trip."

Jonah got back into the truck with a deep exhale as Maya climbed in and sparked the truck forward. Neither spoke until they were well past the gate.

Then Jonah said, "What the hell was that all about?"

"Let's just say it pays to know everyone's weaknesses. Jocine is the other Watcher's wife. She and Percy have been extra friendly lately. You never know when such knowledge might come in handy." She shook her head and turned to him. "You could've told me you were scanned at the hangars."

"I assumed you knew! You're the one who went on with some stupid story about how my truck broke down. If you had just told him I flew in, this wouldn't have been an issue."

"I assumed you'd come by boat like most of the others. Nobody comes in on gliders!"

Jonah tried to calm himself. They were safe, and that's all that mattered. "How does this affect us getting out of here?"

"I don't know. I'm only responsible for getting you *into* the City. Someone else will help you get out. Just tell them what happened."

"Okay." Jonah nodded, then after a long moment he

asked, "Does this ruin your relationship with Percy? Now that you've played your card?"

"I don't think so. But I'll have him killed to be safe."

"Killed?"

"Better safe than sorry. Right?"

"Yeah," Jonah said, not wanting to say what he thought, or willing to worry about one Watcher's fate with all that was at stake.

Another few minutes of driving, then Maya pulled over at an intersection. "This is as far as we go together. Follow this side road west to the market square." She pointed down a sloping path toward a busy outdoors market.

"What am I supposed to do then?"

"I'm assuming someone will meet you, but that's all I was told."

"I don't know why you're helping like this, but I never would have made it inside without you. So, thanks."

"You got it, Lovecraft." She gestured for him to hurry up.

Jonah opened the door and dropped to the road. She pulled away before he could even close the door.

He started walking toward the tented marketplace. Grass along roadside was a brilliant green. He'd seen it from above, but up close, the grass appeared even brighter, and lush, green enough to make him want to cry. Same for the sparkling streets. The asphalt looked like it had been poured the day before. Glass on the tall buildings gleamed in the distance.

Everything seemed so new.

As Jonah made his way into the market square with its large colorful tents and even more colorfully dressed people, he realized how different they were from everyone else he'd ever met. They were almost floating, buoyant without worry, happy to be wherever they were going.

Those who weren't walking stood on mobile platforms, zipping through the market and along every boulevard. Every cobble seemed so perfectly set, Jonah wondered if there was staff to neaten them if they happened to skew.

He entered the first tent fighting his mounting awe. It twitched his mouth at the corners, watered his eyes, made him want to break out in a happy sweat. The tent's interior was one of the most beautiful things he had ever seen. Colorful fabrics were draped behind large pots of orchids, starting in the corners and fanning out along the walls. Pots were stuffed and spilling, like the one City 6 displayed in the square each year on Fertility Day — but that was just one pot, and there were perhaps twenty in this tent alone.

The flowers were decoration, not even what the store was selling. That honor belonged to the abundance of fruit spilling from baskets everywhere around him — on the floor, on top of overturned wooden crates, and along the counter, where a woman brought her small bag of fruit for purchase.

Jonah wanted to feel like he deserved the abundance so he could fit in with everyone else who so obviously did, but in his heart he knew that no one in the world could ever truly deserve so much.

He picked up an apple. It was the most gorgeous piece of fruit he had ever seen: plump and crimson. He drooled, imagining City 1 peaches, then, inspired, wandered the tent until he found some — a giant basket two arms across, piled to the top and crowned with a sign that read, *Bathtub Peaches.*

Jonah sank his teeth into the meat and swallowed the delicious fruit, closing his eyes, rocking his head back and forth before blinking them back open. He wanted to bask in the peach but he had to act like he belonged here. A courier comfortable in City 1 wouldn't be standing around like an idiot gushing over a piece of fruit.

He wandered the tent a bit longer, then went to the front to have his ID chip scanned and charged for the peach before heading back out in search of whoever was looking for him.

Everything was shiny, especially the people. Only after his exposure to their beauty did Jonah realize how truly drab it was behind in City 6. Of course, he *knew* it was dull, but it was one thing to know it and another to live with all the countless blacks, whites, and grays that get trapped in a city made of dreary, lifeless uniforms, chipped cinderblocks, and too many shadows. Citizens in City 1 were dressed in styles that Jonah had never seen, playful patterns and stripes and dots, florals and shapes, even images he recognized from Old Nation movies. Women wore makeup, and their skin was radiant and blemish-free.

Children played games in the middle of the square, rosy-cheeked and waiting their turns. Jonah wondered if they were in school. He tried to remember what day it was and realized that he had no idea. Maybe it wasn't a school day because children here didn't attend. Such a thing was certainly possible in a world turned upside down.

"You're the Hydrangea landscaper?" Jonah heard from behind him.

He turned. A kind-looking man was smiling, his face expectant.

"That's me," Jonah said, the bag in his hand seeming to gain weight.

"Excellent. Then let's get started."

The man started walking.

Jonah fell in step behind him, wondering what else he would see in this strange city.

# FORTY-TWO

# Anastasia Lovecraft

IT WAS hard to believe that just a few days ago Ana had been begging for death. Now she was nearing a reunion with her father in Hydrangea. *If* they could ever find the place.

Ana didn't just feel better. Impossibly, she felt better than she could ever remember feeling before. Healthy, strong, eager.

But Liam was running on fumes. He had carried her, and her burden, setting aside his own needs for too long. Now it was catching up to him. Ana wasn't sure how much longer Liam could keep up. It was only mid-afternoon, but he already looked ready to camp for the night.

He was too proud to admit needing rest. He might also have been scared that if they risked sleeping in the Barrens another night, their luck would run dry and they'd rise in the morning to another Band waiting to attack them.

"It should be here," Ana said. "Are you sure we're in the right place? Maybe we should have turned left at the river instead of right?"

"Positive." He looked bothered, casting his glance

around them at rolling acres of wild hydrangea. "I mean, the flowers are here, so it has to be close ..."

They had been searching for a wall, or sentry towers, or *something* to indicate the village. Two hours later, they'd crossed the entire plot three times each way, hunting for the "patch of brightest blue" they were told to look for.

"It all looks like the brightest fucking blue." Liam was growing more agitated by the minute. About a month before, Ana had suggested that he try cursing less. He had, and his change was immediate and rather remarkable. Ana didn't know if his instant shift was an indication that Liam was capable of shaping habit quickly, or if he cared about her feelings that much. He had barely cursed through their encounter with the Band, even on the rooftop. But now he was back to spitting swears like sunflower seeds.

"There is no brightest blue," came a female voice from behind them.

They turned. A striking woman walked toward them, a rifle slung over her back, accessible but not aimed. She wore thick, metal armored bracelets, bulky but not decorative. They must have some sort of weapon inside them. Although Liam tensed beside her, he left his weapon undrawn — maybe because they were in a field of hydrangea, or perhaps because the woman approached with the rifle still at her back.

Ana whispered, "Think she's a bandit?"

"You ever known one to jabber about the pretty flowers?"

"No, I guess not."

"Looking for the brightest blue keeps you in the patch until you're spotted," the woman explained.

"Then what took you so long?" Liam said. "We've been out here for hours."

"Barely two. We didn't come out because we couldn't.

There are patrols you cannot see. They monitor the Barrens; we monitor them. When it's safe, we show ourselves." To Liam she said, "I'm not a bandit, nor an enemy." Then she turned to Ana and bowed her head. "We are friends, now met."

Even if the woman wasn't a bandit or enemy, she was intimidating to Ana, with jet-black short, spiky hair like a man's, and blazing eyes that looked like they enjoyed a good kill. She seemed almost placid, but with an unsettled serenity that lay just one layer deep, seconds from turning rabid.

Liam stepped in front of Ana, shielding her body with his. Only after he was fully in front of her did she realize that Liam wasn't protecting her from the woman so much as keeping Ana from revealing her wrist.

But she didn't want to hide meekly behind him like a timid child. So she stepped out from behind Liam, bandage on full display. "My name is Anastasia Lovecraft. Sutherland sent for me. I'm supposed to meet my father at Hydrangea."

"Yes, I know who you are, Anastasia. I watched you in the Games." She turned to Liam, her eyes expectant. "And you?"

"Liam Harrow. You missed me in the Games, did ya? And who the hell are you?"

"Are you infected?" She looked down at Ana's wrist, then back up into her eyes, concerned.

Ana nodded.

Liam said, "She's getting better, though."

The woman looked surprised. *"Better?"*

"She was in terrible shape when we left Paradise, close to death just a few nights ago. But after an especially awful night she woke feeling and looking better. The infection had spread almost to her shoulder, but it's retreated and now most of her arm looks normal. It's almost like she's healing or something."

"*Healing*? Impossible. Are you sure she was infected?"

"I think so," Ana said, not sure if she wanted to risk being turned away before getting inside. Oli said Hydrangea was more tolerant of the infected, but she couldn't be sure. "I was bitten by a man we had been traveling with; he turned fast, but I think I'm okay for now. Just tell me what to do and I'll do it. We've come a long way, and I don't know where else to go. We were told that Mr. Sutherland wanted to see me, and that my dad is waiting."

"You have nothing to worry about, Anastasia," she said with a reassuring nod. "Please follow me."

Ana was surprised that the woman didn't ask for their weapons. She didn't see them as a threat, trusted them, or was ordered to bring them in unmolested. The woman didn't look like the type to trust at a blush, so it was likely some combination of the first and last.

They followed her to the far edge of the hydrangeas, where blooms were the dullest blue, then into a clearing. She dipped a hand into her pocket and must have pressed something, because the ground began to shake as a terrible grinding rattled the earth underfoot. A thousand tiny pebbles quivered, then a seam appeared in a long circle around them. The ground rumbled in descent, as it had under Duncan when he saved them from the Games.

Ana stared, awed as the platform lowered them past sewers and tunnels and even deeper underground. She and Liam looked out together as they passed the first level, then the second.

The first had a wide opening that spilled into a long and empty corridor with warm lighting, the second onto a sprawling warehouse where many people worked at long tables, some at machines and some with what looked like hand tools. Others walked the floor in hurried lines. Ana couldn't tell what anyone was doing specifically; they were too far away, but she wanted to know and thought it was probably mechanical work — fixing orbs, perhaps.

"I'm Katrina."

"Hi Katrina. It's nice to meet you. Thanks for helping." Ana shifted on her feet, wondering when they might stop. "Are you taking us to see my dad?"

"Meeting Sutherland is the first thing anyone does in Hydrangea."

The platform stopped on the third level down. They stepped into a tunnel then Katrina pressed a button as she stepped off the platform and sent it grinding back to the top.

"This way." She led them down a long hallway toward a lit door at the end. A man in a dark-blue uniform stood guard in front of it. Like Katrina's garb, it looked more like armor than fabric, and reminded Ana of City Watch.

Katrina nodded at the armored man with a holstered blaster, but said nothing about Liam or Ana or who they were. He returned her nod and opened the door, standing off to the side as he waited for them to step through.

They continued down another hallway. Ana wondered about the size of Hydrangea, and all the secrets hidden behind the rows of doors as they passed them.

"We're here." Katrina turned a knob on her right, not at the hallway's end or in any way marked from the others — a door that might have been described as "one that didn't seem special at all."

Beyond the door was the opposite, the most extraordinary room Ana had ever seen, filled mostly with furniture and textiles in reds and golds, and in more shades than she could have imagined. There were plush chairs and sofas, including what looked to be a throne, with a man standing in front of it.

He smiled at the sight of them, and his large shoulders relaxed. He had reddish scruff on his face and red hair piled onto the top of his head in a top-facing bun. He was the oddest man Ana had ever seen, even without the guns at his chest or the sword on his back.

Liam whispered, "He looks so familiar."

The man spoke before she could ask Liam to clarify.

"Ana Lovecraft and Liam Harrow. I am Sutherland. Welcome to Hydrangea." He held his hands out as he approached them.

Ana had no idea what she expected from Sutherland, but this was nowhere close. Despite his heaving bulk, he broadcast more elegance than any man she had ever met. He oozed charm and manners, but not phony-sounding like Kirk Kirkman. Sutherland's charm seemed both genuine and kind.

Despite their arduous journey, disorientation, and the armored Katrina standing by his side like a personal body-guard, Ana felt an overwhelming sense of relief to have finally arrived. She was about to ask where her father was, but Sutherland distracted her when he looked down and gasped at her arm.

"Oh my! What's this?" He picked up her arm at the wrist and inspected the bandage. "Do you mind?"

"Of course not," Ana said, terrified.

She had no idea what he would do once he found out she was infected, and that she had come into camp knowing it. If he was like Oli, this would be bad.

But he gingerly unwrapped the bandage, allowing the filthy fabric to fall, then peered at her wrist, furrowing his brow and scrunching his nose.

This was the first time Ana had seen her naked wrist in

a while. The skin was dark, and the bite wounds still visible, but her flesh seemed to be healing. Above her elbow, the skin looked normal, save for her most recent sunburn.

Sutherland studied it a while, maybe a minute, before dropping her wrist and looking back at Ana with his eyes full of sorrow. "I'm so sorry, my dear, about your bite. That is a tragedy. But please don't worry. You're in no danger of reprisals. We'll take excellent care of you here and make sure your final days are restful."

"No." Liam surprised her with the defiance in his voice. "These aren't her last days. She's getting better — she's actually healing!"

Sutherland arched his eyebrows and gave him a condescending smile. "And how's that?"

Liam explained that Ana had been on the brink of death, begging him to kill her. His confession of cowardice hit her with a hard wave of sadness. He turned to Ana once done. "Did I get it all right?"

She nodded.

Sutherland looked … interested. "*Fascinating*. This could be truly excellent news … and remarkable timing. We're working on what we hope could be a cure to the zombie virus. We'll have Dr. Oswald and Dr. Liza take a look. Come on, we may as well go and meet them now. Katrina, please lead our new friends to the lab. I'd like to talk on the way."

Sutherland sounded so happy, Ana could picture him jumping up in the air and clicking his heels. She was excited about the cure but more eager to see her dad. She wanted to go to the lab, and to meet Drs. Oswald and Liza, whoever they were, but she wanted to see her father more than anything else in the world.

"Where's my father?" Ana forced the question out, feeling pushier than she wanted to.

They followed Katrina from the room of reds and golds into the hallway.

"Your father will be here soon," Sutherland said. "He's on assignment now."

"*On assignment*," Liam repeated, his voice sharper than Ana cared for. He didn't always have to treat everyone as an enemy, particularly when Sutherland was being so kind. "Doing what?"

"I'm afraid that's confidential, but I can promise you'll be proud, especially you, Ana." Sutherland beamed. "Jonah Lovecraft is doing things to change the world, making history as we speak. Even so, he can't wait to see you. That man lives for nothing else. There will be much to celebrate upon his return."

It was hard to believe Sutherland's message, and of course Liam still seemed skeptical. But Ana felt good. She didn't know if it was because her life seemed to have been spared from Duncan's fate, at least temporarily, or because they were finally below the Barrens and somewhere safe, but she didn't mind that her father wasn't yet there.

She would see him in time. Perhaps the delay was best. She still wasn't sure how she could look him in the eyes after her testimony had sent him to jail.

Ana hadn't yet known the evils of City Watch, or that they had messed with her memories.

Now she hoped he could forgive her.

# FORTY-THREE

# Jonah Lovecraft

JONAH FELT uneasy being passed from person to person —
from Captain Pete to Maya, and now to the mystery man
leading him away from the market and down a fairy-tale
path that cut through a swath of perfectly manicured trees
on either side.

"Why all the shadows?"

The man turned to Jonah and smiled. His features
were almost effeminate, sharp and small, but his walk was
brusque and masculine — perfectly controlled. He looked
around.

"I see few shadows, Mr. Lovecraft. So I'm assuming
you're referring to a pilot who likely left you outside, a
driver who must have brought you in, and now me tending
to your custody?" He smiled politely, waiting for a
response.

Jonah patted his hand on the medical bag's side. "I was
supposed to deliver this and then leave. But now I'm with
my third escort. Can't you just take it and I'll be on my
way?"

Jonah thrust the bag out toward the man, almost violently. "Take it," he repeated, his voice insistent.

He inhaled deeply, straightened his shoulders, smiled at Jonah in a way that made him think the man knew one million secrets, then turned and started walking away.

Jonah had no choice but to follow. When he caught up after a hundred or so strides, the man laughed loudly, like Maya had as she rolled down her window. After catching his breath from the artificial guffaw, he whispered, "Don't do anything aggressive. People are watching. You endanger yourself by existing and endanger me with your proximity. I'm willing to help but won't die by your lack of care."

The man broke from the whisper long enough to issue a louder laugh, then continued, "We have orders and protocol. One loose thread can rip a stitch and ruin the seam. I'm sure you know what happens to the garment after that. Orders and protocol, Mr. Lovecraft, make for stronger thread and tighter stitching."

The man laughed again, even though there was no one around, then led Jonah the remainder of the way down the path, past a group of happy children skipping rope and then a group of chatting people on a picnic, and down to a wide road, freshly paved and at least three times wider than the single vehicle streets inside City 6.

They approached a corner with a lamppost, taller than any Jonah had ever seen. Instead of a light, it held a rectangular computer display. He wondered if it spilled light in the dark. In the daylight the display poured bits of information into a wide grid of letters and numbers that Jonah couldn't make out from where they were walking, though the image did seem to sharpen by the step.

Behind the grid, as if the lamppost were broadcasting specifically for it, was the most beautiful vehicle Jonah could possibly imagine. It wasn't like any car or truck he'd ever seen in person. It was something else, with impossibly shiny black paint. The vehicle's body was wide and sloped in front, rolling forward like the frame was embracing the wheels. The back flared like a woman displaying her backside. City 6 vehicles — all sizes — were metal boxes dropped onto wheels. *This* vehicle looked like a sculpture in the City Museum, or one of the cars he'd seen from the Old Nation movies and pictures.

As they neared the grid, Jonah could see that it was displaying maps, weather, and streaming news with blinking dots and multi-colored lines.

They reached the black vehicle, which looked even more beautiful up close. The vehicle's door opened. The man beside Jonah turned and pointed inside. "Get in. They're waiting for you."

"Why? Why can't you take it? Why do I have to go with one more person?" Jonah looked nervously back at the car, unable to swallow his fright, holding the bag out for the man again, pressing his luck. "I don't like it."

"Everything will be fine, Mr. Lovecraft. I can't promise you one more stop, rules and protocols and such, but I can't imagine you would have more than that, and even if you do, I'm sure it will all be over very soon. Step in the car, close the door, and smile, knowing your duty's been done."

The man smiled like he was selling something, then turned and left Jonah alone, staring at the beautiful car. Like climbing inside a coffin, he got in and closed the heavy door behind him.

"Nice to meet you, Mr. Lovecraft," said a man beside him.

The driver was tall, skinny, and young-looking, beautiful like everyone else. He looked happy from the inside, as if nothing could bother him.

City 1 was supposed to be filled with monsters responsible for the world's misery, but everyone here looked like they wouldn't (and maybe couldn't) hurt a fly. That lie made the omnipresent danger scream louder and the truth that he had no weapons or way to defend himself sit heavy like old food inside him.

"Good to meet you." Jonah smiled and patted the bag. "Do I give this to you?"

The man laughed. "No, that won't be necessary. But I'll get you where you need to go and hardly take a minute of your time on the way. Well, eight and a quarter minutes, to be precise. Ready?"

"Yes," Jonah said.

The vehicle hummed into motion, and Jonah realized the driver wasn't a driver. He sat where the driver normally would, but the vehicle did all the work, keeping pace behind the road's only other vehicle as they drove from one gorgeous scene into another.

Woods gave way to the beach Jonah had spied from the glider. About a minute after Jonah saw water — at what he figured was eight and a quarter minutes after they started — the car hummed to a stop in front of something Jonah had seen only in old movies: an actual house.

The richest people in City 6 lived in the higher apartments. Houses didn't exist. Certainly not anything like what Jonah was staring at. The home was gargantuan, the size of an entire apartment building, but a single sprawling structure, rather than a behemoth chopped into sixty-four boxes per floor. Some of the home's windows looked four stories high; the columns in front were the same size as those at the Capital.

"I suppose you leave me here, and I go in there, right?"

The driver who had done no driving laughed. "Nope, we're going in together."

The man got out of the vehicle. Jonah followed, stepping out onto bright white concrete as a medium-sized wave pounded the shore.

"Follow me," said the man, still impossibly cheery.

He led Jonah through the front doors into what could only be described as a palace. The ceilings were higher than the tall windows, and the staircase was like nothing Jonah had ever seen. Stairs in City 6 were always metal and mostly rusty, except in a few of the newer buildings. The higher apartments were painted routinely, so they didn't look as shabby through the window. The City 1 stairs (at least in this house) were made from some sort of polished stone, rising to meet the second floor with a strip of carpet up the center, so bright white it was like daring dirt to try and sully it, same as the home's ceilings and walls. Color in the room came from ample splashes of art that hung on the walls and accentuated the angular furniture, all of it unusually gorgeous.

They passed the stairs and stepped into a large library on the right. "Now, I leave you," the man said as he opened the door for Jonah. Then he stepped through with a bow of his head. "Thank you, Mr. Lovecraft, for your service."

He ducked out of the way and the door closed behind Jonah.

The room's lone occupant — an ancient man, somehow rich enough to pay for the opulence around him — turned to him with a smile.

Then sounding relieved, he said, "Jonah Lovecraft. I've been waiting forever to meet you."

# FORTY-FOUR

## Adam Lovecraft

Adam clutched the pad tightly to his chest and stepped out from the bathroom, gritting his teeth to keep from slamming the door behind him, again wishing he could carry a shock stick.

"What the hell is this?" he yelled at Michael.

Michael jumped like the couch was on fire, then shoved Adam, hard but not violently, back through the doorway and into the bathroom.

"I told you not say shit in front of the cameras," he whispered as he slammed the door. Then louder: "What do you mean you clogged the toilet? Oh, man, help me fix this before it floods the place!"

Michael had sweat on his brow, and his cheeks had gone pale. His breath was hot and fast. "I said it isn't safe in front of the TV."

"You didn't have to trick me. Why didn't you just tell me what I was going to see? Why did you have to show me like that? What was that, and when is it from? How did you get it?"

"It's new video. Taken the other night. One of our

guys intercepted a transmission from the Barrens. We're not sure who sent it, other than an orb, or who the recipient was."

Adam wasn't sure whether he felt happy or scared. "So Ana's alive? Do you know what happened after the video ended? Did she make it off the roof? Have you heard anything else?"

Adam's questions tumbled from his mouth like one rock pushing the next down a mountain. He had plenty more, but Michael stopped him.

"Calm down, Adam. I'll tell you everything I know, but only if you promise to listen. And trust me. Can you do that, at least for a while?"

"How can I trust you if you wouldn't even tell me what I was going to see?"

"I told you, I couldn't. That's part of trusting me, Adam. I know it's hard to sometimes tell the difference between right and wrong, especially when everything you've been taught is upside down, but that's the first step. Without your confidence we've nowhere to go. So do I have it, or not?"

Adam said nothing.

Michael assumed consent. "We don't know anything more than what you've seen on that video, but that in itself is a lot. The Underground has its eyes and ears waiting for more transmissions. If Ana's alive, we'll know soon — and hopefully where she is."

It was too much to believe, Adam had just started trying and it already hurt. He thought of City Watch, and how they were taught that evidence is subjective. Sometimes people didn't know what they knew, and part of a Watcher's job was to help them remember.

"Can I talk to the people who found this transmission?"

"It doesn't work like that," Michael said. "Besides, there's nothing to say right now. That video was it. All you can do is keep your eyes open, and understand that your world is different than what you think. You're lied to every day. The Academy, City Watch, the State — they all profit when you're in the dark. I keep trying to tell you, keep trying to show you, but you refuse to see."

Adam said nothing.

"Can you see it now? Can you see the truth? They lied about Ana dying. How many other things have they lied to you about?"

"How could they lie about Ana dying? And why? You saw it same as me, she and Liam were dead!"

"No," Michael said. "They showed mangled *remains*. That could have been anyone, it could have been anywhere."

"What do you mean?"

"They make flix, why couldn't they *make* news footage? What's the difference? How would we ever know? How many movies have you seen that take place in the Barrens?"

Adam shrugged. "A lot."

"Exactly. So they shoot that stuff somewhere; it's not live. They could have easily staged Ana's and Liam's deaths."

"But why lie about *that*? Who benefits? The network? The State?"

"The network is the State, and who knows? Maybe it's closure, so one question — Where is Ana Lovecraft? — doesn't lead to too many others. Or maybe just another message letting citizens know not to fuck with the State. They don't want people in the cities to see that Ana and Liam escaped the Games, right? Why give people hope?"

"That doesn't make any sense," Adam said.

"Only because you're still thinking like the old Adam, refusing to see what's in front of your face. If people stand against that system, even if it's as simple as making their own way outside in the Games and not being prisoners to the network, individual freedom could spread like a virus. That's a more terrifying infection than any zombie outbreak for the State."

Adam turned from Michael and looked at the spotted bathroom mirror, staring at his own reflection, feeling enlightened *and* stupid.

He had never been so conflicted. Until recently, most things in his life were a constant. He was happy, so were his parents and Ana. He had no cause to question anything, until he had reason to wonder about absolutely everything. Keller was there to make everything better, to let him know that everything would be okay. But now nothing was okay. If his life was two halves of a whole story, one was a lie.

And one part was dead regardless.

He considered all that Keller had taught him, about ways to be a better Watcher and man. The chief had not only saved Adam from the Chimney Rock bullies, he had been kind to him ever since. He made sure his needs were met, and that he had everything he needed to feel less alone.

Maybe the State *was* lying about Ana, and Keller didn't know. Maybe even he would be surprised to learn this and would help Adam learn what happened.

*There's no way he wouldn't know the truth.*

"Keller's been lying to you since the beginning and has turned you into a puppet for City Watch. Please Adam, *please* tell me you see it now."

It was awful, but undeniable. Adam *did* see it, and the terrible truth made him want to curl into nothing. "Even if everything you say is right — about the network lying, and City Watch grabbing innocent people, about them setting up my dad and sister — that doesn't mean Keller's one of the bad guys. Maybe he's been fooled, just like me."

"He's as corrupt as they come, Adam."

"No he's not." Adam could believe the rest, but he just couldn't make himself see Keller as complicit. "What proof do you have?"

"Proof? Why would I need proof? He's head of City Watch. That's all the proof we need. Do you really need to talk to the Underground again? Hear more horror stories? Oh, the things your buddies do when they go into the Dark Quarter — robbing, raping, murdering."

"Sometimes the good guys have to do bad things," Adam said, clinging to his training. "For the greater good."

Michael turned, laughing loudly with a hand over his mouth. "Is that the sort of horse shit they're feeding you, Adam? Good God. How the hell is robbing, raping, and murdering part of some *greater good*?"

While Adam could *maybe* believe the State had lied about Ana, he couldn't believe that Watchers were doing such awful things in the Quarter. Especially not the last two.

"You said yourself, that you were starting to become disillusioned, right? Why can't you believe what I'm saying? I just showed you video of your sister and Liam, alive. And it *wasn't* made by us, because *we* can't do that. If that doesn't open your eyes, I don't know what will."

Adam returned to the mirror. "Why are you showing me this? Telling me this? What am I supposed to do? Go outside and find Ana in the Barrens?"

"No," Michael said, narrowing his eyes. "You fight."

"Fight?"

"Yes, Adam. Join us."

"Are you crazy? I'm a cadet, I can't join the Underground!"

"That's what makes you perfect, Adam. I can't think of anyone better. You could help us from the inside."

Adam stared, then swallowed the growing knot in his throat.

When the evening started, he'd hoped to discover the truth about Michael. Now he had it, along with an invitation to join the Underground. If Adam was on the clock, then he'd just earned his first bonus.

But the video changed everything, cast doubt on the world he knew.

"Well?" Michael said. "What do you think?"

Adam suddenly knew (in a way that couldn't be doubted, like how the sky sat like a lid on the planet, and that his mom and dad loved him before leaving forever) that everything Michael said was right, and that not helping him would be wrong. "Yes … I'll help you."

"This is perfect," Michael said, louder and more excited-sounding than he likely intended. "When do you want to start?"

"Right now," Adam said, not wanting to give himself a chance to doubt or double back. "What will I have to do?"

"I'm not sure what you're comfortable with, but I know what we need more than anything."

Adam wanted to do whatever that was. He wanted to be a cadet because it made it easier to be the best Watcher. If Adam was going to be in the Underground, he wanted to be best at that too.

"Just tell me what you need."

"We need you to drug Keller."

"Drug the *chief?*"

"The next time the two of you have dinner. It will be easy because he trusts you. I'll give you a stunner; it shoots a paralytic into his blood, along with a jolt of electricity. One shot and he'll have no power over you."

"That won't work." Adam shook his head. "At least not right now."

"Why not?"

"Because he's mad at me. I'm sure he doesn't want to have me over for dinner."

"Do you *know* Keller's mad, or are you guessing?"

"Guessing, but I know."

"Why?"

"Because I stood up for you. When you thought I was ratting you out, I wasn't. Keller asked a bunch of questions, and I lied about the answers, saying I didn't know anything about you being in the Underground. When we finished talking he was short with me and didn't want me around anymore. I could tell by his stare that he knew I was lying."

Adam expected Michael to look upset. Instead, he seemed happy. "That's great!"

"Why is that great?"

"Because this gives you the *perfect* excuse to see him. Tell him you have 'big stuff' to talk about, then ask him if you can meet for dinner at his house, as you don't feel safe talking in public, or even at City Watch. Tell him about me, the Underground, everything else. Set up a mission. It won't matter that you're ratting me out because Keller will be too late to do anything about it. We'll take him somewhere, question him, force him to tell us the truth, and then we'll broadcast that truth to the people."

It seemed like a good idea, if it worked, but Adam wasn't sure. "I don't know. There's no going back if I do this. I'm Underground forever. Maybe I'm too young to hide for the rest of my life. What if he's not alone? Or what if his wife is there?"

Adam didn't want to be a baby or a coward, but drugging Keller seemed stupid. There was no way out if he did that. He would have to sacrifice himself, no matter what. He probably wouldn't have minded before since so little mattered, but Adam wanted to stay alive now that he knew about Ana.

"There's nothing to worry about, Adam. And trust me. Despite the rumors, we never harm innocents. Do this and you won't ever need to go back, or hide. The streets will spill over in revolution, and you'll wake to a new world by morning."

"Will you kill him?" Adam asked.

"No. And we don't even need to hurt him. Though you might want me to once he starts talking."

# FORTY-FIVE

# Dr. Liza Goelle

---

LIZA STARED at Ana's wrist in astonishment.

It was like nothing she had ever seen. If a wound could be beautiful, this one was. Most of the girl's skin was the soft pink of fresh skin, though there was still some faded lavender — barely — where the blackish purple would have flowered under ripped flesh.

Duncan's wound had scabbed like Ana's, but it had taken so much longer, and the slow improvement happened only after Liza had dressed the gash daily. Jonah's daughter and the boy were out in the Barrens for days, yet somehow had managed to reach the second camp better off than when they left the first. Ana had no access to medicine or a doctor, yet she had healed, seemingly entirely on her own.

"This is amazing," Liza said from her seat beside Ana, who was lying on an exam table in one of the medical rooms located across from the main lab on the third level. "I can't believe how much better you look since just two days ago."

Liza had been plenty amazed since her own arrival at

Hydrangea but was most awed by the possibilities present in Ana's blood. And then there was the zombie-cyborg doctor, Oswald, who might help her strain those possibilities into a cure.

She had always hoped to reverse the infection in long-time zombies, despite the odds that their bodies were too far gone for full repair. While the zombies of Old Nation movies were considered reanimated dead, the truth was different: the zombies weren't dead. Rather, they were in a near constant state of dying, and most *should* have been dead, but clung to life, powered by the virus, hungry to spread by any means necessary.

Liza imagined that most people in the Barrens, if cured, would likely die upon healing. Most zombies examined postmortem had brains with severely limited blood flow to all but the most basic parts controlling gross motor function. Even if Liza could cure the long-term infected, they'd likely be vegetables at best. But for the newly infected, and for those not yet infected, she felt genuine hope for both cure and vaccine.

It was still early in the process of experimenting with Ana's blood, and she needed more subjects, but Liza couldn't help but feel encouraged by their prospects. Between Ana and Oswald — who had somehow halted the infection in his own body — stars seemed to be aligning for a breakthrough.

"Do you think I'll be okay?" Ana asked.

"It's still premature, but all evidence points to the virus being in remission." It was so hard to believe that the words still felt odd in her mouth, as if she were a liar for saying them. "I don't want to say you're healed — as far as I know, *healed* is actually impossible with this virus — but your blood is definitely in better shape than Duncan's, both after his initial infection and post treatment."

Liza sighed. This was how it was with science, always a variable or many from the truth. "I wish there were some way I had a sample of your blood from before you began to improve," she said, half to herself, lost in thought.

"What does this all mean?"

"It's too early to say one way or another. Or to know your overall level of infection from the onset to now. I can only monitor what's in front of me. We have to test and measure, mostly wait. Until we know more, it's all speculation."

Liam, standing beside Ana on the other side of the table and holding her hand, asked, "Have you ever seen anyone bitten who only turned a little? This isn't normal, right?"

"I've heard of people immune to the virus. Once their bite is healed, they were fine. But I've never *met* anyone with immunity myself. To my knowledge, nobody in City 6 was immune. And I'm not sure Ana is either. This isn't the standard response to a bite. Typically, a subject isn't affected beyond the regular bite wound, *or* they degrade, and ... never get better. This is ... amazing."

"Why don't you know more? Don't doctors share information?"

"I'm sorry," Ana said, apologizing for Liam with a light punch to the arm.

"It's a legitimate question. The State publishes no data on infection rates. So far as I know, any attempts to find a cure or vaccine have been abandoned by all but those foolish enough to perform unsanctioned experiments."

"Like you?" Ana said with a smile.

"Like me. My only human subject to date was Duncan. And he'd only improved after we treated him with experimental medications."

"Are you going to give me the same medicine?"

"I don't think I need to. I want to see how this plays out untreated."

"So if I'm understanding all of this right," Liam continued, his kind eyes trying to make sense of it all, "it's possible that Ana could get better, and if she does, it's also possible that she could help you to develop a cure?"

*"Maybe."* Liza looked up at Oswald as he entered the exam room.

It was almost a full-time job to stop herself from staring in awe, constantly pretending he wasn't the most amazing (and inspiring) thing she had ever seen.

Oswald examined Ana's arm.

"What do you think?" Liza asked.

He turned his head sideways, examining every inch of her limb. "Looks good."

"I meant what do you think about a cure?"

"Anastasia has me feeling hopeful again." Oswald smiled, though only half of his mouth turned upward. "I can't wait to get some test subjects; that's our next step. The Barrens are full of them, so we'll have more than we need in no time." He turned to Ana. "Your blood could change everything, and we'll know more soon. If a cure can be found, then why can't it be us?"

A cure could tear down the Walls and give humanity a fresh start. It would be easy enough to say that one person was nothing to go on, but *one person* was where everything always started. Cures weren't born, they were discovered. Throughout known history, scientists spent plenty of time looking in the wrong places before stumbling into the right ones.

This *felt* like a breakthrough, and even though Liza had felt such things before, this time she wasn't alone.

Liza would have thought Oswald a genius on sight considering the measures he'd taken to ensure his survival.

She could only imagine the nerves, courage, and raw intelligence it had taken to chop off his own limbs and replace them with bionics. After a few minutes of speaking with him, Liza knew just how special he was. If anyone could find a cure, it would be them, and maybe now.

"So Dr. Goelle," Liam said, "is she gonna live?"

It was obvious how much the boy cared for Jonah's daughter, not just because he was standing close enough to warm her — his every motion seemed articulated for her protection. Ana seemed to like Liam back, but there was something else there too, something she couldn't quite figure out.

Or maybe it was that Ana served as a constant reminder of her father.

Liza felt her eyes getting damp, remembering that once upon a time she swore that his heart beat faster around her, desperately wishing for him to fall into the misdeed she was sure they both wanted.

She had never felt so selfish.

Nor had she wanted to fall for a married man. But she didn't have to have him to herself. Liza would have been fine being his secret, if it meant having some of his attention. She was ashamed to admit that she'd practically thrown herself at him. But he was a good man. As tempted as he may have been, he wouldn't cheat on Molly.

"Why are you looking at me that way?" Ana asked.

Liza turned away, embarrassed. "Because you remind me so much of your father."

Ana blanched. "You know my father?"

Liza nodded. "He's the reason I'm here. He's very brave; you should be very proud."

"How do you know him?"

Liam looked at Liza curiously, a student of the new information.

She turned back to Ana. "We worked together in City 6 a long time ago, when I was doing some work for City Watch. He sneaked into City 6 and asked me to come here, to help find a cure. He can't wait to see you again; it's all he talked about the whole way here, from City 6 to camp."

"I can't believe I'm going to see him. That was all that kept me on our way here. I probably would have turned if I'd known he—"

"That's not true," Liam said. "I wouldn't have let you."

Ana raised her hands and growled. "I would've eaten your face, Harrow, and there wouldn't have been anything you could've done to stop me." He laughed and she added, "You've seen me when I'm hungry."

Liza laughed. Ana reminded her more of Jonah by the moment.

The door opened and Oswald left as Sutherland entered the room with Katrina two steps behind him. "Ladies and gentleman, I'm here for remarkable news. So how is the lovely Anastasia Lovecraft? Quite cured I imagine?"

"Not quite," Liza said. "But maybe someday, and hopefully soon. It does look like she's in excellent shape, and while I can't say for certain that she's in remission since I've no control to compare with, I strongly suspect that she might be."

"That is good news." His entire body seemed to relax. "I am so happy." He turned to Ana. "Does that help make up for the quarantine? Again, I must apologize for that, though I'm sure you understand."

"Of course, and to be honest, I don't mind the quiet at all. I mostly feel like being alone right now, anyway. The only person I really want to be around is Liam, and it's not like I'm quarantined from him."

Ana laughed and looked at Liam. They traded smiles.

"Well, it's a tremendous day for Hydrangea. Katrina, would you please take our newest guests back to their quarters and make sure they get something to eat?"

Katrina nodded at Sutherland and stepped toward Ana.

"Any word from my dad yet?"

"Yes, actually." Sutherland brightened. "Everything is going according to plan. We're waiting to hear more, but it seems your father should arrive on schedule."

Ana smiled and nodded, looking eager yet anxious. Liza could only imagine how desperate she was to finally see her father. She felt the same way.

# FORTY-SIX

# Jonah Lovecraft

THE OLD MAN had endless wrinkles around his eyes and mouth, yet still seemed to have healthy, youthful cheeks. His color was excellent — a warm pink — and while his skin was wrinkled, it wasn't papery.

"How do you know me?" Jonah asked.

"We'll get to that. First," the man smiled as he approached, extending his hand for the bag, "I believe that is for me."

Jonah handed the bag to the man, finally relieved of his obligation.

"Perfect." He looked in the bag and then up at Jonah. "Thank you."

"You're welcome."

"Are you wondering what this is?"

"Not my business." Jonah shook his head. "I was asked to deliver it, and now you have it. That's all I need to know."

He led Jonah to a pair chairs situated on either side of a small circular table. He sat down and looked up at Jonah. "Inside that bag is a cure."

"*A cure?*" he repeated.

"A cure for what ails this world, a solution to the regime's evil ways. Yes," he smiled, "this will most definitely make our blood healthy again."

Jonah didn't want to know any more. He wanted to get out and back to Sutherland's. He didn't care who the man was or how he intended to kill Geralt, nor did Jonah want to know why he had been waiting for so long to meet him.

"You have your cure, now I need to get back. My daughter is waiting."

"Nonsense. Why would you want to go anywhere when *this* is so exciting, here, right now? Do you not open your presents on Nativity?"

He laughed again, then leaned forward, opened the bag, and began to pull out glass vials filled with light-blue liquid. Then he lined them in two neat rows, each with five vials, individually sealed with a cork to hold the toxins inside.

The vials nearly twinkled from light streaming through an ocean-facing window. The old man looked at the vials with enough pride to suggest that he'd filled them himself, or had been waiting forever to see them.

He turned with wet eyes. "I am a big fan, Jonah Lovecraft. Thank you so much for coming to my home. You are a hero. It is a shame that there is no City 7. If anyone has ever deserved to live there, for horrors suffered in the name of his City and under the thumb of this State, it is *you*."

"What are you talking about?"

Ever since meeting Katrina it seemed that the people around Jonah knew more about everything (including him) than he did. He couldn't shake the sense that not only did he know the old man, but that the old man knew him in some way, deeper than the untold number of people across all six cities who had seen him perform in the Games.

"You served City 6 like a man, fulfilled your role with impeccable duty and enviable honor. Then, when the State discovered you were doing your small part to keep the world safe for those standing to suffer most, they set you up for Molly's murder and sent you to die in the Games, offensive as they are. And for what, Jonah? To keep the engines of tyranny running? To keep *him* in power?"

He broke his gaze, returning it to his admiration of the vials, running his fingers along the glass as if waiting for Jonah to speak.

"How do you know they *set me up*? Maybe I did kill her." Jonah felt argumentative for a reason he couldn't explain.

"Well," he said, seeming almost surprised by the question as he looked up, "because I know everything. That's my job. I know that you *technically* killed her, but it wasn't you who programmed the action."

Jonah stood, infuriatingly close to an answer. Egan had sworn that the State had implanted a chip in him. One he assumed had something to do with Molly's death, even if it seemed impossible to fathom a man-made technology that could get him to murder the love of his life, and mother of his children.

"Who programmed it?"

"Please, Mr. Lovecraft, sit." Then, after Jonah sat, "I'll give you one guess."

"Keller?"

"See," the old man smiled, "smart and brave."

"But why the hell would Keller have me kill my wife?"

"You betrayed him by joining the Underground. Keller is a bitter man, particularly since losing his son. He doesn't take kindly to a spy in his nest."

"But why kill Molly?" Jonah felt like he might vomit. "She didn't do anything."

"He wanted to hurt and disgrace you, without the City ever knowing his top Watcher had joined the Underground. But if you need someone to blame beyond Keller, look no further than he who ordered the command."

"Who?" Jonah asked.

"Jack Geralt, of course."

Who the hell was this man?

The old man might have been reading his mind. "My name is Denton Sinclair. And, I'm horrified to admit, I am one of those most responsible for the sad state of your world."

Jonah stared back at him in stunned silence, waiting for him to continue.

"I am nearly two hundred years old ..."

He gave Jonah another long moment to wallow in shock. He needed it; there were rumors of extreme old age in City 1. Jack Geralt was supposed to be nearing that impossible age himself, though no one seemed to know for sure. The State celebrated Jack Geralt Day in honor of his birthday, though his actual date of birth was detailed only as *Before Plague*. But Jonah had never seen anything like this.

"Back in 1975 I was part of a government program called Everlast. We had developed a way for humans to live for hundreds of years. It *sounded* great, but this was at a time when the world's natural resources were nearly depleted. Earth was on the verge of the next world war, prepared to fight over scraps. Why would anyone want to live forever when the world was becoming harder to survive? If we didn't do something, it was only a matter of time before everything was destroyed. So we gathered a tiny percentage of the population, spread out in six underground bunkers in what was then known as the United States of America. Sixteen thousand of the country's best, brightest, and healthiest — those most capable of repopulating a planet primed to thrive. Then, in 1981, we unleashed the virus ... and ended everything."

Jonah stared at the man in horror, couldn't have managed a word, even if he wanted to.

Sinclair continued. "The virus was everywhere. In a matter of days, outbreaks were scattered across the planet. It was a pandemic unlike anything seen before. After the first month, most of the planet was eating itself. The minority who didn't turn were left to fight the final war. Soon enough there was only walking dead outside the bunkers. And just like that, humanity was mostly memory beyond those six bunkers."

"How could you do that?" Jonah finally managed. "How could you murder millions of people?"

With no expression, the old man corrected him. "*Billions.*"

"Why are you telling me this?" he asked, feeling a bad breath from collapsing.

Sinclair stood, went to a shelf with a large paper bag, and brought it back to the table. He pulled out a pair of chambray pants and a crisp white shirt, loose-fitting like Percy's. "I'll need you to put this on. My driver will give you a belt and a shock stick."

Jonah assumed he was being given a City Watch uniform for his exit out of City 1, but his last question still hadn't been answered.

"Why are you telling me all this?" Jonah repeated.

"This is my confession. I don't have much longer, not here in City 1, or anywhere else. Our miracle drug slowed the aging process, but now I'm dying. The original among us, save for Geralt and a few others, are mostly dead. You are here to right what went wrong. Jack Geralt developed the virus. He is the father of the zombies, the architect of death. He must die, and we must bring down this empire I helped to build. This is not the world he promised. America was the land of the free, and home of the brave. Geralt turned it into a mockery, using fear as a prison. Using his Watchers to murder dissent."

Jonah stared, trying to absorb the scope of the old man's story.

"I want to bring down this government, replace it with one by the people, and *for* the people. The men responsible for unleashing the virus all those years ago are still in power, their principles driving the State. I must do my part to end it before I leave. The leaders are gathered at High Tower with some elders from the cities this week. Little do they know that conference will be their last.

"Please, Jonah." Sinclair gestured to the folded clothes. "The uniform."

Jonah put his hand on the impossibly soft fabric. "Let me guess, my ticket out?" But of course he knew that it wasn't.

"You will board the train headed toward the City 1 watchtower. You will walk its length in uniform, slowly releasing the virus by simply pressing a button. Liquid turns to gas, and history is changed. This is a variant of Geralt's original virus; it will spread and destroy everyone in City 1 just as quickly as we wiped out the world."

The old man tapped the glass vials in a row, like keys on a xylophone.

"The hell I will!" Jonah shook his head. "I won't infect innocent people."

Sinclair shook his head, amused but still expectant and saying nothing.

"How do you know it won't spread to the other cities?" Jonah asked. "How do you know you won't destroy the entire world again?" And then he understood. "Oh my God … that's what you *want* to happen …"

"We have some of our best people hidden away underground. They'll restore power once the city falls. They'll kill any remaining zombies, and crush the resistance. Given the Walls and our distance from the other cities, I don't see infection spreading again."

Jonah shook his head and repeated his primary objection. "I won't infect innocent people."

Sinclair turned with a gesture. The wall went from a warm white to full color, filled with a video of Sutherland standing in front of his reds and golds, smiling from his side of the broadcast.

"Hello, Jonah. So sorry that you're on the wrong side of yet more deceit, but I'm afraid I have no other choice. I must lean on you for this one final favor. Please, accept my apology and word that you *will not be harmed*. We've prepared an antidote for you and a select number of people who will aid us in returning City 1 to its former glory."

"*Antidote?*" Jonah repeated. "If you can cure this, then why the hell did you need Dr. Liza?"

"An antidote is not a cure. We've created this variant, which we can better control. We feel close to a cure, but needed Dr. Liza to ensure our success. And now from you, Jonah, we need this one last thing."

"Fuck you, Sutherland. You too, Grandpa."

Sutherland sighed. "I was afraid you'd say that."

He clicked something in his hand and the broadcast cut to Ana sitting beside Liam in a large room, about twice the size of a City Watch holding cell. The room looked comfortable, with neat furniture and full pillows, but a red light above the door proved they were prisoners.

Sutherland returned to the broadcast, with faux sympathy etched on his face. "Yes, Jonah. She is here, and doing quite well … at the moment. I truly hate to do this, but I know what a good man you are, and understand that you might require some nudging. I don't want to be dramatic and detail all the terrible things I could do to your daughter, a smart man like you can imagine."

Jonah tried to reason with the monster. "Why slaughter all of those innocents? Going after those in power will be enough to open the doors to City 1. You're right, this *must* end, power must be returned to the people. But you can't ask me to be responsible for thousands of innocent deaths, not even to save my daughter."

Sutherland frowned. "There *are* no innocents. Every person in City 1 is a direct descendant of the monsters who murdered the world. And each of them deserves to die."

"You're not evil, Sutherland," Jonah argued, needing to believe it. "I've looked into your eyes, and I don't believe you'll kill my daughter."

"Your thinking is small. When safeguarding a species, we must think only in terms of future and past. If you are unwilling to help preserve our future, then you are part of the past and an impediment to all that is coming, Anastasia included. We don't have food to feed what won't be here tomorrow. Besides — there are worse things than killing her."

Sinclair cleared his throat. "You're wasting time, both of you."

So Sutherland concluded his argument. "Fail to do what needs doing and I shall see how many men are interested in a pretty young thing like Ana before she gets a bullet in the skull. I'll make you watch, then we'll still find someone else to deliver the poison."

Jonah felt a sharp puncture at his neck as Sutherland finished his sentence, then turned to see Sinclair holding a needle.

"Enough dillydallying. I have injected you with the antidote. Now you will board the train as instructed, or I will personally see to it that your daughter dies an even harsher death than Molly."

Jonah wanted to take a swing at Sinclair, but he couldn't. They had played him, same as Keller. And now he would follow their orders, like the good little soldier he'd always been.

# FORTY-SEVEN

# Dr. Liza Goelle

LIZA WAS SITTING in the lab, staring into a microscope at a slide with a sample from the latest blood drawn from Ana.

The virus was gone. No sign of it in her blood whatsoever. Oswald stood beside her, smiling to the best of his ability.

"Wow," she said.

Oswald had noticed it first, then brought Liza over to look, seeming more excited than she had ever seen him.

The door suddenly opened, and Sutherland entered. "Well, well, why is everyone so happy?"

"Come and see." Oswald led him to the microscope.

He looked through the lens, then back up at them. "Forgive me, but I'm not sure what I'm looking at."

"It's Ana's blood," Oswald explained. "There's no sign of the virus."

"So, she's cured?" Sutherland asked, his eyes wide.

"I would say so," Oswald said.

Sutherland looked at Liza. "And can we extrapolate this to a cure for the virus? For a vaccine?"

"We had nothing to do with her cure, but I do believe

she holds the key. I'm trying to temper my excitement, but this is highly encouraging. I don't know if it's this lab, Oswald's genius, Katrina, you, or any of this," Liza twirled her finger to indicate all of Hydrangea, "but I've never felt more confident that we're close to a world-changer."

"I imagine it was difficult working in the shadows," Sutherland said. "And lonely, I'm sure. Even disregarding a genius like Dr. Oswald to work alongside you, how much help did you have?"

"I had a few assistants who helped me in the field, but none were doctors, or even medically trained. Just a few members of the Underground I could trust."

Sutherland turned to Oswald. "Are you up to speed? Are you confident you can continue Dr. Goelle's work alone once she returns to City 6?"

"Absolutely." Oswald nodded. "I could start right now."

Liza said, "I do need to take care of a few loose ends, but I would love to come back, perhaps permanently if there's a position for me? I could do so much more great work here."

His face turned blank, charm gone missing. "I'm afraid that's not possible."

"Oh." Liza blinked, confused. "Why not?"

"Because we no longer need you."

"Oh," she said, offended but not wanting to make a scene.

Sutherland drew one of the blasters from under his coat and pointed it at her face. Liza stepped back, suddenly realizing what he meant.

Oswald started to speak as she opened her mouth to scream, but Sutherland's blaster tore through her first.

Liza was dead before she hit the floor.

# FORTY-EIGHT

# Liam Harrow

LIAM WAS INCREASINGLY FEELING like he was swallowing bullshit.

It had been three days since their arrival, and he couldn't help but feel like he and Ana were prisoners beneath the flowers.

Everything was nice. They were taken care of. Comfortable. Safe. Eating better than they had since leaving Paradise. Liam felt rested and strong.

And, according to Oswald, Ana might be the first person cured of the infection.

He should have been happy, but wasn't.

It was probably a childhood spent at the Rock, but the thought of such constant confinement rankled Liam like little else. Even soft, Hydrangea's sheets still felt like shackles.

"You don't see it — at all?" Liam had already asked her the same thing a dozen times, once every couple of hours over the last two days.

"No, I don't see it," Ana answered like always. "At all. I think you're being paranoid. Even if you're right, I don't care, let them keep us prisoner. I'm tired of running, and this is the best life I've had, *we've had*, in a while."

"What if Sutherland is like the witch in *Hansel and Gretel?* Stuffing us fat to serve us at a big feast?"

"Oh please, do you realize how crazy you sound?" Ana laughed at him. "I just want to be happy until my father gets back."

"What if he's not coming?"

"He's coming, Liam. And I wish you'd stop reminding me of how many things could go wrong. I appreciate your concern, I truly do. I know you're looking out for me. And I love that about you, Liam. But let's just enjoy this moment for what it is. My arm is healed."

She held it up as proof, her skin pink like a baby's. "I feel like I could maybe be happy, like *we could be happy*, if you would just stop worrying so much."

She picked up a fat pillow and threw it at him with a giggle.

He finally relented and permitted a smile. "Fine. I'll stop doomsaying and try to lighten up."

After a few beats of silence her excitement returned. "If there really is a cure, and everything works out, do you think we could leave here with my dad and maybe build a life out in the Barrens?"

Then she drew a deep breath and said what she actually meant. "Do you think we could ever have a life … like the one you wanted with Chelle?"

Ana fell silent, her wide-open eyes staring into his, awaiting his response. But Liam didn't know what to think. Of course he wanted that. His obligation to protect Jonah's daughter had turned into more. Maybe it was their shared hell, or nearly losing her a few nights before, but Liam was coming to the startling realization that he was in love with her.

But he couldn't say it. Not now. Not yet.

That would be tempting fate to snatch her away from him. Same as it had done to his baby, and to Chelle. He held her gaze, not wanting to shy away and send the wrong message. He wanted to let her down easy, tell her that she was thinking like a child. But then his mouth surprised him.

"Yes, Anastasia. It's what I want more than anything." His heart and breath had both stopped.

Her cheeks blushed as she looked down. But then she looked back up. Their eyes locked and he thought about how he could stare into them forever, if fate would allow him such fortune.

She moved closer, her lips parting.

But then the door to their quarters clicked and hissed open to shatter the moment as Oswald hurried inside.

He often came to check their blood and ask Ana questions, but only after knocking first. This time the door opened and he barged in like Hydrangea was on fire.

Liam had never seen Oswald without his lab coat. Today he wore some sort of jacket, half fabric with strips of metal and small blinking lights. The mixture of metal and worn fabric reminded Liam of Oswald himself.

"Did you need more blood?" Ana offered her arm.

"I need to talk to you both."

"What?" She looked from Oswald to Liam, her face flinching in worry.

"Go on," Liam prompted him.

Oswald swallowed, his Adam's apple moving up and down the withered and charred tube of his neck. "My jacket will disable the camera, but not for long so I'll need to be quick. If I say the words *thank you* that means I sensed the camera is back online. Just return to normal conversation. Understand?"

Ana looked confused.

"Yes." Liam understood immediately. "Go on."

"You're both in grave danger. Dr. Liza hasn't drawn your blood because she's dead."

Ana gasped.

Liam said, "What?"

"Dead," Oswald repeated. "Sutherland murdered her."

Now Liam gasped.

And Ana said, "What?"

Oswald continued. "Sutherland's not who you think. If someone can cook up a cure to what he's making, he wants that someone dead. Dr. Liza could, so he had to get her here, learn what she knew, then make sure it died with her." His good eye moved to Ana. "You're a bargaining chip for Sutherland to use with your father. Once that no longer has value, you won't either."

"So we need to leave," Liam said.

"No." Oswald shook his head. "We *can't* leave. Not yet."

"Why not?" Ana asked.

"Because we'll have an hour, if we're lucky, before Sutherland would discover that we were gone and send people after us. He has too many people out there. We wouldn't make it to sunrise if we left before dawn."

"What makes you think that he won't kill you anyway?" Ana asked. "Or us?"

"I'm the only one who can manage his vaccine. He needs me alive, at least for now. And he needs you alive as long as I need you alive, which I keep on assuring him that I very much do." He turned to Liam. "And you're alive because of her."

"So what do we do?" Liam asked, sobered from his irresponsible dreaming just minutes before.

"There's not much we *can* do. Your father's in danger, but that will end soon. We'll leave once he returns. I'm confident that Katrina will join us. She too has grown uncomfortable with some of Sutherland's plans."

"What if we take our chances in the Barrens?" Liam asked. "Leave Hydrangea anyway?"

"You would be leaving me here to die," Oswald said. "Sutherland would know I told you. He would kill me, then Katrina to tie every loose end. He'll wait for your father, then execute him the second he enters camp. And the two of you still won't see sunrise."

Liam took Ana's hand. "Just swear that we can leave as soon as Jonah gets here."

"I'll have everything prepared," Oswald promised.

# FORTY-NINE

# Jonah Lovecraft

JONAH HAD ONCE MET with a visitor from City 1 after getting assigned to drive the visitor during his stay behind the Walls. The man had worn a long leather jacket. Something struck Jonah as odd, but he didn't realize what that something was until the third or fourth day of driving the man around. The visitor's jacket was made of real leather, rather than the imitation leather found in City 6. Once he recognized the difference, Jonah couldn't stop noticing it.

He remembered that jacket while standing on the train station platform, waiting for the train's arrival. Like faux leather, he was a sham, walking in a city where he didn't belong. His life, his entire world, was an ugly imitation.

The train pulled into the station, and Jonah entered one of the long cars. Powder-blue doors whooshed closed behind him. The cabin lulled forward with a sound that reminded him of a hovering orb.

Jonah passed many seats with smiling people, their eyes reflecting no worry. They smiled at him, oblivious to his promise of death.

*I can't do this.*

Sinclair chirped at Jonah through an earpiece. He could feel his every move being watched via the train's camera system, ensuring that Jonah live up to his end of the deal.

"Second thoughts are natural, Jonah. You're a good man with a strong conscience, whose life has done much to warp perception. Doubt is expected, but results are still required. I'm sure you don't need a reminder of the inevitable consequences of any unfortunate choices. Keep walking, and press the button ... now, or else your daughter dies."

Jonah put a hand inside his jacket pocket and flipped the cap covering the detonation button. He hovered his thumb, pressing nothing as he looked around at the dozens of people filling the train car — innocents going about their lives heedless of his threat.

He had been to enough crime scenes, including bombings from the Underground when the group was more radical, to know the aftermath of such heinous acts. He'd always wondered what kind of person could do that.

And now he was forced to be that kind of person.

His heart pounded, his throat tightened, and his legs began to tremble. He hadn't been this nervous since his first time sleeping with Molly.

Jonah noticed someone looking at him — a small girl, around six or so. She wore a pretty blue dress, formal, with a matching bow in her hair. Her mother (he assumed) sat beside her, typing into some sort of small rectangular piece of glass, with graphics similar to those broadcasted by the lamppost.

The girl's large brown eyes met his. He thought of how Ana used to look at him, back when he was the man who could do no wrong.

Before he murdered Molly. Before he failed her. Before he wasted a train of innocents, and likely, a city.

*I can't kill this child. Or any of these people.*

But if he didn't, Sutherland and his new cult *would* kill Ana. Hundreds — thousands — of lives to his precious one.

The girl smiled and cracked his heart. He looked away, walked past her two more rows, and then pressed the button.

Jonah couldn't tell for certain if the poison was being released or not. He kept walking, passing by the soon-to-be-poisoned, forcing himself to stare in their eyes.

He passed through the first car and entered into the next, continuing his death march, meeting the eyes of those he was murdering, even though they had done nothing wrong.

People who hadn't chosen a side in this war, let alone known they were in one. People who were probably guilty only of being born into City 1's seat of power by the sea. Sutherland could justify the citizens' guilt by saying they were somehow culpable for living here and doing nothing to rise against their leaders. But that was radicalized bullshit.

Not everything was so black and white. Most people, even people who lived in the "evil empire," were most likely average citizens living their lives, taking care of their families, and waking up each morning to do it all again.

They weren't *guilty*. But that didn't matter now. They were still being sentenced by a coward, ordered to death by a committee of weaklings.

And perhaps he was the biggest coward of all, knowing how wrong this was even as he sentenced these passengers to death.

He stepped into the next car, spreading death with a false indifference.

Three cars from the end of the train, he ran into another Watcher — dressed exactly like him, though clearly more comfortable.

He looked up at Jonah, smiled as if confused, perhaps wondering why there were two of them on one train.

Jonah started to turn around, heart racing, expecting to be outed. He was seconds from discovery, a minute from death.

"Hey, you must be new. I'm surprised they put us both on shift, especially without introducing us." The man laughed and held his hand out for Jonah. "They sure do some funny things sometimes! I'm Andy, good to meet you."

In Jonah's ear: "This man is a threat, eliminate him."

"No," Jonah said quietly.

"Pardon me?" Andy the Watcher asked.

"Nothing." Jonah smiled awkwardly while trying to pass. Again in his ear, but louder, more insistent: "Don't be a fool, Jonah. This man is dead already. Do your job and finish him, then go to the rear car, tell the conductor to slow down, and jump from the train."

Jonah ran instead.

"Hey!" the Watcher called out.

He raced through the doors and into the next car, people turning to look as he tore through the train without stopping.

"Hey!" the Watcher called out again, his boots pounding on the metal floor behind Jonah.

Jonah raced ahead, not knowing what the hell he was going to do. He couldn't jump to instant death and still had to live long enough to ensure that Sutherland kept up with his part of the deal and not harm Ana.

As he bolted into the next car, a large man was making his way toward him, headed either to the bathroom or making a return to his seat. The aisle was too narrow, and the Watcher too close behind, his footsteps pounding a few feet away.

He leapt at the man blocking the aisle then threw him into the coming Watcher, buying himself a few seconds as he pushed through the next doors.

"What's happening?" asked Sinclair in his ear. "The camera feed is stuttering."

"I'm running!" Jonah shouted.

An arc of blue light flashed by, crashing into the roof above, sending fractured, burnt metal chips flying at him. He reached into his holster, rolled to the ground, and came up aiming at his pursuer, squeezing a shot as he did.

He missed, blasting a wide hole in an elderly woman wearing a garish orange-and-yellow dress. He corrected his aim and pulled the trigger twice, hitting the Watcher once in the knee, and a second time in the chest.

He screamed and fell, moments from death.

The old woman in the dress looked down, mouth agape, eyes widening at her incinerated chest as the life drained from her slumped-over body.

A screaming alarm filled the car, with a repetitive, deafening bray — a hunter orb zipping through the aisle in the car behind him, turning its eyes on the passengers. He stared at the orb through two sets of windows.

He had to move quickly before it spotted him. His blaster was no match for the orb, unless he managed to land the luckiest shot of his life before getting vaporized.

He kept moving forward, smashed through the next set of doors, pushed a woman out of his way, apologized with a grunt, then kept on into the next car, racing toward the train's rear.

*What now?* He had planned on ordering the conductor in the rear car to slow enough so he could jump, but if the orb sensed the train slowing or spotted Jonah about to leap, it would chase him down and leave him dead. In the open land outside the train, he would last only seconds.

He kept moving forward, glancing back at the orb, scanning people as it hovered through the car. He saw a man pointing at Jonah, directing the orb toward him.

He pushed through the next set of doors, then saw that the doors into the car ahead were already open. Two people stood in the threshold. A young man in a suit, and a second man, older and dressed in casual, colorful clothes. The older man had wild eyes. He launched forward, biting the suited man in his neck.

The victim screamed as the infected tore a chunk from his throat and swallowed. Behind them, pandemonium — more infected.

*Shit!* Panic filled the car as the situation seemed to dawn on the passengers all in unison. But Jonah couldn't turn back. He'd rather take his chance rushing through the confusion of zombies than risk facing the orb.

There was a mad scramble toward the door to the rear car, stopping his progress dead.

"Back!" Jonah screamed, shoving his blaster in a man's face.

He was too panicked to recognize the threat and pushed Jonah aside before he could squeeze off a shot. His blaster fell to the floor as people stampeded toward the rear, over both Jonah and his gun.

He was buried in legs, arms, and raining bodies. Shrieks filled the air.

Pain exploded through him — limbs, ribs, and head — everything felt battered. He tried to stand, crawl into the safety of the seat to his left, but was shoved down by the mass of people clawing and climbing toward the exit.

Then, new screams. And a worse sound: Jonah could hear the orb vaporizing the poor souls who'd run for safety in the car behind him.

He lifted his head, looked to the seat, and started crawling out of the way. *Too late.* Passengers who had fled the car began pouring back in, trampling Jonah, as they attempted to escape the orb.

Zombies in front, an orb behind, and dozens of scared people on top of him.

His world was pure chaos, his heart racing as fast as the train barreling down the tracks. He expected the orb to catch him at any second.

He had to stand.

The sound of vaporized humans was a devil's symphony behind him.

Pinned to his spot, Jonah looked up to see a woman coming through the doors at the car's front — the little girl's mother, screaming as she tried to pull something off her back.

It was the girl, holding tight, howling as she gnashed at her mother's face, trying to eat her. She bit into her mother's cheek, ripping a chunk away with a furious growl.

Mom screamed and spun, swinging the girl to face her, eyes wet and afraid, her scream desperate.

She raced forward into the row and smashed the back of the girl's head against the glass. The girl screamed. Mom smashed again, repeatedly, until the girl finally fell limp in her arms.

The woman cried out in anguish as Jonah's heart broke, again.

A second later, she was dragged down by yet another infected. A woman fell down in front of him, then stood and kept running until she froze in front of her zombie-filled path.

She looked back and forth, then crawled into the row opposite Jonah and fell to the floor, trying to hide from both the zombies and the approaching orb.

More screams from behind, hot blood and ashes splashing everyone unfortunate enough to be in its path.

Jonah had an idea. He managed to twist himself around and tried to stand.

Another man stepped over him.

He grabbed hold of the man's legs and wrestled him to the floor, pulling him into a choke hold and down for cover in front of the seat.

The man screamed, writhing as he tried to push Jonah away.

"Stop screaming!" Jonah yelled, choking him tighter. "I'm saving you!"

In the aisle, a woman racing by was reduced to her molecules. The orb was attacking anyone and everyone it saw as a threat — anyone running and screaming.

She vanished in a rain of ashen blood.

The man cried out, shaking, trying to break free as her remains spattered around and over them.

Jonah held tight as the orb peered through the open doors and hovered above them. It looked ahead, completely missing them — for the moment.

The woman across the way glanced up at them, shaking as she whimpered.

The orb spun toward her and fired a blast, vaporizing the upper half of her body. Jonah held his hand tight over the man's mouth, hard enough to break his jaw as he whispered in his ear, "*Shut up, shut up, shut up.*"

The orb moved forward and fired, though Jonah couldn't

see the targets from under the man. He heard more blasts, screams, and the sounds of fallen bodies until the orb finally pushed its way through the zombies and into the next car.

Jonah released the man, who jumped off him and ran toward the rear cars.

"Destroy the orb," Sinclair screamed in his ear. The camera feed must have started working again, and Jonah realized the problem: *if the orb killed all the infected, the plan would fail.*

"How?" Jonah cried out.

"There's a jammer in your belt."

"Why the fuck didn't you tell me that?" Jonah screamed as he stood, wiping the blood, ashes, and grime from his uniform.

He walked forward as fast as he could, grabbing the jammer and holding it, same as he'd held the trigger for the poison device only moments before.

He pushed into the car and saw the orb still slaughtering people inside, with no discernment between the infected and uninfected.

Jonah pressed the button and the orb's lights went dark and it fell with a heavy clang.

"Now get off the train!" Sinclair screamed at him. "Quick!"

"How?"

"Head out of the rear car and climb the ladder to the top of the train. You will reach a bridge in about two minutes. There you will jump into a river below. Follow that north until it turns, and you will find your way out of the City; we'll have someone pick you up and return you to Hydrangea."

Jonah raced through the cars until he found his blaster, retrieved it from the floor, then turned around and raced past the cars of corpses to the rear of the train, where the orb had not yet fired on passengers.

He pushed and shoved his way past frightened people blocking aisles, staring ahead and trying to see what was happening.

"City Watch, out of the way!" Jonah yelled, making his way to the rear.

He stopped short at the final car. It was packed with the infected feeding on not-yet-infected, maybe immune. The conductor leaped at him, mouth open and snarling.

He fired into the man's chest, sending him back, taking five people with him. Jonah used the moment to scramble over the fallen before they had a chance to regroup and recognize him as fresh meat. He made his way over the pile and was three feet from the rear door of the train.

Someone grabbed Jonah's arm and yanked the gun from his grip. He turned to see an uninfected woman grabbing him, begging for his help.

He looked down, past her scared eyes and wide-open mouth to the zombie behind her, holding onto her legs and tearing into her thigh.

There was nothing Jonah could do beyond shaking her loose and vaulting ahead. He reached the back door, then pressed through it into the whipping wind outside. The bridge was quickly approaching and past that, a cluster of towers — what looked like City 1's beautiful beating heart.

And the train was an arrow flying toward it.

Jonah grabbed an iron rung and started to climb, clawing to the top one rung at a time as the angry wind beat on his back and threatened to yank him down to the railing.

He nearly fell once — sending his heart up his throat like vomit — and then again, two rungs from the top. The second time he was sure he was dead.

But Jonah reached the zenith just as the train whooshed onto the bridge. There was too much wind and they were going too fast. He couldn't stand.

Jonah thought of everything that had happened to him. Injustice filled him with enough fury to find his feet. He pushed hard against the wind until he was upright, trembling for a few do-or-die moments before the end of the bridge forced him to jump.

He leapt.

The seconds were long as he fell through the cold air, then felt the water blasting him as he sliced into the river, praying he wouldn't smash into a rock.

He plunged deep and stayed under, swimming for as long as possible before gliding to the surface, grabbing a lungful of air, then diving back down below.

The water was a kiss on his skin. He felt clean, washed. Renewed. Almost hopeful. He didn't know what to do next, but the worst of this was over. He had gone inside the City 1 Walls and done what he never could have expected by becoming the monster he was painted as prior to exile.

He had finished the job he was coerced into.

Now he could find Ana, then hopefully Adam after that. He was instructed to follow the river north to his rendezvous. Jonah wondered if there would really be one. They would probably just kill him. If allowed to live, then he would have to secure Ana's safety by making sure that Sutherland was dead.

Jonah estimated two hours in the water when the river finally turned, and he pulled himself up onto a bank to feel his pruned skin baking in an early afternoon sun.

He had no idea where he was in relation to the hangar but figured if nobody showed up, he'd find his way to the coast and navigate back into the City, then secure a vehicle, assuming he could get in safely.

He made it four steps before the hair on his neck was standing. He heard the first orb before he saw. Another seven crowded his view a second later.

The device Jonah had used to cripple the orbs was gone, lost along the way. Before he could react or get his hands in the air, something flew from the closest orb, right into his neck, stinging like an injection.

Then the orb spoke: "You are under arrest by authority of City Watch, Jonah Lovecraft. You've been implanted with an explosive. If you do not follow and stay within range, the implant will be detonated and your body will be blown to pieces. There is no disarming the explosive."

The lead orb hovered ahead of the rest, ushering Jonah from the bank.

He had no choice but to follow, a prisoner shackled to an explosive leash.

FIFTY

# Adam Lovecraft

KELLER SOUNDED happy to hear from Adam, inviting him over as soon as he called. Jacqueline was out with her knitting circle and the chief was only having leftovers, but if Adam didn't mind, he was welcome to join him for dinner. That sounded perfect to Adam ... and Michael.

Michael gave Adam a stunner that sent the drug through a long, slender black-and-purple tube. He had to aim the skinny metal cylinder, then squeeze from its rounded end. Electricity shot through the tube, and if well aimed into a person's body, a single dose could get a victim twitching for half an hour. The device was good for two shots. Even if Adam missed Keller's skin with the drug, the electric charge would still paralyze him long enough for Adam to get a second shot into his skin.

He was scared, even though the plan was simple: Adam was supposed to wait for the perfect opportunity. When Keller's back was turned, and Adam thought he had enough time to draw the tube and squeeze, he was supposed to aim at the back of his neck. Then Adam would call Michael, waiting with a few members of the Underground two blocks outside the high apartments.

The door opened before he could knock. Keller practically yanked him inside. He seemed insistent, not mad. Maybe upset.

He released Adam's wrist and kept walking, leading him through the apartment to his study. Keller stepped to the side at the door, gesturing for Adam to go first, then entering the study behind him. He pressed something on his desk and the wall screen lit to life.

"You need to see this."

Footage started in the middle of something, and that something was awful. There were large seats, two per side each row, running down what looked like a long hallway. It had to be a train, though although Adam had only seen them on Old Nation movies.

Carnage in the train. Men, women, and children in a mass of torn flesh, blood, and chewing. Eating one another alive, tearing at one another.

"What is this?" Adam couldn't believe his eyes and already wished he could forget what he was seeing.

"This is in City 1. From earlier today. This footage is only a few hours old, and top secret at the moment."

"Oh my ..." Adam felt weak in the knees.

"As far as the world is concerned, you've seen the worst. As for your personal world, Adam, I'm afraid that's yet to come."

Adam started to sweat. He couldn't imagine what might still be coming.

Keller swiped a finger and fast-forwarded the video to a man escaping the chaos. He wore a disguise, but it wasn't enough to fool his son, or the man's former commanding officer.

He said what Adam knew was true. "Your father committed this atrocity."

"No." Adam started to cry. "No, no, no! I thought he was in City 7!"

Keller's face seemed somehow hollow, whiter than usual. His beak of a nose was sharper and his face uglier. He seemed … worried.

"I've no idea what happened, or why. But your father showed up in City 1 late this morning, unannounced and unexpected. They say he slipped in beneath the City like a scurrying rat, killing hundreds on a train by unleashing some sort of weaponized virus. It looks like he was trying to bring down the State. Fortunately, he failed. City 1 is fine, and your father is in custody."

"This is a lie!" Adam screamed. "I don't believe it!"

"It's on video. You can't make up video."

"Oh, yeah, what about my sister?"

The chief's face grew even uglier. "*What* are you talking about?"

"The network showed her dead, but she and Liam are *both* alive! The State's creating news, just like they create movies and instructionals."

"What are you talking about?"

"Don't play stupid," Adam said, getting angrier. "I deserve the truth!"

Keller's pale face turned red and blotchy. He was trying to hold his composure as the video of Adam's father unleashing a contagion into a crowded train restarted from the beginning behind him.

"What are you going on about, Adam? I have no idea. *Where* did you see your sister? *Who* is telling you such lies?"

Adam had his answer, but it wasn't what Keller wanted to hear. He reached into his pocket, grabbed the stunner, aimed it at the chief's face, then squeezed the rounded bottom.

A bolt of energy flew from the tube into Keller's neck. He fell to the floor twitching, staring up at Adam with a *why?*, his eyes broadened by shock.

"Adam," his voice rattled. It seemed like Keller's mouth was the only thing he could move in his otherwise paralyzed body. "What are you doing? Please, don't do this."

The *please* sounded like it tore something inside him.

Adam said, "I won't let you lie to me anymore. You *owe me* the truth. You have to tell me now, once and for all." He felt a welling rage inside him. It felt good to add, "You need to stop fucking lying to me!"

His face relaxed. His mouth moved as if ready to speak. The rest of him was as still as a statue. "You're making a mistake. You can't believe your friends, Adam. They're not good people. You know this. Remember the insidiousness? The cancer? *This* is what got into your father, this is what caused him to kill your mother, then to ... to commit today's unspeakable act. Now I'm afraid the insidiousness has infected *you*."

Keller looked like he might cry. His voice was desperate. If Adam didn't know better — if he didn't finally realize that the chief had been manipulating him since day one, just as Michael had said — he might think the man was genuinely concerned about his salvation.

Keller continued, struggling through each word, "I can't believe you would do this ... it's a betrayal of the worst sort. Worse than what your father did because your wrongs have been committed after every kindness was extended to you, every measure taken to ensure your needs are met and future provided for. You're like a son to me, Adam."

"If I'm like a son, then tell me the truth."

Adam kneeled in front of Keller, feeling heavy and horrible and conflicted. His eyes were watery, sore, and (Adam was sure) red. He wanted to blink, but they burned too much. He couldn't cry because there was nothing left inside him, and not a single good feeling for Keller.

His newest lie — showing Adam his father on the train — had drowned his feelings in blood and erased any remaining nice thoughts Adam might have held for the chief.

Keller said nothing, so Adam screamed for him to speak. When he remained silent, Adam shot him with the stunner again, just to see his upper half twitch in shock and keep his lower half frozen. Keller stayed silent, so Adam pulled out his comm.

"Who are you calling?"

"The Underground. I might not be able to get you talking, but I'm sure they can."

"Please don't do this. Set down the comm and we'll talk this out. You don't know what you're doing, and you can't comprehend the consequences of your actions. You're about to make a huge mistake, Adam. *The biggest.* This will ruin the rest of your life. There will be no going back."

Every word from Keller's mouth was a lie, born to confuse or manipulate him. His words were strings at Adam's heart but not enough to drive his murder.

"I don't know if your sister's alive, and it would shock me if she is — how could they do such a thing when we all saw her body? — but *if* she is, and something bad happens to me, you'll never find her. Let me help you, Adam. I *want* to help you. But my help starts with you doing the right thing, like you've *always* done. Do that now, Adam. The right thing. It's what you *want* to do. I'll gladly suffer consequences for my actions, but I can't stand to see you suffer for yours."

"Wow, you're great with this nice guy act," Adam said, tears streaming his face. "And you know what? I *almost* believe you."

He turned away from Keller and called Michael.

"You're going to regret this!"

Adam ignored him, told Michael to hurry, then nervously paced for five minutes until the intercom rang and he buzzed Michael up.

Two minutes later, Adam opened the door to eight masked men storming into Keller's apartment. He wondered how masked members of the Underground could walk high apartment halls in a building where Chief of City Watch lived without worry of reprisal, and realized that the Underground must be larger than he had imagined, and that maybe they had someone on the inside of the high apartments.

And if that was true, maybe there really would be revolution in the streets.

Adam knew which of the masked men was Michael, but did nothing to reveal his identity. The leader was in front, dressed head to toe in black, standing in front of the slightly shorter Michael.

The leader said, "Well, well, well, if it isn't Chief Fucking Keller."

Keller glared at Adam, shaking his head.

"Don't look at him." The leader grabbed Keller by his collar and hoisted him to a sitting position in the chair.

Keller spat, right at the man's face.

The leader balled his gloved fist and swung so hard he knocked Keller to the floor. The leader leapt on him, choking Keller until his face turned purple.

"No!" barked one of the Underground. "We want him alive."

The leader got off of Keller, laughing.

To Adam's surprise, Keller started laughing back. Lying there, helpless on the ground, the chief had the balls to guffaw at a room full of enemies.

"I feel sorry for everyone in this room. Yes, including you, Adam. Everyone in my home right now is a dead man, a worthless pile of shit not fit for the Underground. You're vermin, each of you. And you will all die, either in front of a cheering crowd, or right here and now where no one will mourn you. Do you have a preference? I've learned in my years as the man running this City, sometimes it is best to get the worst over with so the rest of your day will go better."

Keller moved his eyes across the room seeming to look through the men's masks, one at a time. "Which one of you bastards planted the bomb that killed my son?"

The leader stepped forward, raising his fist as if to shut Keller up. "I've no idea who killed your son, *chief*, but whoever did is a national fucking hero."

Adam felt a chill. Now Keller would get really angry. And even though he was the one paralyzed, and there were many guns aimed at his body, he still somehow seemed in charge.

"Are you so cowardly that you can't show me your face? Are you the leader of weaklings and cowards?"

"There are no leaders in our group. We are one: the Underground."

"It's cute when children play games they can't even conceive." Keller smiled and met Adam's eyes, sending a terrible chill through Adam.

"Alert 717!" Keller yelled. "Repeat, Alert 717!"

"What the fuck does that mean?" the leader screamed at Adam.

"I have no idea!" He looked back and forth with the others. From another room in the back of the house, they heard the unmistakable robotic voice of a hunter orb coming to life, saying, *Stop intruders! Stop intruders!*

He ran toward the door, along with everyone else, Michael and the leader included. Metal plates slammed over the windows and door before they reached them.

The orb whirred into the living room, probably from Keller's bedroom. It vaporized the leader first, Michael a half second later.

Adam screamed, ran to the kitchen, and hid behind the sink as the orb kept firing on the Underground members.

He fell to the floor, heart pounding in his chest, breath rapid, and hairs on end. He planted his body on the floor, listening as the men screamed before being vaporized to ash.

Then there was silence, save for the orb's whirring.

He lay still, eyes closed, afraid to do anything. Afraid to do nothing.

The silence was finally splintered by Keller's hysterical laughter. "Oh man, did you pick the wrong side, Adam!"

"I'm sorry! I'm sorry."

The hunter orb whirred into the kitchen.

Adam opened his eyes and looked up as it spun to a stop just above him — hovering, humming, seconds from firing.

"Please!" Adam screamed.

A high-pitched whistling came from the orb, charging its energy.

He wanted to run, dodge, something, anything. But he was as paralyzed as Keller.

"Echo 7, stop. Echo 7, stop." The orb continued to

hover, but the whistling sound withered to nothing. "I am so disappointed."

Adam could hear the man struggling to stand. The paralysis had worn off.

He heard Keller lurch forward, one step at a time, as if every step took all of his energy. Either the poison wasn't as effective as it was supposed to be, or the man was incredibly resilient.

He spoke through labored breathes. "I ... never saw this ... coming. I considered you a son, Adam, and ... allowed that affection to blind me."

"I'm so sorry," Adam said, daring to stand, seeing Keller approaching but unable to meet his eyes.

"I should have known better. You are, after all ... your father's son."

Adam finally met his cold, staring eyes as the man took another two steps forward.

"Once the cancer is in you, it *becomes* a part of you. And it stays there ... forever. Like it did with your father. There's no saving you, Adam. You're gone now. Forever. Just like my son."

"Please don't!"

"Echo 7," Keller said. "Stun."

Then the orb shot Adam.

# FIFTY-ONE

# Anastasia Lovecraft

ANA AND LIAM had been in Hydrangea for four days. Still, her father hadn't shown. She wished Oswald had never said a word. Never interrupted what Ana thought was her best ever moment with Liam — a spark they'd not rekindled since, no matter how many hours she'd wished for it.

She wondered how many more times the world could be turned upside down before she finally stopped believing in good things altogether. A mind could only take so many tumbles before the softer parts tore and everything inside became something else.

Ana was careful not to let Sutherland know she was on to him about Liza or her father. She let him think he was charming. If he knew Ana had unearthed his secret, she'd be dead along with Oswald, Liam, and her father. But it had been four days, and now Ana thought she was safe in asking where Jonah was.

She asked Sutherland if they could talk.

"Of course. How about we do it during dinner," he said, inviting them to their largest meal at Hydrangea so far, with a giant turkey as the centerpiece.

A private spread, just Sutherland, Oswald, Liam, and Ana. Plus four servant women who heeled to his steady commands.

"I want to know where my father is," Ana said, edging the anger from her voice. Liam, sitting beside her, put his hand on hers under the table, squeezing her fingers. "Have you heard anything? Do you have any idea where he is?"

Sutherland looked down at his plate, studied the beast-sized leg, then glanced back up with sad eyes. "Yes, but the news is unfortunate. I was hoping you'd wait a little longer to ask, just in case better news came in."

Ana felt a cold chill. "What?"

"I have reports, many and all corroborating, saying that City 1 has been infected with the virus. Everywhere. The City is down and your father was taken into custody."

"Oh no!" Ana cried out. "What did he do?"

"He went into City 1, boarded a busy train, and unleashed a virus so strong it makes the Original Plague look like the flu. Only those who knew it was coming were spared."

"My father would never do something like that."

"He would and he did." Sutherland smiled as if Ana should be proud and was missing the point entirely. "War is filled with such awful decisions, and in case you didn't realize, we're at war with an old way of doing things, trying to bring something new to this world. Your father's a soldier for the cause and will be remembered for his service forever."

"This is crazy!" Ana's rage was immediate. "What did you make him do?"

Sutherland pulled the pin from his topknot. A curtain of hair spilled from his head. He opened his mouth.

Ana's heart raced as she struggled to still her fists. To keep cool, to clamp her teeth together.

Liam met her eyes and shook his head with barely a twitch. *Not Now.*

Then Katrina — conspicuously absent during the meal — burst into the dining room and spoke to everyone. "Come with me. *Now.*"

Sutherland's face went from bothered to worse. Ana wasn't sure if he was annoyed by the interruption, or nervous about whatever had spooked Katrina. His chair scraped the floor as he pushed it from the table, and in seconds he was on his feet and by Katrina's side.

"Let's go," he said to the others.

They all stepped into the hallway. Ana's fingers were slick against Liam's. She wondered where they were going and what horror might be awaiting them.

The walk was short, maybe two minutes, but after days in isolation, every turn took them somewhere they had never been in the underground labyrinth, until they were finally in a second, larger dining hall.

"So now it's okay for us to be around all these people?"

Katrina ignored Liam and kept walking fast into the mess hall and over toward the far wall, where a swarm of people were huddled in front of a wall screen, all staring.

Ana's stomach boiled with the sight: *Chief Keller.*

"What's going on?" Ana asked.

A large bald man she hadn't seen before looked back and answered in a monotone. "City 1 has fallen. Chief Keller is being sworn in as Acting Head. The State won't admit that, though. They can't. Too much chaos."

Sutherland turned to Katrina. "How long has this been on? Do we know anything else? Any word on Jonah?"

"No. The Darwins were on until a few minutes ago, then the Games cut out and they switched to a live message from the State. They announced ten minutes to prepare. That was about how long it took me to get you."

Katrina nodded up at the screen as Keller, in his pure white uniform — the same one Jack Geralt had worn for so many years — stood in front of two tall boxes, draped in a single red curtain.

*What the hell?*

"What's in the boxes?" Ana asked Sutherland.

"That's the drama," he shrugged. "We'll wait on pins and needles to see."

Keller had to be the only person in the world who looked even uglier when he smiled, Ana thought, wishing she could bash his face in.

"Citizens of the State. Three days ago, vile members of the Underground raided City 1 and managed to infect some of its citizens."

The screen showed a video montage: security footage of a massacre on a train. People turning on people. Infected tearing at one another. A little girl getting murdered by her mother.

Ana couldn't watch, her stomach churning.

Keller's face and voice were back. She looked up to see him speaking.

"Unfortunately, the same disgrace of a man who already spat on law and order by murdering his wife also took advantage of the State's second chances. He was lucky enough to escape his deserved punishment. He won the Games and was rewarded with a new start in City 7 but was so consumed by his hatred for freedom that he couldn't even live his good life in Paradise. Jonah Lovecraft has now committed a new atrocity, one we should have stopped with our vigilance."

He lowered his voice to a hiss. "*This* is what we get for not knowing our neighbor."

Ana watched in disbelief as her father walked up and down the train aisle. Keller's voice spoke over the footage.

"Mr. Lovecraft walked by these men, women, and children, looking each of them in the eye even as he quietly and cowardly murdered them."

Ana's knees buckled. Liam grabbed her and held her against him. She looked on, but only because she couldn't look away.

"Unfortunately, former City Watch Major Jonah Lovecraft's betrayal was such a shock for our One True Leader, Jack Geralt, that he has fallen ill after suffering a mild heart attack. But worry not, citizens. He is in recovery, and we expect the best long term. Right now we will be making some temporary adjustments. More on that in a minute. For now, a few details …"

Keller smiled for the cameras. Her heart was leaking beats as if her lungs were losing air. He paced in front of the boxes, speaking slowly and using his hands to usher one sentence into the next.

"We've been too tolerant. Now we see the results of not knowing our neighbors, and have suffered the folly of seeing our tolerance curdle to weakness. No more! We cannot allow this cancer to spread any further. We've taken care of the situation on the ground, and prevented the infection from eating its way into the City proper. Now we must heal. Now we must show those who stand against freedom that they will be unable to stand at all. We've arrested the two suspects who worked in tandem to orchestrate this attack."

*Two?*

Keller yanked the curtain away with the flourish of a magician, revealing both boxes.

"What is Adam doing there?" Ana cried out.

Nobody answered — every eye on the screen.

The boxes looked like soundproof plastic or glass, like those she and Liam were trapped in before Duncan saved them, when she learned about Liam's lie and chose to spare his life over an innocent girl's.

Her brother and father both had open mouths, screaming in silence, not a note of torment heard. Adam looked older than when last she'd seen him. Taller and stronger. Less like her little brother and more like a man, not scared so much as angry. She would have done anything, given anything, to tell him that everything would be okay.

But it wouldn't be. Not ever. Keller was a monster and about to prove it to every citizen, pretending to keep his sheep safe from the wolves.

"As I said," Keller resumed his pacing, "rules and protocols must be followed. As we all know, treason against the State gets you a ticket into the Darwin Games."

Ana knew what was coming. She screamed. Liam held her tight, pulling her mouth into his chest. She looked up at the screen, helpless.

"Unfortunately, we have another rule in the Darwins. No repeat performances. Not that this has ever been an issue before. Every other player has either perished, or had the sense to enjoy their good life in City 7. But since Jonah Lovecraft was determined to forfeit his freedom, he must also forfeit his life."

"No!" Ana screamed, pulling away from Liam.

He grabbed her from behind and whispered something she couldn't hear over the sound of her own screaming.

Keller drew a blaster from inside his coat as her father's box was opened by a matching set of Watchers. "What do you have to say for yourself?"

Her father stared into the camera. "Please, let my son go. *Please*. He's innocent. He's a good boy who did nothing wrong."

"I'm sorry." Keller shook his head. "Rules and protocols."

Keller's smile returned, looking like a demon as he stared at Jonah, basking in his power as he raised the blaster and took aim at his enemy's head.

Jonah's eyes didn't waver as he stared at the cruel bastard.

Keller pulled the trigger, disintegrating his head into a bloody, ashen pulp.

Her father's headless corpse stood for a few seconds as Ana's heart stopped along with her breath.

His body dropped.

And Ana screamed as she fell to her knees.


## TO BE CONCLUDED IN Z 2136

# A Quick Favor

Thank you for reading *Z2135*.

If you enjoyed this book would you please consider writing a review of it on your favorite bookselling site so other readers might enjoy it too. Just a couple of sentences. That would mean a lot to me.

Thank you!

*Sean and Dave*

# About the Authors

**Sean Platt** is an entrepreneur and founder of Sterling & Stone, where he makes stories with his partners, Johnny B. Truant, and David W. Wright, and a family of storytellers.

Sean is the bestselling author of over 10 million words' worth of books, including the Yesterday's Gone and Invasion series. Sean is also co-author of the indie publishing cornerstone, Write. Publish. Repeat. and co-host of the Story Studio Podcast.

Originally from Long Beach, California, Sean now lives in Austin, Texas with his wife and two children. He has more than his share of nose.

**David W. Wright** is the co-author of edge-of-your seat thrillers including the best-selling post-apocalyptic series *Yesterday's Gone,* the paranoid sci-fi *WhiteSpace* series, and the vigilante series, *No Justice,* as well as standalone thrillers *12,* and *Crash* which was recently optioned for a movie.

David is an accomplished, though intermittent, cartoonist who lives in [LOCATION REDACTED] with his wife and son [NAMES REDACTED.]

He is not at all paranoid.

He is "the grumpy one" on the *The Story Studio Podcast* with fellow Sterling and Stone founders, Sean Platt and Johnny B. Truant.

David writes about books, TV shows, movies, and

video games he enjoys; his struggles with anxiety and OCD; writing; and posts the occasional drawing at his personal blog at davidwwright.com

You can email him at david@sterlingandstone.net

We swear, he almost never bites. Unless you feed him after midnight.

For a full list of his most recent books visit sterlingand-stone.net.

**Z2134**

Z2134

Z2135

Z2136

## The Dead World Series

Dead Zero

Dead City

Dead Nation

Dead Planet

Empty Nest

## The Beam Series

The Beam Season One

The Beam Season Two

The Beam Season Three

The Beam Season Four

The Beam Season Five

## Robot Proletariat Series

En3my

Robot Proletariat

The Infinite Loop

The Hard Reset

Cascade Failure

Reboot

**The Tomorrow Gene Series**

Null Identity

The Tomorrow Gene

The Tomorrow Clone

The Eden Experiment

**Karma Police Series**

Jumper

Karma Police

The Collectors

Deviant

The Fall

Homecoming

**Yesterday's Gone**

October's Gone

Yesterday's Gone Season One

Yesterday's Gone Season Two

Yesterday's Gone Season Three

Yesterday's Gone Season Four

Yesterday's Gone Season Five

Yesterday's Gone Season Six

**Tomorrow's Gone**

Tomorrow's Gone Season One

Tomorrow's Gone Season Two

Tomorrow's Gone Season Three

**Available Darkness**

Darkness Itself

Available Darkness Book One

Available Darkness Book Two

Available Darkness Book Three

## WhiteSpace

WhiteSpace Season One

WhiteSpace Season Two

WhiteSpace Season Three

## Stand Alone Novels

Burnout

The Island

Crash

Emily's List

Pattern Black

Devil May Care

The Secret Within

# Also By David W. Wright

**Z2134**

Z2134

Z2135

Z2136

**Cold Vengeance**

Cold Vengeance

Cold Reckoning

**Hidden Justice**

Hidden Justice

Hidden Honor

Hidden Shame

Hidden Virtue

**No Justice**

No Justice

No Escape

No Hope

No Return

No Stopping

No Fear

**Karma Police**

Jumper

Karma Police

The Collectors

Deviant

The Fall

Homecoming

## Yesterday's Gone

October's Gone

Yesterday's Gone Season One

Yesterday's Gone Season Two

Yesterday's Gone Season Three

Yesterday's Gone Season Four

Yesterday's Gone Season Five

Yesterday's Gone Season Six

## Tomorrow's Gone

Tomorrow's Gone Season One

Tomorrow's Gone Season Two

Tomorrow's Gone Season Three

## Available Darkness

Darkness Itself

Available Darkness Book One

Available Darkness Book Two

Available Darkness Book Three

## WhiteSpace

WhiteSpace Season One

WhiteSpace Season Two

WhiteSpace Season Three

9 781629 553849